Sweet Justice
CHRISTY REECE

ETERNAL
ROMANCE

First published in the United States of America in 2011
by Ballantine Books, an imprint of
The Random House Publishing Group,
a division of Random House, Inc.

First published in Great Britain in 2013
by ETERNAL ROMANCE,
an imprint of HEADLINE PUBLISHING GROUP

1

Cataloguing in Publication Data is available from the British Library

ISBN 978 0 7553 9801 0

Offset in Sabon by Avon DataSet Ltd, Bidford-on-Avon, Warwickshire

Printed and bound by CPI Group (UK) Ltd, Croydon, CR0 4YY

Headline's policy is to use papers that are natural, renewable and
recyclable products and made from wood grown in sustainable forests.
The logging and manufacturing processes are expected to conform to the
environmental regulations of the country of origin.

HEADLINE PUBLISHING GROUP
An Hachette UK Company
338 Euston Road
London NW1 3BH

www.eternalromancebooks.co.uk
www.headline.co.uk
www.hachette.co.uk

For Jim

Sweet Justice

one

Five years ago
Houston, Texas

"Seth Cavanaugh, you're under arrest for the murder of Montgomery Jenkins. You have the right to remain silent. You have the right to an attorney . . ."

Blank-faced stoicism firmly intact, Seth didn't resist as his arms were wrenched behind him and he heard the clink of handcuffs. Staring straight ahead, he ignored the officer reciting his Miranda rights. Didn't need to listen to something he'd memorized long before he'd entered the police academy. For barely an instant, he wondered what Greg Wallace thought as he read his former friend his rights. Greg had already been on the force for several years when Seth started with the Houston Police Department. He'd taken Seth under his wing; now he was arresting him for the murder of a scumbag.

They'd descended on his restaurant right in the middle of the lunchtime crowd. The timing had been no accident. Now an already newsworthy arrest was even more sensational. The television news crews would be outside waiting for him, along with the *Houston Chronicle* and every other news source within the greater Houston area.

He could hear the newscasts in his head: *Well-known businessman and restaurateur Seth Cavanaugh was arrested today for the alleged murder of Montgomery Jen-*

kins, better known as Monty Jenkins. Mr. Jenkins was found dead in his apartment yesterday from a single gunshot wound to his head. According to sources close to the investigation, Mr. Cavanaugh had an argument with Mr. Jenkins earlier in the day. He was seen leaving Jenkins's apartment moments after a neighbor heard a gunshot.

The Houston news outlets were going to have a blast with this one.

"Let's go, Cavanaugh."

Hands cuffed, with a cop on each side of him and one in front, they went through his office doors, down the hallway, and paraded him through the crowded restaurant.

Seth couldn't resist an inner smile at their strategy. Could've taken him through the back door, where only a few employees would have witnessed this, or even through the kitchen, where maybe twenty or so would have been around to watch. No, they'd opted for the most visual and humiliating route.

Even when Ruth's Place was empty, he didn't think it'd ever been this quiet. Tables full of diners, every patron stopped in the middle of their meal to gawk. *Oh yeah, Houston PD is eating this up.*

"You're a fool, you know that, Cavanaugh?" Greg Wallace snarled behind him.

So the man wasn't unaffected by arresting a former friend. Well, he guessed that was something. Responding wouldn't make a difference, so Seth remained silent.

Bright autumn sunlight hit him square in the eyes. Dammit, sunglasses would've been a nice touch, but he hadn't bothered to ask for them. Besides, parading him in front of the half dozen cameras waiting for them to come out wouldn't have near the impact if he'd been able to cover his eyes.

Five microphones were shoved toward his face. "Mr. Cavanaugh, what do you have to say about your arrest?"

"Mr. Cavanaugh, are you guilty?"

"Hey Seth, why'd you do it?"

Wonderful that so many people had faith in him.

Finished with their parade, an officer shoved Seth into the backseat and then slid in behind the wheel. Greg Wallace got into the front passenger seat, gave Seth a hard glare, and then turned his back on him.

As Seth settled back against the seat, the bite of the cuffs on his wrists and the uncomfortable wrench of his shoulders were mere annoyances. Weightier things occupied his mind.

His mother was just now getting the call . . . Sandra would be the one to call her. His sister was his senior by twelve years. The oldest of the Cavanaugh clan, she always took it upon herself to give the bad news to the family. For the first time ever, he wondered about that. Did she resent having to always be the bearer of bad news, or was this something she enjoyed? Guess it didn't really matter, but wondering about it helped take his thoughts off the sheer agony he knew would be going through his mother's mind right now. Her first question would be "What can we do to help?" Mama Cavanaugh always wanted to rescue her babies, whether they deserved it or not.

Then, after Sandra told her, it would go down the line. Sandra would tell Patty, the next oldest, Patty would tell Joel, and so on. Within five minutes, his five sisters and three brothers would know that their baby brother, the youngest and wildest of the Cavanaughs, had been arrested for murder. Houston news outlets had nothing on his family when it came to spreading news, both good and bad.

Someone else would tell Honor. Probably her supervisor. She'd be at her desk working, and the call would come for her to report to his office. There, she would be told that the man she was romantically involved with had been arrested for murder.

How would Dudley George tell her? "Honor, your lover has been arrested for murder. Now, don't you wish you'd listened to me?" Dudley would want to pat himself on the back as he gave her the titillating news. Then he would sit back and watch her reaction.

He'd wanted to say something to her last night. Telling your girlfriend that you were going to be arrested for murder was one thing. Telling your girlfriend who happens to be an FBI agent was a damn sight different. Honor was too intelligent to be satisfied with platitudes and excuses. She would've skewered him with questions. Ones he couldn't answer.

"You want me to call your lawyer?"

Greg's voice stopped Seth from his never-ending obsession of thinking about his family's and Honor's reactions. That had been his one and only regret, but damn, it was a big one.

Pulling his gaze away from the window, he asked, with mild curiosity, "The laws get changed without me knowing? I thought I was allowed one phone call."

"Figured you might want to use that to call your mother."

Despite his need to stay in this cocoon of no emotion, Seth almost grinned. Greg really was a nice guy. Someday, he hoped to be able to thank him for his kindness. For now, all he could say was "Why call and tell her something she already knows?"

"You had everything going for you, Cavanaugh. How could you fuck it up so badly?"

No answer was better than the lie he'd have to give, so

Seth went back to looking out the window at nothing. Might as well get used to it. For the next few years, that's what his life would be. Nothing.

"Stone, got a minute?"

Honor jerked her head up to see Dudley George standing at her desk. Yes, she had a minute, especially since she'd been sightlessly staring at her computer screen for the last half hour, her mind occupied with Seth. Something was going on with him.

"Sure." She stood and followed her supervisor. Several eyes bored into her back as she made her way into his office. At twenty-five, with just two years under her belt, Honor knew that some believed she was too inexperienced to be a field agent. A few thought her family had pulled strings. Telling them that she was mature enough to handle herself or that her family had no influence with the FBI would do no good. Proving herself was the only way to show them.

"Have a seat."

The door clicked closed behind her. Honor sat in the uncomfortable straight-backed wooden chair in front of Dudley's desk. Rumor was, he'd sent back the standard chair that came with his office furniture and bought this one on his own. Definitely set the tone for his meetings.

"I just got some interesting news."

He looked at her, waiting for a response. Dudley had a habit of delivering one-line statements for dramatic effect. Since she had no idea what the news was, Honor waited, too.

Looking a bit disappointed that she hadn't taken the bait, he said, "Seth Cavanaugh has just been arrested for murder."

She almost laughed, the statement was so ridiculous. But from the grim look on Dudley's face, this was no laughing matter. Besides, Dudley wasn't known for his sense of humor.

"There must be some mistake."

"The police don't think so."

Honor could feel her head shaking back and forth in denial but couldn't seem to stop it. "Who . . . how?"

"Montgomery Jenkins, a.k.a. Monty Jenkins. Ever heard of him?"

Dread washed through her. "Wasn't he an employee of Hector Clemmons's?"

Dudley nodded. "Until a couple of months ago, when Hector fired him for stealing. Clemmons didn't press charges. Probably figured that would mean an investigation into his own dirty dealings."

Dammit, she'd warned Seth that having any connections with Clemmons would come back and bite him someday. The few arguments they'd had stemmed from his association with the man. Each time, Seth had shrugged off her concern, saying that Clemmons had a legitimate import company and Seth relied on their business arrangement for his restaurant.

"Seth isn't capable of murder. I'm sure there's a reasonable—"

"That's not the point, Stone." Dudley leaned forward, his mud-brown eyes gleaming. "Your relationship with a man who has such questionable connections and associations has been a source of gossip in this office for months. I warned you what could happen."

Locking her jaw to keep from telling the asshole what she thought of him, she forced a calm response. "Then what is your point?"

"That if you want to advance in the Bureau, you keep your associations clean from now on."

His point was clear: break it off with Seth. As much as she loved her job, she loved Seth more. Standing, she said, "Is that all, sir?"

His expression became slyly speculative. "You given any more thought to that job offer you got last week?"

He was referring to the opportunity to work in the newly formed Child Abduction Unit. Not only was it a coveted position, but the purpose of the unit was the very reason she'd joined the Bureau—something she'd been dreaming about since she was thirteen years old. She had delayed giving an answer for only one reason: Seth.

"Not yet, sir. I was told I had till the end of the month to answer."

"You do. However, with this new development, you might want to consider commiting sooner."

Meaning it could be rescinded. Bullshit. She wasn't going to let Dudley bulldoze or intimidate her. However, pissing him off wasn't the right path either. "I'll take that under advisement. Anything else?"

Dudley shook his head, the light burning even brighter in his eyes. Half the time she thought he was on her side; the other half she could swear he'd just as soon see her leave the Bureau for good.

Honor turned and walked out of the office. She had to grab her cellphone and get out of the building. She needed to call Seth. There had to be a reasonable explanation. Seth Cavanaugh was many things—arrogant, opinionated, and quite often infuriating; an excellent cook, an incredible dancer, and one of the most wickedly handsome men she'd ever known. Those things and a million more made him the man he was. But one thing she knew without a doubt? Seth was not a murderer.

Still looking out the window of the car as it headed to the main jailhouse, Seth heard his cellphone ring. Making every effort not to tense up or show any emotion, he kept his eyes averted. His cellphone had been confiscated at his arrest, so there was no point in worrying about who was calling. No point, but it didn't stop him from doing just that.

Since he had known the arrest was coming, maybe he should have changed his voice-mail message. Something like: "I'm in jail right now. Leave a message and I'll call you back as soon as I make bail. And oh, by the way, I didn't do it."

"Hello."

Seth jerked his head around when he heard those words. His cellphone should have been bagged for evidence. What the hell was Greg doing holding it? Seth's concern about who was calling was buried beneath his concern for Greg. There were only three people, other than Seth, who knew the whole story. The only way this was going to work was to keep it to a minimum. Did Greg know something or was he making exceptions because he figured something was hinky?

He focused on the one-sided conversation Greg was having on his phone. "Yes, it's true." A pause, then: "He's in handcuffs, I can't—" Another long pause and then a sighing "All right. Hold on."

Twisting around, Greg unlocked the barrier between the front and back seats. "Lean forward, I'll hold the phone to your ear."

Seth held back a sigh. The man knew better than to do what he was doing. Not that Seth was planning to escape—that would defeat the whole purpose. Still, Greg had been on the force too long to commit such a rookie mistake.

Since giving him a lecture would seem more than strange, Seth leaned forward and put his ear to the phone. "Yes?"

"Seth?"

Despite his efforts to maintain control, Seth closed his eyes. *Honor.* He hadn't planned on talking to her until he made bail. Had hoped, by then, to be able to come up with something reasonable that she would buy.

"Yes."

"Are you all right?"

"Yes."

"You've been arrested?"

"Yes."

"Hell, Seth, can you say something besides 'yes'?"

Swallowing the pain, he chuckled. "Not much more to say, is there?"

The shaky breath she released sliced into the cloak of coldness he was trying to maintain. Dammit, all his fault for getting involved with an FBI agent. Maybe if Honor had another profession, he could have told her something she would believe . . . maybe she would have agreed to wait. No, that wouldn't have happened anyway. It wasn't just Honor's job that was the problem . . . it was her intelligence.

Twenty-eight years on this earth, and he'd never had strong feelings for or a need to commit to any of the women he'd dated and then, when he was on the biggest job of his life, he falls for a woman like Honor. Irony sucked.

"What can I do to help?"

Shit, not only did he have to fall in love with a beautiful, intelligent woman, she also had the most amazing heart and a deep, fierce loyalty. If there was one thing he could do for her, it was this: "Stay out of it."

"But I—"

"I've got an attorney. The charges won't stick. I'll be out on bail in a few hours. We can talk then."

The silence was painful. He had hurt her, but that had been inevitable. Hell of it was, it was only going to get worse. Dammit, he had known what was coming down.

"Call me," she said quietly, and then the line went dead.

Seth leaned back against the seat once more. He could feel Greg's eyes on him, but refused to engage in any kind of discussion. If Greg did know what was going on here, talking about it in the vicinity of anyone else would be stupid.

"You had so much going for you, Cavanaugh. What happened?"

Seth still didn't look at him. Maybe Greg didn't know. He hoped he didn't. The man was a nice guy, a good cop. Knowing the truth could get him killed.

Three days later . . .

Seth stared out the grimy warehouse window—a perfect match for the filth he felt to his soul. Would this ever end? And how could he even ask himself that, when it had barely begun?

He'd been released a few hours ago. They'd let him sit for three days before setting bail. The fact that Hector Clemmons had posted the bail had been no surprise to anyone. That had been the plan all along.

In those three days, Seth had refused to see his family or Honor. What was the point . . . they were already hurt. It couldn't get any worse, could it? Two days after his arrest, when Honor had shown up at his jail cell, demanding to see him, he'd learned it could get worse. Yeah, a hell of a lot worse.

He turned to the man sitting on an empty crate a few feet away. "I told you to keep her out of it."

"I tried to, man . . . she was one determined woman." Bill shook his head and added, "You knew the risks going in. Bad time to start a relationship."

Jaw clenched in fury, Seth turned back to the window. Bill Keaton was right. He had no one to blame but himself. The minute he'd seen Honor, he'd wanted her. And damn it all, despite every instinct telling him to run the other way, he had pursued her. A relationship that had no future. Honor Stone represented everything good and decent in this world. And because of what he had agreed to do, Seth represented everything vile and corrupt.

"You could always tell her the truth."

Bill's words were said in a normal tone, but to Seth they sounded like the devil's own temptation. As enticing as the words spoken to Eve to lure her with forbidden fruit.

"Exposing Honor to this shit would put her in even more danger than she's already in."

"She's an FBI agent, Seth. It's not like she doesn't know danger or how to handle herself."

That was true; Honor was a trained professional. But the moment he'd met her, he'd had the overwhelming need to protect her. She might have dealt with hardened criminals, but there was a light inside Honor—pure and untarnished. To protect his family, he hadn't told them the truth. Could he do anything less for the woman he loved?

Even if she knew the truth, what future could he offer her? He could just see her face as he said, "Listen, honey, I'm up to my neck trying to bring Hector Clemmons down. I'm probably at least a couple of years away from doing that, and in the meantime, I have to act like this slick, phony sleaze. People are going to assume I'm a criminal. If you continue to see me, it will damage your career and probably endanger your life, so we need to call it quits for a while. And, oh yeah, I probably won't live through it. But in case I do, I'd appreciate it if you'd wait for me."

Sure, that'd go over real well.

"I understand Joel came to see you today." Bill's disapproving tone broke into Seth's thoughts.

"He's the oldest brother. With my dad gone, Joel sees it as his responsibility to watch out for the family. Thinks if he threatens me enough or piles on more guilt, I'll stop torturing everyone and come back into the fold."

"You need to find a way to keep your family away from you."

Seth whirled around and glared. "Don't you think I fucking know that?"

Bill barely raised a brow at Seth's anger. "Do you?"

"What the hell's that supposed to mean?"

"You're knee-deep with Hector now. After this murder charge, you'll be shoulder-deep. Won't be long till you're in his sacred circle. Once you're there, anyone who's attached to you is tainted by association."

"What the hell do you want me to do? I've told my entire family I'm living my life on my terms and if they don't like it, they can fuck off." Seth turned back around before Bill could see the pain on his face as he remembered the stricken look in his mother's eyes. For as long as he lived, he would never forget her expression. No matter how this turned out, he could never forgive himself for hurting her like that.

"You knew what the consequences would be."

Bill's continual reminder did no good. Yeah, they'd told him right off the bat. You agree to this assignment, your life won't be your own. You'll probably lose your family, most of your friends, at least for a while. They'd asked him over and over if he really wanted to take on something that would be so life altering.

But this had been an opportunity unlike any other. A chance to go deep cover and take down one of the most elusive drug lords in North America. The department had never done it before—not this deep, this intricate, or even this quickly. Setting up something so elaborate and multilayered usually took a tremendous amount of effort and resources. But in a relatively short period of time, Seth had gone from respected cop to dirty ex-cop, then a restaurant owner with questionable ties to the underworld. And now murder suspect. Whoever said time flies whether you're having fun or not was right on the money.

The cover had needed to be rock solid and his superiors had believed the restaurant guise would be the most difficult part of the ruse to develop. For Seth, that'd been the only bright spot in this entire operation.

He rubbed the back of his neck where the tension of the last few days had gathered, trying to lock his muscles in place. "How much longer before the charges are dropped?"

"Next day or two should do it. The doubts and suspicions have been cast. Clemmons will be contacting you soon for a solution to your problem . . . strings attached, of course.

"Your not-so-good name has been tarnished even more, greatly diminishing the damage done when he learned you were seeing an FBI agent. With him playing the rescuer, he'll think he's got you by the balls. Once the charges are dropped, you'll be in his debt, right where he wants you."

"You'd think after working with the man for months, I'd have some street cred with him."

Bill shrugged in that nonchalant way that lately had made Seth want to knock the man's teeth down his throat. "We knew going in he'd be a tough sale. With you being a former cop, it made him more wary. Having you leave the force under suspicion of misconduct helped, but he's been around too long to take chances."

And that had been yet another rip in his family's heart. They'd had such high hopes for the youngest Cavanaugh. With a master's degree in criminal justice and a driving ambition to make an impact on the world, he should have had so many choices, so many opportunities. Instead, in lieu of disciplinary action because of several accusations of questionable conduct, he'd resigned. Though all of it was planned and part of his undercover act, both Seth and his family had been publicly humiliated.

Tensions had eased when he'd opened the restaurant. His success had come as no big surprise to the family, since he and all his brothers and sisters had learned to cook very early and had often had cooking competitions at home.

Ruth's Place, named after Seth's mother, had become an overnight success. The Cavanaugh clan had fully supported his new venture. That is, until he'd been linked with Hector Clemmons.

Like most families, they'd made excuses for him, not daring to believe that he'd be associated with a man of Clemmons's reputation. "Murky" and "slimy" were two of the kindest descriptions his family had been able to come up with.

The Houston Police Department knew Clemmons was more than that . . . they just needed proof. It was up to Seth to provide that proof. They'd been looking to put him away for years, and no one had even come close. With time and patience, Seth intended to change that.

"Hey, kid, if you're bored with this undercover stuff and just want to sigh about your girlfriend, let me know. I've got some things to do."

Bill's sarcastic, smoke-graveled voice shook Seth out of his melancholy. As much as he'd like to shove his fist down the asshole's throat, he'd said the right thing. He'd agreed to this job, and a Cavanaugh always kept his word.

Bill's lack of empathy wasn't surprising. The man had no family. No one to hurt if his life went to shit in a heartbeat. Seth had grown up in a large family where everyone knew everything and thought they had a right to share their opinion. Sandra, the oldest, had had her say first, via the longest voice mail in cellphone history. Then his brother Joel had cornered him at the restaurant a couple of hours ago. Wouldn't be long before he heard from the others. His mother would wait. His brothers and sisters were the tenderizers. His mother would be the fire. She would sear him with one look and he'd feel lower than a slug. And he wouldn't be able to give her anything other than what he'd already told her: my life, not yours.

Turning his back to the window, he asked, "How's this scenario going to play?"

"Pretty much what we talked about. Hector's already got some mad love for you. Not only do you look like you could be one of his sons, hooking him up with that little shipment from Venezuela showed him you have the kinds of connections he likes."

"And now he's impressed that I killed one of his former employees," Seth added.

"Yeah, but even though he thinks he's buying your freedom, keep denying it to his face. We want him to think that you might actually have done the deed but can maintain a semblance of your reputation. Hector's got more than enough dirty people surrounding him. He needs you to stay semirespectable."

Seth nodded. Semirespectable would mean something else to his family. His mother had been through so much this year. His dad had died from a massive heart attack less than nine months ago. Having one of her sons under suspicion for murder was going to cause her more pain. And yet, even knowing what he knew now, if he was offered the same job today, he'd take it. Hector Clemmons had gotten away with garbage for years. This was as close as the authorities had been to his inside circle. There was no choice but to go forward.

If he pulled this job off successfully, Seth knew he would be saving lives. Question was, would he have a life to go back to when it was over?

two

The instant the doorbell rang, Honor intuitively knew it was Seth. Not that she'd heard when and if he'd made bail. She was just the woman he was sleeping with . . . why would she know something like that?

Throwing off her anger but determined to get to the truth, Honor opened her apartment door. Wordlessly, she stared at the man she'd fallen in love with almost from the moment she met him. She hadn't seen him since the debacle in the jailhouse. Being told to get the hell out hadn't exactly been the response she had expected. She'd been torn between jabbing her fist between the bars to punch him in the nose and pulling him to her so she could kiss that sexy, unsmiling mouth. She'd done neither. Instead, she'd nodded grimly and done exactly what he'd told her to do: she'd walked out the door. Bastard wanted to act like a bastard, that was his loss.

Now here he stood, and she once again had the same inclination. Instead of acting on her instincts, she stepped back so he could enter. Having a shouting match in the hallway wasn't a good idea. And she anticipated that there would be shouting.

She had known all along that Seth had a dangerous edge. For a girl who never walked on the wild side, he had been a temptation. One she'd never even tried to resist. Despite the fact that it wasn't smart, even now a thrill of anticipation zipped up her spine as she watched him stride into her apartment. Seth was already beyond sexy. Add dangerous to the mix and he was a walking sexual fantasy.

He also looked tired. His thick hair, black as midnight, looked as though he'd run his fingers through it numerous times today. A lock fell across his forehead, and Honor fisted her hand to keep from brushing it from his brow. If she touched him, she knew where it would lead. Though they often fell into bed the moment they saw each other, tonight they had to talk.

Closing the door behind him, she instead gave him a tight smile. "So I guess you're ready to talk now?"

"No 'Honey, how was your day?' No kiss hello? No questions on how the food in jail compares to my restaurant?"

Eyes so dark she could see her reflection in them stared at her hard . . . their usual warmth completely gone. Where was the witty, charming man she'd fallen in love with?

"Is that what you want me to do? Pretend there's nothing wrong?"

He gave a short, dry laugh. "I guess I'd like to see a little faith in your eyes."

"Faith? You want to talk about faith? You're a murder suspect. I'm an FBI agent. Despite all that, I came to see you in jail, where I got the cold shoulder and a 'get the hell out of here' snarl. So don't you dare give me a lecture about faith."

Shooting her another hard look, he passed her and headed to the kitchen.

Her anger now taking full control, she followed him. "Are you going to say anything?"

Still not answering, he pulled a bottle of beer from the refrigerator, opened it, and guzzled half of it with one swallow. That one act froze everything inside her. Seth didn't drink. Hated the taste of alcohol. Said he despised what the abuse of it did to people. Seeing him do something so out of character scared the hell out of her.

Her voice much softer than before, she said, "Talk to me, Seth. Please."

A kitchen chair scraped across the floor as he pulled it out for her. That was so Seth. A man of impeccable manners. Feeling just the slightest bit of ease, she sat down. He sprawled into a chair across from her and gave her an odd, twisted smile.

Hoping they could start over, with a little less drama, she said, "How was your day, dear?"

The smile dropped from his face. "I'm sorry, Honor. I don't want you involved in this. The man was a past business associate of Hector Clemmons's. I went to talk with him as a favor to Clemmons. He was found dead about half an hour later." He paused for a beat and added, "I didn't kill him."

"I never, for a second, thought that you did."

"You get heat at work?"

She shrugged. "Just a few questions. Nothing I can't handle."

He took her hand and kissed it softly. "I'm sorry."

"I know we've talked about this . . . but tell me again. Why do you have to do business with Clemmons?"

"Because I do, sweetheart. He's one of my major suppliers. Some of his other business dealings may be questionable, but—"

"But nothing, Seth. The man is dirty. I've been doing some research on his businesses and I—"

"Stay out of it, Honor."

"I'm just trying to—"

With a suddenness that startled her, he stood, pulled her into his arms, and slammed his mouth against hers. She gasped, and he used that opportunity to thrust his tongue deep.

As anger blurred into passion, she recognized the diversion. Never had she been a pushover. An inner voice told her to back away and demand an answer before this went any further. Under the haze of hot need, the voice was squelched.

Biting at his lips, tugging at his hair, Honor gave in to the heat; Seth's husky laugh fired her blood even hotter. She needed this, wanted this. When it was over, they could talk. But now . . . for now . . . this was exactly what she wanted. Wrapping her arms around his neck, she let her body sink into his.

Seth's hands cupped Honor's butt, pressing her softness to his hardening body. Fitting his erection into the soft, giving V of her mound, he ground against her. She moaned against his mouth and rubbed against him, telling him she was right there with him.

The part of his brain that was still working, where his conscience pounded like a hammer, told him that what he was doing was wrong. Never had he coerced a woman with sex, and Honor wasn't just any woman. She'd stolen his heart from the moment she'd smiled at him across a crowded room. Having her ask more questions that he couldn't answer wasn't an option either. And he couldn't just let her go. Not yet.

His arms tight around her, he headed to her bedroom. A quickie against the wall or on the kitchen table wasn't going to do it this time. Now was a time to savor, to experience the ecstasy that only Honor's body could give. That required no clothes; a soft, comfortable place; and plenty of room to roll around.

Laying her on the bed, Seth pulled away to look down at her. So incredibly feminine, so beautifully strong, so damned sexy.

Her slender body moving sensually, she smiled up at him. "What are you waiting for?"

That growling tone in her voice when she was aroused

got him every time. Seth took the opportunity to appreciate this particular moment. Soon it would be all over, but for right now, he wanted to take his time. Pulling completely away from her, he stripped quickly.

The husky laugh she gave hardened him even more. Hell of a thing—that just her laugh could almost bring him off. He pulled her shoes from her slender feet and kissed the bottom of each foot. Grateful that she was wearing a skirt, he slid his hands up silken legs, spreading them as he went. When the skirt was bunched at her waist, Seth looked down and breathed out a shaky sigh. *Honor's underwear.* The woman dressed as conservatively as any serious federal agent could, but underneath those conventional clothes lurked the sexiest and most provocative lingerie he'd ever seen.

Leaning down, Seth put his mouth at the center of her crotch. She gasped and arched upward. She was already wet . . . her musky scent almost causing him to stop the play and take her hard and fast. Almost. No way was he going to detour from this journey. Especially when the destination was so very worthwhile.

He nuzzled her center with his nose and mouth and felt the ripple of that sweet flesh. She was already on the verge of coming, but that wasn't going to happen for a few minutes. Increasing the anticipation for them both, he stepped back.

"What?" Cat eyes blinked up at him. "Why'd you stop?"

"Too quick, too easy."

"And that's a problem, why?"

"Getting there's half the fun."

Her hands went to her panties. "Let me help you get there faster." She pulled the minuscule thong down toward her knees.

Seth put his hands on her, stopping her. "Not yet." Pulling her arms over her head, he held her wrists with one hand. She opened her mouth, probably to protest, but Seth didn't give her a chance. Covering her mouth with his, he plunged deep. Honor opened her mouth wider and took him, her tongue sliding, licking, and dueling with his. Groans and gasps filled the air—a husky blend of two excited lovers, exploring, seeking ecstasy together.

Seth pulled away to whisper, "We're going to do this slow and easy, baby. Yes?"

"Yes," she sighed with a soft breath.

Back on his feet again, he tugged at her underwear and skirt, pulling them slowly down her long, slender legs. Dropping them on the floor, he took a moment to gaze down at perfection. Creamy, dewy, freckled perfection. Strawberry blond hair covered her mound and the soft, delicious secrets he was throbbing to get to. But not yet.

Wrapping his hands around her ankles, he pushed her legs up and then open, getting a better view of the beauty that awaited him.

Her body arched toward him. "Kiss me," she breathed softly.

"With pleasure." His thumbs spread the folds of her sex . . . he licked at the delicate, wet flesh and then thrust his tongue deep, spearing. With her half scream, half sob urging him on, Seth withdrew and then sank even deeper, eating at her, nibbling, devouring.

Her hands were in his hair, pulling and then pushing him harder as she bucked up into his hungry mouth . . . the cries of her need making him crazy hot.

Lifting his head, he watched her face. Yes, she was close. Her eyes gleamed, sparkling with heat, aroused and needy.

"You ready, sweetheart?"

She nodded and spread her legs wider for him. Seth dipped his head again. Covering her clit, he sucked hard, and then thrust and retreated, over and over. Honor screamed and then she came, throbbing, wet and sweet, against his mouth. Gentling the suckling as she began to recover, his tongue lapped softly, loving her taste, her responsiveness.

Honor returned to reality, enjoying the hot, wet licks of Seth's tongue on her most sensitive flesh. Seth as a lover was unlike any man she'd been with before. Not that there'd been that many, but even if she'd had a hundred, it wouldn't have mattered. Good sex was one thing. Fabulous, wonderful, mind-blowing sex with the gorgeous, sexy man you loved? No comparison.

Seth lifted away from her again, and she took a moment to appreciate the beauty of the naked man before her. Six foot four of pure male power. Broad chest with just the right amount of furring, powerful biceps that could pick her up with ease. Her eyes dropped lower, past the hard, taut stomach to the long, thick appendage that was so aroused, she could see him throb. Her mouth watered.

She rose up, needing to taste him. She took one lick and then strong hands landed on her shoulders, stopping her. Tilting her head, she looked up at him curiously. "What's wrong?"

"Not yet. I won't last five seconds in that hot mouth. You've got way too many places I need to explore."

She smiled, happy with his response. "Who am I to argue with such logic?"

Taking advantage of her sitting position, Seth pulled her shirt over her head, leaving her in a lacy black bra. She watched his eyes grow hotter as they roamed, visually caressing her. Her nipples peaked harder at the hot intent of his gaze—she knew what was coming.

"Take it off."

The words, said in that sexy, growling voice of his, made her burn brighter. Her eyes never leaving his,

Honor shivered with anticipation as she unclasped the front closure and pulled the bra off.

"Lift them up for me."

Cupping her breasts, she lifted them to Seth and gasped as he took one entire breast into his mouth and suckled hard. Seconds later, he released her to give the other breast the same treatment.

She was small-breasted, but with Seth, that had never mattered. He loved her breasts, had told her more than once that they were perfection to him. With a boyish figure and a body covered with freckles, Honor had never considered anything about her body perfect. In Seth's arms, she felt perfect.

"Can't wait any longer," he muttered.

"Good." Lying back on the bed, she watched him hover over her. Her legs opened wider to welcome him home. Seth barely paused before his body covered hers and, with one hard, powerful stroke, plunged deep, filling her to the hilt.

Honor gave a strangled gasp and wrapped her legs around his waist, meeting each hard shove of his penis with an answering rhythm of her own. She let him set the pace, watching his face tighten as he fought to hold off his climax. His eyes, deep midnight blue, locked with hers as he rode her harder and harder. Honor's heart thudded . . . she wasn't going to last much longer. She was at the edge, ready to free-fall into absolute bliss, and the most wonderful thing of all? She knew that Seth would be there, ready to catch her.

Seth ground his teeth, fighting his release. Dammit, he didn't want to come yet, but the tight clasp of her channel, sucking and gripping him, was breaking him fast. He had intended all of this to last much longer. The tasting, the sexy talk, the heat. All of it. But with Honor, his intentions often got sidetracked by just his sheer need to be inside her, holding her as tight as possible. Sensation rippled, then zipped up his spine, and then it was too late. Explosion came quickly. Growling her name, Seth rode the wave of pleasure.

Eons later, he drew the trembling woman to his side. Words choked in his throat, things he wanted to say, promises he wanted to make. He wanted to tell her how special she was to him. That there was no one like her . . . and that in his heart, there never would be again. He had never told her he loved her. The words had trembled on his tongue dozens of times, but he couldn't allow himself to say them. Telling her his true feelings would only make what he had to do a million times harder. And since what he had to do was already going to rip his heart out, he spared them both at least that amount of pain. No, he could give her no words, no promises. *Nothing*.

Breathing in her scent, Seth tried to treasure the rightness of the moment as it was. Very soon, he would be gone and there would be nothing to treasure.

Honor rolled over and reached for Seth. When her hand met a cold space where his body had been, she sat up and looked around. Dawn was creeping through the windows, casting the bedroom in a grayish tint. The room seemed empty without Seth's overpowering presence. Tilting her head, she listened. No sounds in the shower. He must be in the kitchen, drinking coffee and reading the newspaper. One of the many things she loved about Seth was his voracious need to read. She'd grown up getting lost in autobiographies and novels of all kinds. She loved that they had that in common.

Dropping back onto the bed, she stretched and smiled at the delicious little aches in certain muscles. Last night had been beyond wonderful. Sex with Seth was always spectacular. Last night it had been just as amazing, but different, too. There had been an element of need in him she'd never felt before. The connection they'd shared seemed almost otherworldly.

Honor rolled her eyes at her thoughts. Here she was sighing and getting all gooey over what had most definitely been Seth's way to stop her from asking questions. She should resent the manipulation, but she couldn't. Resenting such an incredible experience would definitely be in the territory of "cutting off her nose to spite her face." Besides, they'd have plenty of time to talk today. It was Sunday, and they had nothing planned other than spending it together. Sundays were their special day—the only day of the week they reserved exclusively for each other.

The quietness of the apartment suddenly disturbed her. And if Seth had made coffee, why couldn't she smell it? Bounding from the bed, she grabbed a robe from the hook on the door and pulled it on as she went to the kitchen—the empty kitchen.

Telling herself there could be any number of reasons why he'd left without waking her or at least leaving a note, she nevertheless wandered throughout the apartment looking for one. Nothing. It was as if he'd never been there.

First coffee, and then she would phone him. Maybe he'd gotten called back to the restaurant unexpectedly. She was making excuses for him, she knew that, but after last night, how could she not? Their lovemaking had always been passionate, beyond wonderful. Last night they'd reached a closeness she'd never thought it was possible to reach with another human being. Totally in tune with each other's bodies, each other's needs. A phenomenal experience she'd never forget and one she hoped to repeat often.

The vibration of her cellphone pulled her from dreamy, lustful thoughts. Hating the intrusion of reality, she grabbed up the device. Maybe it was Seth explaining why he wasn't here. "Stone," she said.

"Your boyfriend's been cleared of all charges."

Her heart leaped with relief. She had known there was nothing to the charges. Seth committing murder was almost laughable. She was glad it was over, though, not only for his sake, but hers, too. Dating a murder suspect wouldn't exactly look good on her record.

"Did they catch the murderer?"

"Don't know."

"Do you know any details of why they dropped the charges on Seth?"

"No."

She recognized a certain tone in Dudley's voice. He wasn't that hard to read when something was bothering him. "There's something else. What is it?"

"Nothing other than I can't get anything on why they no longer consider him a suspect. Just seems too damn hush-hush for my liking."

Honor was used to his suspicious nature . . . it went along with the job. But when it came to this, there was no need to be suspicious. No matter how much circumstantial evidence, Seth as a murder suspect had never made any sense to her. She was glad Houston PD had seen that, too.

"I'm just happy it's over."

"Hmm."

The reply wasn't a rousing endorsement, but she hadn't really expected anything more. Dudley had a tendency to want all of his people single and unattached. Honor hadn't had a problem with that philosophy until she'd met Seth.

"Thanks for calling."

Sounding preoccupied, Dudley said, "Yeah."

Honor closed the phone and dropped it into the pocket of her robe. Despite her relief at hearing the news, something still nagged at her. Seth's business required that he associate with all sorts of people, but she still couldn't understand why one of those people had to be Hector Clemmons. Was there more to their association than he was telling her?

Disgusted with herself, Honor went to the kitchen and poured herself a cup of coffee. She had faith in Seth and felt guilty for even doubting him. When he returned, she'd make sure he knew how much she believed in him.

The steering wheel gripped tightly in his hands, Seth focused his eyes on the apartment in front of him. *Honor's apartment*. She would be awake by now, wondering where he'd gone. He'd hated leaving her for the meeting. All warm, cozy woman cuddled up against him— the most beautiful woman he'd ever met. In a few minutes, it would be more than just leaving for a meeting. He'd be leaving forever.

He dragged a hand down his tired face and cursed himself. There was no one else to blame. He'd agreed to this assignment—so damned cocky and self-assured. Sure, he could take down Hector Clemmons. Sure, he could create such a deep-cover web of lies that not even the slickest of Hector's investigators could penetrate it. He was single, had no commitments. When it was all over and done with, he'd explain everything to his family, and they'd understand. *Fuck!*

That was before Honor. Before he'd met the woman he knew without a doubt he'd love for the rest of his life. And his family? Hell, he'd taken them for granted, too. Had assumed he'd be able to lie well enough to head off their questions. Had consoled himself with the idea that he was doing something good and honorable, and that when the time came for them to know the truth, they would forgive him easily and all the hurt would go away.

He was no longer a murder suspect. Not that he ever had been, but it had given Clemmons pause and that's what they'd needed. The man trusted few, and Seth had been well on his way to slipping inside his inner circle. And then Hector had gotten antsy, backed off. Seth's relationship with Honor had come under discussion; questions had been asked. Seth had known something was going to have to be done.

Monty Jenkins's death had fallen into their laps—an opportunity too convenient to pass up. The suspicion of murder had been Bill's idea. Jenkins was a former employee of Clemmons's who'd been fired for stealing. He'd been found dead of a heroin overdose.

Instead of reporting the real cause of death, they'd decided to make it seem that Seth had done the deed. Everything had been a lie, from the neighbor who called in saying that there had been a gunshot and that he'd seen Seth leaving Jenkins's apartment just a few minutes later, to the first on-the-scene detective, who'd reported that Monty had a bullet hole in his head. Then, when Seth was cleared of all suspicion, it would reassure Hector, because now not only was Seth in his camp, having murdered someone for him, but he could slide out of trouble as well as anyone—with a little help from Clemmons, that is.

Being cleared of a murder charge that he had every appearance of having committed wasn't going to be enough, though. It might have eased Hector's suspicions, but the man was still asking too many questions about Honor. And Honor's mention of digging into Clemmons's background had put Seth even more on edge. Having her involved with any of this wasn't something he wanted. Stupid to think he could keep his personal life and professional life separate, especially when his personal life would be nonexistent until Clemmons went down.

Gripping the steering wheel so tight his knuckles went white, Seth shuddered out a breath. She would hate him. But he preferred hatred over her losing her career or her life.

He got out of the car, and on the way to the door, he set his jaw to the hard line of insolence he'd learned over the last few months. With his hand on the doorknob, he paused for a moment and, as crazy as it seemed, whispered a prayer for strength. Breaking Honor's heart was going to require everything he had. He needed all the help he could get.

Honor looked up when the door opened. She'd been staring into her coffee for over an hour, arguing with herself over whether she should call Seth and find out what was going on. Thankful that she didn't have to continue, she stood and waited for him to say something.

He walked into the middle of the living room and looked down at her full cup. "Any coffee left?"

"Yes."

He passed her and went to the kitchen. Huffing an exasperated sigh, she followed him and watched as he poured himself a cup.

"I understand you're no longer a murder suspect."

He took an appreciative swallow and said, "News travels fast."

"Did they get the murderer?"

Broad shoulders lifting in a careless shrug, he took his cup back into the living room, saying, "Hell if I know. Just glad to have them off my ass."

Confused by his strange mood, Honor followed him again. He seemed almost cold, unapproachable. Feeling uncertain with Seth wasn't a comfortable place for her. Especially after last night. Determined to move forward, she said, "So what do you want to do today? I thought we might—"

"I've already got plans."

"What kind of plans?"

He lifted a cool gaze to her. "Plans that don't include you."

Honor jerked in response. "What's that supposed to mean?"

"It means exactly what I said. I've got things I want to do. You're not invited."

"What the hell's going on?"

"Nothing other than I think this thing with us has gotten out of hand."

Her hand dug into the material at the back of the sofa; her lips went numb from shock. "This thing . . . ?"

"Yeah. *Thing*. I mean, don't get me wrong, the sex is good . . . damn good. But face it, babe, that's really all we've got. Eventually that's going to get old." His shoulder lifted in an insolent shrug. "Then what?"

She shook her head and reached a hand toward him. "Seth, you can't—"

As if he didn't want her near him, he backed away, out of her reach.

Honor, who was never at a loss for words, stared mutely at the man she'd thought she would spend the rest of her life with. Everything she'd thought they had, everything she'd thought Seth was, crumbled.

She told herself to get angry, to lash out at him. The fury would come later. For right now, an overwhelming hurt flooded through her. "I see," she managed huskily.

For an instant, a spark of warmth flashed in his eyes. Before she could question that look, his face went impassive, even harder than before. No, she must have imagined the emotion. Now his eyes were cool, aloof, almost mocking. The mouth that had given her such pleasure the night before twisted in a slight smile. "Sorry, babe."

Her vision blurred as hot tears threatened to spill. No! Honor Stone did not lose control in front of others. It was just not done . . . she had to get him out of here. Now! "Get out."

His gaze swept over her body . . . Honor felt the insult to her soul. "Sure you don't want one more round? Just for the hell of it?"

"I said, Get out."

He took another swallow of coffee, then set the cup on the table and winked. "My loss."

Turning her back to him, she heard the door shut. Her gazed dropped to the coffee cup he'd drunk from. Lifting it, she put her mouth in the exact place his lips had been. All warmth had receded . . . only the cold, hard surface remained. Eyes glazed with the tears she could no longer control, she hurled the cup across the room. Her dreams as shattered as the broken cup, Honor turned her back to the mess and walked away.

three

Present day
San Saria Island, Florida Keys

Clemmons is dead.

Seth stared down at the crumpled note. Why he'd held on to it, he had no idea. The fact that Hector Clemmons was dead had made no real difference in his life. Though the man had received the death penalty, he'd survived barely five months of incarceration. A knife to the gut wasn't exactly the easy way out, but it had been much less than what the bastard had deserved.

Still, it hadn't changed Seth's life. Or what his future held. He'd accepted long ago that taking down Clemmons would destroy much of him. Had actually thought he'd be found out before he could accomplish his goal and that he'd end up in the river with cement blocks tied to his legs. Clemmons had done that with a few who'd double-crossed him. Seth had been determined to bring him down but had eventually accepted that he wouldn't live through it. Sometimes he wondered if he had.

Folding the note, he slid it into his wallet once more. At some point he'd get rid of it, but not today.

The calendar across the room pulled him from the edge of the bed, where he'd been sitting for what seemed like hours. Focused on today's date, he moved slowly toward it. He hadn't marked the day . . . didn't see the point. It wasn't like he would forget that today was both her birthday and the anniversary of when they'd met. Without conscious intent, his fingers touched the small white square, but in his mind, he saw only her face. The memory of their meeting was just as clear and vivid as if it'd been yesterday. He'd come to the party to work and be seen. Clemmons and many of his associates were attending, and it had been one more way to get in front of the man.

He had been standing, talking to some of Clemmons's business associates, when she'd walked into the room. Seth had quite literally lost his breath. Job forgotten, his reason for being there no longer important. Mesmerized, he'd walked away in the middle of the conversation, without any explanation.

Honor's instincts had been superb. She'd known instantly that someone was watching her. Those golden-green eyes had settled on him and the world had gone away. As he'd approached her, her eyes had widened. She had recognized a predator. Seth had known his expression couldn't have been pleasant. Hell, he was walking across an overcrowded room full of strangers, dressed in a tuxedo and carrying a full-fledged, cast-iron hard-on. Hell no, he couldn't have looked the least bit friendly. But instead of running, she'd stood rooted to the floor and watched him approach.

He'd stopped about a foot from her and found himself speechless. The glib tongue he'd always relied on to get him what he wanted disappeared. Seth had felt like a fifth grader at his first dance wanting to ask the prettiest girl there to step out onto the floor with him. For a man who'd had more girls flocking after him than he wanted to remember, he'd felt like the dumbest and clumsiest of oafs.

She'd held out her hand and given him a small, simple smile. That's all it had taken for him to fall in love with her.

Silently, he'd pulled her out onto the postage-stamp-sized dance floor and, holding her close, started to dance. Instead of telling him to back off, that he was going too fast, holding her too tight, Honor had put her head on his shoulder and glided with him around the small space.

Later, he'd asked her why she'd gone into his arms so easily. A mysterious smile had curved her beautiful, lush mouth, but she had never answered the question. Seth had instantly forgotten what that question was. When Honor smiled . . . He'd trade an entire fortune, if he had one, for one of her smiles.

A harsh breath echoed in the room. What the hell was he doing? Staring at a blank square on a calendar as if it had some sort of meaning? The past was gone and couldn't be reshaped or relived. He'd made the decision to let her go. She was somewhere else, hopefully thriving and happy. If she ever gave any thought to him at all, expletives and vile curses were probably included.

Contacting her and performing a major grovel occasionally entered his head, but that'd be a damn stupid thing to do. He wasn't the same man he'd been back then. What they'd had couldn't be resurrected. Honor had gotten on with her life. He needed to get the hell on with his, too.

He shook the melancholy away. Fishing, swimming, and diving in the midst of paradise—how could a man ask for anything more? He ignored the small voice that whispered the names of the people he loved, the people he'd hurt.

Disgusted with himself, he twisted around, grabbed his sunglasses, and headed out the door. The sun would be up soon. He wanted to get on his boat and be miles from land before that happened. This was his life now; he damn well needed to get used to it.

Minneapolis, Minnesota

I haven't had sex in over four years.

Of all the things Honor believed one should be thinking when a wickedly sharp knife was being held to your throat, this wasn't one of them. Nevertheless, the thought was there and, sadly, all too true. Today was her thirtieth birthday and her life had become one long workday after another. She was in a serious rut. Though that overregimented, mundane life was about to end if she didn't do something about the idiot holding her from behind and threatening to "spill her guts," as he had shouted in her ear.

"Calm down, Edwin," Honor said calmly. "There's no reason to get more years added to your prison sentence by killing an FBI agent."

"And think of the mess."

If Honor hadn't been standing on her tiptoes to avoid being cut, she would have rolled her eyes. When Miller Moss—or Mossy to his friends—started trying to negotiate with a criminal, there was no telling the outcome. The man had a mind for statistics and facts, but when it came to his negotiating skills, he was all thumbs.

"I didn't kill that girl!" Edwin Simpson shouted.

Honor winced. If she lived through this, she wondered if she could get disability for a hearing impairment. Her right ear rang, making her position even more painful.

"If you didn't kill Shelly Amos, then you don't have anything to worry about, do you?"

"Yeah, like anyone's going to believe me. I made a mistake years ago and paid my dues in prison. Does anyone give me credit for that? No. I can hardly find a job and every time some dumb bitch gets killed around here, you assholes come looking for me."

Honor had almost been feeling a hint of sympathy, until the "dumb bitch" part. Shelly Amos had been a bright, beautiful twelve-year-old child, abducted while walking home from the library. Her bloody clothes had been found, but so far, no body. To have Edwin Simpson, a sleazy pervert down to his black socks and white sneakers, make a comment like that was Honor's tipping point.

With the sincere hope that he really didn't intend to kill her, Honor relaxed, dropping her body slightly. Simpson relaxed, too, but the knife caught her when her feet went flat on the floor. Stung like hell, but she ignored it.

Jerking her head back as hard as she could, she slammed it into Simpson's throat. As he gurgled his pain, his hands loosened and then fell away. Honor followed with a heel kick to his shin, then whirled and slammed her forearm across his face. Blood spurted from his mouth and nose. Grabbing his right hand, she twisted until she heard a satisfying pop and Simpson bellowed like an angry hyena. The knife thudded to the floor and then Simpson fell forward. Seconds later, Honor had him handcuffed.

As she got to her feet, she was surprised by the blurry sway of the room. *What the hell?*

"Honor! Sit down!"

Her eyes blinked up at Mossy. "Why?"

"Because you're bleeding. That's why."

Her fingers touched her neck. Damn. The cut was worse than she'd thought. She figured she could at least make it to the chair a few steps away, but her legs had a different idea. With the suddenness of a falling rock, Honor keeled over. She heard Mossy let out a curse. As the thought flitted through her mind that she would rather he catch her than curse, she fell face-first onto the floor and the lights went out.

*   *   *

Blinking awake, she looked up into her father's face and smiled. When he didn't smile back, she reached up to touch him and found only air.

"Thank God you're awake." Her brother's hoarse voice startled her. What was he doing here?

"Nick?"

"Yeah." He came to stand over her and she was shocked to see tears in his eyes.

"What happened?"

"You almost bled out."

"I did?" She didn't remember anything after she hit the floor.

"Another couple of centimeters and it would have been all over."

She sighed. And on her birthday, no less. Good to know that she was keeping up the tradition of sucky birthdays.

Already knowing, she asked anyway, "Mom here?"

"Yeah, she's in the hallway, talking to Aunt Jenny. Didn't want to disturb you."

Aunt Jenny was loud. Get her on the phone and everyone within twenty feet could hear her.

"Is Mom pretty upset?"

"What do you think?"

She grimaced. Beverly Stone was military, through and through. A former army nurse, she'd left the service and become the wife of an air force pilot and, later, the mother of a marine. She'd stoically seen her husband and son deployed again and again without complaint. She was so very cool about it all. However, when faced with a specific trauma, she had a tendency to hover and worry. Honor had a feeling she was about to get a major dose of mama-henning.

"What'd the doctor say?"

"Two more days after you regain consciousness before you can leave the hospital. Two weeks before you're able to work."

And, no doubt, her mother would want her to come stay with her. Suddenly that didn't seem like such a bad idea. She had some decisions to make. Being fussed over while she did that would please her mom and it would give her a chance to think seriously about several issues she'd been avoiding.

Nick's eyes, so similar to hers, watched her keenly. "Want me to detour her?"

"No, I think I'll go home with her. Think through some things."

"About time, too."

"What's that supposed to mean?"

"You haven't been the same since that bastard."

Anytime her brother referred to Seth, it was only as "that bastard." If he and Seth ever met each other, Nick would probably— Hell, what was she thinking? They would never meet. Seth was never coming back to her. He'd made that more than clear. *Crap, Stone, what does it take to get it through your head? The man didn't want you. It's been five years. Get over it already.*

Honor shook her head. "That's not exactly what I plan to be thinking of."

"Still considering a job change?"

She and her brother had no secrets. He knew all about Seth, had held her while she'd cried her eyes out and cursed him fiercely. And she'd been there for Nick when his best friend was killed in Afghanistan and when Marla, his wife, miscarried. Barely one year apart in age, she and her brother had been best friends almost since her birth.

"I just don't have the excitement and fire for the job like I used to."

"You still thinking about that rescue organization?"

"Every time I talk to Noah McCall, he asks if I'm ready to come on board. I think I might be ready."

"What are you going to tell Mom?"

With generations of military behind her, Honor was one of the few members of her family who'd bucked tradition and hadn't joined the armed forces. It had been a personal, heartfelt decision to join the FBI. One that she had made when she was thirteen years old. Her family had humored her when she was a kid, thinking she'd change her mind. When she was twenty-two and applied to the FBI, it hadn't been as amusing to them.

Though her parents had never tried to discourage her from joining the FBI, she knew they'd never given up the hope that she'd follow family tradition. Even though her dad had been gone for almost five years now and Honor's career choice was no longer under discussion, she knew her mom still harbored some hope.

"I'll explain what LCR does. She's got to support that."

Nick shrugged, his expression doubtful. "Anyway, your friend Moss wants to speak to you. Said he had some information you'd want to know."

Had Shelly been found? Was she perhaps not dead after all? Please, God, let her be alive. Honor was so very tired of being too late to save them. She tried to sit up; agony zoomed through her.

"Hold on, Sprite. Why the hell do you have to be so gung ho with everything?"

If she hadn't been hurting so much, that comment would have earned Nick a snort and an eye roll. They'd been trained from birth to go all out and be gung ho. She'd seen her brother overdo it on multiple occasions.

Lying back against the pillow, she allowed Nick to press the button on the hospital bed to raise her head.

"I'd better let the doctor know you're awake."

"How long was I unconscious?"

"On and off about ten hours."

Funny, she didn't remember the conscious moments, although she vaguely remembered seeing her dad's face. When she was at her most vulnerable, she often imagined she saw him. Wishful thinking? Absolutely, but still it gave her comfort.

"Get the doctor in here before you tell Mom I'm awake or she'll come along with him, giving him instructions and drilling him."

Nick grimaced as he headed out the door. "Too late; she's already done that."

Smiling at the image of her tiny mother shooting questions and advice at her doctor, Honor leaned back against her pillow. After her release, she would go stay with her mom, but it wouldn't take two weeks to make the decision she'd been tinkering with for several years. It was time for a change.

After the horrible experience with Seth, she'd moved on and taken the job offer she'd delayed accepting. And she had continued to breathe, think, and go through the motions. Yes, she'd done some good work, saved lives and put several people behind bars, but she had lost the fire she'd once had. Had she been living in limbo, thinking Seth would come back, beg for forgiveness and they'd live happily ever after? She hoped not, but she greatly feared that had been in the back of her mind.

Well, no more. This incident had been a wake-up call. It was time to let go of the past. Time for Honor Stone to get on with the rest of her life and forget that Seth Cavanaugh ever existed.

four

Three months later

His feet propped on the railing of his balcony, Seth
looked out over the small resort town that was now his
home. Compared to Key West, San Saria had little to
offer other than the beach, a couple of decent restaurants, a nice hotel, and some ratty, storm-damaged
beach houses. He'd lucked into the nicest of the ratty
houses. Making all the repairs himself was taking forever. Not only was he a perfectionist, but he wasn't quite
sure what he would do once he finished. At some point,
he figured, there'd be a day when he wouldn't have a
reason to get out of bed. That thought didn't sit well
with him.

Living in paradise had its advantages, but not having
a purpose, a reason to get up in the mornings was going
to suck. So, to delay the inevitable as long as possible,
he'd make sure every shingle fit just right, every nail was
hammered completely straight, and, what the hell, if he
didn't like one color of paint, he could always repaint.

Seth took another swig of his icy cold Pepsi. This was
what he'd told himself he wanted. And for a while, it
had worked. After years of being immersed in a world
of filth, slime, and murderers, a thick layer of grime had
coated his soul. The fresh salty air and sunshine were
just the cleansers he'd needed.

Once Clemmons went on trial, Seth disappeared. The

man might've suspected that he was the one who'd betrayed him, but he couldn't prove anything. By the time it was all over, they'd had more than enough to convict the bastard and Seth had never needed to testify. For all Clemmons had known, Seth had just jumped ship to avoid being arrested, too.

Handling it like that had worked out well, with one major exception. He had finally been able to tell his family the truth, but they had been unable to share the information with anyone else. Full disclosure was too dangerous. So, to the public at large, Seth had still been a well-known restaurateur who'd dabbled in sleaze on the side. His reputation had never hurt his restaurants, though . . . probably even helped, especially when he put them up for sale.

At first, having his family know the truth changed nothing. Then, slowly, one by one, forgiveness and understanding had dribbled in. His mother, his staunchest defender even when it didn't appear he deserved her loyalty, had been the first to offer her support. To hear his mother tell it, Seth was a hero. Though he knew he was anything but, the deep ache he'd felt for so long had been eased by her defense.

His brothers and sisters had been a different matter. Never had he seen such division in his family. To know he'd caused that dissension only made the guilt go deeper. The last family dinner he'd attended, it'd been like a dam had been unplugged. Shouting, accusations, and anger had spewed. And while it had only been his brother Joel and sister Sandra who'd been the mouthpieces of anger, he'd hated the discourse he'd brought them.

Seth had walked out of his mother's house, figuring it'd be better if he never returned. He shouldn't have tried to come back into the fold and act as if nothing had happened. The easy camaraderie he'd once had with his family was gone. Leaving town seemed a hell of a lot better for everyone than sticking around and pretending things could go back to the way they were.

Dropping his feet to the floor, Seth stood and stepped back into his bedroom. To hell with regrets. He had a hankering for clams casino, and the freshest clams always came in around this time. When he got back, maybe he'd go for an afternoon run on the beach. Then he'd come home and spend a couple of hours in the kitchen. His new stove had arrived last week and he'd barely scrambled an egg on it. Time to christen it with something worth his time.

He was almost to the door when the cellphone on his nightstand vibrated. He was tempted to ignore it since it was probably somebody wanting to rent his boat tomorrow. And since tomorrow he'd be using the boat, why pick up?

Shrugging, Seth stalked over and grabbed it anyway. "What?" he barked.

"Seth?"

Not immediately recognizing the voice, Seth said cautiously, "Yeah. Who's this?"

"It's Joel . . . you know, your brother."

His legs suddenly weak, Seth dropped down onto the bed. Someone in his family had died. That was the only explanation; the only reason Joel would call would be to share bad news. Seth closed his eyes. Before he'd heard who or what, grief and regret already gripped his heart. He forced words from his frozen mouth. "What's wrong?"

"It's Kelli." The thick hoarseness in his brother's voice was unmistakable.

"What's happened?"

"She's missing."

"Missing how? Where? When?"

"From her college. She hasn't been seen in over a week."

And no one had called him? What the hell? Had they thought he wouldn't care? Hell, she was his niece! His mind already working in cop mode again, Seth surged to his feet. Crossing the room, he opened a dresser drawer and began to pull out clothes. "What are the police saying?"

"They don't know anything. The FBI finally got involved, but they can't find her."

"I'll be on the first plane tomorrow. I'll—"

"Wait! I . . ." Joel swallowed audibly. "I know you have connections."

"With the Houston PD? Yeah, I still have a lot of contacts there."

"No, you know people who know people. Slimeballs who can—"

Seth froze. "Shit, Joel, I don't know people who abducted kids."

"You can find out stuff ordinary people can't. You owe us, Seth. This family has never been the same. With Kelli being taken, it's killing us."

Seth swallowed a disgusted sigh and resumed grabbing his clothes. There was no point in trying to explain to his brother that his old contacts with his once sleazy undercover life couldn't help Kelli. Joel's opinion didn't matter . . . Seth's first and only priority now was to find his niece. "Give me all the info you have."

As his brother related details, places, and dates, his mind began functioning at full throttle again—something it hadn't done in a very long time. Pulling a duffel bag from his closet, he stuffed in clothes and shoes. When Joel finally paused for a breath, Seth said grimly, "I'll be there tomorrow morning."

Two weeks later
Last Chance Rescue headquarters
Paris, France

Beads of sweat rolling down his handsome, determined face, the man held Honor's arms above her head and growled softly, "Say it."

Her entire body stretched almost painfully on the floor, voice strained from the effort it took to speak, Honor gritted out one word: "Never."

He kept his voice low and soft, as if speaking to a wild animal he was trying to tame. "Come on, give it up, Stone. Say it and I'll let you go."

Not bothering with words this time, Honor wrapped her leg around one of his and jerked. It was like trying to move a mountain. Dammit, she didn't want to give in, but he'd given her almost a full minute of leeway. Someone less stubborn would have said what he wanted to hear well before now and received some relief. Not Honor Stone.

Though it cost her, she arched an arrogant brow and said, "I've got nothing else on my agenda today."

His chuckle echoed in the small gym as LCR operative Aidan Thorne rolled off her. Determined to show no weakness, Honor sprang to her feet, ready for another attack.

Sprawled on the mat as if it were a bed, his grin as cocky as ever, Aidan drawled, "Just because you didn't say I'm the best doesn't mean you didn't mean it."

"Now, that's the kind of logic I'd expect from a surfer dude."

As he got to his feet, he gave his usual snort of disgust for one of her many nicknames for him.

Honor pulled the elastic band from her sweat-dampened hair and ran her fingers through it. Panting lightly, she smiled at the man she'd almost bested. Aidan wasn't breathing as hard as she was, but still, she'd come as close as she'd ever been to bringing down the big lummox.

His answering wink told her he'd read her mind. "You got close."

Except for his blond, beach-bum looks and the hard, cold expression she'd sometimes glimpsed on his face, Aidan reminded her of her brother. She had never been able to take Nick down, either. Didn't mean she'd ever stop trying. Someday both men would be paying her the hundred bucks they'd promised if she ever accomplished that goal. Never one to back down from a challenge, she intended to collect in full.

Her grin equally cocky, she replied, "One day, Beach Boy . . . one day."

He snorted again and threw her a towel. "In your dreams."

"You two through razzing each other?"

Honor whirled around and smiled at Noah McCall, who stood at the door. In unison, she and Aidan replied, "Never."

Though McCall's mouth twitched in humor, the somber expression in his eyes told her he had something on his mind other than hearing two of his operatives trade insults.

"Honor, can I see you in my office?"

She nodded and threw her towel into a laundry bin. Grabbing a bottle of water, she tossed a grin over her shoulder. "See ya, Goldilocks."

Though Aidan flashed her a smile, she could tell he was disturbed by McCall's expression, too. Feeling a bit more somber she followed her boss into his office.

She'd been with LCR for over two months now, and every day she grew more certain she'd made the right decision. Already she'd been on four rescues—all successful. Rescuing live victims felt damned good.

Not one to wait, Honor dropped into a chair and asked immediately, "What's wrong?"

"You think you're ready to head up a rescue?"

"Absolutely." She might feel lacking in other areas of her life, but she didn't doubt her abilities.

"This might be a tough one for you."

"Why's that?"

"It involves someone you know."

She sat up straighter. Someone she knew was in trouble? Why hadn't she already heard about it? Her heart thudded with dread. "My family?"

"No." McCall paused for a second and then said, "An old friend."

And she knew. Without McCall having to say another word, she knew it was Seth. All breath expelled from her, she collapsed back into her chair. Was Seth in trouble? Hurt? After she'd left Houston, she'd deliberately not followed what happened to him. Hell, he could be in prison for all she knew. But the thought of him hurting or in pain, no matter how much he'd crushed her heart, wasn't something she wanted. Of course she didn't love him, but still . . .

Thankful for the ability to keep her expression neutral, Honor asked calmly, "Who?"

"Seth Cavanaugh."

Of course, McCall would know about her former relationship with Seth. It hadn't exactly been a secret that they'd dated; their breakup had been fodder for Bureau gossip for weeks.

"What's happened?"

"His niece has been abducted. He's asked for our help."

Refusing to acknowledge her immense relief that Seth was apparently fine, she asked, "Does he know I work for LCR?"

"Not yet. I thought I'd leave you to be the one to tell him."

McCall was notorious for getting involved in his operatives' pasts, often reuniting old lovers. Her boss's manipulation was not only unappreciated, but he obviously didn't realize that throwing her and Seth together would not produce the results he normally got. She and Seth had nothing left between them. He had destroyed that when he'd walked out of her life.

"What are the details?"

"The niece is twenty years old. Disappeared from a small private college in Iowa. No ransom demanded."

"How long has she been gone?"

"Almost three weeks now."

"What are the authorities saying? Is the Bureau involved?"

McCall nodded. "They're surmising that she's dead or has run away."

"Seth doesn't believe that?"

"No. As soon as he found out, he started doing some research, and he's uncovered what he thinks is a pattern. A couple of other girls have disappeared under similar circumstances this year. And two last year."

Honor frowned at the oddity. "If there have been four other disappearances, why would the Bureau think she's run away?"

"Other than the ages, there's no real commonality between the victims. Different backgrounds, different races. The locations of the disappearances stretch across the country."

Honor nodded. Yes, there had to be a pattern, some similarity.

"So Seth is asking LCR to find his niece and the other girls?"

"Yes, but only if he can be involved."

"Involved how?" Seeing Seth again was one thing;

having him close by, seeing him on a daily basis, was out of the question. "Seth isn't trained to—"

"He's a former cop."

"That was several years ago. And he's a former cop who resigned under suspicion."

"I think you need to talk to Cavanaugh before you make the assessment that he's not qualified."

Had Seth turned his life around? Five years ago, he'd been teetering on becoming, if not a criminal, at the very least a man with questionable ethics and judgment. Not that it mattered to her if he had or not, but for his family's sake, she hoped he had changed for the better.

"Is he coming to Paris for a meeting?"

"He's already here."

Her heart thudded harder. "Where and when are we meeting him?"

"In about two hours. Here."

Her eyes narrowed as she looked at her boss. She was glad if Seth had taken a new path in his life, but to have him come to LCR headquarters seemed to be taking that assumption too far. Only LCR operatives and people McCall had total trust in were allowed to know this location. Most meetings with clients took place in hotel rooms around the city.

"Do you think that's a good idea?" Honor asked.

"I'm not worried."

Though surprised, Honor didn't question him further. McCall's first priority was protecting LCR and its employees. If he was sure, she wasn't going to argue the point.

The heart that refused to acknowledge any remaining feelings for the man who'd trampled it so thoroughly began to thud harder. Seth was here . . . in Paris.

"Since you apparently know about my past relationship with Seth, are you sure you want me to handle the case?"

"I trust your judgment." McCall leaned forward, his black eyes piercing in their intensity. "Do you?"

"Do I what?"

"Trust your judgment? Can you put the past aside and do your job?"

She wanted to snap out a "Hell, yes!" but bit back the automatic reply and made herself think calmly, unemotionally. Okay, yes . . . the sound of Seth's name sent chill bumps over her skin. The love no longer existed, but she couldn't deny their past. The intensity of their relationship was unlike anything she'd experienced before or since. Could she see him every day and do her job? Of course she could. She was older, wiser. Seth had no control over her life. Not anymore. She had wanted to make a complete break from her past. Well, what better way to do that than to face the nemesis of her heart?

"Yes, I trust my judgment. And yes, I can do my job."

His expression telling her he had expected no other answer, McCall said, "Be back at four o'clock for the meeting."

Honor got up and went out the door. She'd always faced challenges head-on; this would be no different. Rescuing Seth's niece and any other victims was her priority. Completely eradicating Seth Cavanaugh from her mind would just be an added bonus: the final and much-needed death knell to any remaining feelings for the man who'd never deserved her love in the first place.

five

Seth sat in his hotel room. He was a ten-minute walk from the address Noah McCall had given him. He had half an hour before he needed to leave. In that time, he wanted to review his notes. Though he could almost recite them from memory, he nevertheless went over them again.

His niece Kelli, aged twenty, had disappeared from Tyron College, a small private school in Des Moines, Iowa. She'd left for class one morning and never returned to her dorm. Her roommate had reported her missing the next day. The police had scoured the county looking for her, with absolutely no results.

Kelli's sweet, innocent face stared up at him and his heart hurt for her. Where was she? Who had taken her and why? He refused to even consider that she might not be alive. He would find her and bring her back home. There was no other option.

Laying out the photographs of the four other missing girls beside Kelli's picture, Seth once again strived to see the tie . . . the commonality. FBI said one didn't exist. They were treating the disappearances as separate cases. Logically, he knew he should, too. There were no similarities other than gender, age, and that the girls were college students. The disappearances ranged over an eighteen-month time span. There were numerous reasons why each of these girls could have disappeared, and none compared to the others. So why couldn't he look at Kelli's disappearance as a separate entity?

Because that's what everyone else was doing. Fresh eyes, a new take—why the hell not? He had no other leads to go on. Besides, this was what he was good at. Working undercover, never knowing if or when he'd be found out, had trained him to look for nuances, clues that didn't seem suspicious.

The last few months before Clemmons finally went down, he'd drawn his inner circle tighter and tighter around him. The older Clemmons had gotten, the more suspicious he'd been. With good reason. Seth had been on the outer edge of that inner circle and each day that dawned, he had woken with the knowledge that it could be his last. But as far as he knew, Clemmons had never suspected him. Bill had once told him he played polished sleaze better than anyone he'd ever met. The man had meant it as a compliment, but it'd ended up making Seth feel even dirtier.

Maybe the nickname he'd had in school had been a portent for his future. He'd been known as "the dark Cavanaugh" and looked nothing like the rest of his family. Everyone, including his parents, had been golden blond with light blue or green eyes. Seth had gotten some recessive gene, giving him the black hair and dark blue eyes of a great-grandfather. Funny, the man had been a minister.

Throwing off his self-indulgent thoughts, Seth looked down at the photographs. Five young women, ranging in age from eighteen to twenty-four, stared up at him. What secrets lay behind the soft, vulnerable eyes? What hopes and dreams had they had? What had they done to attract a predator? And most important, how the hell was he going to find them?

* * *

Honor stood outside Noah's office. She knew they were in there waiting on her. The sound of muffled male voices came through the door. One of those was Seth's. It had been five years since she'd heard that sexy, rough-edged voice. Five years since she'd gazed into those piercing dark eyes. Five years since . . .

Oh God, what was she doing? He meant nothing to her anymore. Their relationship had lasted barely three months. Three months in thirty years of living. That was nothing . . . he was nothing.

She glanced down once more at her clothes. Her favorite black pantsuit, paired with an ice-blue silk camisole and a multicolored scarf around her neck. She'd taken to wearing a scarf to cover her scar; though it had faded somewhat, it was still there. Besides, she wasn't the most fashionable person; the scarf made her feel a bit more up-to-date.

Professional and serious was the image she'd spent years honing. Today, that image was more important than ever. The last time Seth had seen her, she'd acted like a weak, brokenhearted imbecile—an embarrassment to generations of stoic, unemotional Stones. With the exception of losing her father, that had been the last time she'd shed tears over anyone or anything. Emotional outbursts, wearing her heart on her sleeve—all in the past.

Pulling in every reserved and stony image of generations of men and women in her family, Honor opened the door and walked in. Seth sat across from Noah. Aidan and another LCR operative, Jared Livingston, sat farther away. All eyes were on McCall, listening to a conversation he was having on his cellphone. As unobtrusively as possible, Honor sat down beside Aidan. He gave her a quick wink and then turned his attention back to their boss.

Though Seth never moved his gaze from Noah, Honor

knew the instant he realized that she was there. His expression didn't change, but a small, subtle difference in the set of his broad shoulders told her he knew.

She could see only his profile, but from what she could tell, he looked older, harder. His skin was bronzed, as if he'd spent months in the sun. His hair was longer than it had been before, several inches below his ears. He was dressed in a light blue chambray shirt and jeans. She'd never seen Seth wear anything other than a suit or dress slacks. This new, casual Seth surprised her.

Another subtle shift in his shoulders alerted her that he knew she was looking at him. Not ready to meet his direct gaze yet, she moved her attention to McCall, who seemed to be arguing with someone about getting access to some records. His hand moved rapidly across a sheet of paper as he jotted notes. Without looking up, he put his hand over the phone and growled, "I need you to get on the phone and call some of your contacts. I'm getting the runaround here."

Thankful to have her total focus somewhere else, she asked, "What do you need?"

"Not you, Stone," Noah said. "Cavanaugh."

She jerked her gaze to Seth, who was already pulling his cellphone from the front pocket of his jeans. What kind of contacts did Seth have? Was he back in the good graces of law enforcement, or was this some sort of underground connection McCall thought might be helpful?

Shamelessly eavesdropping—he could have gotten up and left the room if he didn't want anyone to hear—Honor tried her best to see the expression on his face as she listened.

"Yeah, it's Cavanaugh. Let me speak to Larry."

Seconds later, Larry must have answered because Seth said, "We're getting no help from your guys in the Bureau. What's up?"

The Bureau? Seth was talking to Lawrence Atmore, the supervisory special agent in charge of the Houston FBI branch? How did Seth know him?

"Yeah, well, tell them we're all on the same page. Everyone wants to find these girls alive." Several seconds later, Seth closed his phone and looked at McCall. "They're emailing the information to you."

McCall nodded, seemingly not one bit surprised by the help Seth had been able to get with one small phone call. She had thought Seth was the only one who would be blindsided by this meeting, but she was beginning to feel quite differently. Somehow Seth had either turned his life around so completely that he had Bureau heads taking his calls without delay, or she'd tumbled down a rabbit hole and nothing was making sense. What the hell was going on?

Regulating his breathing, Seth did what he'd done for years: pretend. If he allowed any of his thoughts to show, he figured everything would blow up. Flying across the massive cherry desk and knocking the shit out of McCall was a temptation. But since Livingston and Thorne might have a few issues with him attacking their boss, they'd gang up and he'd get the shit beaten out of him. Besides, hard to jump up and fight when you weren't sure your legs would hold you to stand. Just what the hell was Honor doing here?

Stupid question. She was, of course, apparently now working for LCR. No doubt this was a test. For both of them or just him? Didn't matter. He'd passed more difficult tests. You gritted your teeth, stiffened your spine, and persevered.

"Okay, here's what we know." McCall clicked a button on his desk and a wide-screen television appeared on the wall behind him. Then the photographs of five young women were there, one of them Kelli.

"As you can see, all are around the same age. All attending college when they went missing. Those are the only similarities anyone has been able to discover so far."

"Friends, boyfriends, relatives . . . they have no clue?" Honor asked.

"No," Seth answered before McCall could. Might as well jump into the thick of things and show how little it mattered that he'd soon be working with a woman he'd once had sex with numerous times. And really, wasn't that all they'd done? Sex, damned good sex, but that's all it'd been.

"Were you going to add something to that sentence?" McCall asked.

Shit. So much for acting like he had a lick of sense in his head. "Sorry. No boyfriends for any of the women . . . at least none steady. The friends of each of the girls gave no clues. The relatives were even more clueless." He nodded at the folders stacked on McCall's desk. "Everything we have is in those folders."

He tensed when Honor stood and went to pick one up. It was the first time he'd seen more than just her profile since she'd entered. Damn, had she always been so beautiful, so sexy? So coolly untouchable?

She passed a folder to Livingston and Thorne and then sat down again.

McCall's voice drew him back in focus. "Stone is taking the lead on this case. Livingston and Thorne will assist. Cavanaugh, you claimed you have the experience to work this case. I spoke with your former captain; he agrees."

Seth nodded. He hadn't expected McCall to just take his word. However, he could feel the surprise radiate from the woman to his right. Stupid really, but Seth couldn't deny a huge let-down feeling in his gut. She hadn't followed what had happened to him after they broke up.

Clemmons's arrest and trial had been a big news story. Not that Seth had been a part of any of it. By the time it was done, he'd wanted nothing to do with the case and certainly none of the publicity. But the governor had known about his involvement, and his superiors had known. With Honor's contacts, if she'd asked the right people, she could have known, too. She apparently hadn't asked; hadn't cared to ask.

Seth had kept up with Honor's career for a few years and then forced himself to stop. Knowing where she was, what she was doing, had been a form of torture. He hadn't stopped cold turkey—it had been a process of not checking for several days, then for several weeks, and so on. Finally, one day, he had stopped.

Too bad, since if he had continued, at least he might not have been so caught off guard.

Seth had no issues with Honor being in charge of the case. He knew what a professional she was, and before he'd stopped following her career, he'd seen what an asset she'd been to the Bureau. Finding Kelli and the other young women was his number one priority, no matter who gave the orders.

Giving a nod to McCall to show he had no problems with that decision, he looked to Honor and said, "How do we proceed?"

A slightly startled gasp from Honor had an unwelcome response in Seth's body. He remembered her little gasps. Right before she climaxed, one tiny gasp from those beautiful lips had given him warning about what was to come. And now the memory of that gasp had given him a boner hard enough to hammer nails. Just what he didn't need.

Glowering his displeasure, he said, "Do you even know anything about the case?"

Myriad expressions crossed her face, irritation the most prominent. "Since I was just given the case, I think you know the answer to that."

So what if everyone was looking at him strangely? Better they think he was just an ass than a man who had a hard-on from hell. "What do you need to know?"

"I'd like to take a look at the information and then reconvene in"—she glanced at her watch—"about three hours. Does that sound okay to everyone?" He watched her meet everyone's eyes. When she came to his, her gaze dropped to his mouth. Was it because she couldn't meet his eyes or was she perhaps remembering some of the same things he was?

"Works for me," McCall said and stood. "Cavanaugh, would you stay a few minutes? Everyone else, be back here at eight this evening."

Strangely silent, the group of three walked out the door. Seth waited till he heard it close before he turned to McCall, ready to blast him for the dirty trick he'd played. Before he could open his mouth, the LCR leader said quietly, "If you can't handle working with her, we'll still take the case."

Attempting bravado never entered his head. This wasn't about him and his sex-starved libido. This was about finding Kelli and four other young women.

"I'll be able to work the case fine. I'm assuming the surprise with Honor was your way of testing me?"

His gaze coolly calculating, McCall nodded. "If you're not able to deal with seeing an old girlfriend, you sure as hell aren't going to be able to handle working this case. I needed to see your reaction."

Though he didn't like the man's method, he couldn't argue with him. Thankfully Seth was the only one who knew he'd failed McCall's test.

"Finding my niece and the other girls is the only thing I care about."

McCall led him to the door. "With Honor in charge of the mission, I have no doubt that will happen. If you didn't know it already, she's one of the smartest and most professional people I've ever met. I'm just glad she survived that attack."

Before Seth could ask him what he meant, McCall closed the door in his face.

What the hell . . . ? Honor had almost died?

Hidden away in a corner, the conference room was rarely used since it was so small, holding only a table large enough to seat five. Honor found herself working there frequently instead of going back to her apartment. Since she lived outside Paris, wasting time going home made no sense. Besides, she wasn't sure she would have been able to drive.

How could she have forgotten how incredibly gorgeous Seth Cavanaugh was? And not just his looks made her weak in the knees—the powerful effect of his presence was a phenomenon on its own. Within seconds of entering the room, she'd been sweating. The instant she'd heard his voice, she'd become aroused.

Dropping the file on the desk, Honor pulled off her jacket and took a healthy swallow from the bottle of water she'd grabbed from the small refrigerator in the gym. Lusting after a man who'd crushed her under his foot like a bug was one thing; she was the only one who stood to be hurt and humiliated again. Lusting after a man while on a case was completely different. She was a professional and had a job to do; these missing girls needed her full concentration.

Body temperature lowered and her composure finally returning, she opened the file in front of her and became lost in the world of five young women who were either dead or going through hell. Either way, she was determined to find them.

Immersed in her reading, she didn't realize he was in the room until his deep voice grumbled across the room: "McCall said you almost died."

Honor's head jerked up. How the hell could a man so large move so quietly? The heart that had just calmed down returned to its thundering pace. Ignoring her body's reaction, she said, "I think we need to establish some ground rules."

"Like what?"

"The past is in the past. We're both here to do a job." She glanced down at the folder. "This case is our only priority."

He began to move slowly toward her, and Honor had to grasp the edge of her chair to keep from jumping up and running away. Damned if she would let him see the effect he had on her.

"Agreed. But I need to know what happened."

Arching a brow, she said helpfully, "What happened . . . ?"

"You were attacked . . . almost died."

She wanted to ask why he even cared. The intensity of those deep blues eyes stopped her. If she asked, she had a feeling he would give her an explanation she wouldn't want to hear.

"I took down a sleaze a few months back. He sliced my neck . . . came a little too close to the jugular vein."

He was standing in front of her before she knew it. "Let me see."

"Wh . . . what?" Heat washed over her body. She shook her head, her eyes skittering away from that penetrating deep blue gaze. "No, you don't need to see."

"Yes, I do."

She forced herself to look at him. Eyes usually intensely blue now seemed almost black, they were so dark. A thought came to her: *He cares.* And not in a curious, "I want to see your scar" kind of way . . . or even a sexual way. The look on his face was one of deep concern, almost fear.

Her fingers were at her neck, unwrapping the scarf, before she even realized it. Pulling the material away, she tilted her head back. Callused fingertips gently caressed the slightly raised scar that ran across the base of her throat. Honor shivered as every erogenous zone in her body stood to attention, ready to shout hallelujah. With one touch of his finger, Seth has managed to unfreeze five years of denial.

"I'm sorry."

Sweet shards of heat spread from her nipples to her groin. Oh, that sexy, rough-edged voice . . . Then the words registered. "Sorry for what?"

Naked emotion so fleeting she almost thought she had imagined it crossed his face. Then a blank stare replaced the look, making him seem hard and emotionless. But dammit, there'd been something there; she was sure of it.

He dropped his hand and backed away. "I'm sorry this happened to you. I hope you taught the prick a lesson."

Shaken by the odd exchange, she nodded vaguely, her head feeling much too loose on her head. "Yes, he's in prison."

"Good." He glanced down at the folder. "I'll leave you to your review. See you at eight."

Before she could react or respond, he was gone, leaving Honor with unanswered questions, a body temperature well over the norm, and a throbbing arousal that she knew had only one cure.

six

Tranquillity, Wyoming

Alden Pike stood at the top of his mountain and surveyed his kingdom below. What had once been only a dream had become a reality—his fantasy come true. In the midst of a vast wilderness of nothingness, he had created paradise.

No, it hadn't been easy, but he was at last reaping the rewards of all his years of hard work and sacrifice. And because of him, his people were happy and thriving. What had begun twenty years ago with a ragtag group of three men and two women inhabiting a two-room shack a few miles outside Carson City, Nevada, had become a community of over one hundred devout members living a utopian dream.

His people had followed him wherever he led. Fifteen years ago, his dreams had brought him to this piece of land—one hundred and fifty acres of nothing but privacy, beauty, and tranquillity. Lois, his first wife, had chosen the name. And because he'd loved her and indulged her whims, he had gone along with it. Now he couldn't imagine his kingdom being called anything else.

Lois was long gone. Taken by a sadness that swept over her mind and turned her from a beautiful, eager-to-please young woman into a middle-aged shrew with a stubborn streak and a sour disposition. Saying goodbye had been hard for both of them. He'd seen the glaze of tears in her eyes seconds before she took her last breath, but he'd also seen the gratitude. In life, he'd given her the gift of spending her good years with him; in death, he'd given her the gift of peace. What more could a woman ask of her man?

He had tried to replace Lois from time to time, with little success. Each time he'd thought he'd found his queen, she'd turned into just another shrew who grew older and less agreeable, and he'd had to say goodbye. Incredibly frustrating, yes, but settling for anything less than absolute perfection wouldn't be fair to him or his people. They needed his leadership to thrive, and he needed a woman worthy of him to keep him satisfied. A satisfied leader created happy followers. So far, that perfect woman had eluded him. He wanted the very best—that's what his people would want for him, too.

Heavy responsibility weighed on his broad shoulders—the kind few in the world could manage. Like kings of old, if people obeyed his rules, relinquished their worldly goods, and gave him their blind faith, he saw to their needs. Certain people needed to be taken care of and told what to do. Alden had been a young man when the realization had come that he was called to lead.

Caring for his people meant taking care of all their needs and desires, even the most basic. That's why new blood had to be brought in each year, revitalizing and energizing the entire community. Older men who'd come to Tranquillity seeking direction and peace needed companionship. Young boys who'd once played with toy guns and blocks of wood had grown into hot-blooded men who required mates.

When daughters were born in Tranquillity, they were promised immediately. But as the community grew, outside women had to be obtained. It was the only way to sustain his people and provide for their needs. Alden knew all about the urges of men. Cravings as natural as a rising tide could be soothed only by the right woman. Alden took immense care in making sure he selected the best.

"May I approach?"

Alden turned at the lilting tone of Tabitha's voice. So much like her mother, but so much more obedient and joyful. From the moment he'd held her in his arms, he had known what true happiness was. He had nurtured her and taught her all the things she needed to know. And she had become exactly what he'd dreamed.

Holding out his hand, he gestured that it was appropriate to come to him. White-blond hair flowed down her back, her skin a light peach and her expression the sweet one of perfect submission. Lovely beyond reason, she glided toward him, her hand outstretched, a smile of pure radiance on her beautiful face. His angel.

Alden opened his arms wide and she went into his welcoming embrace, cuddling close. He whispered against her silky hair, "I missed you last night."

"The plain one needed someone to stay with her." Her smooth brow furrowed with confusion. "She's more scared than others have been. Having me there to instruct her on her destiny was important."

Alden grunted his approval. Sacrifices were necessary to ensure the health and well-being of new family members. "You will be with me tonight."

Her face lit up. "It would be my honor."

"Good. We'll have a light dinner and then retire early."

She nodded eagerly and then said, "I've promised the girl you might come by for a visit."

Alden frowned, not comfortable with the unusual request. The rules were there for a reason. "That's not the usual procedure."

"I know, but she's doing so much better than she was a few nights ago, I wanted to give her a reward. What greater privilege could there be than to spend some time with you?"

Emotion swelled his chest. How fortunate he was to have his treasure. No matter what woman he eventually took as his wife, he'd always have his Tabitha by his side.

He took her hand and led her down the steep trail. She and two elders were the only ones allowed to visit him while he was at the top, in solitude. From time to time, he glanced at her, relishing the beauty of her slender frame. At twenty, she was a young lady, developed in her body and her mind. Alden had nurtured her from infancy and she had blossomed into even more than he had envisioned. Lois hadn't understood their connection—had called it unnatural. One of the many reasons she'd had to depart this earth.

On level ground now, he allowed her to lead him to the concrete building where their new members began their training. Tabitha opened the door for him and he entered the darkened, silently chilled hallway. Each holding room was small and necessarily utilitarian. The initial training began here. In the back of the building, where privacy could be had, advanced training was conducted.

Alden made his way down the hallway, peeking inside each door he stopped at, checking on the occupants. Only three of the rooms were in use. When the demands grew greater, as he knew they would at some point, they could easily double up and have two girls to each room. It would be an interesting experiment to see how that altered their perception of their new life.

He stopped at a room and Tabitha unlocked the door and pushed it open. The young blonde lay on the small cot, her arms and legs secure, her body nude.

Unclothed, she was much heavier than Alden remembered. Perhaps her diet would need to be adjusted. He would confer with their healer before he made that decision. Also, since he'd yet to select her mate, he didn't want to alter her appearance too much. A few of the men might enjoy a meatier woman.

With his gentle, practiced smile, one he'd created especially for new additions, he gazed down at her. "How are you, my sweet?"

She opened her eyes. Ah yes, now he remembered why he'd chosen her. Such an enchanting color of light blue, almost the exact shade of the sky in the early autumn.

Those eyes clouded with tears as she whispered, "Please, let me go home."

"This is your home, my sweet." Lowering his head till his mouth touched the delicate shell of her ear, he whispered softly, "One you'll never leave again."

Feeling considerably better, Seth entered McCall's office at exactly eight o'clock. A five-mile run and an ice-cold shower had been a necessity after his brief talk with Honor. He never should have touched her.

At a small noise behind him, he looked over his shoulder to see Honor, Livingston, and Thorne come in behind him.

McCall stepped around to the front of his desk and sat in the seat Honor had occupied earlier. He gestured at the floor. "All yours, Stone."

Her demeanor solemn and all business, Honor stood next to the screen that revealed the five faces of the young women who were missing.

"Drenda Greene, Karen Hatcher, Anna Bradford, Missy Meads, and Kelli Cavanaugh. Drenda has been missing the longest—about eighteen months. Karen was reported missing three months after Drenda. The other three, Anna, Missy, and Kelli, disappeared this year. The police and FBI have been involved in each case. Since the disappearances are spread across the country, separated by months with the only similarities being that the women were in college, the cases are not considered related."

She pointed at a girl with brown hair and dark brown eyes. "This is Anna Bradford, from Halo, Arizona. She's twenty-four and disappeared from Durrant University in Harristown, Oregon."

Pointing to another photograph, she said, "Missy Meads, from Bloomington, Indiana. She has no family and, from what her file indicates, no friends. No one reported her missing until her landlady went to collect the rent and realized she was gone. It's possible that she was missing at least two weeks before her disappearance was noticed."

As she went through the skeletal biography Seth had been able to dig up of each young woman, he was once again reminded of Honor's competence. No matter his personal feelings; he was damn glad she was on the case. The compassion was there, but tempered with a fierce determination. A determination shared by him.

"The last one to go missing was Kelli Cavanaugh, Seth's niece." Intelligent, golden-green eyes settled on Seth. "I'll go over the background we have on her. After that, if you have anything to add, please do."

Seth nodded. "Thanks."

All eyes were on the screen as the photograph of a blond-haired, blue-eyed Kelli appeared. "Kelli is a twenty-year-old sophomore. Her home is in Houston. She attended Rice University last year, but transferred to a private college in Iowa this past semester. According to her parents, she's shy and has only a few close friends. She's studying computer science. The day she disappeared, she went to all of her classes but the last one. She never returned to her dorm."

Seth hadn't seen Kelli in over a year. Joel had given him the most recent picture he had of her, but he didn't think she'd changed a lot from the last time he'd seen her. Still that sweet, shy smile, the inevitable Cavanaugh dimple in her right cheek, and the slightly up-tilted nose that all of his sisters had lamented over when they were growing up.

A poignant memory tugged at him. When Kelli was little, maybe about six, Seth had been teaching her how to ride a bike. She'd panicked going down a small hill, lost control, and wrecked. His heart had been in his throat, but she had been up on her feet before he could get to her. Blood had been running down her leg from a badly scraped knee and she'd had an angry-looking scratch on her chin. Instead of crying, she'd grinned and said, "I reckon I forgot to brake, Uncle Seth." He'd grabbed her and hugged her hard, afraid it'd be weeks before she'd be willing to try again. Instead, she had insisted on getting back on her bike immediately.

She had been a tough kid . . . he hoped to hell she was still tough.

Aware that Honor had finished with Kelli's bio, Seth leaned forward and told them what he remembered about his niece. "She is shy around strangers, but with her family or those she feels comfortable with, she's very outgoing. She's compassionate and loves animals of all kinds. Has a great sense of humor, doesn't do well in sports, but is a whiz at computer games." Realizing he'd shared almost nothing helpful, he added, "I haven't seen her in a while. Most of these are the things I remember about her when she was younger."

The sympathy on Honor's face had him swallowing hard. He hadn't realized how emotional he'd felt until he'd started talking.

"Stone, you have a plan you're ready to share yet?" McCall asked.

Moved by Seth's obvious affection for his niece, Honor cleared her throat and turned back to the group. Focus was always an important element while on a mission . . . during the next few weeks, it would be even more so. Working this case was going to be hard for Seth. For the plan she was about to recommend, it was going to be hard for her, too.

"I'd like to send Jared to both Missy Meads's and Karen Hatcher's homes and their last known locations. Since those places are only a few hours apart, he should be able to cover both within a few days."

Aware that Seth might disagree, she nevertheless turned to Aidan and said, "I'd like for you to go to Houston and interview the Cavanaughs, talk to Kelli's friends, former teachers, and classmates at Rice, and then head to Iowa and talk with her teachers and classmates there."

Reasonably prepared to handle whatever objections Seth might throw at her, she looked at him and said, "You and I will interview Anna Bradford's and Drenda Greene's families."

Though she saw surprise on his face, all he said was "When do we leave?"

Noah answered for her: "I'll have the jet available at nine in the morning."

She nodded her thanks to Noah and then looked around the room. "Any questions?"

All of the men shook their heads. "Good. We'll meet on the plane at nine." She shot a look at Noah. "I'd like to talk to you for a few minutes."

Noah nodded and stood. "Good luck, everyone, and be safe. If these disappearances are related, whoever is doing this won't go down without a fight. Be vigilant."

Honor deliberately didn't look behind her as Seth, Aidan, and Jared left the room. Hearing the door click behind her, she allowed herself one small, relieved breath.

"Everything okay?" McCall asked.

Honor turned to her boss. It had taken two years and a near-death experience for her to decide to come work for Last Chance Rescue. Known for her professionalism and coolheadedness at the Bureau, she wanted to bring those same qualities to the first op she was leading here.

"I just wanted to reassure you that my past relationship with Seth won't interfere with this mission."

"If I thought it would, Honor, I never would have assigned it to you."

She had known that, but had felt the need to reassure him. Hell, maybe she was just reassuring herself.

And yet she continued to explain: "I assigned him to work with me. I know Aidan's and Jared's abilities and training. I don't know Seth's."

McCall's mouth relaxed into a half smile. "Again, Honor, you don't need to explain your actions or how you make your assignments. I trust your judgment."

"Any hope of getting Dylan's help on this one?"

Something odd flickered in McCall's expression. Most LCR ops were done on a need-to-know basis. However, it had been months since she'd seen Dylan Savage. She'd worked with him on a couple of rescues before she'd started with LCR, but none since. It was almost like he'd gone into hiding.

"He's working a case that's taking most of his time these days."

She nodded, knowing McCall would reveal nothing else. Changing the subject to something she'd meant to ask him this morning, she said, "How's Samara feeling?"

"She's doing great. Morning sickness is over, thank God." A full-fledged grin brightened his face. "Now she's driving me crazy with names. Since neither one of us wants to know the sex of the baby, she's got double the names she can't decide on. And since Shea and Ethan's baby girl was born, Shea's giving her suggestions, too."

She laughed softly at the slightly bemused expression on her boss's face. The tough-as-bullets Noah McCall loved his wife and son to distraction, and it was obvious he was thrilled about the new addition to the family. One of the many reasons she had wanted to work for Last Chance Recue was the humanity she'd seen in McCall.

"Any last-minute suggestions on finding these young women?"

"Trust your gut. I followed the cases when each of the girls disappeared. Based upon the number of young women who go missing each year, I agree with the FBI's assessment that these particular cases have few similarities."

"Then why are we treating this case as if they are related?"

"Finding missing persons is our job. Even if they aren't related, if, in our investigation, we can find just one, we've accomplished a lot."

"But if we find them all . . ."

McCall's eyes gleamed. "Then we've accomplished a miracle."

Seth stepped onto the Gulfstream G650 and took a moment to gaze around at the surprising luxury of LCR's jet. Ten chairs plus a couple of narrow sofas, all covered in cream-colored leather, were scattered throughout the cabin. A small table against one wall held coffee and pastries; another table in the corner held a large-screen TV.

He turned to see Aidan Thorne coming down the aisle toward him. Carrying a cup of coffee in one hand and a doughnut in the other, Thorne flashed a grin. "Nice ride, huh?"

"Very."

Downing half the doughnut with one bite, Aidan shrugged. "LCR has some wealthy benefactors. This particular jet used to belong to a prince in the Middle East. Last year we rescued two of his children. This was his thank-you gift."

Seth had done his research on LCR. Not only was their organization's rescue success phenomenal; cases were never turned down because of an individual's inability to pay. In his opinion, whatever they received, money, gifts, or special favors, they deserved.

After more than a week of dead ends in his own investigation of Kelli's disappearance, he'd realized he would have to go for outside help. He had the experience to find her, but not the resources he knew it'd take. After a couple of days of researching rescue organizations, Last Chance Rescue had been his first choice.

Seth handed his bags to a smiling flight attendant and then helped himself to a cup of coffee. Taking a seat across from Aidan Thorne, he eyed the seemingly laid-back LCR operative. Yesterday, he'd observed a warm camaraderie between Thorne and Honor. Were they something more than co-workers or friends? A couple of times they'd finished each other's sentences, as if they had some kind of connection or special bond. Was he not only going to have to work with Honor but also be subjected to seeing her with a lover? Another degree of hell he hadn't expected.

A sound to his right brought his head around. Jared

Livingston came through the door like a dark, ominous cloud. Wordlessly, he handed the flight attendant his bag, grabbed a cup of coffee from the table, and then sat down several seats away. Without acknowledging anyone, he lowered his head and proceeded to read the documents in the folder he'd brought with him.

Seth got the impression that the black-haired, silver-eyed operative was a loner. In yesterday's meeting, though he'd asked pointed questions and offered intelligent observations, he'd engaged in no small talk or joined in conversations with anyone. Solitude surrounded him like an impenetrable shield.

"We set?"

Seth watched as Honor made her way down the aisle to them, and swallowed past an immediate dryness in his mouth. He'd spent five long years trying to forget that loose-hipped walk that somehow exuded both competent professionalism and gorgeous, sexy femininity. Dressed in another pantsuit, this time navy blue and just as serious-looking as the one she'd worn yesterday, paired with a white blouse with ruffles. One of the many things he'd loved about her was the paradox between her professional persona and the woman outside the job. As his lover, she'd not only been feminine and sweet, she'd been the sexiest and most giving woman he'd ever known.

"All set," Aidan answered.

Jared Livingston lifted his head, offered a grim nod, and went back to reading.

Seth gave her a nod, too, and then, forcing himself to look away, pushed the past where it belonged. Last night, he'd spent considerable time lecturing himself about working with Honor. A lecture he fully intended to remember and abide by. And her behavior yesterday was an indication that she'd put the past behind her, too. She'd been professional but pleasant. Seth told himself he could do the same. Okay, so the pleasant part would require some work, but dammit, he would try.

Lifting his gaze from the folder whose contents he had memorized, Jared Livingston turned to the window to watch the building's blur as the jet taxied, then zoomed down the runway for takeoff. This was his favorite part of flying . . . the exhilaration of speed. Damn, he loved that belly-dropping moment when the wheels went up.

Though he enjoyed that moment, he was also aware of what the other occupants of the plane were doing. Aidan was pretending that flying didn't bother him by cracking a wise-ass comment. Jared had come to work for LCR six months ago, and one thing he'd learned about Aidan Thorne was that you should never believe the surface of the man. Behind that cocky grin and bad-boy demeanor lay secrets. But that was Aidan's business. Digging deeper and knowing the man better wasn't on Jared's agenda. Who didn't have secrets?

Eyes still on the blurring view outside the window, Jared turned his attention to Honor Stone. He'd met her a half dozen times and had worked one rescue with her. She seemed competent, if a bit too soft. Since she'd been an FBI agent and had dealt with some seriously dangerous criminals, he assumed the softness was a façade. Again, everyone had their secrets.

Seth Cavanaugh sat to the right of Stone and was doing his best to act as if he wasn't totally aware of her. They had a past. Didn't take a genius to see that or to know that the chemistry was still there. Jared saw past the chemistry to the hurt both of them refused to acknowledge. Their story wasn't over.

The jet leveled out. The small jolt of excitement over, Jared returned to the file for Missy Meads. He'd be interviewing her employer and people who knew her in Indiana before he went on to Michigan to interview Karen Hatcher's family and friends.

Last night, he'd spent hours on the files . . . knew them by heart now. However, Missy Meads's story continued to draw him back to her. Each time he read it, the details made him angrier. How the hell could a young girl be gone for two frigging weeks and no one report her missing? He knew the answer, but it only infuriated him more. Truth was—nobody gave a damn.

No family; she'd been raised in an orphanage. Had few friends, if any. Lived alone in a small, cheap apartment off campus. Worked at a pizzeria that had closed down for repairs about the time she went missing. Hell, even her professors didn't notice when she didn't show up for class. Apparently no tests had been given during that period. The girl had been invisible.

Jared knew he was empathizing with Missy's circumstances, perhaps more than he should. That wouldn't keep him from finding out as much as he could about both Missy and Karen. But Karen had people who cared for her, wanted her to come home. Missy didn't have that. Jared vowed to be that person.

Honor stood in the aisle so she could see everyone's faces. "I know we've got a long flight ahead of us, but let's go ahead and get a discussion under way. The drop-off itinerary is as follows: We'll land in Indianapolis and drop Jared off, then head to Houston for Aidan. Seth and I will then fly to California. Rental cars should be waiting for all of us. The local authorities know we'll be in the area. All have expressed their willingness to work with us and offer assistance where needed, but they'll have eyes on us at all times." She fixed Jared Livingston in her gaze as she added, "No going solo into dangerous

situations or pissing off the locals. We need their coop-
eration."

Livingston gave a small nod of acknowledgment, but
still Honor worried. She knew the man had come to
LCR fully trained and ready to kick ass. He was more
than capable, but she'd seen evidence of a wild streak.
Lone Ranger heroes were not her favorites to work
with. However, McCall trusted him, and she trusted her
boss's judgment.

"I'm assuming everyone had an opportunity to review
not only their assignments but the information on the
other girls. Any questions or observations come up?"

"I have one," Aidan said.

"What's that?"

Instead of looking at her, his golden-brown eyes focused on Seth. "Out of all the people who go missing
each year, why do you think these five were related?"

Seth shrugged. "After my brother called to tell me
about Kelli, I spent days researching before contacting
McCall. Though I didn't have access to all the information, just what I could dig up or get out of my contacts,
these five seemed to separate themselves out because of
a lack of commonality, as opposed to similarities."

"How's that?" Livingston asked.

Seth blew out a sigh. Leaning forward, elbows on his
knees, he took in everyone's gazes. "With the exception
of their ages and that they're college students, these girls
have nothing in common that we can see. Right?"

Everyone nodded in agreement.

"In my opinion, that's a commonality that's not been
explored enough."

Intrigued by his reasoning, Honor sat down across
from him. "So the fact that there's no reason to think
they're related makes you think they are related?"

"Something like that."

Eyeing him thoughtfully, she nodded. "Looking at things backward sometimes helps."

Seth's mouth twitched. "It's definitely a different perspective."

"You think it's deliberate?" Jared Livingston asked.

"Yeah, I do. The guy's got to know the authorities would look for similarities. What better way to keep them off his ass than to give them none."

Honor shot up from her seat and began pacing, thinking out loud. "Okay, we know the similarities are the gender and age of each victim and that she's a college student. We'll assume the college-student aspect is just because it gives him a large pool to work within. But the age . . . he wants women of about the same age. Is that his preference or does he need that age group for another reason?"

"Not for material gain," Seth said. "The girls range from having nothing to very well off. And ethnicity doesn't matter. Drenda is Hispanic, Karen's African-American, and the other three are Caucasian."

"And I hate to say it, but it's one of those nonsimilar similarities: looks don't seem to matter, either."

Surprised that Livingston was the one to bring this up, she said, "What do you mean?"

"All the girls, with the exception of Missy, are attractive and slender. Missy is . . ." He looked down at the folder in front of him and shrugged. "She wears no makeup, is about twenty pounds overweight, and looks like she just came in from a cattle drive."

The other girls had several photographs in their files. Missy had only one, and Jared was right: it did look as though she had been doing something that not only involved dirt but was also very difficult. Filth and mud covered her jeans; the too tight white sweatshirt she wore had numerous stains.

"Makes me wonder who took this picture," Seth said.

If possible, Jared's face went even grimmer. "That'll be one of my first questions."

Honor observed the men as they continued to discuss Seth's theory and offer input. Each man was as committed as she was to finding these young women. Question was, were they still alive to be found?

seven

Tranquillity

"No, I don't want any of them."

His first instinct was to lash out in frustration, but Alden held his anger in check. His children were completely opposite in temperament. His daughter went out of her way to please him in every way she could. His son, especially lately, did everything to oppose him. Not for the first time, he wished he'd spent as much time training John as he had Tabitha. Now his son was a greedy, ill-tempered, spoiled brat. Alden had no patience for such a person.

"You have three females to choose from, John. Other men have been waiting longer, and are several years older than you. Since you are my son, I'm allowing you to choose first. You should feel privileged—instead, you complain about your choices."

The mutinous expression on John's face was becoming a permanent affliction. "As your son, it's my right to go before others. None of these women will do for me. I wasn't even allowed to go on the hunting trips. My choices shouldn't be limited to the few bitches you drag in here for the others. I deserve only the best."

Alden didn't lose his temper often because when he did, he lost all control. John knew this about him, but the older his son became, the more often he challenged

Alden's decisions. The boy's arrogance was becoming problematic.

Alden's followers weren't allowed to question his authority, and his son was one of those followers. Though he often gave John leeway he wouldn't give others, he refused to allow this.

"I make the mating decisions for Tranquillity, not you."

Brown eyes, so like his, narrowed. "Fine, but at least let me go with you to get the last one for the season. I'm sure I can find one to suit me."

Alden opened his mouth to object, but John stopped him with "You're not the one who's going to spend the rest of your life with her . . . I am."

As much as he didn't want to give in to his son's childish demands, he had to admit that he made a good point. There was no such thing as divorce in Tranquillity. Women and men were bound together until death.

Alden was the only man who was allowed the outlet of divorce. Staying satisfied and free of worry enabled him to be a better leader. He'd made that clear to his people from the beginning. Not that he would ever consider divorce. A man who could not control his woman was not a man. He'd had only three wives . . . all of them had agreed to his requests that they leave him. Once a month, as a show of respect, he visited their graves.

"Very well. The men, starting with Nathaniel, will place bids on the three we have now. In a week or so, we'll go out and you can make the selection yourself."

"A week? Why not—"

Alden sprang to his feet. "Silence!" The temper he'd been fighting spewed forth. "I will not allow more questions. My word is law. Understand?"

John's sullen nod told him that it wasn't over. Alden opened his desk drawer, and before he knew it, the small whip he kept inside it was in his hand. Swinging hard, he slashed it across his son's face, leaving a bloody crevice on his cheek.

Tears stung his son's eyes and his breath hitched rapidly as he tried to control his emotions. The boy knew he had done wrong. It usually took Alden only one strike to get his point across.

Composure finally achieved, John said quietly, "I'll await your instructions, Father."

Satisfied that, for the time being, the matter was settled, Alden dismissed him from the room with a nod. If John complained again or continued his arrogant ways, he wouldn't be as gentle. However, the fire continued to burn inside him, needing an outlet.

Pressing a button on his desk, he called the one woman who had the ability to calm him in the best ways possible.

"Yes, Father?" Tabitha's voice came through the intercom.

"I have need of you."

"I'm on my way." He could hear the happiness in her voice. Keeping him satisfied made her happy. And Alden enjoyed making her happy.

Piney Ridge, California

Honor collapsed onto the bed in the sterile-looking hotel room. She felt as if she hadn't slept in days. Flying internationally always did that to her, but the extra stops in Indianapolis and Houston had been a bit much. Of course, it hadn't helped that Seth had been beside her all the way, either. Not that he had done anything wrong. In fact, he had been polite, had said nothing inappropriate or controversial, and once had cracked a joke that had been funny. Even Jared had lifted half of a lip in a smile.

Seth was behaving like a complete professional, and he was irritating the hell out of her.

No explanation of what he had been doing for the past five years. No information about why Noah McCall thought he was totally qualified for this job. Not once had he offered her anything other than that one touch in the conference room, when his finger had caressed the scar on her neck and he'd said he was sorry. Shivers ran up her spine at the memory.

She could come right out and ask him. She would at some point, if he didn't volunteer the information. How to pose the question was the sticking point. Asking a question without any seeming interest in the answer wasn't something she had a lot of practice with. When asking questions, she always made it clear she was interested in the answer.

Over the years, she had studiously avoided knowing anything about Seth and what became of him. Oh, she'd come close on several occasions. Once, in the middle of the night, she'd woken throbbing and aching from a much too realistic sex-filled Seth dream. She'd slunk into her small office, turned on her computer, and Googled his name. The instant Ruth's Place, his restaurant, popped up, she'd slammed the laptop closed and marched back to bed, furious at herself.

Others had known about her antipathy to his name. After their breakup, a few people had tried to question her about what went wrong. When she'd cut them cold, word had gotten out. Honor had developed the reputation of being fair-minded, professional, and easy to work with . . . as long as one man's name was never mentioned. Now she regretted being so hard-nosed about it. What had she missed? Should she try another

Internet search and this time have the courage to actually read the information?

Blowing out an exasperated sigh at her own foolishness, she got to her feet. She needed to get her butt in the shower; she was meeting Seth in the lobby in half an hour.

They were going to see Drenda Greene's family. Since LCR wasn't a law enforcement agency, they were somewhat limited in their scope of authority. People didn't have to talk with them. That had been a difficult adjustment for Honor. As an FBI agent, she'd been used to people having to talk with her, whether they wanted to or not. Fortunately, the Greene family was interested in getting help any way they could. Their daughter had been missing for well over a year; any additional offer of assistance not only was welcomed but revived hope in what had become a hopeless situation.

Tomorrow they would interview the Bradfords, who weren't going to be as cooperative. Yes, they loved their daughter and wanted her back home. However, Anna's parents were in the middle of a bitter divorce, and talking with Honor and Seth was apparently one more thing they couldn't agree on.

She would be meeting with Anna's mother. Seth would go to the next town over and talk with the young woman's father.

After those interviews, it would be on to the colleges the girls had attended.

Opting not to wash her hair, since blowing it dry would take too long, she finished her shower and was ready to dress in minutes. She stood at the closet and barely paused for thought before selecting a light blue pantsuit. Seth used to tease her about her pantsuits, telling her she must have a closet full of them. The first time he'd spent the night with her, he had discovered how right he'd been in his assessment of her wardrobe. She still remembered the morning he'd walked buck naked into her closet, thinking it was the bathroom. He'd turned on the light and burst out laughing. Seth had a great laugh.

Her eyes rolling at where her thoughts had once again headed, she dressed quickly. Makeup was a light foundation, mascara to darken her lashes, and a colorless lip gloss. Pulling her hair back into a low ponytail, she stepped back to access her appearance. Unimaginative and much too bland, but also coolly professional—an image that would inspire confidence in others. Not only that—seeing Seth again had put her emotions into a tailspin. Dressing in this manner gave her a much-needed feeling of normalcy.

She fastened a side holster at her waist, slid her SIG Sauer inside the pocket, and snapped the buckle. Shrugging into her jacket, she stepped back once more and gave a final nod of approval. Attractive, competent, and businesslike. In no way did she reveal that her insides were experiencing a mild earthquake at the thought that, in a few minutes, she would see Seth again.

Get a grip, Stone. Satisfied with the mini-chastisement, she turned away.

She had deliberately not listened when Seth had checked in, not wanting to know where he would be sleeping. When she opened her hotel room door, she froze. A lot of good that had done; Seth was coming out of his room right across from her.

As if he had known her thoughts moments before, his eyes swept up and down in a hot, thorough glance. "Nice pantsuit. New one?"

The glare Honor shot him could've melted his gun. Now, what the hell had he done to set her off?

Mentally shrugging at the intricacies and intriguing layers of the beautiful woman glaring daggers at him, he headed to the elevator. "You want to grab dinner after we talk to the Greenes?"

Honor entered the elevator first. The instant the doors closed, she said, "I think we need to do more than just have dinner."

Seth went hard instantly. Did she mean . . . ? He snuck a glance at her face. Of course she didn't. Her beautiful face held an expression he'd seen more than once when they were dating. She had questions and wanted answers. And hell, if anyone deserved answers, wasn't it this woman?

He nodded. "You're right."

She released a long sigh, as if she'd been holding her breath. Had she thought he would refuse? Probably. Their last time together hadn't exactly been pleasant. He'd said things he never expected forgiveness for.

Despite how he'd hurt her, he knew it couldn't have ended any other way. Not only would Honor's career have been permanently tarnished if they'd stayed together, but Clemmons would have gladly used her to manipulate Seth. And if the man had tried that, the game would have been up. No way in hell would he have allowed Honor to be used as a pawn or to be hurt. He would've killed Clemmons.

Little had he known that his biggest regret would be in not killing the bastard when he'd had the chance. If he had, at least he would've been spared the nightmares.

The elevator door opened. As if they'd read each other's minds, they exited wearing the same expression of seriousness. The past could be discussed and dissected another time. Now it was time to get to work.

Drenda Greene's family lived in an upper-middle-class neighborhood just outside the city limits of Piney Ridge. Her father was a plumber, her mother a real estate agent.

She had one sister who was still in high school and a brother in middle school.

Evelyn and Marty Greene greeted them with hope in their eyes. Seth had listened to Honor on the phone when she'd set up the appointment. She'd given them a brief rundown of why LCR was on the case. Not in any way had she been encouraging or discouraging about the chances of finding their daughter. But the Greenes were grasping at anything, and LCR's involvement gave them renewed hope.

Sitting in the Greenes' living room, sipping tea and eating cookies, seemed incongruent with what they were discussing, but that was the nature of this case. What the hell kind of refreshment do you serve when you're discussing your missing child?

"So you said that someone hired your company to look into my Drenda's disappearance?" Mrs. Greene was a slender, middle-aged blond with a nervous habit of blinking rapidly when she spoke.

In a compassionate but firm voice, Honor said, "Not only your daughter's disappearance but several others' as well."

"So there's a possibility somebody took our Drenda and is holding her along with other girls?" Mr. Greene was a stout, ruddy-faced man with deep lines around his mouth. The worry in his eyes indicated his grief over his daughter's disappearance.

"That's what we're looking into," Honor said.

Feeling Honor's eyes on him, Seth explained: "A few weeks ago, my niece Kelli disappeared. I'm a former cop, so my brother called me for help. I have the experience to find my niece, but I don't have the contacts. Last Chance Rescue specializes in finding missing people. I felt getting them involved was my best bet in finding my niece."

"But what does that have to do with Drenda?" Her eyes filling with tears, Mrs. Greene added shakily, "Our daughter's been missing for a year and a half."

"We don't know that the person who took Mr. Cavanaugh's niece is the same one who took Drenda; however, that's what we're trying to determine."

Mr. Greene leaned forward, his expression one of desperation. "If there's anything we can tell you that will help you find our Drenda, all you have to do is ask."

Mrs. Greene nodded. "The FBI delved into everything, from our personal life to Marty's and my business associates."

"We appreciate that, Mrs. Greene," Honor said. "What I'd like to do is start with Drenda. Tell us about your daughter."

Seth stayed quiet as Honor led the couple through a discussion of their oldest daughter. Her soft voice and open-ended questions soothed even as she dug deeply into Drenda's personal life.

With tears and a smile, Evelyn Greene talked about how she and her husband had despaired of ever having children and the moment they'd seen a photograph of the Hispanic baby girl who'd been put up for adoption, they'd fallen in love.

Marty Greene chimed in to brag about what a good daughter Drenda was and how she'd been such a good role model for her two younger siblings.

Two hours later, as they stood to leave, Seth felt as though they had a good understanding of the young woman. Drenda was quiet, somewhat shy, had a few close friends and no steady boyfriend. After eight years of lessons, she played piano like a dream and attended church regularly. She had an affinity with animals and planned to be a veterinarian. All of these things were important for victimology and determining a commonality to tie the disappearances together. Unfortunately, he still saw no real relationship between hers and Kelli's disappearances. That gut feeling he'd had that they were related was fading fast.

After shaking both parents' hands and assuring them that if any information about their daughter's whereabouts became available, they would be contacted immediately, he and Honor went through the door and headed to their rental car.

Doing what he'd been taught to do from the time he was strong enough to handle a door of any kind, he opened the passenger door for Honor. She barely acknowledged the gesture, and Seth could tell something was on her mind that she wanted to discuss. He had an empty feeling in the pit of his stomach that he knew what that something was. Not only were they on a wild goose chase, but they'd probably given hope to Drenda's parents when there was no hope.

Seth got into the driver's seat and put the key in the ignition. Instead of starting the engine, he looked over at her. "This is pointless, isn't it?"

Turning to face him, her eyes dancing with excitement, she practically shouted her answer: "Are you kidding? We're on to something, Seth, I know we are."

eight

Seth stared blankly at Honor. It was obvious he'd missed the connection. He confirmed it with "We are?"

Out of the corner of her eye, Honor saw Mrs. Greene peeking out from beind the blinds of the living room. Since she didn't want to get the woman too optimistic until she checked the information on the other missing girls—seeing them have an animated discussion might well do that—she said, "Let's get out of here and I'll tell you."

Seth started the engine and pulled out onto the road. As he maneuvered through the subdivision, she collected her thoughts. *This had to mean something . . . it had to.*

The Greenes' upscale neighborhood had a large park exclusively for the residents. They'd passed it on the way in, and Honor instinctively knew that was where Seth was headed. As he turned onto the paved parkway, she pondered her ability to read him after all these years. Which seemed odd, since she didn't think she'd read him well when they were together.

He parked the car under a shade tree, turned off the ignition, and faced her. "Okay, what'd I miss?"

"Did you hear Mrs. Greene talk about how Drenda hadn't liked the college she was attending the year before and transferred to a smaller school last year, just a couple of months before she disappeared?"

"Yeah . . . so?"

"That's a similarity, Seth. Remember, Kelli did the same thing this year."

The expression on his face wasn't encouraging. "So what? Lots of kids can't settle in one school and move to another to finish up. Two of my sisters did the same thing."

"But it is a similarity . . . something that ties these girls closer together."

"Hell, honey, that's a stretch."

She did her best not to show a reaction to his endearment. It meant nothing. Seth was from Texas. She used to live there, too, and had gotten called "honey," "sugar," and "darling" a hell of a lot more than "Honor." It meant absolutely nothing. But when Seth said it, in that gravelly bedroom voice she remembered so well, her body took it a different way.

Pushing past the need, she said, "A stretch, but still something."

"So, even though they have this similarity, how does it connect them? They went to different schools, all across the country."

Refusing to be discouraged by his underwhelming response to her theory, Honor shrugged. "I don't know. I'm going to call Jared and ask him to check. If he hears the same thing about Karen or Missy, it could very well mean the beginning of a new thread."

Muttering under his breath with what sounded like a "Pollyanna" slur, Seth started the car and continued through the subdivision.

Honor pulled her phone from her purse and punched in speed dial for Jared. Until she heard differently, she was maintaining her optimism. Because right now, it was all they had.

Bloomington, Indiana

Jared took his time closing the cellphone and returning it to his pocket. The conversation with Honor should have eased his fury. Her disappointment had been palpable, reminding him that he wasn't the only one who cared about finding these young women. Though it seemed a thousand miles past a long shot and barely a point to ponder, the fact that Missy Meads had never transferred from one college to another had seemed to deflate her optimism immensely.

"You want another soda?" a cheerful female voice asked.

The young woman, probably about Missy's age, had a cheerleader's enthusiasm in her voice. Pretty, bubbly, and way too damn perky, she flitted from table to table in the pizza parlor, like a butterfly stopping at flowers.

Carmen Endicott was the pizzeria's newest employee, and judging by the lecherous glances of the two men who owned the joint, they were extremely satisfied with their selection. She had been a replacement for an employee both were happy to see leave, no matter how it was accomplished: Missy Meads.

For twenty minutes, while he pretended to enjoy the greasy pizza, he'd listened to the owners of the restaurant discuss Missy as if she were a stray dog that it would have been best to put down. Yes, she had worked there for two years and, yes, she was a competent employee, but she was shy, awkward with customers, and did nothing to make people want to come back to the restaurant. Certainly she was nothing like their new employee, Carmen.

That wasn't what had set Jared off. He had no real issues with hiring attractive employees. That was the way of the world and their own business. What he didn't like was the answer to his question about the photograph in Missy's file. The only picture anyone had of this girl was atrocious.

Since Missy had no family or friends, her employers were the only people who might know about the photograph. After he'd heard them talk about her like she was little more than garbage, Jared figured they'd have a clue about the picture. Turned out he was right. The photograph had been taken just outside their door by one of the owners.

The man seemed proud of the picture and even chuckled when he saw it in Jared's hand. "Yep, took that right after a snowstorm blew in one night. The girl didn't have any chains on her tires and ended up in a ditch. She called and told me she was going to be late. I let that slide, even though it was stupid not to have chains on your tires in the middle of winter. But when she got here two hours later, looking like that, I couldn't resist snapping the shot. Girl was butt ugly to begin with, but with all that mud and gunk all over her, she looked like some kind of swamp monster."

Jared had turned the photograph facedown then, refusing to allow the bastard to laugh at it anymore. Wanting to get the full story, he asked quietly, "How did she get so muddy?"

He shrugged. "Didn't call a tow trunk and had to leave the car in the ditch. Ended up walking to work. Said she fell down a couple of times." He grinned. "Looked more like a couple of dozen times to me."

"Did no one here offer to help . . . maybe to pick her up?"

"Hell no, we got a strict policy here. If you can't make it to work under your own steam, you're out of a job."

The man had been friendly up until Jared had asked softly, "And if Carmen called and told you the same story, would you have given her the same answer?"

Flushed with anger, the man said, "I think it's time you left."

"As soon as I finish my soda."

The look Jared gave the man had the bastard backing away, saying, "Yeah . . . well, there's no hurry. You stay as long as you need to."

Disgusted with himself for shutting off an avenue of communication, Jared threw down money for his pizza and drink and walked out the door. Missy didn't need him beating up her former employer because the guy was an asshole. She needed to be found, along with the other girls.

Once outside, Jared took a cleansing breath. He'd learned long ago to compartmentalize, separating his thoughts from his actions. Working for a government agency few people knew existed had honed those skills. The last few years, though, he'd gotten soft. Being married, working as an investigator for Kane Enterprises, he had lowered his defenses, allowed himself to grow weak. That life was behind him now. The longer he worked for LCR, the harder he could feel himself becoming again. He wasn't there yet, as evidenced by his overreaction to Missy Meads's circumstances. But the hardness would return.

Cocooning himself into a world where only adrenaline and the thrill of the next op existed, he would return to the coldhearted, hard-edged bastard he'd once been. He looked forward to the day when he once more didn't give a damn.

Seth had barely sat down in his chair across from Honor before he said, "I'm sorry I called you 'honey' before."

Honor lowered the menu she held, her golden-green eyes sparkling with humor. "Don't worry about it. I've been called worse. Besides, I've lived in the South a lot; you get used to those words."

"What states have you worked in besides Texas?"

"Georgia and South Carolina. My last assignment was in Minneapolis."

Remembering her love for sunshine and warm temperatures, he grinned. "Bet you nearly froze to death."

She scrunched her nose. "Yeah, a little too cold for my blood."

"How long have you been working for LCR?"

"A little over two months."

"I figured you for an FBI lifer."

She shrugged and dropped her gaze. "I needed a change."

Didn't take a menu smacked over his head to tell him he was getting into territory she didn't want to go to. No one had ever accused him of treading softly. "Did you leave because of the close call?"

Sighing, she put the menu down and leaned forward. "Listen, I'll be glad to share all the things I've been doing for the last five years. Spill my guts, tell you all my secrets. I'll even try to remember what I had for breakfast for the past one thousand, eight hundred and twenty-five mornings if you'll tell me one thing."

Stupid, but it took every ounce of self-control not to cup that beautiful face in his hands and cover the delicate snarl on her lips with his mouth. No one could ever accuse Honor of treading softly, either. One of the many things he admired about her.

Though he figured he already knew, he asked anyway. "What's that one thing?"

"Why the hell do you think you have the right to know anything about me?"

She had him there. He had no rights when it came to her. Had given all of them up to do a job. She had every reason to be pissed, but what was done was done.

"You're right, I don't."

He almost thought she would drop it and not say anything else . . . she had looked that angry. Finally, she said quietly, "Why, Seth?"

Before he could answer, their waiter came to the table. Honor gave her order and as he gave his, she sipped her martini and seared him with that direct gaze that always fired his blood.

After the waiter left, Seth took a long swallow of his iced tea and suddenly wished he didn't hate the taste of alcohol. Anything to get him through the next few minutes.

"Letting you go was one of the—"

She raised her hand. "Let me stop you right there. If you say that letting me go was one of the most difficult things you've ever had to do, I'm getting up and leaving."

"Do you want answers or not?"

She nodded.

"Then let me talk. Okay? I hated letting you go, but it was the only thing I could do."

"Why?"

"You remember Hector Clemmons?"

"Of course. I understand the man finally ended up in prison."

"He did. I helped to put him there."

Eyes wide with shock, she leaned forward. "What are you talking about?"

"I was undercover."

"You're saying you were still a cop when we were together?"

"Yes."

"What about your restaurant?"

"It was mine, but I had some help getting it started. The restaurant was my cover."

"What was your job?"

"To infiltrate, get as close as I could, earn his trust, and then use every means possible to bring him down."

"If that's what you did, why wasn't your name mentioned in the news? I didn't follow the case closely, but I know your name would have caught my attention."

"For one, to protect my family. Even in prison, Clemmons still had contacts. I didn't want to risk them. And by the time it was done, I was so sick of the shit, I wanted nothing to do with it. I just wanted out. Getting credit was the last thing on my mind."

Publicly acknowledging his involvement would have meant interviews, speculation . . . questions. Dredging up memories that he'd give any amount of money to forget.

She went quiet for several moments. Seth withstood her intense scrutiny, figuring if she got up from the table and wanted to kick his ass, she had the right. Just because he wouldn't have done anything different didn't mean she didn't deserve to be both furious and hurt.

Finally she broke the silence with probably the hardest question she could have asked. "When did the job start?"

He shrugged. "The setup took several months. I—"

"But well before you and I met, though. Right?"

Seth nodded, already knowing what was coming.

"You knew you were going to end it with me before we even started seeing each other, didn't you?"

"I knew it was a good possibility."

"And yet you pursued it anyway. Why, Seth?"

What could he say? Anything he said was sure to set her off, because he had no excuse for pursuing her. Hell, what was the point in trying to be evasive? She already despised him. "Because I wanted you."

She laughed. Not her usual pretty, soft laugh, but a hard, angry sound. "That's just great. So I guess once you'd had enough, you figured it was time to end it."

"No, that's not the reason." He'd had years to think about this. Even though he never figured he'd get the chance to explain, the least he could do was have words prepared that weren't going to crush her all over again.

"Then why?"

"Because each day the job became more dangerous and complicated. Clemmons thought I killed a man for him. I didn't, but having that kind of reputation with him . . ." He shook his head. "I couldn't take the risk that he'd ask me to do something to you, just as a show of loyalty or because he thought he could get away with it. He would have used you any way he could."

"I was an FBI agent. You could have told me the truth. Or did you not trust me?"

"Of course I trusted you, but what good would telling you have done?"

She stood and dropped her napkin onto the table. Shoulders straight, with the dignity she wore so well wrapped tightly around her, she said quietly, "You wouldn't have broken my heart . . . that's what good it would have done."

Her movements jerkier than she would have liked, Honor turned away from the table, from Seth's too knowing eyes, and made her way swiftly out of the restaurant. Tears swam, blurring her vision, but she'd be damned if Seth saw them fall.

Okay, so getting up and stomping out the door didn't exactly scream "mature woman totally over her man," but it beat sitting there, sobbing into her salad.

Ignoring the couple that joined her in the elevator, she focused on the floor numbers as they flashed. Once she got to her room, she could lock herself away, have her little pity party in private, and then it would be over. She'd get back to work on this case and forget that once again, with barely any effort at all, Seth had managed to crush her.

The dinging of the elevator door opening was a welcome relief. Just a few more steps to her room and she could let go. Key card in hand, she inserted the device into the slot and pushed the door open.

"Honor."

The breath whooshed from her body. Dammit, he'd taken the next elevator. Refusing to face him, to let him see the pain, she spoke to the door. "Let it go, Seth."

"Hell . . . I can't let it go. You don't know what it did to me, letting you go—"

Whirling around, she snapped, "Did to you?" She shook her head, barely able to make out his face for the tears blurring her eyes. "No, you don't get to be sad or hurt. You're the one who made the decision for both of us. I slept beside you for almost three months. I gave you more than I'd ever given any man, and you just threw it away."

Instead of walking away or telling her to stop behaving like a wimp, he moved closer and nudged her body. The door behind her swung open and Honor stumbled into the room. Seth came in after her.

"What are you—"

His mouth slammed down onto hers.

Honor grabbed his shoulders and pulled him closer, holding him tight. Her tears still falling, she tasted them, along with Seth. So long. Dear God, it had been so long.

Pushing her gently, Seth walked her backward toward the bed. A small voice in her head told her this was a bad idea. A louder, more needy voice told her to take what he was offering—she deserved this.

His hands were everywhere, pulling off her jacket, sliding under her blouse, caressing and kneading her bare skin. She gasped into his mouth when his hands covered her breasts and his fingers tweaked her nipples.

Backing away slightly, she gazed up at the face she'd dreamed about for years. Her arms were wrapped around the body she'd ached for so much that the first few months after their breakup, she would hold her arms around a pillow and cry herself to sleep at night. And here he was for the taking—what she'd dreamed of, wanted for what seemed like forever.

Dropping her arms, she stepped sideways, away from him. "I can't."

His surprise obvious, he growled, "What?"

"I can't fall into bed with you just like that."

"I see."

"Do you?"

"I hurt you, Honor, and I'm sorry. I wish circumstances had been different. If I—"

She shook her head in disbelief. "You still don't get it, do you? It wasn't circumstances that made the choice. It was you. Your decision . . . about my future."

That intense blue gaze scorched her for long seconds. Then he sighed and backed away. "You're right." He turned and walked toward the door. "I'll see you in the morning."

His name trembled on her lips; she fisted her hands to keep from reaching out to him. She didn't want to let him go, but she needed distance. Having him close clouded her thinking. She managed a hoarse "I'll meet you in the lobby at seven."

Without turning back, he went through the door. As soon as she heard it click close, she dropped onto the bed. Emotions she hadn't allowed herself to feel for years had sprung to life, but they blended with new anger and hurt.

Not only had Seth lied by omission, he had made decisions for her. How could she forgive something like that? Hugging herself, she rocked back and forth, dealing with information she'd never expected and another blow to her fragile, never-healed heart.

She'd faced everything else in her life with fortitude

and determination, confident in her path. Seth was the only person she'd allowed herself to be vulnerable and open with. And look where that had gotten her.

Sighing, she pulled herself up and straightened her shoulders. All of these rampaging emotions would have to wait. She had a job to do. Letting personal issues get in the way went against everything she believed in.

She changed into her pajamas, brushed her teeth, and washed her face, all without allowing herself to think about Seth. Then, taking the files she wanted to review one more time, she settled into bed. Files on her lap, she forced her mind into career mode. She had taken this job to save lives . . . that was what she would damn well do. Seth and his lies would have to take a backseat.

Self-lecture over, Honor opened the first file and began to read.

nine

Seth stood in the lobby, waiting for Honor to appear. She was late. He'd already checked out of his room and put his bags in the car. He would've knocked on her door and asked if she wanted him to take her luggage down, too, but figured she'd just as soon cram her suitcase down his throat as put it in the car.

Last night, after he'd walked away from her, he'd gone for a run. Their heated encounter required more than just going back to his room and ordering room service. Clearing his head and releasing the pent-up, explosive emotions surging through him had been a necessity.

That kiss had been ill-advised, stupid, and the best thing that had happened to him in five years. He never should have followed her to her room, but seeing the hurt in her eyes when she'd gotten up from the table had been too painful to just let go. He'd told himself he was going to apologize again, like that was going to make a damn bit of difference. Instead, he'd pushed her into her room and attacked her mouth like a marauding pirate after the sweetest of treasures. He was lucky she hadn't slugged him.

She had responded. Oh hell and damn, had she responded. Her passion and need had been so hot, she'd almost blown his head off. And being the prick he was, he hadn't tried to soften the kiss, romance her and tell her how good it felt to be with her again. Oh no, not horny Seth. He'd immediately started taking her clothes off. If she hadn't stopped him, he would have been inside her in seconds.

Seth closed his eyes and ground his teeth till his jaw ached. Just what he needed, a Texas-sized hard-on in the middle of a busy hotel lobby.

He glanced at his watch again. Five more minutes and he was going up after her. So she was only seven minutes late, but for Honor, that was unheard of . . . not like her at all. She was the consummate professional. Her tardiness was just one more indication of how badly he had hurt her. The shimmering tears in her eyes had haunted him all night long. Sleeplessness had been a way of life for the last few years, but it had been necessary. Never knowing when Hector might learn the truth, Seth had never let his guard down.

Last night, the sleeplessness had been for a different reason. He had known he'd hurt her but never realized just how much.

A soft sound behind him had him whirling around. Dressed in another black pantsuit, this time with a dark orange blouse, Honor looked both beautiful and coolly composed. The serene expression on her face seemed to be etched in ice.

She gave a small nod. "Sorry I'm late. I just got off the phone with Anna Bradford's father. He's going to meet us at Anna's mother's house. They're going to talk to us together."

Good. That saved him from having to rent another vehicle to go to the next town over. "You had breakfast?" he asked.

"Yes. Have you checked out?"

The polite, frigid conversation set him even more on edge. Seth nodded and reached for her bags. "I'll put these in the back with mine."

She'd been holding the bags in her hands, but when he

went to grab them, she let them drop to the floor. The message was obvious: *Don't touch me.*

Regret a bitter taste in his mouth, he picked them up and said quietly, "Ready?"

She gave a stiff nod and walked toward the sliding glass doors that led outside.

"Honor."

She turned around. With that blank, polite mask firmly in place, her brow slightly arched, she silently waited.

"I'm a prick."

Several gasps a few feet away told him he'd made that admission much too loudly in a lobby filled with families. Ignoring them, he kept his eyes locked on hers, waiting for a crushing insult or even another cold shoulder. What he got was Honor Stone at her best.

Her mouth curved and a slight twinkle came back into her eyes as she said, "They say admitting the problem is the first step."

Admiration vying with the sinking reminder of what he'd given up, Seth followed her out the door.

Honor took the keys Seth held out at her request. Driving would keep her hands occupied, since she alternated between wanting to punch him for his arrogance and to caress him because . . . well, because he was so damned caressable.

His admission of being a prick had softened her defenses. She wasn't a pushover, but why did the man have to be so charming when she still had a major, completely justified mad going on?

This morning, she'd woken prepared to have the minor pity party she'd delayed. Then her eyes had caught sight of the files she'd reviewed late into the night. Each one represented a missing girl. Like magic, her weepy, self-serving tears had dried up. How dare she have a meltdown over something that happened five years ago, when these young women, if they were even still alive, were going through hell?

Missing dinner last night had left her with a massive hole in her stomach. After dressing for the day, she'd gone down to the hotel restaurant and had breakfast. And since she'd walked out of the restaurant after she'd ordered last night, she had apologized to the manager and offered to pay. She'd been assured that it had already been taken care of by her handsome dinner companion.

Turning left at the entrance to the interstate, she was more than aware of that handsome man beside her. He had been silent since they'd gotten into the car, probably figuring he'd said enough last night. That had been the sketchiest of details. Today, she wanted facts—all of them.

Keeping her eyes straight ahead, she said quietly, "Okay, I'm ready."

He didn't even pretend to not know . . . he just started talking. "Not long after I joined the force, I did a short undercover stint. Turns out I was good at it. I was cocky, sure of myself, thought I could handle anything. When they offered me the opportunity to bring down the elusive Hector Clemmons, it was like being offered the Triple Crown. Take down a murdering son of a bitch, impress my superiors, and feed my ego.

"We started the ruse with me being under suspicion for taking bribes. Nothing major . . . just enough to taint my reputation, have people question my ethics. And then I supposedly resigned under pressure."

"What about the restaurant? You said the department helped you set that up—that took some serious cash, didn't it?"

"Yeah, but it was actually something I'd always wanted to do. I told you my mom taught all of her kids how to cook. I'd always thought if I hadn't decided on being a cop, I'd like to own a restaurant." He shrugged. "The department put up half the cash . . . I paid them back with interest within a year."

She shot him another look, this one of surprise. "Wait a minute. You were looking at opening another one when we were together."

"Yeah. The department only set up the first one. Turns out I really enjoyed it. I ended up owning three."

"And Clemmons?"

"He was scum, but he also had some legitimate businesses. One of those was importing gourmet foods. I started slow with him. He knew I'd been a cop, so he was even more suspicious. The taint of me being a dirty one helped, but it was slow going, earning his trust."

"And the murder charge?"

For the first time since they'd been talking, he hesitated. She might be furious with him for his deceit, but she knew Seth. He wasn't a murderer. And then it hit her. "It was because of me, wasn't it?"

"Hector heard about you. Stupid of me to think I could keep my private life private. Bill, my handler, warned me. I didn't listen. Hector made some comments about you. Started asking questions. We knew we were going to have to do something to throw him off track." He shrugged. "And then Monty Jenkins just kind of fell into our hands."

"How's that?"

"He was the low man on Clemmons's ladder. Got caught stealing some goods; Clemmons fired him but, surprisingly, didn't seek retribution. Jenkins's landlady found him in his apartment, dead from a heroin overdose."

"And the gunshot?"

"Never happened. The landlady only saw the bottom part of his body. She called the cops immediately, so she didn't know how Monty died. We invented the neighbor hearing the gunshot, the one who also saw me leaving the apartment. But we let Hector think I killed Monty as a way to prove myself to him and show my loyalty."

"Then, I'm assuming Hector was the one who came to your rescue in jail?"

"Yeah. Worked just like we planned. Hector put up my bail. And then, as you know, the charges were dropped."

"But what about the dead guy's family? How did they—"

"Fortunately for us, Monty didn't have a family. And even more fortunately, Hector never asked to see the body. He not only posted my bail, he also paid the coroner to say it was a self-inflicted gunshot wound. Or, rather, Clemmons thought he paid the coroner to say that." His mouth moved in a tight smile.

"So the coroner was in on your plan, too?"

"Yeah, my captain had a long talk with him. He was getting close to retirement . . . planned to move away anyway. Though he was in no real danger. Clemmons fell for it like a dream."

"What about your family?"

Even without looking at him, she knew he stiffened . . . could sense the tension in his body.

"What about my family?"

"Did they know any of this?"

"Not until it was over."

"So they . . ."

"Pretty much disowned me way before Clemmons went down. The only way we could get this to work was for everyone, including my family, to think this was all legit. And it was the only way to ensure their safety. If Hector had thought he could use my family against me, he would have. I made it clear to everyone that I wanted nothing to do with them. It worked just liked we'd planned; the entire family backed away from me completely. My mom held out the longest, but even she stopped trying to see me after a while.

"Of course, when they found out I was actually on the right side of the law, they got pissed for a whole new reason."

"But they forgave you, right?"

"Most of them have . . . things are still strained, though."

"With Clemmons dead, they can tell others. Right?"

Seth shrugged. "Too little too late."

"But your brother asked for your help."

"Kelli was missing a week before he even called me. The only reason he did it then was because he thought I might have some connections that could help them."

"But why didn't someone else in the family let you know?"

"I asked the same question when I went home. My mother thought Joel had called me right after it happened." He turned toward the window, but she could see his jaw working as he added, "I don't think any of them believe I'm someone they can depend on to help anymore." He shrugged. "Years of trying to defend a scumbag relative took its toll on everyone."

"I'm sorry, Seth."

She could feel his surprise even before he said, "Hell, Honor. You have as much right to be angry as they do."

"I didn't say I'm not mad anymore. But I know what your family means to you."

He gave a stiff nod of acknowledgment, and she wasn't surprised he changed the subject. "What about your family? Your parents still living in Virginia?"

"Not anymore. My mom didn't want to stay there after my dad died."

He twisted around to face her. "Your father died? I'm sorry, Honor. I know how much you loved him."

Swallowing the lump that always accompanied talking about her dad, she said, "Thanks. It was a shock for all of us. He went on his regular run one morning and just dropped dead. Aneurysm."

"When did he die?"

"A few years ago."

Recognizing evasiveness in her too brief answer, he asked, "When?"

"A few weeks after you and I broke up."

Seth blew out a sigh. So he'd broken her heart and then she'd lost her father not long afterward. Was it any wonder that she hated him? "How's your mom doing?"

"She's been the rock in our family forever, so pretty much the same now. It was hard at first. They had so many plans."

"And your brother?"

"Got another six months left in Afghanistan. Then we're hoping he's stateside for good."

"Wasn't your sister-in-law pregnant when we were together? They have any more kids?"

"They have none. Marla lost the baby and suffered some complications. She can't get pregnant."

"God, that's tough."

She threw him a tight smile. "Lots of things can happen in five years."

"Guess so."

"So what are you doing now . . . do you still work for Houston PD?"

"No, after Clemmons was arrested, I left."

"What about your restaurants?"

"Sold them."

"And?"

"Moved to a little island south of Key West."

She shot him another look, her eyes now dancing with laughter. "Seriously?"

"Yeah. Why?"

"Because my mom moved to Sarasota a few years ago. Her sister lives down there. When I was visiting her not long ago, we went to Key West for the weekend."

What would he have done if he'd been walking down the street and had seen Honor? Hell, what would she have done? Shoot him? No, but she probably would have wanted to.

"So if you're no longer a cop, what do you do now?"

"Not much of anything. Fishing, diving. Bought a boat, rent it out some. Teach scuba diving."

"Sounds . . . peaceful."

He snorted. "Sounds boring, I know." He shrugged. "I needed to get away."

"Did it help?"

Having no answer he wanted to give, Seth gazed out of the window. What could he say? Nothing had helped, would ever help. Whether he lived in Florida or Texas, the past couldn't be altered. Forgetting what had happened . . . not only what he had done, but what he hadn't done. Hell no, didn't matter where he lived; that was never going to change.

ten

Tranquillity

The deafening blare of the warning siren woke Alden from a dreamless sleep, causing him to jackknife from the bed. A second later the phone beside the bed rang. He answered with a furious growling, "What's happened?"

"One has gotten away."

"Who?"

"One of the new ones. The brown-haired one."

Shit, she was the one he'd been the least sure about. Not only did she seem too worldly and street-smart for his liking, she hadn't displayed the kind of helpless lone-liness he liked to see in the women he chose. But Tabitha had convinced him to take her. Said she'd be a good match for one of the more strong-minded men in the community. And, dammit, he had acquiesced.

"How did she get past the guards and through the gate?"

"She stole the keys from her keeper. Guards must've not seen her go through."

"Are the dogs out?"

"Yes. She won't get far."

"Call me with an update every fifteen minutes."

"Will do."

"What's wrong?"

Alden turned and backhanded the woman standing

behind him. "Damn you. She's the one you talked me into taking and now she's escaped. Just how did that happen?"

She withstood his fury, as she had many times before. "I don't know, Father. I double-checked all the doors myself. They were locked."

"I'm deeply disappointed, daughter. Get your clothes on and help with the search. You do not return to my bed until she's found. Understand?"

Wasting no time, she gathered the clothes she'd folded and placed on the chair when she'd come to him last night. Dressing rapidly, she pulled on her shoes and ran from the room.

Alden took his time putting his clothes on. Hopefully, by the time he was dressed and had his morning coffee, the girl would have been rounded up. How hard was it to keep a skinny bitch chained or a damn door locked? Tabitha had received her just punishment. After the girl was located, he'd find out who'd been on guard and have a very stern discussion with him.

Eerie sounds in the distance caused her to stop abruptly. Gasping another breath into her overtaxed lungs, she leaned against a pine tree and listened. Bloodhounds howled. Terror increased the shivers running rampantly through her body. She'd heard the siren a few minutes ago, and now the search, including dogs, was apparently on. Were they the kind that tore humans to pieces? No, she couldn't let herself think about that. She had to keep on going. Besides, being torn apart by ravenous beasts would be better than what she'd been through the last few weeks. No way was she going back there. Ever.

Despite the fear, she couldn't help but feel a small sense of triumph. She'd been gone for hours and they had just discovered her absence.

The pants she'd stolen were much too large; even the leather belt she'd knotted at her waist barely kept them up. She didn't care; they were clothes—the first ones she'd had on in days. The silent, odd-looking man had come in to give her the nightly injection and she had rammed him with the lamp beside the bed. He'd only been stunned the first time and had tried to make a grab for her. She'd managed to evade him and get in more bashes. On the third one, he'd gone down with barely a whimper. Then she'd taken the damn needle and injected him instead.

Getting the keys from the belt at his waist had been easy. Even stripping his clothes off and putting them on hadn't taken that much time. It was the stops she'd made on the way outside that had slowed her down. She'd had to try to save them; it had been useless. The two girls were so out of it, she'd been able to wake them for only a few seconds. If he'd given her the injection, she would have been the same way.

After she'd run into the night, she had been stunned to discover that she was in the midst of a small community. For an instant, she had considered knocking on a door and asking for help. She had resisted that temptation. Several of the buildings looked too much like the building she'd just escaped from. Meaning there were probably no people around who would help her.

When she'd reached the gate, she'd been doubly glad she hadn't asked for help. The entire area was a fortress. She'd ended up crawling the last few yards to the gate on her stomach and had prayed with all her might that one of the keys fit the lock. Her prayers had been answered.

It would be daylight soon. If she'd been able to wear the man's shoes, she could have run faster, but his giant shoes had swallowed her small feet.

Holding her hand to the painful stitch at her side, she looked around. Dawn was breaking, giving her an opportunity to see her surroundings better. She appeared to be in the midst of a forest. Giant trees surrounded her, as far as the eye could see.

If only she could find a road somewhere, maybe she could wave down a car. Once she got to the police, she could tell them about these people. They would save the other girls.

The throbbing in her feet made her look down at them; she winced. Though the light was still dim, she could see well enough to tell that they were a bloody mess. She couldn't let that stop her . . . she had to keep going.

Pushing away from the tree, she broke into a flat-out run. There had to be a way out of here. There had to be.

Halo, Arizona

Electricity crackled in the air. Honor sat beside Mrs. Bradford on the sofa. Seth sat in a chair across from them. Mr. Bradford paced back and forth in front of the window, half the time looking like a grieving father, the other half like a five-year-old on the verge of a temper tantrum.

"You're the one who suggested she go to that school in the first place," Joe Bradford snarled.

Her eyes glistening with bitter hatred, Elaine Bradford snapped back, "So all of this is my fault?"

"If she was living with me, she wouldn't have changed schools. If you—"

"Mr. and Mrs. Bradford, arguing isn't going to help us find Anna." Honor used the tone she'd honed to perfection to deal with overemotional, grief-stricken parents. "If we can just concentrate on Anna and—"

"If you hadn't slept with that slut, this never would have happened in the first place."

Seth shot to his feet. "Hell, this is getting us nowhere. If you people want to behave like two squabbling idiots, that's your problem. We're more interested in saving your daughter."

"You can't talk to my wife like that."

Honor resisted rolling her eyes. Between the Bradfords blaming each other for their daughter's disappearance and Seth's justified fury, she was wishing she had a gavel to bang.

"Mrs. Bradford, could I perhaps have some more tea?" she asked, shooting a speaking glance at Seth.

Elaine Bradford jumped to her feet. "Of course."

"I'll help you." Honor followed the older woman into the kitchen. Hopefully, by separating the spouses, who'd been sniping at each other nonstop since she and Seth had arrived, half an hour ago, they could get something out of them other than bitterness.

Family strife and one parent blaming the other for a missing child wasn't unusual. Combining those issues with the fact that the Bradfords were in the middle of a messy divorce only made it more volatile.

"I'm sorry. I know what we're doing is childish and not helpful." Mrs. Bradford's red-rimmed eyes and trembling mouth made it hard for Honor to be angry. Her grief was apparent, as was the tremendous hurt she obviously still felt about her husband's infidelity.

Honor sat at the kitchen table and watched the older woman flutter around nervously. The goal was to keep her out of the living room, where, she sincerely hoped, Seth was getting somewhere with Joe Bradford. And while Anna's mother busied herself with making tea, Honor concentrated on learning what she could. So far, they'd gotten almost nothing from either parent.

"Tell me about your daughter."

The woman's face lit up, making her look years younger. "I know I may be prejudiced, but Anna isn't like most young women her age."

"In what way?"

"She's much more responsible, more mature. That's why I knew almost immediately she was missing." Her mouth twisted bitterly. "I couldn't get the police to believe me, though."

Honor nodded in sympathetic understanding. She had read the police report, and this was the only thing Mr. and Mrs. Bradford had agreed on. Anna was twenty-four, the oldest of the missing girls. The police had thought she might have gone off with friends and chose to wait twenty-four hours before declaring her a missing person and beginning their investigation.

Relieved to be getting to the heart of their reason for coming, Honor asked a leading question. "Anna is a year or so older than the average college student . . . ?"

"She worked for a couple of years before she decided to start college."

"Where did she work?"

"At the mall, a real estate office, an insurance company, a bank. It seemed every three or four months she was looking for something new."

"She was trying to find herself."

Mrs. Bradford smiled. "That's what we figured, so Joe and I didn't say anything. We trusted that she would find her way eventually."

"What did she finally decide on?"

As the woman turned to adjust the kettle on the stove, Honor could see only the side of her face, but it looked twisted with grief. "Criminal justice." She faced Honor, her eyes swimming with tears. "Isn't that ironic?"

"Is Anna an outgoing person?"

"Yes, but she's smart, too. She wouldn't just go off with a stranger." Mrs. Bradford shuddered and turned away. "She would have had to been taken by force. After all that training, someone still took her."

"Training?"

Mrs. Bradford poured the boiling water into the teapot. "Starting in high school, Anna became interested in martial arts. We encouraged it because we thought it could save her life."

"It might still save her life. You can't give up hope."

She nodded. "I know. That's what I keep telling myself."

Honor touched the hand that clenched nervously on the counter. "Then hang on to that. It sounds like Anna is an amazing young woman. And she sounds like a survivor."

The smile that brightened Elaine Bradford's face was almost too painful to watch. Honor prayed that she wasn't giving the woman false hope.

"I need a break. How about you?"

Honor eyed Seth. He'd been quiet since they'd gotten into their car, half an hour ago. Since they'd been with the Bradfords most of the day, they hadn't had much breathing room. Even before he'd said the words, she'd been thinking that he needed to get some air. He looked close to explosion.

"The hotel we're going to has a gym."

There was a barely perceptible pause before he said, "Sure. And then maybe a run after?"

One of many things she and Seth had enjoyed when they were dating was working out and running together. After they'd broken up and she'd moved to Atlanta, Honor had gone almost a month without working out, which had made things a thousand times worse. Not only had she felt like crap, but when she started working out again, she'd realized how stupid she'd been. Working out had been a great way to get over Seth.

"A run sounds good, too. After drinking all that tea, I need to get rid of some of this excess energy."

"And I need to expend some energy that doesn't include slugging Joe Bradford in the face."

Honor grimaced an apology. "Sorry about leaving you to deal with him alone. I figured the only way to get any information was to separate them."

"No apology necessary. You were right to do that. It was obvious they couldn't be in the same room together without arguing. I'm just glad you got something useful." Seth snorted with disgust. "Bradford's number one concern is himself. Even after I had a very frank talk with him, if I didn't keep him focused, he'd go back to talking about himself."

"Mrs. Bradford was more than happy to share. I don't know if I'm more encouraged or discouraged after talking with her, though."

"Why?"

"The college transfer . . . that's a commonality. But Anna is different from the other girls. Not only in age, but maturity and life experience."

"Yeah, but you've got to admit that out of the five girls, so far we know three transferred to another school. I know it's small, but I still think there's a thread."

"I agree. I'm just not sure how big of a thread it is." She turned into the parking lot of a large chain hotel. "I've scheduled a conference call with Jared and Aidan for nine tonight."

"Good. If we find out about another transfer, I think we've got to do some research on how they're done and what's involved."

Honor nodded absently as she got out of the car. Yesterday, she'd believed it was something, but now that she'd thought it through, that one small thing seemed insignificant—useless information that would lead them nowhere. As far as she knew, transferring from one college to another didn't constitute much of anything other than paperwork. She hoped Seth wasn't getting his hopes up over something she wished she'd never brought up.

As they rolled their bags into the lobby to check in, Seth blew out a ragged, silent breath. He'd told Honor he needed a break, which was true. What he couldn't say was that he needed some time away from *her*. Last night's kiss had reminded him of how good they'd been together. She had tasted as good as he remembered . . . better, actually.

Except for the time they'd separated the Bradfords to talk with each one individually, he and Honor had been together for most of the day. He was more than aware of her scent, the delicate arch of her chin when she disagreed with him. That small smile that sometimes curved her mouth when she was thinking. So mysterious, so damn sexy.

He needed to do something physically demanding to deal with all the explosive thoughts he'd been having. That sure as hell didn't include seeing her work out in a gym or running beside her, watching that beautiful body move with her natural grace while her creamy skin dampened and glowed.

Suddenly feeling like a mountain lion that'd been deprived of breakfast, Seth grabbed his key card and growled a thank-you to the sweet-looking lady behind the counter. She looked a bit startled that he'd gone from pleasant to caveman in a matter of seconds. He grimaced a smile of apology and turned away.

"So I'm in room 412," Honor said. "What about you?"

"Tenth floor," he growled. Hell, he sounded like a grizzly.

"Everything okay?"

Just got a major boner thinking about you. Yeah, Cavanaugh, tell her that. It'll go over real well. Jerking his bag toward the elevator, he nodded. "Just want to get to my room."

"Okay . . . well. Do you still want to work out?"

Hell, Honor was the least insecure woman he knew, but she sounded uncertain, decidedly hurt. He turned back to her and made the effort he should have made before. "Sure. Give me about fifteen minutes to change. Want me to come to your room?"

"No, we can meet in the gym."

Stretching his mouth into a semblance of a smile, he punched the elevator button to go up and was relieved when the doors opened immediately. Honor got in beside him, still eyeing him as if he were an alien.

The doors opened on her floor and, thankfully she got out before he could grab her and show her exactly what had been bothering him for the last half hour.

"See you in a few minutes."

Seth nodded and let the doors close in her face. Better to be rude than pull her back into the elevator, push the stop button, and strip her naked. Although, judging by her expression last night, he'd probably get a black eye instead of satisfaction.

How in the hell had he expected to work with the one woman he'd never been able to forget?

eleven

Tranquillity

"We can't find her."

Using the glare he'd developed in prison to save his ass and intimidate the hell out of others, Alden slowly shook his head.

Ben Hamilton, one of the largest of Tranquillity's men, had likely been elected to deliver the news to Alden. News he refused to accept. The girl had to be found; there was no other option.

Though it was true that she could be dead, eaten by wild animals or from falling off a bluff, he couldn't take the chance. Their community was nestled in a remote area, between two large mountains, their access road well hidden. However, she must be found, dead or alive. Until he saw her body, or at least a piece of it, he couldn't rest. If she somehow survived and was found, she would tell. He'd worked too long and hard to create his ideal life to let it fall apart on him. One little bitch would not destroy his dreams.

"How many do we have looking?"

His face going slack with relief that Alden hadn't punished the messenger, Ben answered eagerly, "Twenty."

Leaving the community undefended was worrisome, but Alden had little choice. The girl had to be found. "Call together every able-bodied male over the age of sixteen to help with the search. Cancel all classes. Stop all entertainment at the stable. Any work that has to be done, the women will see to it. We need to go on full lockdown mode until the girl is found."

"This is our marketing week. Our supplies are low."

"Tabitha and two of the younger boys can go. She knows what we need, and the boys can carry the heavier supplies."

Brother Hamilton swallowed audibly as he glanced hesitantly at the closed door behind Alden. "She is up to the task?"

Alden raised both brows at the question. How he reprimanded his children was no one's business and had never been cause for discourse. Perhaps it was time to remind the citizens of Tranquillity that while he was a gentle-natured man, his word was law and never to be questioned.

"You have a problem with how I've disciplined my daughter?"

His eyes widening slightly, Ben swallowed hard again. "I came by earlier. The screams were quite loud. I just wasn't sure—"

"The screams released the demons within her. Tabitha knows she was responsible for the girl's escape. And she accepted her punishment as a woman should."

He moved closer to Ben. At six foot four, Alden could intimidate most people with just one look. Brother Hamilton was not only shorter and less bulky in frame, he had nothing on Alden when it came to determination and discipline. "If you're questioning my authority, you would do well to recommit to our purpose here."

Ben backed away awkwardly; he knew he had crossed the line. "I overstepped my bounds, Brother Pike. Please accept my most humble apologies."

"Tell me, Ben, are you pleased with your woman?"

A look that hadn't been there before sparked in his eyes: fear. "My woman pleases me greatly. We've been together for over two years now. She fulfills all my needs."

"That is good to hear. I would hate to have to remove her from your care. A woman who isn't satisfying her man isn't a happy, fulfilled woman. We want our women happy . . . do we not?"

"I assure you, my Lucy is extremely happy and fulfilled."

"Good. Still . . . perhaps it would be helpful for you to spend some time in solitude, reviewing my manifesto and our purpose."

"If that is your wish."

Alden kept his expression benign. "I, of course, only want what you want."

"Yes, that's what I want. Thank you for suggesting it."

"Of course." Alden gave the man his special smile, a blend of condescension and kindness. "Why don't you get started this evening?"

"Don't you need my help finding the girl?"

"I think solitude will be more beneficial than your help in finding one wayward lamb. Don't you?"

"Yes, yes. Thank you again for suggesting it." Brother Hamilton wisely almost ran from the room.

There were certain advantages to having everyone terrified of him. Not that he punished unjustly. Actually, he almost never punished the men anymore—it just wasn't worth his time or energy. Their women were another matter. He'd learned long ago that most men were led around by their dicks. When and if they did behave incorrectly, the root cause could always be traced back to a woman. Besides, the men behaved so much better if their women were brought to heel occasionally. It always amazed Alden what a man was willing to do for his woman.

Being a follower meant obedience to the leadership. Brother Hamilton would return in a couple of weeks with a renewed sense of purpose. And if not, there were other ways to ensure his obedience. Alden had enjoyed taming Lucy once; he had no problem with giving her a refresher course.

She eased her feet into the ice-cold spring, hissing out a soft curse at the biting pain. She couldn't decide which hurt worse, the freezing temperature or the sting of the water on her torn, bruised flesh. A breath shuddered from her as she pushed past the initial agony. Lowering her hand into the water, she rinsed her meal—the wild huckleberries were a godsend. Though tempted to stuff the entire handful in her mouth, she made herself eat one at a time, relishing the burst of flavor on her tongue, the texture of each berry . . . the sheer pleasure. They were the best things she'd eaten in weeks.

Even though she'd been fed twice a day, each meal had been shoved through a slot at the bottom of the door and had always landed inches out of reach—intentionally, she knew. Forced to stretch every part of her body to reach the food, she found the process excruciatingly painful and, as it was meant to be, dehumanizing.

An hour after sunrise, she'd stopped running long enough to climb to the highest point she could reach. Beautiful rolling hills and majestic mountains stretched before her in every direction. She had been here before. Not in this exact spot, but she thought she recognized the terrain as either Wyoming or Montana. Years ago, when they'd still been a family, before her parents had turned into two bickering people she didn't recognize, they'd vacationed in Montana. And last year, she'd gone backpacking with a group of friends in Wyoming.

So she knew approximately where she was . . . she just needed to figure out how to get out of here. And once she did, she had to lead people back to where those monsters lived.

After placing the last berry on her tongue, she took a breath and looked down at her feet. She'd held them in the water as long as she dared. They were numb from the cold, but at least they no longer throbbed. She lifted them from the water and winced at their appearance. Now that the blood had been washed away, she could see that they hurt for a good reason—a multitude of bruises and cuts.

When she'd picked her berries earlier, she'd found some thin, flexible vines she thought would come in handy. Pulling them from the pants pocket, she took off the shirt she'd stolen from the guard. With her teeth, she tore two large strips off at the bottom of the shirt, wrapped the rags around each foot, and secured them with the vines. Not exactly great protection, but better than nothing.

Both feet now wrapped, she pulled the ragged shirt back on and pushed herself up to stand. Hours had passed since her escape. She had covered her tracks as much as possible, and though it had been a while since she'd heard the howling dogs, she knew, without a doubt, that she was still being hunted.

She straightened her shoulders and took a deep breath as she plotted her next path. The spring was small, maybe just two feet wide, but it meandered around a curve and looked as though it flowed into a larger body of water. If she found a lake, maybe there would be people fishing or camping.

She took a step and swallowed a cry at the agony in her foot. Then she took another step and another. Gaining speed, with the drive to survive growing stronger and stronger, Anna Bradford headed down the stream, hoping and praying for freedom.

* * *

Honor stood at the entrance to the hotel gym. Seth was already at the bench press, and despite all her self-lectures over the past couple of days, she couldn't help but stare at the man who'd been the subject of numerous steamy dreams. When she slept, her subconscious somehow didn't care that he'd broken her heart. In her dreams, she remembered the heat, the passion . . . the sheer beauty of Seth Cavanaugh.

Dressed in a gray, sweat-dampened Dallas Cowboys T-shirt and black gym shorts, the real Seth Cavanaugh made every erotic dream she'd had of the man inconsequential and silly. Years before, Seth had been lean and well-defined. This Seth had matured not only in definition but also in bulk. Taut muscles in his arms and shoulders bulged as he moved the heavy bar up and down over his torso.

The deep concentration of his expression turned her on as much as his perfect body. Now, that was a look she remembered all too well. When Seth made love, he had the same kind of concentrated intensity on his face. Always determined that she find pleasure first, he'd set a course for her arousal as if on a quest. And Honor remembered eagerly answering with just the response he'd sought.

Feeling a throbbing between her legs, her nipples peaking, her entire body now on fire, she was tempted to strip and jump into the pool instead of working out. Only problem with that was, she had no swimsuit with her, and as much as she wasn't shy about her body, stripping down to her underwear in a hotel pool wasn't in her makeup.

Afraid he'd look up and notice her lascivious stare, Honor walked over to the nearest machine—a butterfly press—and sat down. Taking a breath, she concentrated on her own need to work out. Expending energy this way was so much healthier than starting something up with Seth. Okay, not as enjoyable, but mentally, so much sounder.

She couldn't let herself love him again. Taking pleasure for pleasure's sake could last only so long. When the heartbreak came again, as it inevitably would, it would be bad; she refused to be caught in that tidal wave again. She'd been there, done that, and still had the crack in her heart to prove it.

Lifting her arms into position, she stared straight ahead, pressed hard, and repeated. Counting her reps, concentrating on her breathing, and focusing on the blank wall in front of her, she was able to get into her workout. No use trying to forget or ignore Seth. Her concentration skills were good, but not enough to overpower the gorgeous hunk of masculinity sweating and flexing only a few feet away. Besides, a woman could look without touching, couldn't she?

Seth's breath almost exploded from his chest when Honor finally started working out. How the hell was he supposed to lie here and lift weights when she'd stood at the door for a solid five minutes and stared at him? Her gaze had been so hotly caressing, he was surprised his body wasn't steaming. The longer she'd stood there, the harder he'd gotten. He was just damned glad they were the only ones in the room. The giant bulge in his shorts sure as hell wasn't meant for anyone other than the sexy strawberry blonde with the burning look of need on her expressive face.

She still wanted him. He'd recognized that last night. That kiss had almost set him on fire, but she'd been the one to pull back . . . the one to say no. It had been the right thing to do. As much as he wanted her, he couldn't do what he'd done before. When this was over and Kelli was home and safe, Honor would return to Paris and he'd go back to Florida. What they'd had before couldn't be re-created. They were two different people now. Too much water under the bridge—or whatever the hell other cliché described a hopeless, too-late scenario.

His muscles stinging with just the right amount of burn, Seth sat up. Still rock hard and hurting, he turned to Honor, who had gone from the butterfly press to the rowing machine and was working up a fine sheen of perspiration all over her cream-satin body.

Hell, he had to get out of here, or in a few minutes both Honor and the hotel management were going to be severely shocked.

Getting to his feet, he headed toward the door that led outside to the parking lot. "I'm going for a run." He didn't wait to see if she followed. He figured she wouldn't . . . he hoped to hell she wouldn't. No way could he run in the condition he was in now, and if she went with him, his condition was only going to worsen.

A coolly challenging voice said softly, "Or are you just running away in general?"

In mid-stride, Seth turned around and stared. "Excuse me?"

With a grace few people could pull off, she rose from the rowing machine in one smooth move. "You've had a bee up your butt for the last couple of hours. What's your problem?"

Despite the challenging words and his explosive urges, Seth fought the need to laugh. "Baby, if I had a bee up my butt, I'd be doing more than running."

She burst out laughing. "I guess you're right."

Seth sighed inwardly. That was one of the many things he'd loved about Honor. She could be as mad as a sore-toothed hound, but she could also laugh spontaneously, ridding herself of that anger in a flash.

"So you want to tell me what's wrong?"

"Honey, if you can't figure it out by looking at me,

then you're either not looking in the right spot or your eyesight isn't what it used to be."

He watched her gaze drop to his shorts, where the raging hard-on still raged and then grew even harder at her perusal.

"What are we going to do about that?"

Was that an invitation or his wishful thinking? Testing her, he said, "You got any suggestions?"

She walked slowly toward him. Seth stopped breathing. Every argument he'd just given himself about ships sailing and water under the bridge disintegrated. If she wanted him, he'd fall on his knees and love her like she'd never been loved before. Hell, the management could call the cops on his sated ass for all he cared. He just wanted Honor now, no matter what.

Reaching him, she used a slender finger to trace the lines around his mouth. "These are new."

"Holy hell, Honor. Don't touch me if you don't want this. I'm about to go off like a rocket."

A rare show of vulnerability flickered in her eyes. "And what then, Seth? If we appease this hunger we obviously both have . . . what then?"

She had him there. Beyond the hour or so he wanted to spend inside her, he didn't have an answer. Would it sate his lust? For the time being, yes, it would. But the need would return. And then what? Again and again. Just when would it end? When he walked away from her for good?

He didn't want to talk . . . he wanted to taste those sweet lips again. But he had to ask, "What do you want?"

"I want honesty. Can you give me that?"

"Yes." That had been an easy one. The only lies he'd given her before were out of necessity. "What else?"

"That when it's over, we'll walk away with no regrets."

The crushing blow surprised him. He hadn't planned on reigniting more than a physical fire and satiating a need they both had. So why the hell did her comment hurt like a fist had been slammed full force into his gut?

Seth ignored the pain . . . he would consider it later. Now all that mattered was quenching the fire burning through him. "Yes, I can do that."

Her mouth trembled slightly. "I know you can."

"What the hell is that supposed to mean?"

"Nothing."

"Don't give me that. Was that a real question or another way to rub the past in my face? If you think I walked away with no regrets, then you've got a lot to learn about me, Honor. I did what I had to do."

"And damn the people you cared about."

Shit. Turning, he walked a few feet away from her, then came back. "Hector Clemmons was responsible for more deaths than most small wars. He didn't discriminate, either. If it got him what he wanted, women and children were included, too. Someone had to get inside his inner circle. And even though my personal life went to shit and I gave up the only woman I've ever loved, if I was asked to do it again, I would."

He glared down at her, feeling furious and too damn exposed at the same time. "If you think I walked away with no regrets, then you never knew me at all."

Turning away again, he went out into the parking lot and took off running. If he stayed, he'd either kiss her senseless or throw her over his shoulder and run back to his room, where he'd kiss her senseless and a hell of a lot more. And then what? Who the hell knew. He only knew he couldn't risk finding out.

twelve

I gave up the only woman I've ever loved. Frozen in place, Honor heard those words echo through her brain. Seth had loved her. She didn't know if she should be happy to learn that or wish he'd never admitted it. What was she supposed to do with that information? Forget about it? No way in hell. But neither could she let it influence her now. She had tested him with the question of walking away with no regrets. Something her dad had often warned her about. Never ask a question unless you're prepared for the answer.

Seth said he could walk away with no regrets. She believed him. There might have been regrets before, but that was because he'd loved her. Those feelings were gone. The attraction was still there, but the tenderness she'd once seen in his eyes was missing.

Honor shoved her hands through her hair and turned away from the door Seth had just stalked through. Running with him was out of the question, but since she now had even more excess energy to burn, she had little choice but to go back to her workout.

An hour and a half later, soaked with sweat, limbs shaking with exhaustion, she felt better physically, less tense, but that was about all. Chugging down a bottle of water, she headed back to her room. Aidan and Jared would be calling at nine; she wanted to go over the interviews she and Seth had conducted with the girls' parents one more time.

As she let herself into her room, she came to an abrupt stop. Seth sat at the desk by the window, the notes she'd taken over the last few days spread out before him.

"How did you get in?"

"Told the housekeeping lady I'd locked myself out."

And it had always been that easy with Seth. One look from those wickedly sexy eyes and women fell at his feet. She was no different. The moment he'd looked at her across the room at that party, she'd been putty in his hands. Descended from generations of warriors and soldiers, Honor had always prided herself on her iron-willed discipline. Seth tempted her like no one ever had.

Being angry that he'd broken into her room would be pointless. Especially when he'd done it to work on the case. Rescuing his niece was his priority. Honor might not appreciate his methods, but if he found something helpful in her scribblings, then she'd gladly give him a key to her room. She mentally shook her head at that thought. Better not go there.

"I need to shower. Want to grab dinner before our conference call?"

He looked over his shoulder at her. "Why don't I order something from room service? That way it'll be here when you come out."

Sitting across from him in a crowded restaurant was hard enough. Being in a small hotel room, with no one around and a bed within a few feet, was so not a good idea. So why did she hear herself say, "Salad, no dressing, grilled salmon, steamed veggies, and iced tea."

He grinned. "Still the healthiest eater I know."

She snorted. "I'm probably still the only healthy eater you know." Grabbing a pair of jeans and a white button-down shirt from the dresser drawer, she turned to the bathroom. "Be out in fifteen minutes."

In much better spirits, Honor stripped and stepped into the steaming hot shower. She refused to ask herself why she was suddenly lighthearted. Lying to herself by giving credit to her workout for her better mood wouldn't fly. The reason for her lighter mood had a name—one she refused to acknowledge.

Seth dropped the phone back into the handset after ordering their meal. Honor was no longer angry with him, which was a plus. And his run had returned some sense to his blood-deprived brain. Starting anything up with her right now would be foolish. Pointless beyond the pleasure of the moment. Concentrating on finding Kelli and the others should be his only focus.

The notes Honor had made were neat and precise. In comparison, his notes looked like the scrawls of a child. Though messy, they still held important information.

Yesterday, in their meeting with the Greenes, they'd taken down the same information. Today that had changed. While Seth had been grilling Joe Bradford, trying to get him to focus on his daughter and not his bitterness, he'd learned a few things. Judging by Honor's notes from her visit with Elaine Bradford, she'd been much more successful.

"You find anything interesting?"

Seth turned to see Honor standing in the bathroom doorway. Slightly damp from the shower, her thick strawberry blond hair was piled on top of her head in the casual, sexy way she often wore it. She had on no makeup, and the freckles she hated but he'd delighted in were more apparent than ever. Her creamy skin looked moist, dewy, and delicious. *Hell.*

Turning away, he looked back down at her notes. "You got some interesting things from Mrs. Bradford. You're right, Anna's much more mature than the others. And she's had training. Sounds like she could handle herself in any given situation."

She came closer and looked over his shoulder. "I agree. Unfortunately, when you have a gun to your head or a knife at your neck, survival is the name of the game. You have to choose the right time to fight."

"Yeah, I just hope to hell she found the right time."

The knock at the door pulled them away from that grim thought. After signing for the meal, Seth rolled the cart to the middle of the room, placed a chair on either side of it, and waited for Honor to sit down.

As she took her seat, she smiled up at him. "Who was responsible for your impeccable manners? Your mom or your dad?"

Seth snorted out a humorous breath. "By the time I came along, both my parents had despaired of teaching their kids any manners. My two oldest sisters, Sandra and Patty, took it upon themselves to share their wisdom."

"How'd they do that?"

"By telling me about their bad dates . . . about how rude and disrespectful the boys were. They made me swear I'd never treat a woman like that." He shrugged. "Guess it stuck."

She laughed softly as she removed the silver dome from her plate. "All boys should have such helpful sisters."

"I'm sure my sisters would agree with you." Seth removed the cover from his meal and took his time unfolding his napkin, feeling an odd, nervous anticipation as he waited to see what would happen.

"Holy hell, Seth. What did you order?"

Hiding a satisfied smile, he took a bite of his loaded potato and gave a moan of appreciation. "Damn, that's good." Scooping another bite onto his fork, he held it out to her. "Want some?"

They used to play this game all the time, and both of them always pretended it was the first time. Two or three evenings a week, they'd eat at his restaurant. The chef would always prepare a healthy, nutritious meal for Honor, while Seth usually had something heart attack–inducing. And every single time, he'd end up sharing half of his food with her. They never talked about it, never planned it. Just one of those habits that couples get into that come as natural as breathing. To think that they could fall back into the same sweetly familiar routine made his chest tighten with emotion.

She looked down at her spartan meal and then back up at him, her eyes gleaming with shared laughter. "Maybe just one bite."

He held the fork out, and when Honor opened her mouth, he put the potato on her tongue. Watching her lips close over the fork and hearing her appreciative moan made him throb like hell.

Her eyes locked with his as he slowly pulled the fork from her mouth. Endless seconds passed; wordlessly they shared a moment of the past, without pain, without guilt. His entire body clenched. How he wanted to push their meal away and take her right here, right now. Relive the passion, the heat.

She drew a trembling breath and dropped her gaze to her meal. Reality returned, and with it came the inevitable memories.

Disappointed, but refusing to feel bitter, Seth returned his attention to his meal. He cut a quarter of his porterhouse steak and placed it on her plate, along with a generous helping of potatoes.

And Honor, doing what he expected of her, dug into the potato and said, "You need to start eating healthier."

He took a generous bite of his steak. "You're right."

With the poignancy of the memory still hanging heavy in the air, they continued their meal in silence. Finishing up well before Honor, he unwrapped the generous portion of chocolate cake he'd ordered and divided it. Before he could slide half of it to her, she said, "No thanks."

He didn't bother to try to convince her otherwise. Her favorite dessert now tasteless in his mouth, Seth only took a few bites, then pushed it aside.

Hell, she was right. He did need to start eating better.

The Wyoming wilderness

Like a blanket covering the sun, night fell quickly. Anna figured she'd traveled at least four to five miles. Not a lot of territory but when your feet were almost twice their normal size, pretty impressive. Since she could do nothing for them, she had ignored the agony most of the day. Now that it was nighttime and she'd gathered leaves and branches for a bed, she had nothing else to do but try to stay warm and think about how much they hurt.

Had she made any progress toward civilization? She didn't know. The sounds of dogs howling might have disappeared, but she knew better than to think they had stopped looking for her.

As she lay on the hard ground, she thought about the day she'd been taken. How long ago that was, she had no idea. In captivity, days ran together. At first, she had tried to keep track, but after they'd started drugging her, time had blurred and she'd lost count of the hours.

What they planned for her and the other girls she didn't know—and, actually, didn't want to know. The first few days, she had been locked in a small room with only a commode and a small mattress on the floor. A single lightbulb hanging from the ceiling had been her only light, and it had been turned off most of the time, with the exception of when she was fed. The food had been surprisingly plentiful, if bland. It was their delivery system that sucked. Twice a day, a small slot opened and a plate, along with a carton of milk, was shoved through. She imagined that wild animals at zoos were treated with more dignity.

Then a man had appeared one morning. With her foot chained to the floor, she hadn't been able to get close enough to do any damage, but she had gladly screamed the most vile, atrocious language she could come up with. That had been a mistake. She should have cowered, acted beaten. Her temper and the indignity of her circumstances had overcome her good sense.

He had quickly closed the door. A few minutes later, he had returned with another man. That man had had a needle in his hand. While one had held her down, the other had injected the drug.

That had happened twice before she'd finally wised up and realized that the only way to get away from them was to let them think she was subdued and resigned to her captivity. Finally only one man appeared to give her the injection. She'd been weak but determined . . . and she had taken him down.

Which brought her back to the day she'd been kidnapped. It had started on a sour note because she'd argued with her dad that morning. He had been angry with her mom and, as usual, she'd been the sounding board for the two of them.

The call had put her in a bad mood, so when the young girl at the coffee shop approached her, she paid little attention at first. Her forensics lab exam was only two days away, and studying for it occupied her thoughts.

Then she heard a soft, tentative voice: "Excuse me. Do you mind if I sit here?"

Anna jerked her head up. She'd been so immersed in her reading, she'd forgotten where she was. She cast a glance around, saw that all the tables were full, and shrugged. "Sure, have a seat."

Hoping the girl wasn't the chatty kind, she bent back to her book.

"I'm new here. This is my first year."

She drew a silent breath. So much for studying. Raising her head, she smiled at the young girl. She didn't look older than eighteen and had such a delicate, angelic quality, Anna couldn't help but feel protective. She knew how it felt to be thrust into a world of busy campus life where everyone seemed to know where they were going and what they should be doing except her. Which was one of the reasons she had attended a small social the day before. Not that it'd done any good. She'd felt years older than everyone there.

"What's your name?" the girl asked.

"Anna Bradford. What's yours?"

She held out her hand. "Call me Tabitha."

She thought nothing of Tabitha not giving her a last name. They chatted about the small town of Harristown and how it differed from where they'd grown up. Tabitha said she was from somewhere back East. Their conversation lasted for about half an hour, and then Tabitha said, "Can I ask a favor?"

"Sure."

"This boy asked me out the other day . . . I really like him and want to look good for our date, but I'm hopeless at picking out clothes. Do you think you'd have time to go shopping with me, just for about an hour?"

Anna glanced down at the words on the page she'd been reading. What was the point in pretending she could get her concentration back? Maybe an hour of window shopping wouldn't be such a bad idea. Besides, though Tabitha was a beautiful girl, her outdated cotton dress did scream for fashion help. She could play fairy godmother for an hour, couldn't she?

"Sure." Packing her books into her backpack, Anna stood. "You want to go to the mall?"

"There's actually a little vintage shop about a mile from here. I found a dress that I think will look perfect . . . I just need a second opinion."

Okay, well, vintage clothes weren't exactly her thing, but with Tabitha's looks, she could probably pull it off quite well. "That's fine. Do we need to drive?"

She nodded eagerly. "My car's out front."

"I could follow you."

"No really, it's not that far. I'll bring you back to your car as soon as we're through. Promise."

Anna shrugged and followed her out the door. What could it hurt? Two minutes later, she found it could hurt quite a lot. The instant she sat in the passenger seat, a giant hand came from the back of the car and covered her mouth with a noxious-smelling handkerchief. She woke to find herself in the trunk of a car with her hands and feet tied. Furious and scared, she made such a racket that the car had stopped. And that was when she saw him for the first time. A giant, mountainous man with the most vile, evil gleam in his eyes. What scared her even more was the loving smile he gave her as he injected a needle into her neck.

When she woke up the next time, she was in a small, cold, empty room, naked and tied to a wooden board. The groans, screaming, and cries of pain that surrounded her gave her the first indication of what she'd walked into and what they had planned for her.

Anna forced those nightmare thoughts away, and

tightened the curl of her body under the pile of leaves. With fantasies of finding her way out and making those monsters pay comforting her, she closed her eyes and let sleep take her to a land where life was fair and justice overcame evil.

thirteen

Honor looked down at Seth's bent head as he reviewed the notes from their phone conversation with Jared and Aidan. Though both men had information to share, no significant leads had been discovered other than that Karen Hatcher was also a transfer student and that the real reason Kelli Cavanaugh had transferred to another college was because of a broken heart. Breaking up with a boyfriend her parents hadn't even known she'd had and wanting to get away from seeing him date her best friend was an interesting piece of news, but no one felt it had anything to do with her disappearance.

After ending the call, Honor had watched Seth withdraw, his expression almost austere. She knew the reason; she just didn't know if he was going to be open to talking about it. Aidan's casual comment about how several members of Seth's family had questioned why he wasn't there investigating his niece's disappearance had put the scowl on Seth's face. But an instant before that, she'd seen the flicker of hurt in his eyes.

Treading softly, she said, "See anything?"

"Nothing. The more I look at the evidence, the less sure I am that any of these disappearances are related."

"Don't do that to yourself, Seth."

His head jerked. "Do what?"

"Punish yourself because of your family."

Dark brows drew together in an ominous frown. "What are you talking about?"

"You're second-guessing yourself because of your guilt, not because there's not a connection."

Seth pushed his chair back, stood, and went to the window. Pulling the drapes, he stared out at the night. "I don't need you psychoanalyzing me, Honor."

"I'm not. I'm just trying to help you understand where your doubts are coming from. Believe me, I know. There were cases where I became attached to the family and their pain became mine. That made me question everything I did. Should I have gone in a different direction? Was I seeing things that weren't there just because I wanted to bring their children back to them?"

Her heart clutched . . . she hadn't thought of those cases in a long time. The ones where no matter what she'd done or how much she'd wanted it, she hadn't been able to solve the case fast enough or do enough to save the child. Yes, most times she had brought in the pervert responsible. But not always. And it had eaten at her, just as it was eating at Seth. Only for a different reason.

He turned to face her, and instead of the anger she'd seen seconds ago, there was understanding and compassion. Was it any wonder that she had once loved this man so very much?

"I'd forgotten that you worked with the Child Abduction Unit. My God, the misery and pain you must have seen."

"Sometimes it was unbearable, but most times, the parents' pain did what it needed to do. It drove me, helped me to stay focused, and made me even more determined."

Seth twisted around to stare out the window again. "I just can't get over the feeling that I should go to Houston and at least give them some kind of update."

"We will, when we have something to give them. Going there now, without any concrete evidence, will only frustrate them more. Let's get our preliminary investigation out of the way. Then, when you go, hopefully you'll be able to give them hope."

"You're right."

Feeling on firmer ground now, she asked, "Have you talked with anyone in your family, since this happened, other than Joel?"

He nodded. "The day after Joel called me, I went to his house to talk to him and his wife, Beth. Mom and my sister Ally were there, too. I think they came in case things got heated between me and Joel." He shrugged. "I felt like a stranger with them."

Honor couldn't help but hurt for him. Her family meant the world to her; what would she do if she couldn't call them, rely on them to be there when she needed them? Seth hadn't had that for a very long time. The decisions he'd made for his job had cost him his close relationship with his family. And even though his actions had also broken her heart, she felt an unexpected anger at the Cavanaughs. Families were supposed to love and forgive you no matter what.

"When you told your family the truth about Clemmons, what did they say?"

"It's what they didn't say that was the most telling. Even though Clemmons didn't know I was the mole, he still had enough money and influence to come after me if he found out the truth. I was still a target. After he was arrested, I told my mom, brothers, and sisters the truth, but they had to keep it to themselves. I know they were relieved that I wasn't the sleaze they'd thought I was, but I could tell they were pissed, too."

"Because you hadn't trusted them with the truth?"

"That, and the fact that I had basically put my entire family at risk."

"But that's why you separated yourself from them, to protect them."

"Yeah, well, that didn't stop them from being pissed."

Honor watched as he stared intently out the window. Her room faced the parking lot, and it was pitch-dark outside. He wasn't looking at the view; he was looking inside himself, questioning and hurting. And Honor hurt for him even more. Yes, his family had suffered for what he'd put them through, but so had Seth.

"I would think they'd be proud that you did something so dangerous and selfless."

"My mom defended me, but the things I had to say and do to keep them away from me are hard to forget." He sighed. "Even though everything makes sense to them now . . . there's still a divide.

"Most of the family never understood why I wanted to be a cop in the first place. I come from a long line of accountants, cooks, and realtors. Good, honest professions, but not exactly edge-of-your-seat excitement. I wanted something more."

Without telling her legs to move, Honor found herself standing behind him. Putting her hand on his shoulder, she gave him something his entire family should have but hadn't. "I think you're a wonderfully brave man."

He turned and looked down at her, puzzlement and something else in his expression. "After what I did to you, you can say that?"

"I'm still angry and hurt about that, but I also realize the sacrifices you made. Takes a strong person to be that committed."

His mouth twisted into a semblance of a smile. "I really am sorry I hurt you."

"I know you are."

She gave him her own twisted smile and dropped her hand. If she didn't get him out of her room, she was going to do something supremely stupid. Seeing this side of Seth made her want to ease his pain. Doing that now would involve more than just physical release. Making love to him would open up the part of her heart she'd sworn would be closed forever.

Honor backed away. "Guess we'd better call it a night. We need to get an early start tomorrow."

Knowledge flickered in his eyes. He understood exactly why she'd moved away from him. Despite her determination to feel nothing, a lump developed in her throat.

"I'll see you in the morning."

As she watched him walk out the door, Honor literally had to grab on to the desk beside her to keep herself from running after him.

Years ago, she'd loved him with an intensity and fervor that had rivaled any great romance. Today, maturity and experience made her pause and assess every move, every word. After Seth, she had promised herself she'd never again fall so hard and so fast. Never feel so deeply. Now here she was, five years later, and not once had she felt for anyone close to what she had felt for Seth.

With an explosive sigh, Honor turned to the lackluster view beyond the window. She was in so much trouble.

In the late afternoon of the fourth day of her escape, Anna stood in the midst of the wilderness and, for the first time, began to question whether she would survive. She had no idea where to go, what direction to head in. She could live on berries and nuts—they were plentiful. And so far, finding water had been no problem. However, her physical condition was deteriorating. An hour ago, she had given up on the cloth covering her feet, which was just as well, since it really had provided little protection. But now she feared infection or worse. Her feet throbbed with a never-ending pain, and several of the cuts were red and inflamed. If she didn't get help soon, she wouldn't make it.

Last night had been her worst yet. The temperature had fallen with a rapid pace she hadn't expected. She'd huddled beneath all the branches and leaves she could find, but the area she'd wound up in had been devoid of trees, except for a few, sparsely spread out. She had resisted stopping until it was too dark to see and then, when she had, she'd discovered that she had little protection from the elements. This morning, she'd woken sore and stiff from trying to stay warm.

She had hoped that going downhill would mean something. So far, all she'd found were more valleys and hills and absolutely no signs of civilization. Sitting down and having a good cry was a temptation, but where would that get her? Nowhere.

Chin jutted out to prevent those useless tears, Anna set her sights on what looked like a clearing beyond a small patch of trees. She headed to the opening. Seven steps later, she stopped and listened. An unfamiliar sound hit her ears. Beyond the birds chirping, the wind shuffling the leaves of the trees, and small animals scampering and foraging, she heard something distinctly human: whistling.

Frozen in place, her breath halted, she waited. Had she imagined the sound because she wanted it to be true? No, there it was again. Some kind of vaguely familiar tune. Someone had hiked this far into the woods and would be able to help her, get her back home. She could call the police, save the other girls. Choking back a sob of thanksgiving, Anna ignored the pain in her feet and ran toward the wonderful sound of another human being.

She stopped at the edge of the clearing. Having learned her lesson the hard way, she refused to just explode through the trees until she knew what she was getting into. After all, it could be people from the hunting party of those monsters she'd escaped from.

The man appeared to be in his late thirties. Tall and broad-shouldered, he whistled as he set up a tent in the middle of the clearing. Totally focused on his job, he never looked up from his task of pounding a steel stake into the ground. When he stopped pounding for a moment, Anna recognized the tune he was whistling as an old Dean Martin love song. She sighed her happiness. That song had been one of her great-grandmother's favorites; she was going to be rescued.

Gingerly, she made her way toward the man. Not wanting to startle him, she stood a few yards away and waited for him to notice her. Several seconds later, his body stiffened and she knew he had sensed her presence. He lifted his head and stared at her as if she were an apparition.

With her oversized ragged clothes, no shoes, and wild hair, she probably looked like a scary woodland creature. Anna gave him a bright smile, hoping to lessen the impact of her appearance. "Thank God I found you."

The man continued to stare, making Anna wonder if she looked even worse than she thought. "Don't be afraid. I'm lost and need to get back home." She took a step closer and said, "Do you have a cellphone, by chance?"

He shook his head.

"Can you help me?"

He nodded.

She moved closer. The expression on his face so wary, she wondered if he thought she would harm him.

Apparently finally finding his voice, he said, "Are you hungry?"

"Starving."

He turned and pulled several items from a canvas bag. "I have cheese and crackers. As soon as I get a fire started, I'll heat up some beef stew."

Anticipation and hunger brought her even closer. "Thank you so much."

He nodded at a folding chair. "Have a seat and I'll get you fed in no time."

Almost crying, her relief was so great, she sat down and savored the moment. She was going home; she had survived.

"My name is Anna Bradford. What's yours?"

"Ben Hamilton." He smiled for the first time as he added, "And I'm very pleased to meet you, Anna."

She looked around at the supplies neatly laid out on a small strip of canvas. "So are you up here for some fishing or hunting?"

The smile spread even wider. "Yeah, you might say that."

fourteen

Seth stared at the white dry-erase board and tried to see something he knew wasn't there. There was almost no real commonality between the five young women. How the hell could he have thought otherwise?

He and Honor had visited the colleges Drenda and Anna attended. They had gone to the places they were last seen, had interviewed professors, friends, and acquaintances. Other than someone remembered seeing Anna at a local coffee shop talking with a young blond woman, there was nothing. The coffee shop didn't have surveillance cameras, so other than that she was pretty, no one knew what the hell the girl looked like. A pretty blond wasn't exactly on their list of suspects. Problem was, no one else was, either.

He and Honor had flown into Tampa a few hours ago; after checking into their hotel, they'd both wanted to come to LCR to prepare for tomorrow's meeting. Thorne and Livingston would be arriving tomorrow morning. Noah McCall was flying in from Paris and would be there as well. Between the five of them, he hoped like hell someone would see something. What that something was, he had no idea.

Honor spoke from behind him: "Let's head back to the hotel and catch some sleep."

"You go ahead."

She sighed. "Seth, we've looked at the evidence from every angle. Nothing is going to magically appear. With fresh eyes and additional people, maybe we'll see the connection we're missing."

He whirled around. "And if we don't? What then? Do we just drop it? LCR goes on to something they can solve?"

A sort of stubborn pride sparkled in her eyes. "No, that's not going to happen. We don't give up."

"Why not—that's what you thought I should have done, isn't it?"

"What?"

"With Clemmons. You think I should have just dropped it and gone on with my life. Forgotten about the promises I made and let him get away with his shit."

"Did I ever say that?"

"No, but—"

Cheeks flushed, her eyes gleaming even hotter, she advanced on him. "Don't you dare use your guilt and frustration to make me out to be the villain." Inches from him, she stopped. "I never said I thought you should give it up. I've seen people like Clemmons . . . I know what they can do."

An odd expression flickered across her face as she backed away. "If you're not interested in sleeping, let's at least work off some of this excess energy."

Exhausted from his worry for Kelli and the lack of clear-cut leads, he went still at Honor's words. Aching with a need for her that would never die, Seth studied her beautiful face. Did she mean . . . ? She gave him a look, vulnerable but yearning. Hell yes, she did. Always semi-hard in Honor's presence, he moved on to full-fledged arousal in an instant. He shot a quick glance around the conference room, judging where the most comfortable place would be. "Where? Here?"

She shook her head. "Follow me."

Figuring he'd follow her over a cliff if she swayed her beautiful ass like that, he trailed her out of the conference room, down a hallway, and into another room.

Seth stopped at the door while Honor went to the middle of the room, turned, and smiled. "It's a great gym, isn't it? I figured I'd have to join one when I moved to Paris, but all the LCR offices have fully equipped ones."

"You want to work out?" He couldn't keep the incredulity out of his voice . . . he was past pretending. He was already brick hard and getting harder by the second.

She arched a brow. "You want something else?"

He advanced into the room, his fingers tugging at the buttons of his shirt. "Yeah, I want something else. So do you."

She didn't argue, which was a relief. A small smile tweaked her mouth, but her eyes were solemn, searching. "Just sex, right?"

His fingers stopped at the last button of his shirt. "What do you mean?"

"No promises, no talk of the future. Nothing beyond this moment."

He told himself he wasn't disappointed in her request. He sure as hell wasn't looking for a relationship. Sure, if things had been different five years ago, he probably would have married Honor; maybe they'd even have a couple of kids by now. And they would have been happy, he knew that without a doubt. But that was all in the past . . . a future with her didn't exist any longer. Didn't matter. No way in hell would he refuse her invitation.

"Mindless, meaningless sex? Sure, I can do that." Isn't that what he'd done before and after Honor?

Moving slowly toward him, that sexy walk of hers heating him to boiling, she stopped before him and said softly, "Just so you know. Sex with you could never be meaningless."

With a groan, Seth pulled her close and covered her mouth. She opened willingly and his tongue went deep, meeting, tangling, and licking at hers. His hands were equally busy, pulling and tugging at her clothes. In seconds, she was beautifully, gloriously nude. Unable to stop himself, Seth stepped back to appreciate what he'd only been able to fantasize from memory for the last five years. Cream silk and freckles—his fantasy come to life. "You're even more beautiful than I remembered."

Her smile sexy, her eyes gleaming with need, she took his hand. "Let me show you what I found the first time I visited this office." Pulling him toward a wall, she pressed a small panel and a door appeared. Seth followed her in to find a few more pieces of equipment.

"You got a sex swing back here?"

Her expression one he'd go to his grave needing, she shook her head and started pulling at his clothes. "Much better."

"What's better than a sex swing?"

She drew back, her eyes alive with laughter. "Have you ever tried a sex swing?"

"Hell no."

"Me either. This, on the other hand, is perfect for us."

Taking his eyes off the beauty in front of him, he looked around again. "What are you talking about?"

"Get your clothes off and then I'll show you."

No additional encouragement was necessary. Seth stripped to nothing and then sucked in a breath when Honor's soft, cool hand closed around him. "Baby, I can't—"

"Then come with me." With one last caress, she let him go and walked naked toward a door in the corner. His eyes on her delectable ass, Seth barely knew how his feet were moving. All available blood had zoomed to his groin. If Honor wasn't in front of him, promising sweet relief, he'd probably fall to his knees.

She opened the door and turned, offering another enticing smile. "Come with me."

Since he felt as though he could come at any moment, her words seemed more likely as the seconds passed. Shifting his gaze, he realized she was leading him into a sauna.

Seth followed her inside. Immediately, a fine sheen of warm moisture covered his skin. Unable to wait any longer, he pulled Honor back into his arms and claimed her mouth again.

Wrapping her arms around this man she'd never been able to let go of, Honor swallowed a groan of need. Yes, this was what she wanted, what she needed. Seth. Only and always Seth. As he ate at her mouth, Honor's hands slid down his broad shoulders, loving the feel of his hard, slick skin beneath her fingers.

His hot mouth lifting from hers, he began to trail his tongue down her neck. Honor tried to bring her mouth back to his, but he shook her head. "Not yet . . . I need to taste you." He pushed her backward until the backs of her knees met the bench behind her. She sat down and Seth went to his knees in front of her. Honor pulled him to her and attacked his mouth again—she could never get enough of Seth's kisses.

Holding her head with his hands, he gave her what she wanted. He thrust his tongue deep again and again, and Honor chased his tongue, sucking, dueling. The heat of the sauna was nothing to the heat Seth's mouth was creating inside her.

Finally, she had to pull back to catch her breath. Seth nipped at her lips, and when she would have gone after his mouth again, he growled "I forgot how damn good you taste" as he moved his mouth down her neck, to her breasts. Licking a nipple and then taking it into his mouth, he suckled hard. Honor gasped and held his head as he devoured first one breast and then the other.

He pulled away again and Honor blinked to focus on the man in front of her. Beads of sweat slid down his face, and that expression of intense concentration that promised ecstasy made her want to throw herself back into his arms and let him take her hard and fast.

His deep blue eyes locked with hers, she felt his hands on her butt, pulling her closer to the edge of the bench, and then his hands were between her legs, spreading her. "Seems like I've dreamed about this forever."

So had she. How many times had she woken aroused, swollen and wet, throbbing with need, because she'd dreamed about Seth's mouth, his hands, his body? Too many times to count.

The first flick of his tongue on her clit sent her to the edge of climax. Honor leaned her head back against the wall, closed her eyes, and gave herself to his devouring mouth. And then, in an effortless, dreamy fashion, she was there—bright lights behind her closed lids exploded; her only thought, her only focus was the pleasure zooming through her. A keening scream of ecstasy bounced against the walls of the small room.

Long seconds later, she opened her eyes to see Seth still on his knees before her, a tender expression on his face.

She leaned forward and kissed him softly, tasting herself on his mouth. "I need you inside me."

With a swift motion, he stood and jerked her up from the bench. Whirling her around, he sat down and pulled her over him. "Then take me."

With her knees on either side of his hips, Honor once again locked her gaze with his as she lowered herself. Seth cupped her butt, easing her onto to his erection. Her breath hitched as she felt the tip of him slide into her.

"Easy, sweetheart," Seth whispered.

She didn't want easy, she wanted hard and fast, but it had been such a long time for her. When he was halfway in, Honor stopped and leaned her forehead against his shoulder, panting with exertion.

"You okay?" he asked.

"Yeah, it's just . . ."

"Shhh." He lifted her up again and inserted two fingers inside. Spreading her gently, insistently, he worked the eager flesh surrounding him. Honor rode his fingers, feeling herself loosening, opening more for him. The throbbing desire intensified with each thrust of his fingers; she had to have more, needed more . . . she needed all of him.

Apparently agreeing that she was ready, he withdrew his fingers and eased her down over his erection again. She gasped a welcoming sigh. Yes, this time he went in easier, until he was almost totally buried within her.

"Okay?" he asked gruffly.

"So very okay."

"You ready?"

"Yes."

His big hands cupped her butt again as he worked her up and down, allowing her to take him a little more with each downward slide. Heat built. Gripping Seth's slick shoulders, she began to move up and down on her own, letting him use his hands to close around her and bring her breasts up to his mouth. Gasps, groans, and cries of delight filled the small room. Climax zoomed, fierce and sweet, carrying her away on a wave of pleasure and searing, burning heat. Crying out his name, Honor exploded around him. Seconds later, Seth let out a low, growling groan and she felt his release flood her.

Clasping her arms tightly around him, she pressed her face against his neck and licked his neck, his collarbone, everywhere she could reach. His taste seemed beautifully familiar, yet wonderfully new—this was Seth before and this was Seth now. A man she'd never stopped wanting or needing.

As her body shook with satisfaction and exhaustion, Honor acknowledged that for the first time in years, she felt whole and at peace. And now, the biggest question faced her: how in the hell was she ever going to let him go again?

fifteen

Bellefonte, Pennsylvania

Alden sat in the most comfortable chair the RV provided. Traveling around in the contraption wore him out almost as much as finding the right woman each time they went hunting. He was eager to return home and begin his favorite part—the initiation and then the training. With feigned patience, he eyed his son. "Have you made a choice?"

"There are two that I want."

"You can only have one."

A sly gleam entered John's eyes. "You've often had two women at a time, sometimes more. Our people expect me, as your son, to have more than they do."

Alden's fake tolerance vanished. "You're barely man enough to handle one woman, much less two. Now choose or I'll do it for you."

"I've often handled three at once. Ask the stable girls if you don't believe me."

Alden snorted. "Do you honestly believe that a hard dick is the only way to satisfy a woman? Women have to be controlled, shown what to do, what to think. If you let them lead you by that hard thing between your legs, they'll take advantage. To keep them happy, you have to show them what makes them happy. Doing that with more than one woman would be a difficult task for anyone. For someone who's barely a man, it's an impossible task. Now choose or I will."

John glared his displeasure. "I'm more than man enough to please half a dozen girls."

Too late, Alden recognized his mistake. He never should have agreed to let the boy choose a mate this soon. Should have let him sow his wild oats with the eight women who earned their keep by providing relief to his community of men. The single men visited the stable frequently; the married men were allowed to go there only when their women were unavailable due to pregnancy or their monthly flow. John was only nineteen, much too young to find the right woman to settle down with and take to wife.

However, Alden could not admit that mistake. Admitting errors could make his people think he was flawed. His word was law. If he went back on his promise to his son, they'd question his decision. Might start questioning other things, too. That couldn't happen.

He gave a philosophic mental shrug. When his son realized he'd chosen the wrong woman, Alden would find a way to make her disappear. Two of his three wives had contacted a mysterious, incurable disease. Having the girl get a similar ailment should be easy enough.

However, he refused to weaken on one particular issue. "You must choose only one."

"Very well. I want the blonde."

Alden barely refrained from rolling his eyes. John's choice only reemphasized the boy's immaturity. Both girls were attractive and looked as though they could bear healthy children. However, the blonde had large breasts and bleached hair. The other one, a brunette, was petite, small-breasted, and seemed to have the more pleasing personality. Trust an immature kid to look at the physical appearance as the most important quality.

"Very well." Alden turned to the young woman sitting

at his feet. "Tabitha, do you know which one your brother desires?"

"Yes, Father. The one with the giant ass."

Alden swallowed a chuckle. This was the second year Tabitha had provided assistance in selecting the females. His angel resented bringing him the women, fearful he would choose one to replace her. He never could, of course. Yes, he would eventually marry again, if for no other reason than to set an example for his followers. And at some point, he'd like to breed another child or two—his gift to the community.

Another woman, however, could never replace Tabitha. But he did adore that jealous streak.

Alden stood. "Let's bring her in today. I'd like to be home by week's end."

He would leave his daughter in charge of setting the trap. She was the craftiest of women when it came to pretense. One look from those innocent baby-blue eyes and people fell over themselves trying to please her. Little did they know that only one thing pleased his Tabitha, and that was keeping her father happy.

The Internet café streamed with people, most of whom didn't seem to care to get on a computer. Young people were entertaining to watch. Years ago, before he'd served his time in prison and long before he had envisioned Tranquillity, he would often go to the hangouts the local college kids frequented. He hadn't attended the university, but he had enjoyed the activity of campus life.

He should have stuck with just watching, but when one of the young women had given him signals that she wanted to get to know him better, Alden had become a bit overeager. Screwing her up against the brick wall at the back of the building had been a mistake. Should've taken her somewhere else. No, he should've smothered the bitch when she'd screamed. His luck hadn't been with him that day. An off-duty policeman had been there seconds later. Alden still had his pants unzipped and the bitch had started jabbering about rape. Before he knew it, he was in jail and then prison.

Three years in prison had not only perfected his self-control skills but had given him a lot of time to think. And in that time, Tranquillity had been born in his mind. A place where he ruled everything and everyone and when he wanted to screw some girl, then he damn well did it.

After he was released, he hooked up with some low-lifes and tried out his new powers of persuasion. Turned out, he was very good at it. Within a month, he had four followers. In a year, he had twelve. Now, twenty years later, he had over one hundred and could have more if he wanted. He didn't want more. The ones he had were devoted and devout. The three or four girls he added each year to keep his men satisfied was all he needed. Babies were being born all the time, and as soon as they could comprehend anything, they knew he was their leader. Over time, the population had grown all on its own. And each and every person there would give their life for him. He'd made sure of that.

His dream had come true.

The angelic vision in front of him caught his attention, pulling his thoughts from the past. Alden sat in the corner of the café and, with anticipatory delight, watched his daughter work her magic. The overblown female John had chosen, Mallory Roland, looked up as Tabitha said something to her. He supposed the girl was attractive enough, in a too obvious way. The white-blond hair, large breasts, and ample bottom made her look like a cheap imitation of one of those old-time movie starlets. Before he'd realized his calling, he'd lusted over such women. Once he'd even put up a poster in his bedroom of some blond bimbo actress and had gotten the hell beaten out of him by his whore of a mother. She hadn't appreciated the competition.

Soft laughter drew his attention back to the girl. Tabitha was probably sharing an anecdote or joke. His daughter was good at making people feel comfortable. Mallory laughed appropriately, but the more Alden watched her, the less he liked her. His son was going to have trouble with this one, he could already tell.

Yesterday, Tabitha had attended a newcomers' gathering. The tiny camera attached to her collar, disguised as a ladybug pin, had done a good job of picking up the features of several promising candidates. His son had barely looked at the women before settling on two of his favorites. The final choice of the blonde was no real surprise; still, Alden wished his son had better taste. Once the boy realized what a mistake he'd made, perhaps he would listen to his father more often.

The two young women got to their feet. As prearranged, Tabitha would lead the girl down an alley, ostensibly to her car—the shopping ruse had worked quite well for them this year. When the girls arrived in the alley, John would be waiting and would meet his mate for the first time. Since privacy was of the most import, it would have to be a short, quick meeting. Alden would pick them up in the RV within minutes.

Five minutes later, Alden left a 20 percent tip for his coffee and roll and stood. Leaving too much or too little money would make him memorable. Leaving the correct amount helped him blend in with the rest of the crowd. Since he was decades older than most of the occupants, he tried to do as little as possible to attract anyone's attention.

Keys in hand, he slipped out of the café and walked the short distance to the RV he'd parked in front of a convenience store. He started it up and headed toward the alley behind the coffee shop. Things were going so smoothly, they should be on their way home in a matter of minutes.

As Alden drove around to the back, he knew immediately that something was wrong. Tabitha stood several feet away from the car, the expression on her face one of sheer panic.

Putting the RV in park, he kept the motor running and got out. "What's wrong?"

"I think John was too rough."

Alden's rage surged, but the need to control the situation was imperative. He ran to the car to see John thrusting inside the woman's body. The idiot was doing her here?

"Are you crazy? What . . . ?"

Rarely at a loss for words, Alden stood by, stunned, and watched as his son finished with the woman, then climbed off her half-clothed body. What was supposed to have been a simple matchmaking event had just turned upside down on them. In the RV, John could have had the bedroom to acquaint himself with the woman. Instead, he'd chosen the backseat of their rented car.

His son's lack of self-control could well destroy Alden's entire world.

"You fool! What have you done?"

Huffing with exertion, John crawled out of the backseat and snarled, "The bitch laughed at me when I told her she was coming home with me. I lost control."

Alden looked down at his son's crotch. "You couldn't control yourself yet had the presence of mind to put on a condom?"

"Bitch didn't deserve my sperm."

Alden's rage bubbled. His hands fisted tight at his sides, the urge to beat the little prick within an inch of his life almost overwhelming. But this was not the time, and the middle of an alley behind several businesses was not the place. That would have to wait until they returned home. And after Alden finished, it'd be a long time before John put his dick into anyone or anything.

"We'll take her back and put her in the stable," Tabitha said quickly. "No one has to know this was supposed to be John's mate."

Before Alden could respond, John snarled, "Hell no."

"That's not your call to make," Alden snapped. "You just gave up your right to make any decisions about the girl."

His handsome face marred by arrogance and hatred, John shook his head. "She'll laugh at me whenever she sees me. She'll tell others."

As much as he didn't want the boy's input, Alden had to admit that John had a point. No matter how furious he was with his son's unthinking selfishness, having a woman mock their leader's son would be bad for morale.

"Fine." He glanced down at the barely conscious girl and then swept his gaze around the empty alley. There was no way they could just dump her here; nor could they have her telling the police what had happened. "Here's what we're going to do." He glared at his son. "And I swear, if you fuck this up, the same thing's going to happen to you."

A tinge of worry flickered on his son's face. At last, he was comprehending what a royal screwup he'd made of a very simple procedure.

His anger on temporary hold, Alden drew his children close and described his hastily made plan to clean up his son's mess.

sixteen

Tampa, Florida

The sound of Seth taking a shower waking her, Honor rolled over in bed and stretched with the sheer pleasure of being alive. Delicious aches all over her body were a delightful reminder that Seth Cavanaugh was still an exquisite lover. After recovering from their steamy lovemaking, they'd dried off and put their clothes back on. Since neither of them had slept in almost twenty-four hours, they'd headed back to their hotel rooms. She had stopped in front of her room and never even considered that Seth wouldn't follow her inside. The minute the door had closed behind them, she'd gone back into his arms. And that was where she'd stayed till morning.

What did any of this mean? What did Seth feel? She refused to allow herself to think about the future. The here and now with Seth was more than she ever thought she'd have again. Speculating on where this was heading was a sure path to disaster.

Being with him again had felt so good, so right. She'd had only one very brief relationship in the last five years. If one could call a weekend fling a relationship. A few months after she and Seth had broken up, she had worked with LCR on a case and had met Cole Mathison, an LCR operative who had reminded her of Seth. Cole had lost his wife and daughter a few years earlier and was still suffering. And, at that time, she was still crying into her pillow each night. That weekend fling had been as much about comfort as about pleasure.

Since then, she had focused solely on her career, with almost no social life, and had dated no one. How ironic that she'd made the decision to leave the Bureau in an effort to finally put the past to rest, only to find Seth roaring back into her life. She refused to consider that this was fate's way of allowing her to finish with him once and for all. She couldn't think about that right now.

"Good morning," Seth said in that early morning growl she remembered so well.

Sitting up, she leaned against the headboard and smiled up at him sleepily. "Morning."

"Coffee?"

"Please."

When he turned to the small counter behind him, Honor held back a sigh at the somber, too serious expression on his face—an indication that his thoughts were back on the case. One of the reasons she'd let her defenses down and made the invitation to him last night was because of this. They had so little to go on, and the frustration of not being able to find Kelli was killing him. They both knew that the longer it took, the more their chances of finding her alive dwindled.

Honor also knew that, coupled with his need to give his family back one of their own, he was feeling hopeless. Seeing Seth's despair wasn't something she could handle.

He brought the coffee to her and sat on the edge of the bed as she took an appreciative sip. She hadn't needed to tell him how she liked it . . . a small thing, yes, but still a nice reminder that while she hadn't been able to forget anything about him, he at least still remembered she took her coffee black with one packet of artificial sweetener.

"How are you feeling?" he asked quietly.

There were two ways to play this. As if it had been a monumental, earth-shattering event or just an enjoyable reunion romp with the sexiest man she'd ever known. Seth had enough drama in his life right now . . . she didn't need to add to it. She smiled. "Deliciously sore."

He chuckled and leaned in to kiss her softly. "Yeah, me too."

Relieved that she had chosen the right response, she said, "Guess we need to grab some breakfast."

"Why don't you shower and I'll order it. You still like the same thing?"

Even though she hated being so predictable, she couldn't help but be thrilled that Seth had apparently remembered that, too. "Yes. Thanks." She took another long swallow of her coffee and then sprang from the bed.

The thought of being self-conscious barely entered her mind. Seth had explored every part of her body, and though she was normally a modest person, with Seth, that had never concerned her.

Grabbing her underwear from a drawer, she headed to the bathroom. Seth's "Honor" stopped her. She turned at the doorway to look at him.

"Thank you," he said quietly.

There was no need to ask what he meant. Giving him a smile that came from her heart, she answered with a soft "My pleasure."

She turned and stepped into the bathroom before she was tempted to offer another bout of comfort. If she did that, he would quickly realize that her offer had less to do with the need to give them both some relief from their stress than it did with the unresolved feelings she had for him. Again, more drama than either one of them needed right now.

When the door clicked closed, Seth let go of a long-held breath. He'd made so many stupid mistakes in his life, why should one more surprise him? And the hell of it was, he wouldn't change a thing. Years ago, sex with Honor had been the best he'd ever had. Last night had been even better. So, stupid? Hell, yeah. But give him another chance and he'd take it again . . . and again.

Arousal surged, and he closed his eyes. There should be no life left down there, at least for several days. But when it came to Honor, his body had a way of defying biology.

Cursing under his breath, Seth grabbed the phone. He could either stand here lusting like a fifteen-year-old or behave like a man who had more to do than just satisfy a never-ending desire.

Assured that breakfast would arrive within the next fifteen minutes, Seth poured himself another cup of coffee and walked out to the attached patio. Autumn in Florida could still mean steamy and hot, but today promised to be on the mild side, with a pleasant mid-seventies temperature.

What was it like where Kelli was? Was she hungry, exhausted, scared? He still refused to consider that she wasn't alive. That had never been a possibility to him. Even though they'd come to a standstill in the investigation, Seth still firmly believed she was alive.

Optimism wasn't exactly his thing—never had been, really—but he damn well refused to accept any other option. No, he didn't consider it optimistic as much as determined. Kelli was alive and he was going to rescue her, no matter what.

The knock on the door and a male voice announcing "Room service" brought him back inside. Seth opened the door and took the rolling cart from the man. After signing the bill, he pushed the cart into the center of the room and called out, "Breakfast."

Unsure if she'd heard him, he opened the bathroom door and froze. Having always prided himself on being able to keep his thoughts to himself in any situation, he knew that at this moment, without a doubt, his face showed exactly what he was thinking. How could he have forgotten Honor and her underwear?

Last night, he'd been too far gone to do more than get everything off her as quickly as possible. Now he took the time to fully appreciate the drop-dead-sexy woman in provocative lingerie. Seth stopped breathing as his eyes roamed freely. The ice-blue scraps of lace and satin barely covered her beautiful breasts, and the small panel of cloth at her mound covered just enough to make his mouth water.

Turning away before he acted on the need to remove those tempting pieces of cloth and taste her again, he growled, "Breakfast," and closed the door.

He grabbed a couple of chairs and placed them on either side of the cart. The mindless task of uncovering their meal and arranging silverware did nothing to ease his arousal. He knew only one thing that could do that, and for right now, that couldn't happen.

Five minutes later, Honor emerged. Dressed in a brown pantsuit, she looked coolly professional. Only Seth was aware that beneath the sedate clothes, a sexy nymph existed.

Acting as if she weren't aware of the volcano of sexual need bubbling inside him, her expression coolly neutral, Honor sat down in the chair Seth pulled out for her and started on her meal of oatmeal, orange juice, and coffee.

Seth dropped into the chair across from her and dug into his own meal of a western omelet and toast, appeasing one hunger while another continued to rage.

Almost finished with his breakfast, he raised his head to see a bemused expression on Honor's face. Swallowing the food in his mouth, he asked, "What's wrong?"

"Nothing. Just wondered if you were going to breathe in between bites."

He gave a wry grin and sat back in his chair. "You said you'd worked with LCR on some cases before joining them. Were they all child abduction cases?"

"Yes. The last one we worked together was over a year ago, in South Carolina. Two children, four-year-old twin girls, were abducted from a playground, right in front of their mother."

Yeah, he remembered that all too well. The case had made the national news. He'd made the mistake of watching the news one night and had caught a press conference about the investigation. Honor had been front and center, answering questions. He'd sat there, stunned, because it was the first time he'd seen her in years. Instead of changing the channel or getting up and leaving the room, he had devoured every expression, every subtle shift of her body as she talked about the case.

The press conference had lasted about ten minutes. Seth had found himself still staring at the television an hour later, barely aware that another program had started. When he'd finally pulled his head out of his ass and realized what he was doing, he'd turned the television off. He hadn't watched the news for the rest of the year.

He had, however, found himself following the case in the newspapers. When her name had been mentioned, Seth had studiously overlooked it.

"I remember reading about that case. The kids were found, weren't they?"

"Yeah, but by LCR, not us."

"I don't remember LCR's name being mentioned."

"That's what they prefer. Getting credit or press is something they'd rather avoid."

"Was that a hard adjustment for you when you got to LCR?"

Her nose scrunched up. "I hate press conferences. Even though they can be helpful in an investigation, being on camera and answering the same question, posed in twenty different ways, was one of my least favorite things."

That was too bad, because Honor had the kind of face the camera loved. Beautiful, high cheekbones, a heart-stopping smile, and the kind of earthy sensuality that would attract people to tune in to a press conference if only to see her on their television screen.

She had a timeless beauty, almost flawless. His gaze dropped to the scar on her neck. It was still fading, but he doubted it would go away completely. She had almost lost her life and he'd never known it. Might not have ever known if she'd died.

"The bastard who cut you. What were you after him for?"

"We went to question him about several young girls who'd been abducted and murdered. A new one was missing, but we were out of leads and down to talking to one-time offenders. This guy had served time for molestation of a minor a few years back. Idiot went berserk. We found out why, later. He wasn't responsible for those murders, but turns out he had moved a block from an elementary school and was back to stalking little girls."

"Did you find the girl you were looking for?"

She dropped her gaze to the meal in front of her, but not before he saw the answer in her face. Hell, he wished he hadn't asked. Was finding Kelli and the other girls alive just as hopeless? Was he just fooling himself?

"Did you at least catch the bastard?" Seth growled.

"Yes. The week before I left the Bureau, he was

stopped for a minor traffic violation. The cop noticed a pair of panties on the floorboard. That was information we'd never let leak to the press—that the guy kept the underwear of his victims."

"If that hadn't happened, you might not have found him."

She leaned forward and grabbed his hand. "I know what you're doing. You have to stop. We will find Kelli. I swear to you . . . we will find her."

"How do you know that?"

She released his hand and gave him the quietly confident words he needed to hear: "Because I won't stop until we do. And neither will you."

Honor rose from her chair and stood at the front of the large LCR conference room. The four men sitting at the oblong table before her had completed their review of one another's files. Now it was time to brainstorm and figure out, within the mass of notes, observations, and theories, just how these disappearances were related. If they could tie them together, see a thread or pattern, their chances were a hell of a lot better.

Before she could begin, Noah said, "Just want to alert everyone that there's a new disappearance."

"Related to this case?" Seth asked.

Noah shook his head. "Don't know yet. She was reported missing yesterday. She has a live-in boyfriend, and when she didn't come home, he called the police. She's a student at Penn State. Fits a couple of the similarities of the other victims. She's twenty and a transfer from a smaller school. I've got a call in to the campus police. As soon as I know something more, I'll let you know." He shot a look at Honor. "Let's get started."

If possible, the room was now even more somber. She gazed around the table at everyone. "Okay, if the new one is related, the more we can learn about these disappearances, the better our chance of helping the new victim, too."

At their agreeing nods, she continued: "I'm going to detail our investigation. Everyone please jump in and add anything that comes to your mind. Nothing is off the table or too crazy. What we're hoping for is some commonality we might have missed."

As Honor went through the litany of each girl's disappearance, family and friends' interviews, and personality profile, everyone listened intently, looking, as she was, for a thread. If there wasn't one, then, by rights, they were going to have to let go of all of the investigations, with the exception of the one they'd been hired to do—for Seth's niece.

"We've also checked to make sure the girls didn't know each other. They had no sororities in common, no people in common." Honor shook her head, suddenly disgusted with her own lack of ideas. "Hell, from what I can tell, they don't even like the same foods."

Without a word, Seth abruptly stood and went to the dry-erase board to her right. Before the meeting, she had attached the photos of the girls, along with a time line and the location of where they were last seen.

"You see something, Cavanaugh?" Noah asked.

"Not yet." He flashed a look at Honor that sent an odd chill up her spine. Something was definitely on his mind. "Keep talking. Let me think."

Trusting he'd share what he was thinking when he was ready, Honor returned to the discussion.

"What about the transfer thing?" Aidan asked. "With this new disappearance and the girl being a transfer student, could there be something to that after all?"

Honor sighed and shook her head. "I just don't know. Four of them transferred. Missy's the only one who didn't." She shrugged. "There's nothing really special

about a transfer that would cause students from different parts of the country to have anything to do with
each other."

"Except having no friends."

Honor turned at Seth's soft murmur. "What?"

"Missy's the only one who wasn't a transfer, but she's
also the shyest, most introverted of the girls. And she
had no friends, no family support. She's completely
alone." He shot a glance at Jared. "Right?"

His expression grim, Jared nodded. "Yes to all."

"Okay." Seth began to pace in front of the board. Not
wanting to be in his way, Honor stepped aside and sat
down at the table.

A magnetic kind of energy surrounded Seth as his
eyes, gleaming with excitement and optimism, swept
over the room. "Go with me on this. Okay?" Without
waiting for an answer, he turned back to the board. "All
of these girls were in some sort of transition or crisis
mode."

Picking up a marker from the tray in front of him, he
began to jot facts underneath the girls' names. As he
wrote, he said, "Missy wasn't a transfer, but as Jared
said, she's shy and awkward. She was also out of a job
until the pizza joint opened again." He turned to Jared.
"I'll bet if you check some kind of employment data-
base, Missy had been trying to get employment else-
where. Problem is, jobs are tough enough to come by for
anyone. As shy and socially awkward as Missy is, she
probably really struggled to find someone to hire her.
Which could make her even more vulnerable and open
to a predator."

Honor glanced around the room. The varying expressions told her the men were listening intently but were
also not seeing where this was going. She had the same
doubts, but after working with Seth, she trusted him to
lead them somewhere significant.

Seth continued: "Drenda, Anna, Kelli, and Karen were all transfers. Meaning, whether they were confident young women or not, they were dealing with uncertainty. Drenda went from a large university to a small one where people probably already knew one another. Friendships that were formed in the local high schools probably carried over to college.

"Anna moved two states away." He looked at Honor as he added, "And Honor and I both believe she did it to get away from her parents, who are going through an acrimonious divorce. Most likely using her as a pawn to hurt each other. Which means, even as confident and mature as Anna is, she's got some major anxiety going on."

The atmosphere in the room suddenly changed as everyone began to see where Seth was headed. Honor looked around again. Where there had been confusion and doubt, there was now a cautious hopefulness.

"Karen's parents indicated that she had a terrible first year at Michigan State," Jared said. "They hoped the smaller school would suit her personality more."

Her excitement growing, Honor said, "And Kelli transferred because of a breakup with her boyfriend. New school, broken heart, away from her family for the first time. All leading to a very vulnerable mental state."

The approving look Seth shot her sent ripples of excitement through her. Her silly, foolish heart leaped for joy.

Aidan's grim voice penetrated the increasing enthusiasm in the room. "Being the cautious voice of reason is damn uncomfortable for me, but I just gotta say two words: so what? The majority of young people are going through some sort of transition or trauma in their personal lives."

Seth acknowledged the other man's concern with a nod. He appreciated the question . . . and Thorne had a right to wonder where this was going. Seth just hoped to hell his thought process was leading them in the right direction.

"You're right, Thorne. But there's one place two of the girls went a day or so before they disappeared." He turned back to the board and pointed at the scribbles he'd added. "Drenda went to a new student support group. Mrs. Greene told us she'd been struggling to find new friends and thought this might introduce her to some people who were feeling the same way.

"And when I spoke with Joel, Kelli's father, he said something I didn't think was significant until now. Kelli was having problems settling in, but she told her parents she was looking into some student support groups to help her adjust better."

Turning back to the group, he gave his conclusion: "I believe this man is targeting vulnerable young women and that he's using groups such as those as his method of finding them."

Before anyone could question or object to this vague hypothesis, he added, "Before we go further, I'd like us to stop to see if we can determine if the other three girls might have done something similar. A social group, new student orientation . . . hell, even a party. Anywhere a young woman might feel safe going to find new friends or get better adjusted."

Giving no indication that it bothered her that Seth had taken over her meeting, Honor nodded her agreement. "I'll give Mrs. Bradford a call and ask her about Anna." She turned to Livingston. "Jared, you okay with getting that information as soon as possible on Karen and Missy?"

"Yeah. I should be able to get it on Karen quickly. Missy might be another matter."

Seth breathed out a silent sigh. Having no friends or

family made Missy the odd person out even within this group of missing girls.

Honor stood. "Do what you can. Let's get back together when—"

"Damn," McCall growled.

Everyone turned. McCall had been the most silent person in the room since the meeting started. His expression was now even grimmer than before.

"What's wrong?" Honor asked.

He held up his BlackBerry. "Text message on the missing Pennsylvania girl. Unless the guy's evolving into something even worse, I don't think the young woman's disappearance is related."

"Why?" Seth asked.

"Her body was found floating in a river, close to the campus. She'd been raped and strangled."

seventeen

Tranquillity

The shrill screams that had threatened to shatter the windows of the house were less frequent and had grown weaker. Breathless and feeling the exhilaration that comes from the release of pent-up fury, Alden drew back a muscled arm and cracked the whip against his son's naked back once more. Forty lashes so far and still he wanted to do more. The little SOB had tried to ruin it for him. Everything he'd worked so hard for could have gone up in smoke.

Feeling that fury reignite again, he put everything he had into the next swing of the whip. John cried out in misery again, but with much less force. Alden walked around to the front, where he could see his son's face. Tears poured from his eyes, combining with the sweat that dripped from his chin. Having him strung from the ceiling gave Alden the opportunity to use the whip on his front as well as his back. From his shoulders to his feet, John was covered in welts of punishment. Days, maybe weeks would go by before the idiot could lie down comfortably.

"Have you learned your lesson, John?"

"Yes, Father."

"And what is that lesson?"

"To abide by your wishes, no matter what they are."

"Excellent. And now that you've learned that lesson, it's time for another."

John's head had been drooping against his chest, but he lifted it and managed to ask, "What?"

"Do you think this measly punishment is all that you're due to receive? Son, when I get through with you, you'll wish you were lying alongside that little dead bitch in Pennsylvania."

"No, Father, please, I beg of you. I've learned my lesson. I promise."

Alden smiled. "Then let's just call this a reinforcement." He turned to the woman at the door. "Is the healer here?"

"Yes, Father."

Turning back to his son, he gave him the information he would need before the next event. Soon he would be in such severe pain, he would hear nothing but his own screams. "You will not die from your punishment, John. The healer is here to make sure that doesn't happen. However, this will be your final warning. Defy me again, do anything that could bring worldly attention to our community, and even the fires of hell will not be as painful as the punishment I will give you."

"Please, Daddy," John sobbed. "I'm so sorry."

Alden stiffened. His children never called him "Daddy." Something fluttered in his chest at the term. Before he could wonder at his strange response, Tabitha was there beside him, touching his hand. He looked down to see the satisfaction on her face. Her expression confirmed that he was doing the right thing. Children needed discipline. Tabitha had received hers, and now his son's punishment must be completed.

Taking the knife his daughter handed him, he went to his son and cut his ties. Before John fell to the ground, Alden caught him in his arms. Carrying him like a baby, with John sobbing against his shoulder, he took him to the tub that had been prepared.

He gave the healer a nod of approval. The possibility of death was minimal, but he wouldn't take the chance of John dying. What was the point of punishment if death was the final outcome? Kissing his son's furrowed, sweaty brow, he lowered him into the tub of liquid—a mixture of lemon juice, vinegar, and alcohol.

Shrill screams once again echoed through the house. And then there was blessed silence as John succumbed to unconsciousness.

"Check him for shock and then revive him."

Watching the healer carry out his orders, he caught a glimpse of his daughter's face. Pure happiness brightened her features.

"His vital signs are steady and he is awake." The healer reported the observation in his dry, matter-of-fact way.

"Excellent." Alden stood over his son, who lay back against the rear wall of the tub, his eyes only half open. "Your punishment is at an end, son. You stood up quite well." He turned back to the healer. "Get him to his room, tend his wounds. Give him what he needs to recover."

Satisfied that John had indeed learned his lesson, Alden turned his back on him and walked out of the room. The only thing that had saved the young fool's life was the fact that Alden had waited till they returned home to give him the punishment he deserved. Hundreds of miles of roadway had returned his control and lessened his fury. The boy would be scarred, but he wasn't dead. Anyone else, he would have killed outright. John should be grateful for that favor.

Tabitha had also been punished, but to a much lesser degree. She should have been able to detect the young woman's cruel streak and warned them. His daughter knew she had failed and had taken the punishment as a lady should. Because of her submission, she would be able to return to her regular duties in a day or two. His son was a different matter. Weeks would go by before the boy didn't feel the agony of his father's wrath.

And now Alden would do what he should have done in the first place. He would choose John's woman for him. The window of opportunity was about to close. Early fall was the best time to find women in a college setting. Young, vulnerable, and needy of friendship, they were like plucking ripe apples from a tree. Practically fell into his hands. He had planned to add four to their numbers this year, but only had three so far. The other men in the community trusted him to bring in healthy, amiable woman of childbearing years. Because of John's immaturity, he had squandered his right to choose his own. Never send a boy to do a man's job.

With weeks of recuperation ahead of him, John would have an opportunity to evaluate how he'd handled the situation, and it would also give him the chance to mature. By the time the woman was trained and ready for her new husband, John would be wiser and less inclined to lose his temper, ensuring a more harmonious marriage.

Initiation and training could take up to three months, depending on the particular young women's needs. Adaptation to their way of life was not always easy; some needed more convincing than others. He used to train them individually, but he'd found it too time-consuming. The first time he'd trained the women as a group, he'd realized he had been missing a great opportunity. Not only did he enjoy it more but the women were able to witness what the others went through. When their turn came, they behaved so much more obediently.

"Brother Alden, may I speak with you a moment?"

Alden turned at the soft, respectful tone and words.

Ben Hamilton had returned to the compound with a new reverence and appreciation of their ways. Alden had planned to take his wife, Lucy, away from him for a short time, just to reinforce his message of never questioning his authority. However, Ben had come back from his sanctuary trip much earlier than he had planned, bearing a gift. A lost lamb—the young woman who had escaped—had returned to the fold. Returning the runaway had earned Ben special privileges—Alden had allowed Lucy to see to her husband's needs immediately. Ben had been appropriately appreciative ever since.

Wiping his bloodied hands on a cloth, he asked, "What brings you here, my brother?"

"I have a special favor to ask."

That so startled Alden, he stared at the man for several seconds. His followers weren't granted favors. He allowed them the occasional special privilege because he was a good and benevolent leader. However, to have a member ask for a favor? He wasn't sure anyone had ever done that before. If someone had, he was almost certain the punishment had been severe and just. Did this man think Alden had gone soft because he'd rewarded him for finding the girl? If so, the man was about to learn the hard way that rewards can be revoked as quickly as they are given.

Knowing that if he revealed his thoughts, Ben would back down, Alden kept his expression bland. "What favor might that be?"

"I would like to be involved in the training of our new female members."

Now he was even more intrigued. Ben had never indicated an interest in the grueling lessons that each new female must go through. Not only did it take a great amount of time and energy; it was also not for the faint of heart. Few members knew exactly what went on inside the training facility. The women, once they had completed their instruction, never remembered the methods he had used to tame them. The pain-filled training was stopped almost immediately as soon as they pledged their obedience and loyalty, and afterward, they never acted as though they knew what had happened.

Somewhat gruesome tactics had to be used to bring the women to the understanding of their purpose in the community. As leader, Alden oversaw all of the training. He had studied the human psyche extensively, but even better, he had a special gift of reaching inside a young girl's mind and getting her to react exactly as he needed.

Alden knew his gifts were special and that few had them. However, he couldn't deny the thought that sharing the enjoyment with others might well increase his own pleasure. Tabitha certainly enjoyed it when he allowed her to assist. Why deprive Ben, if his proclivities led him to the same type of pleasure?

Still, was Ben up to the task of the more "vigorous" type of teaching? "And exactly what kind of training would you like to do with them?" Alden asked.

"Showing them around the community . . . helping them understand how fortunate they are to have been chosen to live here in Tranquillity, with you as their leader." His smile brightened as he added, "Lucy would like to help, too."

Ah, just as he'd thought. The man had no idea that the lesson plan included much more than a hospitality tour of their new home. When Ben had arrived in Tranquillity, he'd endured a few of the milder lessons himself. Perhaps he thought that was all that was involved. Little did he know that creating perfection in women was a time-intensive and laborious endeavor. But so very worthwhile.

Ben's wife, Lucy, had endured three months of intensive training herself before she'd been ready to meet her new husband. About three years ago, Alden had spotted the bright-haired Lucy at a mall in Seattle. And now Lucy didn't remember her former life, nor did she remember the training it had taken to help her forget that life.

Feeling quite kindly toward Ben, since without his knowing it, he had reinforced to Alden how very successful and brilliant his training really was, he said, "In a day or two, I'll allow you and Lucy to take one of the girls and show her around Tranquillity."

"Thank you, Brother Alden. This is an area I've been interested in for many years."

Alden dismissed him by turning away. He might be feeling kindly toward the man, but he was still the leader and, as such, had to be kept separate. Fraternizing with the members was not acceptable.

A pain-filled moan from the room behind him was a reminder that he still had another responsibility to handle. Finding his son a wife. Once that was done, the community would be at peace for another year. He could stay home with Tabitha and get back to doing what he did best: leading his people.

Honor could feel waves of tension bouncing off Seth. She sat quietly beside him in the taxi, wishing she could come up with something remotely encouraging. She had nothing. The news that the young woman who'd gone missing yesterday had been found dead had stunned everyone. Though remote, the possibility still existed that she'd been taken by the same person who'd abducted the other girls. And if that was so, had he killed them, too?

They were taking a much-needed break. Until Jared confirmed that Missy and Karen had visited some kind of social or support group at their school, Seth's theory was nothing but a vague hope that they were on to something.

Honor had made a quick call to Anna's mother, but had come up empty. Mrs. Bradford had no knowledge of Anna going to any kind of social meeting at her new school. And though that poked a hole in their theory, she refused to let it destroy what she felt was finally a thread. Anna hadn't fit the profile in other ways either, but everyone still felt that her disappearance was related.

While they waited for word from Jared, she and Seth needed to get away and Honor had the perfect solution. If he would go along with it, that is. Whether he would admit it or not, he needed some downtime. Learning about the girl's death had floored everyone, but it had devastated Seth.

Maturity and experience had given her insight into reading Seth, skills she hadn't had when they were together before. Though he didn't say it and maybe hadn't even admitted it to himself, Honor had seen the desolation and terror in his eyes. He was doing what family members and loved ones of missing victims do: imagining the worst. Going to places in his mind he didn't want to go but couldn't prevent himself from visiting. What hell was Kelli going through and would they find her in time? Seth might not admit to it, but he needed a respite from those thoughts.

She was about to make a suggestion she sincerely hoped she wouldn't regret. However, there were several reasons she thought it was a good idea. She just hoped to hell her libido wasn't secretly involved in the decision making. With Seth, it was hard to tell. Mentally shaking her head, Honor took the plunge. "I'd like to go see my mom. Would you come with me?"

He shot her an incredulous look. "Are you serious?"

"Just because we're not standing in front of a board or reviewing files doesn't mean we won't be thinking about this case. She's only an hour away and I need some downtime."

He shook his head. "That's not why I'm surprised. I agree that a couple of days away might clear our heads."

"Then what?"

"I'm just surprised you'd want me to meet your mother."

"Why's that?"

"Because of what I did to you."

Oh hell, she was in so much trouble, because once again, she had the overpowering desire to hug him. "I'm not saying my mom's going to open her arms wide in welcome the minute she sees you, but she's been through a lot of things. My dad worked on several missions he wasn't able to talk about."

"So does that mean you understand why I did what I did?"

She wasn't ready to have this discussion. The hurt and pain were still there, and she wasn't sure they would ever go away. However, she had to give him this. "I do understand why you felt you had to do what you did."

"But you can't forgive me. Right?"

"Let's not go there right now. Okay?"

He nodded stiffly and turned his face to the taxi's window.

Honor held back a sigh. Part of her wished she could tell him that she had forgiven him. Problem was, she didn't know if that was possible. Understanding why he'd done something wasn't the same as forgiving him or believing he had done the right thing. He had made a decision for her that had monumentally affected her life.

"So do you want to go with me?" And because she hated seeing that dark, grim look come over his face, she added teasingly, "My mom's apple pie is out of this world."

His mouth tilted in a half smile, but his eyes remained serious. "Sounds great. Thanks."

The taxi pulled up to the front entrance of the hotel. Seth got out and then held out his hand to her. That one small act stopped her cold as something flickered in her mind. The hand, almost twice as large as hers, darkly tanned, with a sprinkling of black hair and blue veins, looked so strong, so capable. Lethal when necessary, but it had only ever been infinitely tender with her, giving her incredible pleasure.

Blaming her odd thoughts on mental exhaustion, Honor took his hand. After a couple of days of sleep and a few of her mom's home-cooked meals, both she and Seth would get back on the trail. Dwelling on her past with Seth would get her nowhere other than on a path toward a broken heart. And that was one place she'd sworn she would never go again.

Tranquillity

Darkness and light became one interminable time span of nothingness. In the deepest recesses of her mind, Anna knew she was drugged. Reality was blurred, leading to confusion, nightmares that never seemed to end. Pain existed, but with the drugs, she could almost not acknowledge its existence. Where she hurt and why, she didn't know. The aches were there, but her blurred mind refused to summon the will to find its location.

The man she'd thought would be her savior had betrayed her. That much she remembered. One moment she had been enjoying her first hot meal in days, and the next, she'd been draped over a mountainous shoulder, being carried somewhere. Her instincts had told her to fight, but her weak limbs had ignored the order.

The dimness receded, and as her thoughts became more coherent, questions clamored in her head. How long had she been here? Were her eyes open or closed? What had they done to her while she was unconscious? Her body ached, but once again, she couldn't locate the pain, nor could she acknowledge it as distinctly painful. It was just there, hovering.

The man who'd brought her back . . . he'd said his name was Ben. She had tried to ask him questions. Once she'd realized that shouting and then begging wouldn't sway him, she had tried to get information. His answers had been infuriatingly vague. They were a community of believers, living in harmony with nature. When asked what that belief was, he couldn't say exactly.

The more questions she'd asked, the less accommodating he had been. Finally he'd threatened to knock her out to shut her up. Since staying awake and alert had been imperative, she'd kept her mouth closed. Not that it had done her a lot of good. The moment she'd been carried inside the giant gate, two men had grabbed her and a needle had been jabbed into a vein in her arm.

From the brief, uninformative conversation she'd had with Ben, she now understood that she was in some sort of commune. She and the other girls had been abducted. What these creeps planned to do with them was something she didn't dare contemplate. Best thing she could do was concentrate on escaping again. And this time, she would make it stick.

Distant voices reached her ears. With the darkness surrounding her, she couldn't tell if she was in a large room and the people speaking were in another part of the room or if she was closed up in a small room and the people were outside. Shuffling sounds came closer. Anna tensed. Was she about to get her questions answered?

The terror she'd been able to hold at bay leaped forward like a rabid animal, tearing viciously into her façade of bravery. Her tough inner talk disintegrated, and once again she was a terrified young girl wanting to be held in her mother's arms and told it had all been just a bad dream.

A dull light appeared above her and a soft, whispery female voice said, "You're awake."

Anna blinked, but was unable to see anything other than the dark outline of a body. "Who are you?"

"My name is Lucy."

"Where am I?"

"You're in Tranquillity."

Anna almost laughed, but humor, even the sarcastic kind, escaped her. Besides, pissing this woman off by laughing at her wouldn't accomplish anything.

"Why am I here?"

"To serve."

That didn't sound good. "Serve who?"

"We don't know yet."

"We?"

Though she couldn't see Lucy's face, Anna felt the hesitation in her body. Afraid the woman would just go away without giving her more information, Anna went on to another question—hopefully one less threatening. "Would it be possible for me to go to the bathroom?"

"Why?"

Surprised at such a stupid question, Anna couldn't help but say, "The obvious, of course. I need to pee."

"But you have a catheter attached."

Anna's entire body jerked at that information. Who had dared do something so intimate and invasive? If she were in a hospital, it would be different. But this wasn't a hospital, and she sure as hell wasn't a patient.

"Who did that . . . put a catheter in me?"

"I did . . . with Tabitha's guidance."

Now, that was a name she recognized. Tabitha, the bitch who'd been instrumental in her abduction.

Tired of the cat-and-mouse questioning, Anna went for broke. "Can I sit up? Get some water? Food? See something besides this damn lightbulb?"

"I'll check. We've been given special permission to assist in your training, but I don't know what's allowed yet."

"Training?"

"Yes."

"Training for what?"

"To be what you need to be."

"I'm quite happy being me; I don't need to be anyone else."

A gasp was the only answer Lucy gave. Obviously, that was a foreign concept to this woman.

Footsteps that sounded like they belonged to a heavy man came closer. "Is she awake?"

Anna recognized Ben's voice. The asshole who'd returned her to this psycho place. "Get away from me, you bastard."

Lucy gasped above her, and then Anna felt a small, painful pinch on the inside of her arm.

"Dammit, that hurt," she snapped.

"You cannot talk to my Ben like that."

Laughter sprang to her mouth before she could control it. Lucy had acted like such a sweet, shy creature, but here she was defending a man who was almost twice Anna's size.

"That's okay, Lucy," Ben said. "She'll be mad until she understands that we're only here to help her."

"You pretty much pissed on your chance to help me. Your kind of help I can do without."

"Lucy, turn on all the overhead lights so Anna can see we're not the evil people she apparently thinks we are."

Biting her lip, Anna said nothing. Being able to see was too important to risk him changing his mind if she pissed him off. If she was going to get out of here, she had to know as much as she could about this place. Being able to see seemed like the best place to start.

Lights flickered on above her. Anna blinked at the brightness, her eyes watering. She looked around, unsurprised that she was in a small room with no furniture. Instead of being chained, as she had been before, she was lying on a bed and her arms and legs were tied to it. She glanced down, relieved to see that she was at least covered by some kind of nightgown.

Ben stood beside the bed, an odd smile of encouragement on his face. She found his attitude so weird that she barely paid attention to the woman she sensed coming closer.

"Is that better?" Lucy asked.

Anna turned her attention to the woman now standing beside Ben and swallowed a gasp. Tall, slender, and stunningly beautiful, Lucy gazed adoringly at Ben as if he were her god.

Ben, who had to be almost twice her age, said, "My Lucy asked you a question. You must answer her."

"Yes, it's better." Figuring she needed to stay on their good side, at least for the time being, she added, "Thanks."

Ben nodded. "You're going to fit in just fine. Once you go through training, like Lucy did, you'll be much happier."

"Training?"

His smile bright but his eyes oddly vacant, Ben nodded eagerly. "Perfection training. My Lucy is perfect and someday soon, you'll be just like her."

What the hell?

eighteen

Sarasota, Florida

Seth stood in the driveway of the two-story, plantation-style home that belonged to Honor's mother. Why had he come here when he could have just as easily hopped a plane and been at his own home in less than an hour? He shot a glance at the woman at his side and mentally shrugged. No point in asking himself that question. Downtime with Honor trumped being by himself by a million miles, even if that included a firm dressing down from her mother.

"Don't be nervous." Honor winked. "I'm almost positive she won't shoot you."

"Shooting would be kinder than what I would imagine she'd rather do."

Grabbing his hand, she pulled him with her to the front door. "I think you're overestimating my mom's revenge quotient." She flashed a bright smile back at him and added, "My brother, on the other hand, would find several creative ways to punish you. Thankfully, Nick's not here."

Seth was grateful for that, too. Going head to head with a marine was not his idea of relaxation, especially when he wasn't so sure he didn't deserve a thrashing for breaking Honor's heart.

The front door was flung open and a petite, middle-aged, red-haired woman, her freckled face beaming, shouted, "Honey!" as she ran toward them.

Letting go of Seth's hand, Honor ran to her mother and threw herself into her arms.

Before Seth could step back and give them more privacy, Honor turned to him, grabbed his hand, and pulled him closer. "Mom, this is Seth Cavanaugh."

Holding himself straight and rigid, Seth withstood the piercing green stare of Honor's mother. He had never met Honor's parents, and even though he had known the relationship wasn't going to last, he had regretted that. Honor had obviously adored her folks and had talked about them often.

As the stare continued, Seth got the idea that this was a test. Problem was, he didn't know exactly how to pass it. Did she want a full confession and an apology for breaking her daughter's heart? About to give her just that, he opened his mouth. Before he could speak, she said, "Are you hungry?"

Seth couldn't help but smile. That question was exactly what his mother would have said. And he knew exactly how to respond: "Yes, ma'am, I am."

Her expression one of approval, she glanced at her daughter. "Come on in and get settled. The pot roast is ready. I'm just waiting on the corn bread. I put Seth in the bedroom at the top of the stairway. Yours is at the end of the hallway."

Flashing the beautiful smile he'd fallen in love with, Honor pulled him into the house. He stood in the foyer and watched Mrs. Stone head toward the back of the house, then disappear around a corner.

"Let's get our bags upstairs; then I'll show you around."

The anticlimactic meeting with Honor's mother leaving him feeling oddly unsettled, Seth grabbed both bags and followed her upstairs. He came to a halt when she grabbed his sleeve and stopped him in front of a door. Her voice low, she said, "Separate bedrooms. Okay?"

He had expected nothing different . . . it would have been the same in the Cavanaugh home. "Your mom's nice."

"I think so. She's been through a lot, especially the last few years, with my dad dying." Honor shrugged. "She's always been our rock, but when we lost him, I thought for a while that we were going to lose her, too."

"How long were they married?"

"Thirty-seven years."

"My parents were together for forty-two."

"I wished I'd been able to meet your father."

He wished that, too. But his dad had been gone for several months before Seth had met Honor. Of course, he had resisted like hell Honor meeting anyone in his family. Not that his mother had listened . . . at least, not at first. Ruth Cavanaugh had taken matters into her own hands. He still remembered the tightness in his chest when he'd explained that he and Honor were not a permanent thing and he had no real feelings for her. One of the many lies he'd had to tell that had carved a scar on his heart.

Hell, for a man who hated dwelling on his past mistakes, he'd been reminding himself of a lot of them lately.

"I'll go put my bag in my room," Honor said. "After dinner, we can take a walk on the beach, if you like."

Suddenly morose and pissed at himself for the feeling, Seth stepped into his assigned bedroom. He knew Honor stood at the door for several seconds before she walked away.

Seth gazed around and didn't wonder in the least why he'd been put in this particular room. It was full of Honor. Photographs covered the walls and trophies filled the shelves. Mrs. Stone was making a statement, one he understood and had lived with daily: *Look what you gave up*.

Honor dropped her bag in the room she'd stayed in when she'd come here to recuperate. Funny, her mom must have decided to redecorate and packed her stuff away. The room was almost bare except for a few new decorative pieces she'd never seen before. After this case was over, she'd ask her mom to send some of her most treasured framed photographs to Paris. The bare walls of her apartment there were beginning to wear a bit.

She took a few minutes to freshen up in the attached bathroom and then headed back to Seth's bedroom. His reaction to her mother had been amusing but poignant, too. How many times had she suggested a weekend trip so Seth could meet her parents? Each time, he had put her off with excuses. The reason he hadn't wanted to meet them was now clear: Seth had known their relationship wasn't going to last. She hadn't known the truth and had been disappointed in his reluctance not only to meet her family but for her to meet his.

Seth's mother had had other ideas, though. About a month after they'd started dating, Ruth Cavanaugh had called Honor at her apartment and invited her to Sunday dinner. Honor had eagerly accepted and had called Seth to tell him, figuring he would think it funny. Being so hopelessly in love with him, she hadn't clued in to his odd, unenthusiastic response at her news.

The dinner had been delightful, noisy, messy, and full of laughter. Even Seth seemed to have a great time. That had been the first and last time she'd seen anyone in his family. Looking back on it now, she knew he had probably talked with his mother and advised her that their relationship was only temporary.

Honor stopped a few feet from Seth's bedroom door

and purposely waited for several seconds. Being angry with him about his deception and past actions would get her nowhere. One of her dad's favorite sayings was that dwelling on the past was a sure way to ruin the future. Not that she had a future with Seth, but she did need to be able to work with him.

She knocked, and when his voice said "Come in," Honor opened the door. Seth was standing across the room, gazing at a wall full of framed photographs. A swift look around the room had her laughing softly. Her mom had been busy . . . now she knew where her things had gone. Beverly Stone had a flair for making a point.

By the chagrined expression on his face, Seth knew that, too. "Your mother makes quite a statement."

Honor crossed the room to stand beside him. "Sorry about that. She has a tendency to be quietly dramatic."

Seth pointed to a small grouping of photographs. "Who's that?" The pictures were of Honor as a child—riding her bike, swimming in the community pool, skateboarding, water-skiing on Watkins Lake. And in each shot, another young girl was with her. Dark hair, brown eyes, and a mischievous grin . . . such an incredible zest for life. It had taken Honor years to be able to look at these photographs without sobbing.

"Marnie Simmons, my best friend."

"She's the one you told me about? The reason you joined the Bureau?"

Honor nodded, now able to smile at the wonderful memories she and Marnie had made together. Her mother had packed the photos away, telling her she would want to see them again someday. A few years after Marnie's death, Honor had pulled them out and, after grieving again, bought frames for many of her favorites and put them up on her wall. She had even carried several of them to college with her. They had been her incentive.

"Odd, but we only knew each other for two years. My parents moved to Kentucky a few weeks before school started. I met Marnie the first day of school, and we were friends from that first hello."

"How old was she when she was murdered?"

"Thirteen. Her birthday had been the week before. Since our birthdays were so close together, we combined our birthday parties."

"She was killed on your birthday, wasn't she?"

"Yeah. Her mom dropped her off at my house so we could swim together at the community pool. Marnie went to get a soda from the vending machine and never came back."

Despite the years that had passed, Honor still remembered the emotions of that day. The fear when she realized Marnie was missing. The guilt of not having been there to protect her friend. And then the overwhelming grief when Marnie's battered body was found a few days later by hikers. She'd been raped and stabbed repeatedly.

Barely two hours after Marnie had gone missing, the FBI had arrived. Honor had watched intently as they'd gone about their investigation. Two days after Marnie's body had been found, a part-time worker at the city pool had been arrested. The bastard was still in prison today, and if Honor had anything to do with it, he would remain there until he died.

She had been immensely impressed by the FBI investigators. Their commitment to finding Marnie and then her killer had been obvious. The week after Marnie's funeral, Honor had announced to her family that instead of joining the military, she planned to become an FBI agent.

"Honor, Seth, dinner's on the table."

Her mom's voice bringing her back to the present, Honor grabbed Seth's arm and pulled him toward the door. "Let's go. My mom's a drill sergeant when it comes to meals."

When he didn't budge, she looked up at him in surprise. "What's wrong?"

"You're a remarkable woman, Honor Stone. Did you know that?"

Honor laughed. "Mom will be so happy to know that she was not only heard loud and clear, but that you wholeheartedly agree with her. She loves it when that happens."

Seth shook his head. "That wasn't your mom's statement. She put me in here to show me what a damn fool I was. And you know what? I wholeheartedly agree with that statement."

As Honor rinsed the dishes for the dishwasher, her mother put away the leftovers. The meal had been surprisingly upbeat. Seeing Seth devour her mother's food and his appreciative, complimentary words had done something to Honor's heart.

"That was a marvelous meal, Mom."

Wrapping up what was left of the roast, Beverly Stone lifted her head from her task and smiled. "You and Seth both looked like you needed the nourishment."

"It's been a difficult few days for him."

"And for you, too? Seeing him again must have been a shock."

Honor snorted. "That's an understatement."

"You told me a little on the phone . . . about why he did what he did. My question to you is, what are you going to do about it?"

In mid-rinse of a casserole dish, Honor stopped to shoot a questioning look at her mother. "Do about what?"

"Now that you know he had a good reason for breaking your heart, what are you going to do about it?"

"He had a good reason for taking on the job. Breaking my heart was another matter. Not telling me the truth was wrong."

"Sweetie, when men are thinking with their hearts, not their heads, common sense gets put to the side. He was trying to protect you."

"I was an FBI agent. I didn't need protecting."

"Honor, you weren't an FBI agent to him. You were the woman he loved. There's a big difference."

Honor turned back to the sink, that statement cutting deep into what she'd considered her carefully thought out and justified anger. When Seth had told her he'd lied to her to protect her, she'd been insulted. She hadn't needed protecting. Now, with her mother's words blurring that anger, she allowed herself to consider his actions in a new light.

She had never been in love before Seth . . . had never even come close. For most of her life, she'd been focused on achieving one goal or another. Romantic entanglements had been something she'd steered clear of—her eyes always on her objectives.

Her parents had raised her to believe she could accomplish anything. She had never doubted their love, but they had never coddled her or treated her with less than the highest of expectations. They'd raised her brother the same way. Sure, they would have come to her defense if she'd needed them. So would Nick. But she'd never thought of herself as a person who needed to be protected.

Finishing up the last of the dishes, Honor dried her hands and grabbed her mom for a quick hug. "You're a brilliant woman. You know that?"

"But of course I am. How else could I have a daughter like you?"

Honor grinned and walked toward the doorway. Her mother's voice stopped her. "You know, I put you in separate bedrooms because I didn't know how you felt about each other."

Not sure where she was going with this, Honor said, "Okay . . ."

Giving the mysterious smile of absolute knowledge her family had often teased her about, she shrugged. "Just saying . . ."

With a snort, Honor walked out of the kitchen. If they stayed here any longer, she'd no doubt be giving pointers to Seth, too. Her mother had a tendency to dole out wisdom and advice. And this time, just like in most other cases, her mom made way too much sense.

nineteen

Salty air, heavy with the threat of an early evening thunderstorm, blew across Seth's face. Honor strolled on the beach beside him, her expression faraway and solemn. Years ago, she would have told him what was on her mind. Dealing with secrets had been part of her job, but when it came to sharing herself with Seth, she'd been totally open. He, on the other hand, had shared as little as he could get away with.

The dinner with Honor's mother had been enjoyable. The pot roast, mashed potatoes and gravy, green beans, and corn bread had been out-of-this-world incredible. What had surprised Seth was how much Honor had eaten. When she'd seen him gawking at her second helping of mashed potatoes and gravy, she'd laughed. "I'll be overloaded with carb guilt tomorrow, but somehow I can't make myself care about that right now."

Beverly Stone apparently thought she'd made her point with the bedroom because she had treated Seth like an honored guest during dinner. Her questions and comments had been related only to current news events. Not once had she asked about the case he and Honor were working on together or said anything about breaking her daughter's heart.

Watching Honor and her mother together had given Seth a rare insight into Honor's life. The love and respect were obvious, as was the ease they had with each other. In a way, it reminded him of the big, boisterous Cavanaugh gatherings of the past. Though the noise quotient was often at decibels above what the human ear could handle, the enjoyment they had in one another's company more than made up for the pain. Seth could document to the day when that atmosphere had changed forever.

Pulling to a stop, Honor faced him and asked quietly, "Want to talk about it?"

In the past, he would have come up with something glib or tried to take her mind in a different direction by kissing her. Not that he didn't want to kiss her right now, but not having to hide behind a façade anymore felt damned good.

"I was thinking about my family . . . comparing mine to yours."

"In what way?"

"About how easy you and your mom are with each other. We used to be like that."

"What changed it?"

He shrugged and looked out at the ebbing tide of the ocean, his mind on a past he couldn't change. "The setup for my undercover job . . . the accusation of taking bribes. There was no way to prepare my family for that. No way to assure them that I really wasn't the dirty cop the press was portraying me as. My dad probably took it the worst. He'd been so proud of me, becoming the first policeman in the family."

"Did your family believe you when you told them you didn't take the bribes?"

"Yes. I knew they would, but the rumors hurt." He shrugged. "We'd always been so damn lucky. No major catastrophes or illnesses. Hell, even my great-grandmother was still alive then. We sailed through life without the typical angst of divorces, teenage pregnancies, drugs, infidelities. All of those things that tear families apart didn't exist for us."

Her expression gently understanding, she said, "You think you started it all, don't you?"

"Hard not to think that. A month or so after the accusations, I quit the force, as planned. Broke my family's heart, because to them it looked like an admission of guilt.

"When I opened the restaurant, things settled down and the family was excited about my new venture. But still, the atmosphere at family gatherings was different." He shrugged again. "Like we'd lost something . . . maybe an innocence. Not long after that, my great-grandmother died. She was elderly and it wasn't unexpected, but it's like I started the ball rolling and it hasn't stopped since."

"Other than Kelli's disappearance, what else has happened?"

"Let's see. Two divorces, one affair, a DUI, and one shoplifting charge. And that's just the stuff I know about."

"You can't seriously believe you're responsible for these things."

"I know I'm not responsible for other people's bad decisions. I just hate being the first one to tarnish the Cavanaugh name."

"For a damn good reason, too."

Seth couldn't help but grab her and hug her tight. Of all the people who had a reason to defend him, Honor should be the least likely. But again, Honor Stone was not an average, ordinary human being. He'd known that the moment he'd met her. There was something pure and bright about Honor. An untouchable goodness.

Burying his face in her hair, Seth breathed in a subtle

fragrance he'd always associated with Honor. He'd never been able to identify it and she'd sworn she never used anything special. Nevertheless, it was a scent he'd never been able to forget.

She tightened her arms around his waist and flattened her body against him. Arousal surged hot and urgent. She groaned and rubbed against him like a cat seeking warmth. Cupping her butt with his hands, he pressed into her softness, loving the sound of her increased breathing in his ear.

"We're not exactly alone," she whispered.

Yeah, he'd known that, but hadn't really cared. Getting Honor in his arms made everything else secondary, including having an audience.

"Don't suppose we could go back to your mom's house and send her to the movies, could we?"

She pulled away from him, laughing. "My mom has heard every excuse from my brother and me. She's never fallen for one yet."

"Can we go someplace? To be alone?"

"Where are we going with this, Seth?"

Dropping his arms, he stepped back. Hell, that was a question he hadn't wanted but one she had every right to ask. Where was this going after they found Kelli? The sex between them was as hot as ever, but so much had changed. He wasn't the person he used to be. A washed-out ex-cop with a run-down beach house, a fishing boat, and absolutely no future.

"You're right." Ignoring her searching eyes, he gazed over her shoulder at the seemingly endless ocean. "I'll see you back at the house. I'm going to take a walk."

He turned away and didn't look back.

Honor wrapped her arms around herself as she watched Seth's long strides take him farther down the beach. She could stop him, tell him she didn't want promises. Tell him whatever he needed to hear just so he'd hold her close, kiss her, and make love to her. She could tell herself that she could have sex just for the pleasure, but lying to herself had never been her thing. As she'd told him yesterday, sex with Seth could never be meaningless.

And there was another issue she hadn't yet faced. One he'd asked about earlier and she had purposely avoided answering. She hadn't forgiven him for what he had done to them. Yes, she could understand his reasons, but that was a long way from forgiving. He had deliberately misled her. Not only that, he'd gotten involved with her knowing full well it wouldn't last. For a woman who'd been making life decisions for herself well before the norm, having Seth arbitrarily decide her future not only infuriated her, it insulted her.

Her mother's words returned to taunt her self-righteous anger: *You weren't an FBI agent to him. You were the woman he loved.*

The buzzing cellphone in her pocket was a welcome distraction. Torturing herself over the past was her least favorite pastime.

She checked the screen: Aidan. When she and Seth had left Tampa, he'd been headed to Pennsylvania to get information about the college student who had been found dead. There was no real reason to suspect that the abductions were related, but everyone wanted to be sure.

Holding the phone to her ear, she began walking back toward her mother's house. "Are you in Bellefonte?"

"Just landed. Had to fly commercial, so it took longer."

"What's up?"

"Just something that came to mind I wanted to ask Seth. He's not picking up his cellphone. I thought you might be able to reach him."

Honor jerked around, looking where Seth had headed. Reception on the beach was often spotty. "What do you need? I can ask him for you or get him to call you."

"You and Seth are taking some downtime together?"

The gentle amusement in his voice would have stirred her ire if it was anyone else. Not with Aidan. From the moment they'd met, they'd teased and joked with each other like a brother and sister would. Considering that Aidan looked liked a sun god dropped from the sky and could be as charming as he could be deadly, not being attracted to him seemed ludicrous. But there it was.

"We're staying with my mom."

"Hmm."

"What's that supposed to mean?"

"Now, don't get your bloomers in a bunch. I figured there'd been something between you two. Neither one of you is very good at hiding those heated, furtive looks."

She snorted. "Did you really have a question to ask Seth or did you just call to needle me?"

She could almost see his grin as he said, "A little bit of both."

"Then what's your question."

"I wanted to ask him if he'd looked beyond last year for any similar disappearances."

"I don't know. I'll ask him, but I would think the Bureau would have done that."

"Probably did, but since they don't even think the most recent disappearances are related, why would they think others were?"

He had a point there. "Okay. Let me see if I can find Seth. I'll call you back."

"Did you lose him?"

Honor closed the phone without answering, but her

answer would have been yes. She'd lost him a long time ago.

Seth looked down at the folders they'd spread out on the dining room table. He'd met Honor on the way back; she'd been looking for him. He hadn't even realized his cellphone wasn't working. That had been a reminder he shouldn't have needed. Going over mistakes he had or hadn't made wouldn't do a damn bit of good. Finding Kelli and the other girls had to remain front and center. Yeah, the downtime had been a nice change of pace from the breakneck speed of the last few days, but now he needed to get his head back to where it should be.

"Noah's checking missing persons records going back ten years." Honor stood on the other side of the table from him.

Seth shook his head. "I can't believe I didn't search further than last year."

"You were focused on finding Kelli, not looking for a multitude of abductions."

"Aidan say how he came up with the idea that there could be more?"

Forgetting that it was after one in the morning, Honor pressed a button on her cellphone. "Let's find out."

Aidan answered on the first ring. "What's up?"

"Hey, I've got Seth here. We were wondering why you thought there could be more related cases."

"No real reason other than if no one even thinks these cases are related, how many more of them could there be? What if the guy didn't just start this last year?"

"Noah's checking back over the last ten years," Honor said.

"That should give us something . . . if there are any. I just got to my hotel room. I have an appointment with the detective in charge of the case tomorrow morning. I'll call you after that with an update."

"Okay, thanks." Honor closed the phone and looked at Seth. "So, seems like it's more just a supposition than anything else."

"The man's got good instincts." And because he couldn't leave well enough alone, he said, "Something going on between you two?"

"Yes, I'm sleeping with you and him, too." Bright jewels of golden-green fire seared him. "Why would you even ask that?"

Well, hell. He used to be better at keeping his stupid thoughts to himself.

"You have an affectionate rapport with him." He shrugged. "Sorry. None of my business."

Hurt dimmed the brightness of her eyes. Again, he'd said the wrong thing. Hell, he needed to get some rest before she kicked his ass out on the street. "I'm running on no sleep," he added.

Looking like she wanted to say something but wouldn't, she glanced at her watch. "It's almost two. Let's get some sleep and then hit it hard again tomorrow. If Noah does get some leads, we'll head back to Tampa."

Gathering the folders, he stacked them together and turned away, then turned back and picked them up again. One more review couldn't hurt. Yeah, he knew them almost by heart, but in the mass of notes, police reports, and theories, there damn well had to be something they were missing.

Honor watched Seth as he preceded her up the stairs. The folders in his hand told her that sleep wasn't exactly on his mind tonight, either. The man needed rest. His question about her and Aidan had infuriated and hurt her until she'd noticed his glazed, bloodshot eyes. He was running on adrenaline and nothing more. She knew how that was. You said and did stupid things.

So, after she'd followed him up the stairs, she stopped in front of his room and, blaming it on her own exhaustion, said softly, "Sleep with me tonight."

Whirling around, he stared at her. "What?"

"If you go in there, you'll stay up all night, reading those files. You need to get some rest."

Sensuality and arousal erasing the exhaustion from his face, he advanced toward her. "So sleeping with me is really for my health?"

Okay, so that hadn't been the best come-on line in the world. Hell, what was the use in pretending? Why not just lay it all out and if he couldn't accept it, that would be the end of it. "Fine. I want you, but I don't know that I'll ever forgive you."

Stopping inches from her, his mouth hovering so close that she felt his breath on her face, he asked quietly, "And if I told you I want you more than my next breath but sex is all I have left to give you . . . what would you say?"

The warning bells in her head went on shutdown. "That for now . . . tonight, I don't need any more than that."

Seth settled his mouth against hers. Groaning, Honor wrapped her arms around him and let the world fall away. Regrets would come later—acknowledgment of her weakness, maybe even a promise never to let this happen again. But for right now, in Seth's arms, she didn't care about any of that.

His mouth lifted slightly. "Your bedroom or mine?"

"Mine," she whispered. "Yours is directly over my mom's."

Surprising her, Seth lifted her into his arms and in five long strides was at her bedroom, carrying her over the threshold.

He dropped her feet to the floor and then closed the door behind them. The click of the lock was a signal to both of them. Here, inside this room, it was only them, only the present. Neither the past nor questions of the future existed. Only need consumed by desire would give them peace. Peace she'd only ever been able to find in this man's arms.

Their hands and fingers worked with frantic speed, their clothes magically disappearing in a matter of seconds. Seth's eyes roamed over her entire body, heating Honor everywhere his gaze touched.

Unable to wait, Honor wound her arms around his neck and pressed against him, groaning at his heat, loving the feel of his hard, naked body.

Holding her loosely, gently, Seth let his mouth travel from her cheek down her neck, to the hollow of her shoulder. "You know what I used to fantasize about?" His voice was the rough, sexy growl of a fully aroused male.

"What?" Honor asked softly.

"Remember the first time we danced?"

"Yes." She smiled at the memory. "Seconds after we met."

"I used to replay that moment in my mind, with some subtle differences."

She pulled back to see his face. "And what were those differences?"

Glittering midnight-blue eyes roamed over her face. "We were completely alone. And totally nude."

"Mmm. Maybe we could make that fantasy a reality. Want to?"

Instead of answering her with words, he pushed her backward until her bare bottom met the bookshelf. She smiled, knowing he was reaching for the Bose radio on the second shelf.

His mouth tilted in a teasing grin, he said, "Got it set already?"

"Of course." Seth knew she had a weakness for sappy old love ballads. When they were together, he used to tease her that she and his grandmother liked the same music.

She heard a click and then, as if she'd made a special request, Nat King Cole's velvet voice began to sing "Unforgettable." No song could have captured her thoughts better. Seth was unforgettable. No matter what happened in the future, she would never forget him.

Moving her away from the bookshelf, he led her to the middle of the room and began a slow, swaying dance. Melding herself to him, Honor lost herself in Seth's fantasy. Her eyes fluttered closed as big, callused hands glided down her back to cup her bottom. Hard, hot, and throbbing, his erection pressed up against her stomach.

She rubbed her face against his chest and murmured, "I'd forgotten what a good dancer you are."

"It helps to have the perfect partner."

Her heart clenching at his words, she tightened her arms around his neck, loving the feel of the muscular, sexy male body moving against her. Endless moments passed as they glided around the small bedroom, allowing the music to take them away, to another place, another time.

As the last notes faded, Seth stopped. "Ready to move on to another fantasy?"

Aroused to the point of no return already, she asked, "And what would that one be?"

"The one where I kiss and lick you all over until you're screaming for me to come inside you."

Her breath hitched in response to those sexy words said in his slow, rough-edged voice. Whispering soft kisses over his chest, she murmured, "Sounds wonderful. And then let's do my fantasy next."

"Which one is that?"

"Where I let you lick and kiss me all over and then scream for you to come inside me."

"Damn, that sounds even better than mine." Lowering his head, he covered her mouth with his. Honor opened, inviting him inside. Tangling her hands in his hair, she gave herself up to the heat and incredible desire.

What tomorrow held, she didn't know. All she could concentrate on now was that she'd ached for Seth for five years and if tonight was all she'd ever have of him, she was going to make memories that lasted as long as she lived.

Seth breathed in Honor's scent, a blend of honey, spice, and sensual female arousal, a fragrance that grew sweeter with each passing moment. Holding her silken, slender body in his arms and gliding around the room was a fantasy come true. How many nights had he woken, so hard and aching that he could barely breathe from the want? This had been one of his most frequent dreams. He just hadn't known that the reality would be so much better.

His hands moved down the satin-soft skin of her back and then lower, to cup her beautiful ass. Lifting his mouth from hers, he watched the play of desire on her face as one of his hands moved around to her silky stomach, then traveled down to brush lightly at the soft curls between her legs. Her eyes, usually a mix of gold and green, were now a dark, solid green, shimmering with heat. His fingers gently caressing her, Seth carefully watched her expression as arousal took control. He loved the flush of her cheeks, the way her beautiful mouth opened slightly with her increased breaths. When he pressed his fingers into the moist folds, her breath hitched, and then she gave a low, sexy feminine moan of approval.

Throbbing with need and close to explosion, Seth refused to give in so soon. Dropping his hands, he stepped back.

"What are you doing?"

He went to his knees before her, pressed a soft kiss to her belly, and swirled his tongue around her navel. "Enjoying myself," he murmured. "Got a problem with that?"

Laughing softly, she threaded her fingers through his hair. "Absolutely not."

While another old love ballad soared around them, Seth lowered his head. Spreading the soft folds of Honor's sex with his thumbs, he used his tongue to spear deep and then dance inside her. The gasps and soft pleas from the woman above him blended beautifully with the music as he played and flirted, teasing her arousal to the next level.

Needing more, Seth lifted her leg and propped her knee on his shoulder. Growling "Hold on," he delved deeper. Thrusting and retreating, he licked at her, loving her taste, the quivering, throbbing response in the slick knot of nerves at the top of her sex. His tongue gliding and dancing, he led her to the brink and kept her suspended and on edge, her gasps and groans sweeter than any music he'd ever heard. Then, unable to wait any longer, he suckled hard, pushing her over. Soft, hitching sounds came from her throat as she tugged on his hair, then reaching her peak, she let out a soft, keening cry.

Seth couldn't wait any longer. Surging to his feet, he scooped her into his arms and carried her the few steps to the bed. Dropping her gently onto the mattress, he followed her down, and with one powerful stroke buried himself deep.

Surrendering his mind to the soft, warm, giving body beneath him, Seth knew there was nothing left for him to lose. He'd lost his heart long ago to this brave, beautiful woman.

Little did Honor know that she'd always had him. And no matter what happened in the future, she always would.

twenty

Tranquillity

"And this is where the community comes together for our weekly meetings."

"What kind of meetings?" Anna asked.

"We meet once a week, sometimes twice, if it's deemed necessary, to hear Brother Alden speak on a variety of subjects."

Lucy's deliberately vague answers were wearing thin, but since she was the only one Anna was allowed to speak to, she had little choice. For someone who didn't seem to have a thought in her head other than what her husband or the mysterious leader known as Brother Alden had put there, Lucy was surprisingly deft at steering away from topics she didn't want to discuss.

This morning Anna had been untied, allowed a delicious if too brief shower, and given some clothing. Wearing an ankle-length, white corduroy dress and soft leather flats similar to Lucy's, she had stepped outside, where she'd been introduced to the "community" she was to become a member of . . . "when the time was right."

Since she was just as determined that the time would never be right to be part of this oh-so-freaky community, she wanted to learn as much as she could. The more she knew, the better her chances of a successful escape.

The moment she'd walked out into the bright sunlight, she had been stunned by her surroundings. This was a thriving, busy community. At least a dozen large buildings lined a wide paved street. Another street held about twenty or so smaller structures that were apparently houses for the older members of the community. Still other members lived in a communal house about the size of a small hospital.

"Here's our garden," Lucy said. "In the spring, once the coldest nights have passed, we work in shifts to get everything planted."

At least three acres of land, if not more, spread out before them. "Who works the garden?"

As if reciting a mantra, she said, "Every able-bodied person old enough to hold a tool in his or her hand is to assist."

"How many people live here?"

Lucy shrugged and turned away. "As many as there needs to be."

Resisting the urge to roll her eyes, Anna followed her once more and then paused when Lucy stopped in front of one of the smaller houses. "This is where I'm allowed to live with my Ben."

"Allowed?"

Lucy turned toward her, hurt gleaming in her eyes. Okay, so she shouldn't have put so much sarcasm into that word. But, dammit, did the woman have an independent thought in her head? Why would she want to be with a man who was not only twice her age but treated her like a puppet?

Hoping to repair the damage, Anna quickly said, "It's nice. Do you have children?"

"Not yet. Ben says we will soon."

Biting back another sarcastic comment, Anna asked, "How long have you been married to Ben?"

"A little over two years."

Lucy couldn't be older than nineteen. "How did you two meet?"

"A mutual friend introduced us."

Mutual friend, my ass. Lucy had most likely been taken just like she had. Were all the women in the community kidnap victims? If so, how was it possible that these people had been getting away with abducting women all these years? And just what the hell did this perfection training involve? Had Lucy been a normal teenaged girl before these freaks got hold of her?

"Where did you live before you came here?"

"My life didn't begin until I moved to Tranquillity."

Anna didn't know if she should weep for this beautiful, obviously brainwashed girl or snap at her to stop being so damned stupid. "How long has this community been here?"

"I don't know. Since as long ago as Brother Alden created it, I guess."

Another non-answer. Anna gazed around as they continued to walk. Since they'd begun their tour this morning, she'd seen a dozen or more people performing various tasks. Repairs on one building, painting another building. Three women watched over a handful of children in a small play area. Everyone seemed so focused, like worker bees, intent only on their own tasks. The few times she'd tried to meet someone's gaze, the men had looked straight through her as if she didn't exist and the women's eyes had skittered away.

"This is where I spend much of my time."

They stopped in front of a medium-sized structure. "What is it?"

"Our school."

"Are you a teacher?"

"Not yet. I don't have the knowledge and experience to teach, but I help as much as I can. Perhaps Brother Alden will allow you to assist, too."

The cliché "over my dead body" fit so well here, but Anna had a feeling that this wasn't a foreign concept to these people. If they were bold enough to kidnap and brainwash people, murder wouldn't be that much of a stretch. Her best bet was to keep as low a profile as possible until she could figure out a way out of here.

"How many children live here?"

"I don't know. Fifteen or so, maybe."

So not only had women been abducted, they'd been forced to bear children. Anna hadn't thought she could get more furious or terrified.

They continued on a path that led to some steep steps. Lucy stopped at the bottom of the steps and pointed upward. "Just on the other side of the hill is where Brother Alden lives."

Anna tensed. Was she ready to meet this mysterious leader everyone seemed to worship? Was he the man she'd seen when she'd first been taken? That evil, slimy grin would live in her memory for years. What would she do if she saw him? Since she had returned, she'd been drugged frequently. Her limbs were weak and her feet were just now recovering from her barefoot escape. Could she find the strength to destroy this monster if she had to confront him?

"Are we going up there?"

Lucy looked both horrified and astounded by the question. "Oh no, we're not allowed to venture anywhere close. Ben goes occasionally, but the women of the community must stay away unless sent for."

That was just fine with her. Being summoned to the palace of the king—or whatever the hell "Brother Alden" thought he was—wasn't something she wanted. Getting the hell out of here was her one and only focus. If she could escape without ever having met him, she could definitely live with that.

They turned away from the steps and Anna swallowed

a startled yelp. Ben stood behind them, along with another man.

Giving her that oddly gentle smile that made her want to punch him out, Ben asked, "What do you think?"

"Think about what?"

"Tranquillity. You'll enjoy living here. I'm sure of it."

Was there a right response to that arrogant comment? If she said yes, would he even believe her? After babbling when she'd first met him about the crazies who had abducted her, she knew better than that. However, telling him there was no way in hell she ever planned to live here would most likely get her punishment of some sort.

Using Lucy's tactics of a non-answer, she said, "It's certainly thriving."

She watched warily as Ben gave the man beside him a look. The man, a little smaller than Ben, fortyish, with fiery red hair and an equally fiery handlebar mustache, grinned at Anna. "I think you're right, Ben. I believe she will do me just fine."

"This is Brother Harbin Meeks. He's going to bid for you."

Comprehension came instantly. *Like hell!* Anna whirled around, took a leaping step, and rammed into a broad chest. Looking up, she stared with wild-eyed terror at a giant. The man who'd abducted her.

Brown eyes glittered down at her with the most terrifying expression she'd ever seen. "Going somewhere?"

With her heart pounding so hard she could barely hear over the noise, she heard Ben say from a distance, "Brother Alden, what an honor to have you join us."

His gaze never leaving her face, he said, "Has she been behaving?"

"She'll never leave us again," Ben said. "We'll make sure of that."

A wide grin spread across his face, but his cold eyes narrowed in speculation. "That's good to hear. But I'd like to hear those words from her."

Anna remained stubbornly silent. Maybe that was a stupid thing to do, but pretending that she wanted to stay in this psycho community went well beyond her limited acting skills.

The man nodded, looking oddly satisfied at her defiance. "Now I know why Tabitha was so insistent on this one. My daughter enjoys training the stubborn girls the most."

"Brother Harbin is going to bid for her."

"Excellent. I believe she'll have several men vying for her." Finally lifting his gaze from Anna's, he looked at the men standing behind her. "Brother Meeks, prepare your petition, along with your preferred names."

A big hand came toward Anna's face, and she couldn't help but flinch and jerk away. The hand grabbed her hair and held her in place. "Someday soon, you'll be kneeling at my feet."

Too scared to even pretend bravery, Anna could feel her eyes glazing over in tears. When one rolled down her cheek, the man reached out his other hand and lifted the teardrop with his finger. He looked down at the glistening drop and then brought it to his mouth. "Delicious." Lowering his head, he whispered softly, "I'll make sure it's your first of many."

LCR branch office
Tampa

Honor stared at her neat scribbles on the dry-erase board, a careful optimism making her heart thud harder. She and Seth had gotten in an hour ago and come to the office immediately. Aidan, Jared, and Noah had arrived a few moments later and now sat, along with Seth, at the conference table.

Everyone had significant information to share, and though they'd briefed each other on the phone, Honor wanted to get it all written down in front of them so they could begin a discussion.

"Okay, with everything we have now, let's start over again. Aidan, you go first."

"Mallory Roland was the young woman abducted and found dead in Pennsylvania. She was twenty years old and was last seen in an Internet café a couple of miles from the Penn State campus."

"And the similarity to the other girls?" Seth asked.

"Age and she was a transfer. She started at Penn State this year to be with her boyfriend, who's a junior there."

"Anything else?" Honor asked.

Aidan nodded. "I talked to a couple of people who saw her at the café. She had a long conversation with a young blond woman. They walked out together. That was the last time anyone saw her."

Seth grabbed one of the files for the missing girls and opened it. "Kelli was seen talking to a young woman prior to her disappearance. She didn't leave with her, but the woman left and then Kelli left about ten minutes later. That was the last time Kelli was seen. No one knew who the woman was . . . just that she was a young, attractive brunette."

"So you're saying a woman could be responsible for these abductions?" Jared asked.

"Not solely responsible, but she could be the lure." Seth surged to his feet and began to pace. "So let's go back to our theory. These young, vulnerable girls are lonely and looking for friendship. A beautiful young woman befriends them. They have no reason to think she's anything other than another college student.

They're eager to make friends, they're not looking for a predator. She lures them somewhere, and that's when they're taken."

He went back to the table and flipped through the other files. "All the other girls were seen talking to a young woman before they disappeared. It didn't register with us because the women had different descriptions."

"It's easy enough to disguise yourself with a wig and a different demeanor," Honor said.

"Okay, but how does this help us?" Jared said. "We don't know what she looks like really, except that she's young and pretty. There're a hell of a lot of young, pretty women on college campuses."

Honor nodded, not minding a bit having a naysayer in the bunch. Poking holes in their theories would keep them focused. "You're right. But it's not something we'd considered before. And it makes me wonder about the motivation for the abductions. Before I was thinking human trafficking. Now I'm not so sure."

"But why did he rape and kill Mallory?" Aidan asked.

"I don't know. Maybe something went wrong. Could be she fought back . . . harder than the others. Maybe the guy lost his temper. Lots of things could have happened. I'm just not willing to say this isn't our guy, just because he wasn't successful with this abduction." She glanced at Aidan again. "Any evidence left on her body?"

"No, the coroner said the water washed everything away."

Tapping her pen against the table, Honor said, "Okay, so we know that the five girls, plus Mallory, were seen talking with a young woman no one knew, prior to their disappearance. Which to me is the most telling piece of all."

"What?" Noah asked.

"If she's that attractive, why didn't anyone know her?

Of all the people we've talked to, why was it that not one of them had any idea who she was?"

The room went silent as everyone absorbed and considered her statement. Finally, Seth said, "Okay, so we've got that. What else?"

Noah and Jared looked at each other. Noah gave a nod, indicating that the other man should proceed.

Pulling a thick stack of papers from a small box on the floor, Jared slid a smaller stack of stapled pages across the table to each of them. Honor took hers and ran her eyes swiftly down the first page. She turned the page and again read quickly. Each turn of the page was successively faster as an ache developed in her stomach. Reaching the last page, she raised her head and saw her feelings reflected on everyone's faces.

"How far did you go back?" she asked.

"Ten years," Jared answered grimly.

"Okay . . . now wait, help me out here," Aidan said. "I see some similarities, age and such, but the MOs are all over the place." He picked up his stack and flipped to a page. "This girl was only seventeen, a popular high school cheerleader, and the last time she was seen was at a mall in Seattle."

"Take a look at the other two girls who went missing that same year," Jared said. "Look at their last known location."

Aidan turned another page. "Shit. A mall," he murmured.

Noah stood and went to a two-sided whiteboard. "Jared and I worked on this last night." He flipped the board over to reveal a map of the United States. "We've tagged the states where the girls have gone missing, using a colored pin to show the year and the last known location." He shook his head. "I'm the biggest doubting Thomas there is, but it's hard for me to say there's not something there."

As Honor drew closer, she could feel everyone else come up behind her. All eyes were glued to the map and the horrifyingly numerous and different-colored pins dotting it.

Seth's deep voice broke the stunned silence. "So what we're looking at is at least ten years' worth of abductions. Each year, he changed the MO and the number of victims he took."

"Exactly," Jared said from behind them. "And, as you can see, they're all over the map, which is probably the reason no one's ever connected them before. The year a girl went missing in Nevada, he took another one in Tennessee and the next in New York. None of them close enough in location or time frame that the authorities would suspect that the disappearances could be related."

"A video arcade, fast-food restaurants, coffee shops, malls, movie theaters," Noah said. "Anywhere young adults hang out a lot."

"Okay, I'm willing to concede that the disappearances have some similarities," Aidan said. "But how are they related to this case? The girls we're looking for have gone missing from a lot of different places."

Honor nodded. "True; the similarity is each girl is a college student and a young woman is the lure."

Seeing that a smattering of doubts still lingered, she said, "Okay, let's see where this takes us." She repeated all they'd learned: "He never hits the same state twice. One year, he hit four states; another year, two states. In a ten-year time frame, that's forty-three states. Let's rule out Hawaii and Alaska simply for remoteness and difficulty of travel. This year he's hit Iowa, Oregon, and Indiana. And most likely Pennsylvania. If he continues this pattern, there's only one state he hasn't hit."

She pointed to the state without a pin. "Wyoming."

She turned back to the table and sat down. "That's where we need to concentrate our efforts."

"That's a damn big state," Jared said.

"True. But it's a much smaller area than we had before. And we know to look at college campuses."

"So we're going to go to colleges in Wyoming and search for good-looking women who talk to other women?" Aidan asked.

"When you put it like that, it does sound hopeless and far-fetched. But that's exactly what we'll be doing. Except we're going to have LCR females do that. This creep isn't looking for guys." She glanced over at Noah. They'd discussed this on the phone this morning after he'd given her the bare basics of what he and Jared had learned. "Noah is bringing in eleven female operatives to help."

Sitting across from Seth, she saw his jaw clench, and the rigid set of his shoulders became even tenser. They hadn't talked about this yet; he was learning about the plan along with Aidan and Jared. By the look on his face, he disapproved.

Apparently picking up on Seth's feelings, Noah asked, "You got a problem with the plan, Cavanaugh?"

Instead of answering immediately, Seth gave Honor a hard, searching look. He wasn't an easy person to read, but she knew something had disturbed him. However, his answer to Noah was "No, this might be our only chance of catching the guy this year."

Noah stood and addressed them all. "Exactly. That's the biggest concern. Look at the dates of each abduction. He's never taken anyone after mid-November or before mid-March. We're two weeks away from the window closing until next year. If the Pennsylvania case is related, and I think we all agree that there's a strong possibility, he failed at his last attempt. And—"

Seth finished his statement: "And if we don't get him in the next two weeks, our chances of finding Kelli and the other girls this year are almost nonexistent."

Silence permeated the room as everyone absorbed that grim statement.

Doubt suddenly washed over Honor. Either way, their choices sucked. If they were wrong and none of the previous disappearances had anything to do with this case, then they were wasting valuable time. Time they couldn't afford. And if they were right, their odds were even suckier. A two-week time frame to cover an entire state filled with several large and small campuses looking for one pretty woman who was being used as a lure to attract lonely young girls.

The optimism she'd felt at the beginning of the meeting dwindled considerably. No way in hell was this going to work.

twenty-one

Tranquillity

Alden sat in his favorite chair, oversized for his large frame and with enough room for an additional, more slender body for those times when he wanted company. He'd had it placed at the floor-to-ceiling window that looked out over his community. Here he often sat for hours and, with the help of powerful binoculars, watched his people work. Like tireless minions, they toiled and slaved, all to make their lives better and more fulfilling.

Soon winter would arrive and they would truly become a community once again. During the warmer months, there was a separation, a disconnect. The men would hunt wild game, the women would tend the garden and fill their time with canning and freezing. The warm weather gave them the opportunity to prepare for the winter. But it also meant there were absences, and when that happened, the community suffered. All of its members were needed.

His own absence was the worst, he knew. For the last ten years, he'd had no choice. Young women were necessary to increase their numbers and keep the men's baser needs satisfied. In turn, the women were given the opportunity for their own fulfilling destiny. What greater gift could a woman have than serving her man?

He was glad that his travels for the year were almost over. If not for his wayward son, his work would have been completed last week. And since they were running behind schedule, he was going to do something he had promised himself he'd never do: he was going to hunt close to home. Not that the authorities would have any idea of where to look, but just the idea of bringing any attention to the state where Tranquillity resided bothered him immensely. He'd learned long ago that you don't piss in your own backyard. There was nothing he could do about it, though. Traveling to another state would take too much time. After the first solid freeze, winter would set in, and the heavy snows would make traveling difficult. Besides, he had too much to do here to be gone for very long.

John had truly made a mess of things. Secretly, he agreed that the girl had deserved severe punishment—having her laugh at his son could not be tolerated. Still, John should have had more self-control. It shamed him to realize his son had repeated the mistake Alden had made years ago. But that mistake hadn't been Alden's fault. If he'd had someone to guide or assist him, as John had, he never would have made such an error in judgment.

His son had enjoyed all the advantages Alden had missed out on, and still, he'd made the asinine blunder. His boy was fortunate he had a father who could clean up his messes. John better have learned his lesson. Alden wouldn't be as lenient if anything like this happened again.

Too bad they'd had to put the girl down; she could have been useful here. There were only eight stable girls. Many of these women had been taken from the streets or strip clubs and had required virtually no training to fulfill their job requirements. The Pennsylvania girl might have needed some breaking in, but very little training was required to work in the stable. The women performed the tasks that came natural to them . . . it was what they'd been born to do.

Yes, another female in the stable would be a welcome addition. The last time he'd visited there, the women had looked a bit worn. Bringing in a fresh one would've been nice. Perhaps he would find a couple of new ones next hunting season.

But for this year, he would concentrate on bringing in the last one and then he could enter into his favorite time. Training had to begin by the end of the month at the latest. By early spring, the men who'd submitted the winning bids would be ravenous, ready to take their mates.

"Father, may I approach you?"

Smiling his welcome, he opened his arms. Tabitha flew toward him and flung herself into his embrace, as she had almost from the moment she could walk. Alden held her tightly to him, his heart overflowing with love. A surge of arousal quickly followed, and he laughed softly as she rubbed up against his hardening body. "Later, my angel. For now, tell me how your new charges are doing."

Settling onto his lap, she gave him an update. "Extremely well. Each girl has toured our community at least twice. They're eating well and exercising to maintain their shape and good health. The healer has checked their teeth and overall health. And the ugly, fat one has even lost some weight."

"Don't let her lose any more. Royce caught a glimpse of her the other day and I believe he wants to bid for her. He's sending me his offer soon."

"The stable girls say Royce can be quite brutal. This girl is shy and submissive. They will make a good match."

Tabitha was such a romantic, always looking for the perfect match for each person in the community. "And what about our little runaway? How is she faring? I saw her the other day. There's defiance in her."

"When training day arrives, I fully expect she'll be as cooperative as the rest."

"And Ben and Lucy? Are they a help or a hindrance to you?"

"Oh, they're extremely helpful, especially with the runaway. She obeys their commands almost immediately." Something wonderfully wicked flickered in her face as she added, "I often have to use a bit more coercion."

Alden inwardly smiled. His angel had a hint of the devil in her. This unique characteristic had revealed itself early. Lois, Tabitha's mother, had been the first to fall victim to her creative talents, carrying bite marks, scratches, and bruises on her skin for days.

When Alden had recognized his daughter's unique appetites, he'd taken her under his wing and shielded her. Another downfall of his first wife—she hadn't fully appreciated their daughter's specialness. It had been one of the many reasons he and Lois had had to part ways.

He remembered that day well. Tabitha had been there at her mother's bedside during her last moments and Alden could still picture the little smile of satisfaction curving his daughter's mouth. Though only twelve at the time, even then, she hadn't wanted competition from another woman.

"So you've chosen the runaway as our teaching aid this time?"

She grinned. "Yes, and I think she may well be our best yet. You know that kind of defiance always makes for good teaching points. Her punishment will give the others excellent examples."

"And give you enjoyment."

She shrugged. "Finding enjoyment in one's job is important. You taught me that."

Alden leaned forward and put his mouth to her ear. "And you were an excellent student."

"Thank you, Father." Placing her head on his chest, she snuggled against him.

"Are you ready for our trip next week?" Alden asked.

"Yes. Having you all to myself for a few days will be a special treat."

"Have you chosen our location?"

She nodded. "Since we have to stay close to home, I've chosen a small college two hundred miles southeast of here. If we can identify her early enough, we might possibly be home by the end the week."

"Excellent. I'll leave all the details to you."

Shifting slightly, she put her lips against his neck and spoke against his skin. "May I stay with you awhile?"

Rarely able to refuse his angel, Alden slid his hand under her dress and then up her soft thigh. "You know that whatever pleases you pleases me."

With a soft, gratitude-filled sigh, Tabitha's hand went to his zipper. Alden closed his eyes and allowed her to have her way.

Seth stood at the window of the LCR conference room. The city of Tampa sprawled out before him, but he saw nothing other than the words forming in his head. Words that would no doubt create an argument. Damned if he'd keep them to himself, though. Fortunately, everyone but Honor had left—all preparing to take their plans for the stakeout and deep cover to the next level.

"What's wrong?"

She stood behind him, all soft woman, all once his. He

had no right to ask her to step back. Honor was a
trained professional. In the years they'd been apart,
she'd been involved in dozens of dangerous cases. But he
hadn't known about them . . . hadn't allowed himself to
know. Now, with this job, he was the one responsible
for bringing her into danger.

"Seth?" she asked again.

Without turning, he said, "How many female operatives does LCR have?"

"I'm not sure. Thirty, maybe. I've never asked. Why?"

Taking a breath, he turned and tried for evasiveness
and logic, at first. "Having an additional female operative on the case would be helpful."

Her smooth brow furrowed in confusion. "Noah's already designated eleven more female operatives, plus
two additional men, Gabe Maddox and Jordan Montgomery. Along with Aidan and Jared, that's sixteen operatives, not counting you and Noah. That's a hell of a
lot of people for one mission."

"One more can't hurt."

"Why do you think we need one more?"

"Because you're in charge of the entire operation. You
need to be coordinating everyone's efforts, not have
your time split between that and working undercover,
too. Your focus will be off."

"Are you trying to protect me?"

He didn't know which surprised him most—her soft
voice, the hand she put on his arm, or the tenderness he
saw in her expression. He'd figured she would be furious.

Feeling hopeful, he asked, "Would that be so bad?"

"My mom said that's why you lied to me before. To
protect me."

"I told you that." He blew out a sigh. Going down
this road again would probably not help, but if it made

her look at things from a different perspective, he'd try anything. "If I had told you what was going down with Clemmons, what would you have done?"

"I don't know. I only know that you took the choice away from me."

Seth nodded grimly and turned back to the window. She was right; he had taken that choice from her. And if he had the same decision to make again? He'd do the same damn thing. She said she didn't know what she would have done with the truth; Seth had known. Honor would have stuck around, tried to help, gotten involved. And in the process, she could have become a target, trained professional or not. He had loved Honor, and the need to protect her overrode everything else.

"Seth, look at me."

He turned to her again. With an expression of earnest resolve on her beautiful face, she took both of his hands in hers. "Let's put what happened in the past behind us and look at it from today's perspective. I won't go into boring detail about the number of cases I've worked, the arrests I've made, or the commendations I've received. When we were together before, I was green, I admit. Maybe I would have screwed everything up back then, I don't know. However, what you need to remember is that now I am a trained professional, with lots of field experience under my belt. I can do this job. What I need from you is to not only believe I can handle the job; I need you to promise that you'll let me do my job."

Seth held back the words of protest clamoring to get out. What was the point? She just didn't see it, would never see it. He knew she was a trained professional, even deadly when necessary. But when he looked at her, he saw the sexy, beautiful, freckle-faced woman who'd stolen his heart years ago. The softly, vulnerable woman he'd held in his arms, the sweetly fragrant woman he'd licked, tasted, and savored. He'd felt the delicacy of her satin skin, knew the vulnerability and softness of her slender body.

To the rest of the world, Honor might be a tough, hard-nosed, no-nonsense woman with a gun. To Seth, she was simply his heart.

If he told her those things, he knew what would happen. She would suggest that he work with another team. No way in hell was that going to happen. Honor didn't believe she needed his protection. Whether she needed it or not, she was going to get it. No matter how this case went down, whether they saved Kelli and the other girls or not, Honor would be safe. This he swore.

"Seth, can you do that?"

"Yes, I can do that. I have all the faith in the world in you."

Giving him the smile he'd fallen for long ago, she leaned forward and kissed him softly. "Thank you. Now let's go find Kelli."

As Seth followed her out the door, an odd sense of inevitability washed over him. Fate had brought Honor back into his life for a reason. He was beginning to comprehend what that reason was, and in his gut, he knew that what was about to take place was meant to be.

Two days later, Honor stood in front of the room again, this time facing a much larger group of people. Along with Noah, Jared, Aidan, and Seth, two other male LCR operatives had been added to the mix—Jordan Montgomery and Gabe Maddox.

Prior to coming to work for LCR, she had worked with both men, but hadn't had a chance to do so again since she'd become an operative. Both Jordan and Gabe had taken several months off to handle some personal matters. Jordan and his wife, Eden, had recently adopted a little boy from Thailand. And Gabe, who'd reunited with his wife last year, had spent most of his time in Tennessee, building their new home. When Noah had told her they'd be on the case, she'd been happy to have two such seasoned operatives added to their numbers.

Of the eleven female operatives Noah had called in, none were familiar to her. Though she would have preferred to know at least a few, she wasn't worried. All LCR operatives were well trained, and she knew Noah McCall; he wouldn't assign a job to anyone unless he had full confidence in that person.

"Okay, here's what we know." Honor turned to one of the boards and pointed at their list. "We figure he's been at this for ten years. He never hits the same state twice. Each year, he uses a different venue to grab his victims, and he's not consistent in the number he takes. The first year we've tracked him back to, he took three; the second year, five; the third year, three again."

"How is it that he's not been targeted by the authorities by now?" Gabe asked.

"For one thing, his preferences are all over the place. Though he does seem to like them in their late teens or early twenties, he doesn't target one particular race, background, or even body type." She shot a glance at Seth. "One of the things Seth noticed immediately before he contacted LCR was how there were so few similarities."

"So, all totaled, how many women has he taken?"

"He's hit forty-seven states."

Several gasps and curses exploded in the room. They were experiencing the shock she had felt two days ago. She allowed several seconds for that information to sink in before she continued: "We believe he hasn't hit Alaska and Hawaii just because of the sheer difficulty of transporting his victims."

An operative who'd been introduced as Julie Rose said, "What's the other state he hasn't hit?"

"Wyoming."

"Any reason for this?" Jordan asked.

"We have a couple of theories. He either simply hasn't gotten to that state yet or that's where he lives and he doesn't want to hunt so close to home."

"And that's where you think he's going to hit next?" Jordan asked.

"That's what we're counting on." She prayed to God they were right. They were basing this premise on simple math, and because of their limited time frame, they had no choice. They had nothing else to go on.

"We also believe we have a short window before he stops for the year." Looking back at her list, she said, "His hunting time is early spring through late autumn. If we don't find him now, it'll be months before he goes on the hunt again. Months these girls don't have."

She drew a breath and continued: "Here's what we don't know. We don't know why he's doing this or what he's doing with the girls."

"So what's the plan?" Gabe asked.

"Each female operative will go to a campus. I'll review your covers and locations before we adjourn. Noah will be our point person. We'll have twelve operatives working the campuses. And six operatives will be backup and assist when needed."

"What are we looking for?" asked Andrea Johnston, a tall, lanky blond. "Most campuses are ripe with guys trying to pick up girls."

Honor glanced at Seth, who took up the reins and said, "The MO has been different each year. This time he's not only targeting college campuses, he's targeting young girls who are particularly vulnerable. The two girls last year and two of the three missing this year, including my niece, were transfers. We think he's using a young woman as a lure."

"How's that?" Gabe asked.

As Honor reviewed the ruse they believed was being used, Seth observed the women who would be going undercover. Most of them looked young enough to be in college, which surprised the hell out of him. Where had all of these young women come from? What made them willing to risk their lives to rescue others?

He glanced back at Honor. She was probably the oldest here, but of all the concerns he had about her going undercover, looking like a college coed wasn't one of them. Honor in the right clothes, with the right expression on her face, would look as young as any college freshman. He wished that she did look too old to take part in the operation. Sure as hell would make him feel a lot better.

As she began to make the assignments for each operative, Seth pulled out his map of Wyoming. They'd fallen exhausted into bed last night and hadn't discussed which campus he and Honor were going to take.

"We have fourteen campuses to cover," Honor was saying. "A couple of them have a low female attendance, so two of you will cover two campuses each. To stay below radar and have a good pool to choose from, I think he'll want to target a larger female population."

She passed out individual assignment sheets to each person, noting, "I've included everyone's name, location, and cell number." She took a breath and looked around the room. "Our goal is for one of us to get taken."

Gabe Maddox, who'd been sprawled in his chair, sat up. "So you want an abduction to take place?"

"Yes. We need him to lead us back to where he's taken the other girls."

Jordan Montgomery said, "You're assuming he's holding these girls in one spot. You got any proof of that?"

"No. However, that's what we're hoping he's doing." She held up a small wristwatch. "Each operative will be equipped with a watch like this one and an earbud. The watch has a microphone, so you'll be able to communicate with your 'go to' person at all times. And it has a GPS tracking device that will transmit for up to a thousand miles. If you get taken and no one's around, we can track you."

A young brunette who'd been introduced as Sherry said, "So, if I'm taken, what's my agenda?"

"First and foremost, stay alive," Honor said. "The last thing we want is for anyone else to be hurt. Our biggest advantage will be in tracking you to his location and coming in after you and the other girls. Since you'll be able to communicate via your watch, give as many clues as you can without being obvious. If you see any of the other girls and can find a way to let us know, that's fine. But don't put yourself at risk to do so. You will have accomplished the most important part. Let us do the rest."

Seth glanced down at the assignment sheet, looking for his and Honor's names. When he came to his name, he was shocked to see that she had assigned him to a location in Laramie with another operative. She was going to Camden College in the northeastern part of the state. Hundreds of miles from him.

"No."

Though well aware that his voice had been loud and

abrupt, Seth didn't care. Everyone was looking at him, but he had eyes for only one person. When she slowly turned to face him, he saw the knowledge in her expression. She'd done it on purpose.

"Something wrong, Seth?"

Though Honor had asked the question, he turned to McCall. "I'm working with Honor."

McCall's mouth twitched, but he shook his head and nodded at Honor. "Stone's in charge of the case. Take it up with her."

"Fine." Seth stood and approached Honor. The flare of panic in her eyes told him he'd shocked the hell out of her. He was going to do more than just shock her if she didn't change the assignments.

Stopping a foot from where she stood, he said softly, quietly, so others couldn't hear, "Reassign me to work with you."

She shot an uneasy glance around. Seth could feel the stares of sixteen pairs of eyes boring into his back. His intent wasn't to embarrass her or undermine her authority. McCall was right, it was her case, but he'd be damned if she was in one part of the state, putting her life on the line, and he was in another.

"Do it, Honor."

"Seth, I don't—"

"You've got two choices, babe. Make the reassignment or I'm going to do something that these LCR operatives will be talking about for years to come."

Her temper making her eyes gleam like green diamonds, she snapped, "You wouldn't dare."

"Try me."

She glared for several seconds and then said, "Fine, you're with me."

Knowing the argument that would come later, he didn't feel the least bit of triumph about his victory. He nodded and said, "Thank you."

He turned back to the room and said, "Sorry for the interruption." Going back to the chair he'd vacated, he listened intently to the rest of Honor's instructions. Although acutely aware of the curious glances in the room, Seth continued to ignore them. He had more than enough concerns to occupy his thoughts. And one of the biggest was, why the hell had she separated them?

twenty-two

Camden College
Parkersville, Wyoming

They sat in the dining area of the RV and reviewed their choices. With a student body of less than ten thousand, their options would be limited. Alden wasn't worried, though. Except for the girl in Pennsylvania, Tabitha had proven herself an excellent judge of female flesh. He had no doubt she'd find the perfect woman for the last trip of the year.

"There are only four school-approved social clubs catering to females," Tabitha said. "Two of them meet today, one this morning, in about an hour. Another one meets this afternoon. The other two don't meet until two days from now."

Alden grunted. "That'll eat into our time. If we want to be home by the week's end, it would be better if you could find the girl as soon as possible."

"I'll do my best. There are also a couple of non-school social events I think might be worthwhile to check out. Only problem is, the most promising one isn't until Thursday."

Alden sighed. No matter how anxious he was to go home, getting the right girl was the most important factor. "Tell me about them."

She slid two flyers to him. "This one is a mixer. A

chance for boys to meet the new girls. The more attractive girls will probably attend. And they'll look their best to catch the boys' attention." Her full, red lips pinched together in disapproval. "As if wearing makeup is what attracts a man. However, it will broaden our choices."

"It's tonight."

"Yes, I'll go for a little while. If I don't see anyone in the first hour or so, I'll return here."

"What about the other one?"

"That's the one on Thursday. It's an all-girl event, about a mile from campus. The description sounds intriguing. I think it might give us our best chance at finding the right one."

Alden read the flyer, his excitement ratcheting as he saw the event description:

New to Camden? Have trouble meeting new people? Feeling a bit homesick? Come meet other newcomers just like you. Food, music, and a chance to make new friends. What are you waiting for?

Alden nodded. "This sounds ideal."

"That's what I was thinking. Even though it's not until later this week, it should attract the right kind of female for Tranquillity's needs."

"Excellent, my angel." He checked his watch. "You have a few minutes before you have to leave. Would you like to pleasure me? I know that always relaxes you."

"Actually, I have something to discuss with you."

His Tabitha had never turned down the opportunity for pleasure. Whatever she wanted to talk about must be of enormous consequence.

"What is it, my love?"

"You know that I will do anything for you, don't you, Father?"

Alden nodded. "One of the many reasons I love you."

"And you know that anything I ask from you is only

to make your life easier and Tranquillity the perfect home for you and your followers?"

Becoming more curious by the moment, he said, "Yes, I know that. What is it you want?"

An unusual expression hardened the lovely features of her face—one he rarely witnessed, but when he did, something interesting always happened.

"John needs to be put down. He's a weakling and has caused you nothing but problems since his birth."

Alden couldn't say he was surprised by her request. Tabitha and John had never been close siblings. He remembered the time a fifteen-year-old John had tried to crawl into his sister's bed. Tabitha's fury had been awe-inspiring. Even Sarah, his third wife, had been appalled by John's behavior. Having Sarah on Tabitha's side had been a unique pairing; they'd sparred like two felines in heat most of the time. And while he understood his son's desires—after all, he had them, too—he wouldn't share Tabitha with anyone. She belonged to him.

To please her, he had put Tabitha in charge of John's punishment. She had wanted a public flogging in the town square, but Alden had refused that request. Having the community witness his son's punishment would make him look bad as a father. His people needed to see him as omnipotent. If he couldn't control his household, what kind of a leader did that make him?

Tabitha's second choice had been truly inspired. With his help, she had tied John down and then plucked his fingernails out with pliers. And while he'd been screaming in pain, she'd poured lemon juice over his bleeding fingers. He remembered John's screams of agony all too well. An excruciatingly painful punishment, but it had worked. John had never crossed Tabitha again. Or had he?

"Has John made advances toward you again?"

"Oh no, he knows better than that. However, his mistakes have caused you problems. And now you're here trying to find him a woman, as if he is fully forgiven."

"He still suffers from his punishment. It'll be at least another week before he's able to be out in the community. And his attitude is much more subservient than it was before."

"But that's not enough." She moved around the table to sit beside him. Placing her soft hand on his groin, she caressed him lightly. "His demeanor will stay that way until he's no longer in pain; then he'll be the same. He'll never really change." She leaned forward and whispered softly in his ear, "He's a bad seed, Father. You deserve so much better."

Alden swallowed a moan at the magic of her hands, the sound of her sultry, enticing voice, and found himself unable to argue with her profound statement. John was a troublemaker and Alden did deserve so much better. "How and when?"

Her hand continuing to stroke him, she smiled up at him. "I'll take care of it. No one but you and I will ever know."

"What about our hunting trip?"

"We still need to add another female. Your goal was four for this year. Brother Baker's wife died in childbirth last year. I heard that he visited the stable girls the other night. He would probably appreciate a young woman who could bear him children—without dying this time. Don't you think?"

Alden shook his head in wonder at Tabitha's brilliance. Not only was she going to make his life easier by ridding him of his wayward son, she was thinking ahead for the community.

"You are a true treasure."

She blinked innocently up at him. "You know that whatever makes you happy makes me happy."

She was right. Looking out for his happiness was her

gift and her responsibility. Everything she'd suggested was only to make his life easier and better.

"Then you have my permission. You may kill your brother."

"Thank you, Father." Her beautiful smile one of extreme satisfaction, she lowered her head to his lap to show her appreciation.

Parkersville, Wyoming

Every available flat surface in the small bedroom suite was covered with maps, brochures, and information about Camden College, whose small campus she and Seth would cover.

Two LCR jets had flown the entire team into Casper yesterday. At the airport, the operatives had dispersed, each taking a rental vehicle that the indispensible Angela, LCR's receptionist, had arranged. There'd been little conversation during the flight. Each operative knew the importance of the mission, and Honor had left the airport with a secure sense that if dedication and commitment were the most important ingredients for success, they would indeed rescue all of the victims.

Unfortunately, she also knew that luck would play a huge role in this mission. If this guy wasn't in the right place, at the right time, where a trap could be sprung, then this whole thing would be a wasted opportunity. And they wouldn't get another chance until the spring.

Tension knotted the muscles in her neck and shoulders. Though much of the anxiety came from worry over whether this was the right course to take, she knew that wasn't the only reason. She had seriously screwed up with Seth.

She glanced over at the too-silent man sitting by the window, reading a Camden newsletter. They'd both done as much research on the small school as possible, hoping to find the most likely prospects that this creep would target. But since the meeting yesterday morning and that much too public confrontation, he hadn't spoken directly to her.

So yes, she had screwed up. She should have told him before the meeting that she thought it best to assign him to another location and not with her. Clouded judgment could compromise an operation. Honor had told herself she had made the decision strictly for that reason only, but deep down, she had acknowledged that it wasn't the only reason.

What was going to happen to them after this case was over? They'd agreed to no promises, no commitments, but how the hell could she separate that agreement from what was going on with her heart? She loved him . . . had never stopped loving him. Problem was, Seth had given no indication that he wanted more after this was over.

Assigning him to another person had been an attempt at separating herself from him. She hadn't counted on Seth's determination or that he'd make his opinion known in front of the entire group. And while she'd been embarrassed and shocked, she had recognized something in Seth's expression she hadn't expected. *Hurt.*

Late yesterday afternoon, when they'd checked into the hotel, she hadn't said anything to him but had told the front desk that they would need only one room, instead of the two that had been booked. Seth hadn't objected.

Shopping for clothes in Tampa to wear in Wyoming had been out of the question. So while Seth had stayed in their room, Honor had gone out for a few hours. Not only had she needed to find clothes that would help her blend in on the college campus, she had needed breathing space, away from Seth. She had been much more successful in her shopping than she'd been in escaping Seth's presence. He hadn't been with her physically, but he'd been on her mind all the same.

She'd returned to the room last night exhausted and tense. Again, Seth had been quiet, speaking only when she asked him something outright. Too exhausted to deal with the argument she knew was coming, she'd delayed its inevitability. Taking only enough time to brush her teeth and wash her face, she'd fallen into bed. Sometime during the night, she'd woken to feel Seth's arms around her and had fallen back asleep, content.

This morning, she was refreshed and energetic, ready to begin their search. But first, she had to address what she'd been delaying.

Aware that his anger still simmered, she raised the question tentatively. "Can we talk about it?"

Without looking up from the page he was reading, he asked, "What's there to talk about?"

"I should have discussed it with you beforehand."

"That would've been a nice touch."

"I'm sorry I didn't tell you."

He looked at her then. "But you still think you did the right thing."

"I just thought if we weren't working so closely together, our focus would be clearer."

"You thought I'd be less concerned about you if I was hundreds of miles away from you, as opposed to being close enough to know what was going on?"

Shit. The way he put it made her decision sound not only wrong but downright stupid, too. "Fine. It was a stupid, ill-thought-out decision. Can we get past it?"

That intense blue stare pierced her for several seconds. Finally, he nodded and said, "Yes. And for the record, I apologize for embarrassing you in front of your coworkers."

"Apology accepted. We both did things we regret."

"No, Honor, you misunderstood." He went to his feet, and in one swift movement, pulled her up and into his arms. "I didn't say I regretted what I did. I said I apologize. Big difference. If that was the only way I could get you to change your mind, I'd do it again. Understand?"

Shivers of arousal dueled with outrage at his arrogance. She opened her mouth, sure that she would come up with a stinging put-down. Instead, no words came, only a sighing moan.

Answering her moan in the best way possible, Seth's mouth moved whisper-soft along her jawline. Her entire body now a throbbing, melting mass of want, Honor almost sobbed as his mouth finally settled softly on hers. When she tried to take the kiss deeper, Seth wouldn't let her, continuing those tender, whispering kisses that caused a chain reaction to every nerve ending. Until, finally . . . oh, sweet heaven . . . finally, his lips covered hers firmly, drawing her tongue deep into his mouth, where he lashed at it with his, then sucked.

Moments later, Seth drew back and rasped gruffly, "We'd better get ready."

Ignoring the vehement protest of her overaroused body, Honor pulled away. Seth was right. The fact that he didn't look any less pained eased her mind. The hard evidence of his erection pressing against her stomach was a clear indication of his need.

"We'll continue this later," she whispered.

He didn't answer, but the hot gleam of promise in his eyes gave her the response she needed. Blowing out a shaky sigh, Honor gestured toward the shopping bags on the floor. "I need to get to work on my outfit. Looking younger might take me some extra time."

His expression revealing that he was back in mission

mode, too, he said, "I'll order a light lunch for us and then put together an itinerary of events."

Honor turned to the closet, where she had hung up a couple of her new things last night. At thirty, she knew she wasn't the typical, age-appropriate college student. With the right clothes and demeanor, she felt confident, she could pull it off.

Half an hour later, she stood in front of the full-length mirror in the bedroom and wondered if she had been a bit too confident.

"Damn, babe, you look good enough to eat."

She whirled around to see Seth eyeing her like she was a steak-and-lobster dinner and he'd been on a weeklong fast. Grimacing, she turned back to the mirror. "I'm not so sure that's a good thing."

"Guess that wasn't the most politically correct compliment, but it was sincere. If I'd gone to college with a girl who looked like you, I never would've graduated."

A foolish grin spread over her face. Okay, so the comment had been a bit sexist, but when it came from Seth, instead of taking offense, she felt her heart thud and her legs go weak.

Honor ran her gaze over her outfit again. The jeans molded her body like a second skin; the western-style sky-blue long-sleeved shirt wasn't tight, but emphasized her assets quite nicely.

"You think it's too sexy?"

"No, the clothes look almost identical to what we saw when we drove by the campus yesterday. My comment was for the woman inside the clothes."

Her heart made another leap. If he didn't stop, she was going to have to seriously consider turning around and kissing him again. "What about my hair?"

"I like it pulled back like that. You look sweet and innocent."

Since that's what she'd been going for, she felt infinitely better. "What's on the agenda? Anything other than the three coffee shops, the Internet café, and then the frat party tonight?"

"A couple more. Let's eat and we'll talk strategy."

Ignoring the need to hold her in his arms one more time, Seth pulled out a chair for Honor at the small dining table where he'd placed their lunch. He'd thought that reminding himself at least a dozen times just since he'd woken this morning that she was a trained professional had helped, but when she'd stepped out of the bathroom dressed like a shy innocent, his protective instincts had flared full force once more.

As she nibbled on her fruit-and-vegetable plate, Seth slid the agenda he'd worked up across to her. "Two of the coffee shops are on campus. Since we don't know how long this guy watches his prey before he pounces or where he'll be, probably be a good idea to visit these shops at least twice each day."

Biting into a celery stick, Honor nodded. "I agree. You think about an hour in each one is enough?"

"I think it's going to have to be. Even though this is a small campus, there're numerous places kids can hang out around here."

She glanced down at the list again. "Hmm, the Internet café . . . that's the sort of place where Mallory Roland, the girl at Penn State, was taken. Wonder if he might be too skittish to try one again so soon."

Seth took a bite out of his cheeseburger and nodded his agreement. "Good point. Let's try it for only about half an hour. There're a couple of other places I'd like you to try this afternoon. A Laundromat not far from campus that a lot of kids use . . . it's attached to a diner. Also, there's an ice cream parlor in the middle of campus I thought we might try."

"About the frat party: I never went to one when I was in college. Do I just walk in the door?"

Seth took another bite of his burger to hide a smile. No, he couldn't see the too serious, totally focused Honor Stone hanging with a frat crowd. His freshman year, he'd done his share of those kinds of parties. While some of them had been fun, most of them were ones he'd like to just forget. Guzzling beer and then puking his guts up hadn't been the wisest use of his time— something his dad had made clear when he'd seen Seth's first-semester grades.

"We'll look for a group going in the door; you can attach yourself to them. No one's going to question your right to be there. Believe me."

"That's one place I won't have to pretend that I'm ill at ease and nervous."

"All the better. If our guy is there and sees how uncomfortable you are, you may hook him."

"Or her?"

Seth nodded. "Yeah, it's going to be interesting to see exactly how he's making the selection. Is she doing it for him? Or do they have some sort of camera device and he tells her which one he wants?"

She finished her meal and stood. "If he's directing her in this, I've got to think he's calling the shots."

"Since she knows his type, could be she's an expert at picking the right ones."

"Except Anna. I still can't piece together why they would have chosen someone who doesn't fit the profile."

"Hell if I know. Kelli fits it to a T."

"Once you bring Kelli home to your family, what happens then?"

Seth jerked at the unexpected question. "What?"

"Don't you think it's time to mend the rift between you and your family?"

"How do you think I'm going to do that? They know the truth. I can't take back the past."

"No, but you can give them another chance."

"Another chance to tell me how I screwed up the whole family? Thanks, but I've heard it all before. My only aim is to give Kelli back to them. That'll give them a hell of a lot more peace than me going back and pretending like nothing happened."

Her eyes narrowing, she tilted her head. "What happened to you?"

"What are you talking about?"

"The man I met five years ago wouldn't have just given up."

"I didn't give up. There's no point in rehashing something I can't change."

"There's more to it than that. You never really talked about what you had to do while you were undercover."

Yeah, well, there was a reason for that. Reliving hell and his past sins wasn't exactly on his "to do" list. "I got the job done."

"I've done undercover work, Seth. I know how easy it is to lose yourself. You had almost six years of being one of Clemmons's associates. That must've had a severe impact."

"Never said it didn't."

Golden-green intelligent eyes speared him. "Why can't you tell me about it?"

"This isn't the time or the place to go into a discussion of an old case. But you're right about one thing: I'm not the same man I was five years ago."

He could see the questions trembling on her mouth. He had, not so successfully sometimes, pushed those memories to the back of his mind. Yeah, he still had frequent nightmares and, no, he'd never forget. Talking about them would do no good.

He stood and grabbed his keys. "We need to get started."

The hurt on her face was hard to take. The judgment in her eyes would be a hell of a lot harder. Tell her what happened? What he regretted on a daily, sometimes hourly basis? No way in hell.

twenty-three

Propped up against a mountain of pillows in the bedroom of the RV, Alden sipped a soda and watched the live feed of the party as Tabitha made her rounds. His daughter really was a marvel. So intriguing how the young men reacted to her beauty. First they looked at her angelic face, then their eyes would drop to those plump red lips, go lower to her tight, firm breasts, and then take in her beautifully shaped ass. By the time they made it back up to her face to speak, they were drooling.

He never felt the slightest jealousy. They were young and their fascination with her beauty was understandable. Only once had he felt the slightest anger, and that had been last year when a young man had touched her. Actually, the anger had been more than slight. After Tabitha had been rightly punished for allowing the young prick to get that close, Alden had gone out and hunted him down, just as any good father would. As the kid had gasped out his final breaths of life, Alden had whispered in his ear the sin he had committed. The young man had died knowing justice had been served.

They had never talked about that night, but Tabitha had seen the blood all over him when he'd returned to the RV. She'd simply run him a bath and washed it off. That had been the end of that, and she'd never allowed anyone to get close enough to touch her ever again.

Alden was pulled from his musings as Tabitha whispered into the microphone attached to her collar. "There is a young woman on the stairway. She looks out of place and alone. Would you like me to approach her?"

"Get closer. I can't see her clearly."

The image of the woman became clearer as Tabitha walked toward her. The girl was moderately attractive. Heavy makeup and ill-fitting clothes took away from her looks, but she had potential.

"She's a possibility. Talk to her . . . see what you can find out."

Before Tabitha could approach her, a young man ran up the steps toward their prospect. The girl's face brightened, her relief obvious.

"Looks like she's a no-go," Tabitha muttered.

Alden sighed. "Walk around for another few minutes. If you see no one, come on back. We'll try again tomorrow."

"I'm sorry, Father."

"Not your fault, my angel. We'll find the right one soon."

As Tabitha made her way through the overcrowded room, Alden kept an eye out for any interesting-looking females, as well as any men who made improper advances toward his daughter. A party such as this, with people drinking and doing all sorts of vile things to alter their minds, there was no telling what some imbecile would do to a beautiful young woman like his angel.

After about ten minutes, it was obvious that Tabitha was not going to find the right young woman there. The party was getting louder, more boisterous. Fools were going to get more foolish as the night went on.

"Come back now, Tabitha. We'll start again tomorrow."

"See you soon."

Disappointed but not overly so, Alden relaxed against the pillows again. Finding the right one to bring back to his people wasn't an easy task. He had made several mistakes in the early years, not only in selecting girls but also in training them. A couple had ended up as stable girls. Others he hadn't been able to tolerate, so he had put them out of his or their misery.

Having Tabitha help him had been a brilliant idea. Not only did she look like an innocent, she could spot certain aspects of a woman he'd never looked at before. Qualities that only another woman might be able to identify.

No doubt about it. She would continue to travel and hunt with him each year.

Honor stood in front of the mirror and tried out several expressions, hoping to come up with the right one. For three days straight, she'd made herself as visible as possible. At the beginning of the week, she'd been confident she could look and act like an insecure, lonely college student. Through several long, exhausting afternoons and evenings, that confidence had disappeared. She had attracted plenty of guys, but not the one she had wanted to lure. The shy, awkward persona wasn't as easy to give off as she'd thought it would be.

"You ready?"

She turned to Seth, who stood behind her. After that brief, uninformative talk about Clemmons, he'd been much too quiet. Whenever she made a statement or asked a question, his comments were terse, to the point of rudeness. And though they slept together each night and he held her in his arms, they still hadn't made love.

She tried to tell herself that his worry for his niece and his focus on the mission were to blame for his standoffishness. While part of that could be true, she knew that wasn't the whole story. Whatever had happened to Seth during his years of undercover work continued to eat at him.

Why hadn't she delved into that experience before now? She'd seen the changes in him, including a hardness that hadn't been there before. The answer to her question wasn't one she was proud of, but it was the truth. Getting specifics would have meant digging deeper into their past. Other than reminding herself daily that he'd lied to her, she had skirted the issue of what Seth had endured. Pain avoidance was a selfish reason, but there it was.

Now not only did she need to play catch-up, she had to figure out how to get him to talk. He'd made it pretty damn clear that the subject was off-limits.

"You look nice."

Quite different from his previous compliment. Stretching her mouth into a smile at the watered-down flattery was difficult. They were back to behaving like strangers. She hated that. However, until this job was over, she could do nothing about it. Once they'd found the young women and the creep who'd taken them, she promised herself, she and Seth would spend hours of uninterrupted time together . . . with their clothes on.

"It's a little less sexy than the other outfits I've been wearing. I bought the shirt at the mall in Casper and the jeans and my jacket at a thrift store."

"You could wear a sack and still look beautiful."

Her heart clutched. Now, that was a Seth compliment. And only with him had she ever felt beautiful. He had made her feel that way, and not only by how well he treated her; his attention to detail was phenomenal. He'd notice minute things, like her perfume or a new shade of lipstick. Once he'd complimented her on a new belt she'd bought. She knew enough about guys to realize how special Seth was.

He'd told her that having five sisters had trained him well. She just wished to hell they'd trained him to open up more.

Her hands smoothed the emerald-green blouse. "You always know the right thing to say to make a woman feel special."

"It's easy when the woman is special."

Biting her lip to keep it from trembling, she turned around and gave him a brilliant smile. "So, I guess we'd better go over everything one last time. Okay?"

His expression tightened. "First, we'll hit the two coffee shops and the diner again. This afternoon, we'll go to the library, another bookstore that's got an attached café, and let's try that ice cream shop again. Tonight, there's a small newcomers' get-together not far from campus."

She grimaced. "Hopefully better attended than the frat party."

"Yeah, that was a bust."

The party had been a dozen or so guys getting drunk and no girls. Honor had made one quick glance around the room and sped out of there before she was seen. Drunk college boys weren't on her list of suspects.

"If we have any spare time, I'll wander around the campus a little more today. Maybe if I'm seen walking alone through campus, that'll catch his eye."

"Let's test the mic one more time."

Part of her wanted to roll her eyes at him; the mic had worked perfectly each day. And today, they'd already had three tests. However, not only did she understand how important it was to have the equipment working properly, she also knew Seth needed this reassurance. If it eased his concern for her, then she would grit her teeth and test it another half dozen times. Anything to erase those grim lines around his mouth and lighten the shadows in his eyes.

"How about I go down to the lobby and grab us some coffee and a couple of those homemade chocolate chip cookies we saw yesterday?"

Though his eyes remained somber, a small smile lifted his mouth and eased the lines somewhat. "Make that four cookies and a large coffee."

"Gotcha." Adjusting the watch at her wrist, she winked at him and went out the door.

The instant the door clicked shut, Seth released an explosive sigh. He used to be better at hiding his thoughts. Honor knew something had happened with Clemmons . . . something he still couldn't talk about. Only a few people knew the whole story. After the son of a bitch went down and Seth left the force, he told himself he never had to think about it again. What was done, was done. He couldn't change the past, no matter how much he wished for it. Didn't stop the nightmares, though. He doubted anything ever would.

Clicking on the small receiver in his ear, he heard the elevator bell ring, telling him that Honor was probably in the lobby. Distant noises hit his ear, and he envisioned her walking through the lobby toward the coffee station.

"Hmm." Honor sounded eerily close. "Only peanut butter and double chocolate today. My favorites, but not what the grumpy man in my room asked for. Guess he's out of luck."

"Get your sweet ass up here with those double-chocolate cookies before I have to come down there and—"

She gave an overexaggerated gasp and Seth hardened. How was it that one small sound from Honor could turn him on so fast when he'd had other women strip naked to give him lap dances and he'd felt nothing? Hell, did he really want to answer that question?

She laughed softly. "My sweet ass is on its way up. You hear me okay?"

"Yeah, hear you fine."

"Everything okay?"

"Yeah. Everything's fine."

She went silent again, but the abrupt quietness wasn't reassuring. She wasn't going to stop asking questions and trying to find out what had happened. He told himself that Honor was a professional. There was probably very little that surprised her. However, to dig deep and share the things he'd seen, the things he had done to survive and get the job done? Could he open up and spill the darkest, deepest, filthiest part of his soul?

The door opened and Seth turned to see Honor struggling with two white foam cups and a napkin-covered plate of cookies. He strode quickly to take them from her hands.

"Thanks." Her eyes sparkling with good humor, she grinned up at him. "I got six of each. Thought you could use a little sweetening up."

The punch to his gut went clear to that battered, dirty soul and he knew the truth. This beautiful woman might have seen the worst of what humans could do to one another, but beneath that tough-girl attitude was the optimistic and idealistic young woman who still believed in goodness and doing the right thing.

No way would he tell her that in hell, the right thing didn't exist.

Honor's mouth ached as she smiled and said for the tenth time today, "Thanks for asking, but I have a boyfriend. Nice to meet you, though."

Had the boys been this horny when she was in school? Sadly for her, she knew they had been. However, she'd been a skinny, freckle-faced, too serious girl when she was in college. Dating had been one of the least important items on her agenda. Yes, she had dated occasionally and had even managed a couple of steady boyfriends, one in high school and a less serious one in college. Not one of them had ever touched her heart. Not until Seth.

As if she'd conjured him up, she heard him sigh. "Honor, if one more pimple-faced kid or muscle-bound jock asks you out, I'm coming inside to pass out pamphlets on abstinence."

Swallowing a startled laugh, Honor lowered her head to the book she'd been pretending to read. "They're just lonely, Seth."

He snorted. "Lonely, hell. They're horny kids and you're a hot babe who looks like their nighttime wet dream."

Honor didn't know if she should be insulted or complimented. Deciding not to even comment on that, she said instead, "I've been here for over an hour, and other than a couple of girls who came in for coffee and then left, I haven't seen anyone who could remotely be the woman we're looking for."

"Yeah. I agree. What's next on the agenda?"

"I'm going to walk around campus."

"Okay, sweetheart, I got your back."

Arousal hit unexpectedly, taking her breath. Heat flowed through her entire body and then pooled between her legs, causing a slow, steady throb. She squirmed in her chair. A room full of horny young men was not the best place for her to be right now.

"What's wrong?" Seth asked.

"Huh?"

"You groaned. Everything okay?"

Telling him the truth was out of the question. "Yes," she said instead. "Guess I've just been sitting for too long."

"I'm in the parking lot. Are you headed outside yet?"

The answer would be no, she was sitting here lusting after the owner of the gruff, sexy voice in her ear. Telling herself to get her act together, Honor stood and went out the door. On the sidewalk, she stopped for a second for a sweeping gaze around. She saw no one suspicious, nothing out of the ordinary. A few students walking to classes, three girls giggling in the parking lot, cars driving by. And as she'd figured, she didn't see Seth. The man was excellent at hiding.

"Where are you?" she murmured.

"Across the parking lot from you. Sitting in a grassy area, with my back against a tree, pretending to read some boring book about what some group of people did to another group of people in the Middle Ages. Figured if anyone saw me, I'd better look like I was a professor or something, instead of a stalker."

"Okay, I'm headed to the student union. It's the large two-story building on State Street."

"Right behind you."

Walking through the middle of the moderately busy campus, Honor took her time, hoping to give the impression that she had no appointments, no place to go, and no one to meet. Putting herself into the lonely, "I don't have a friend in the world" persona was wearing and somewhat depressing. Sad that there were young people out there who felt this way. Not that she'd had loads of friends, but she had a couple of close friends she could call on a moment's notice. She also had her family. Even so, she wasn't generally one who became morose and moody. Whenever she'd felt that way in the past, a good book or movie had usually changed her attitude.

That wasn't quite the way she'd handled herself when she and Seth had broken up. No book, movie, or bracing talk could fix her blues. Then, a few weeks later, her dad had suffered an aneurysm during his daily jog. That time had been the lowest point in her life. The relationship she'd had with her dad was special. Not a day went by that she didn't miss him.

She had eventually been able to overcome the sadness, immersing herself in her work and getting on with her life. Now when she thought about her him, though there was still the sense of missing him, she could smile at the wonderful, warm memories she had of the man who'd always been her hero.

With Seth, that hadn't been possible. Though losing him had felt like a death and she had mourned the loss of the bright future she'd envisioned for them, she had never been able to look back and think fondly of their time together. There had been too much bitterness and bewilderment. Way too much pain.

When she'd seen him again, she'd told herself this was an opportunity to finally put her past to rest, to put him behind her for good. But what had she done? She'd slept with him, become involved with his problems with his family, and had done the one thing she had promised herself she would never do. She had fallen back in love with a man who had no intention of having a future with her now, any more than he had five years ago.

Had she really told herself she was smarter and wiser? If she had, Honor knew she'd lied. When it came to Seth Cavanaugh, there was no smart, no wise. There was just this inevitable, deeply abiding, and hopeless love she would never overcome.

twenty-four

"I don't see anyone suitable, Father. I might as well leave."

Alden held back a disgusted sigh. He knew it wasn't Tabitha's fault they hadn't found the right one yet, but her whiny voice was wearing on his already frayed patience. Time was running out. Almost five full days of hunting and still no real prospects. They had to find someone soon or he would have to return home empty-handed. That had never happened before, and he refused to consider that within this mass of female flesh, there wasn't at least one young woman who would meet his community's needs.

"Father, did you hear me?"

Swallowing the biting comment that came to his mind, Alden feigned patience. "Just one more sweep around the room, my love, and then you can come back to me."

As Tabitha made her way through the large room filled with women, Alden strained his eyes. This event had been his most hopeful one. The advertisement for shy, young women new to the area and looking for friendships had seemed tailor-made for them. However, Tabitha had already been there for over an hour, and other than a vague interest in a couple of girls, there'd be no one remotely viable.

Having her stay long at any event was never a good idea. As attractive as she was, people always wanted to talk with her, ask her questions, even flirt with her. She deterred them well—his angel really wasn't much of a conversationalist. However, he didn't like to chance it for too long.

And once they found the right girl, attracting attention was out of the question. If someone remembered her conversing with a person who'd disappeared, people would begin to talk, become wary. Tabitha often disguised herself, but at some point, there could be speculation. Thankfully, this would be the last time they hunted at a college campus for a long while. He hadn't yet decided on next year's venue.

Tabitha's loud, disgusted huff hurt his ear, but it was her whiny "I see no one and my feet are beginning to ache" that set his teeth on edge.

Giving his own, less obvious huff, Alden relented. "All right, yes, you may leave. We'll start again tomorrow morning. I just hope—" His heart kicked up an excited beat as he caught sight of the beauty headed toward the camera. "Wait. See the reddish-blond-haired girl with freckles?"

"Where?"

"Walking toward you. What about her?"

There was silence as Tabitha evaluated the girl. "Perhaps. Let me get closer."

Alden leaned forward, his heart pounding unusually loud in his chest. The girl had a freshness to her that he hadn't seen in a while. From what he could tell, she wore no makeup and her clothes, though they fit well enough, were cheaply made and looked worn. The expression on her face was one of loneliness, almost desperation. She would soon learn that he had a cure for both.

Accompanying his interest was an unexpected surge of arousal. Usually while on a hunt, he was looking for women to add to the community, not occupy his bed.

Suddenly, he wanted to make an exception. "I believe I would be very interested in knowing more about her."

"I can think of no man in the community who she would suit. I thought we'd agreed to find a mate for Brother Baker. This woman does not seem his type."

"That's not for you to decide," Alden snapped. "Stop stalling and go talk to her."

"Yes, Father." Though her tone had a sulky edge to it, she knew better than to argue.

Mesmerized, Alden was spellbound as the young woman's face became clearer on his television screen. Fresh, delicate, and innocent, but with a sensual beauty. Oh yes, he definitely wanted to know more about this one. He waited in anticipation as his daughter made contact.

"Hi, I'm Tabitha. Are you new to Camden, too?"

The soft, almost childish voice stopped Honor in the middle of making her exit. Having decided that the party was a bust, she was anxious to try out a couple of more places before calling it a night.

Hating to be rude to such a sweet and shy-sounding person, she turned and smiled. The young woman was lovely. Long, white-blond hair fell halfway down her back; full, pouty lips held just a hint of pink lip gloss, and sky-blue eyes sparkled. She might be shy, but Honor figured it'd take the young men of Camden only about five minutes before they started asking her out.

Honor shook the girl's delicate hand. "I'm Maggie. And yes, this is my first year here."

"Mine, too." Tabitha looked around the room and then said, "Want to go sit on the porch, where it's not so noisy, and talk?"

Telling herself there was no way someone who looked like she belonged on a doll shelf could be helping abduct young women, Honor nevertheless said, "Sure." She knew better than to make a judgment on appearance alone.

Seth growled in her ear, "What do you think?"

As they walked through small groups of laughing and chatting girls, toward a door that led outside, Honor carefully assessed Tabitha. She'd seen more than her share of people pretending to be one thing when they were something else. Could this lovely girl really be the lure or was she just lonely and in need of a friend? Time would tell.

Tabitha opened the door and smiled, allowing Honor to go first. In that moment, Honor felt an unusual chill wash over her. Of course, she'd been working all day. Could be exhaustion. She went out onto the porch and sat on the top step, anxious to see where this discussion would lead.

Tabitha sat down beside her and gave her another sweet smile. "Where are you from?"

"Outside Cheyenne," Honor answered. "What about you?"

"I'm from here." She gestured vaguely with her hand. "I live just up the road."

"Oh, then you must know lots of people at Camden."

Tabitha grimaced. "Not really. I went to school out of state for a couple of years, but my parents wanted me to come home."

"It must be nice to have family so close. It's just my dad and me at home, but I really miss him."

"Oh, it is." The girl glanced at her watch. "In fact, I'm supposed to be home soon." She jumped to her feet. "I'd better go."

Honor gave her a kind smile and stood beside her. Apparently it had been exhaustion making her suspect someone so harmless-looking. The poor girl was just lonely and in need of a friend. "It was nice to meet you, Tabitha."

Instead of returning the farewell with something equally bland, Tabitha gave her a distracted, almost worried look as she walked away. Figuring the girl was concerned about getting home late, Honor turned away. With her foot on the first step, she opened her mouth, ready to tell Seth where to meet her. A hand on her arm had her twisting around. Tabitha stood before her. "Would you like to come have dinner with my family?"

Another chill washed over her, this time even stronger.

Seth cautioned quietly in her ear, "Careful. Don't seem too eager."

"Oh, thanks," Honor said. "I didn't know what they'd be serving tonight, so I ate before I came. It was nice to meet you, though."

Tabitha looked out to the dark street and then back at Honor. "Do you mind walking me to my car? My parents made me promise not to walk by myself in the dark."

Confirmation settled into Honor's mind. "Sure. I'd be glad to."

Tabitha's expression was one of such apparent relief, for an instant Honor doubted her suspicions.

As they headed down the steps and out onto the walkway, Tabitha gushed, "Thank you so much. And then I'll drive you to your car. That way, we'll both be safe."

Honor eyed her carefully. There was almost a desperate tone in the girl's voice. Or maybe a fearful one?

"My car's down that street and around the corner. I didn't get to park as close as I wanted. It's really dark out tonight, isn't it?"

As Tabitha continued a chatty monologue, Honor heard Seth's reassuring voice in her ear: "Looks like this is it. I'm going to pass by slowly. Whatever happens, sweetheart, I'm right behind you. You need me, I can be there in seconds."

Though her adrenaline was spiking, a surge of warmth

and love went through her. She knew how difficult this must be for Seth. Despite that, his voice never changed from its even, normal tone.

She continued alongside Tabitha until the girl made an abrupt stop in a particularly dark area of the sidewalk. "Wow," Honor said, "this is a really dark place to have parked." She looked up at the dim streetlight. "I wonder why—" Sudden, acute pain speared through Honor's body. She let out a strangled cry as her legs collapsed and she dropped to the ground. As her entire body jerked with agony and every muscle spasmed out of control, her mind told her she'd been Tasered. Having no choice, she rode it out.

In the midst of the agony, she heard Seth in her ear. "What happened? It's too dark for me to see you. Do you need me to help? Talk to me if you can."

She and Seth had decided upon several keywords to relay her status—innocuous ones that no one would suspect. But damn, she couldn't remember the one to tell him she was fine, that everything was going according to plan. The pain was unbelievable. She'd been Tasered once before, but this seemed a hell of a lot worse. Dammit, what was the word?

A sting at her neck barely gave her a warning before a cloak of numbness began to wrap her in a terrifying, paralyzing embrace. Her vision blurred, tunneled toward darkness. Screams formed in her head . . . a calm voice stopped them. Told her to calm down and think. She had to alert Seth . . . *Think, Honor. Think!* Struggling with all her might, Honor stretched, searching for the correct word. What was . . . ? And then it came to her . . . so very fitting.

Praying that her brain was communicating the right one to her rapidly numbing mouth, she mumbled a garbled "Bastard."

And then darkness took her.

* * *

Gripping his Glock in one hand, Seth grabbed the door handle of the Jeep with the other, ready to push it open. Only ten yards away from her. *Ten fucking yards!* And he didn't do a damn thing but watch. Never had he felt more helpless.

Though it was dark, he could see the shadowed movement of bodies—two people, plus Honor. Unable to make out any facial features, he waited . . . listened. When Honor's fractured voice finally mumbled, "Bastard," he gripped the door handle tighter. That was their agreed-upon word . . . that meant she was fine, but dammit . . .

"Take her feet," a male voice whispered harshly. "Hurry. I think I hear someone coming." A heavy door slammed shut, and several long seconds later, a midsized RV pulled onto the road.

Every instinct screamed at Seth to go after her, to save her. He couldn't. This was what they'd hoped for, planned for. But never had he imagined the gut-wrenching horror of hearing the pain in her voice and being unable to do a damn thing.

Pushing past the fear, he followed the RV at a discreet distance as it maneuvered through the light traffic. He'd tailed enough people in his day to know how to stay out of sight. And while he followed, Seth listened intently.

"Why this one, Father? She doesn't seem our type."

"I believe you're wrong. You fought me on this, daughter. I could hear the defiance in your voice. You almost let her escape. Your insubordination won't go unpunished."

"But I—"

"Silence! We have a long trip ahead of us and there's a snowstorm headed our way. We'll talk of this when we arrive home. Secure the female."

"Yes, Father."

Father and daughter . . . holy hell.

Seth heard heavy breathing and obvious exertion. The girl, Tabitha, must be maneuvering Honor's unconscious body. A couple of minutes later, he heard the girl softly humming a familiar-sounding tune.

Grabbing his cellphone, he punched a button for McCall. The instant the LCR leader answered, Seth said, "Honor's been taken. I'm following them."

"She got her tracker on?"

"Yes."

"How'd it go down?"

"We were right. Bastard had a young woman lure her. The freaks are calling each other father and daughter. I couldn't see what was going on. From the sound of it, I think she was Tasered and then maybe drugged." Seth clenched his jaw, determined to hold it together. "Her speech indicated that she was in pain and was having trouble thinking coherently or forming words."

"An effective way to disarm anyone."

"Yeah. He's traveling north in an RV. I only got a partial plate." Seth gave the first three numbers of the tag. "Wyoming tags."

"Hopefully, he does live in the state then."

"He told his daughter they had a long drive ahead of them, so we'll see. There's some sort of dissension between them. She told him Honor didn't seem their type. He disagreed and told her she'd be punished for defying him."

McCall grunted. "Sounds like she may be a victim, too."

"Could be."

"He also said that a snowstorm was coming. Can you check that? Maybe that'll help narrow down where he's headed."

"Hold on."

His eyes on the taillights of the vehicle ahead of him, Seth did his best to focus on the job at hand. Thinking about Honor, what she'd gone through and might still have to endure, would do little good. Best he could do was remember that she was a trained professional . . . that she could take care of herself. And that very soon, both she and Kelli would be home safely.

"Damn."

McCall's growling curse gave Seth a new cause for concern. "What's wrong?"

"Entire state's under a winter storm warning, but the northern part is going to get hit the hardest. High winds and heavy snowfall."

Seth had gear in his backpack that could see him through rough weather. Would the RV be able to make it if the weather turned severe? The mental image of watching helplessly as the large vehicle slid off a mountainside chilled him. Seth tried to shrug it off. He had enough to deal with; thinking about what could go wrong wouldn't help a damn bit.

"Okay," McCall said. "I'm calling the entire team in. The jet will be on standby in Casper. The instant you can detect his destination, let me know."

"Will do."

His hands tight on the wheel, Seth stayed five car lengths behind the RV. Assuming the mic on Honor's wristwatch was still working and she was within the sound of the bastard's voice, he'd be able to hear if the man thought he was being followed.

Though the girl had said she was unconscious, he couldn't help but try to talk to her. "Honor, can you hear me?"

No response.

"Sweetheart, moan . . . make some sort of sound to let me know you're awake."

Still nothing.

They had to have knocked her out with something. A Taser gun incapacitated but shouldn't cause unconsciousness, unless it was a stronger charge than normal.

When she was conscious again, he knew, she'd tell him everything she could. They still had no idea what this bastard did with these girls. What was with his daughter saying that Honor wasn't their type? Hell, was this some sick, twisted sex game he and his daughter played with the young women?

Seth blew out a disgusted sigh. He could speculate all night and still not come up with the right answer. Thinking like the sick, perverted bastard would get him only so far.

The best he could do was be ready to go after her if this went to shit. Yes, he would save Kelli and the other girls, too, but damned if he'd sacrifice Honor to do it. If it appeared she was in mortal danger, he was going after her. No matter what.

The elevation of the road rose with each mile. Did this guy have a cabin in the mountains? Was that where he'd taken the other women?

As the RV started up a winding road, a light snow began to fall and Seth held back a little farther. This late at night, with the possibility of bad weather, there were few enough vehicles. He didn't want the guy to get even an inkling of a suspicion that he was being followed. The road was curvy, but he could see well enough.

He'd wait and hope that Honor would wake up soon. And if sugar went to shit, he prayed he'd be close enough to save her.

twenty-five

A strange lethargy pulled at Honor as she fought for consciousness. Unable to process where she was or what had happened, she remained still and quiet. Waiting. Seconds, minutes later, memory trickled like the slow drip of a faucet. A young woman . . . Tabitha. Walking beside her . . . pain . . . her body spasming out of control. Tasered.

Abducted . . . she had been taken. How odd that she was so unconcerned about it all. Shifting to a more comfortable position, she realized her hands and feet were tied together in front of her, much the way a steer is tied. Even that knowledge didn't produce the furious reaction she knew it should.

Drugged. There could be no other explanation. What should have made her spitting mad and screaming at the top of her lungs barely drew an emotional response.

Blinking, she tried to focus on what she could see. She was in a dimly lit room. Lying on her side, she could make out a bed above her, so she must be on the floor. Moving her head slightly, she spied a dresser and a mirror. Straining her neck . . . a television. She must be at someone's house.

No, not a house. She felt movement beneath her. They were traveling. An RV?

A little voice whispered: *That's how they transport them.*

Them? Who was "them"? Why did that come to her mind?

She shook her head rapidly. Comprehension at last flooded through her, and the thick haze of confusion cleared. She had been taken by the bastard. Dimly, she remembered the girl's voice . . . Tabitha's voice.

Seth! Where was he? Behind them? Yes, he would be following. She looked down at her arm and saw that her watch was still on. Praying that her earbud was still in place, she spoke softly: "Seth?"

"Honor? Thank God. Are you okay?"

"I'm fine. Are you behind us?"

"Yes. You've been traveling for several hours. Looks like he's headed up into the mountains. Right now, you're on the Cody Highway, headed toward Yellowstone."

"Did you alert Noah?"

"Yeah, he's gathering the team. As soon as the RV stops, I'll let him know where you are. How are you feeling? You were out a long time."

"I'm okay. Got Tasered, then shot up with some sort of knockout drug. I'm fine now."

"Are you tied up?"

Honor grimaced. If only he knew. "Yeah."

"As soon as you get a chance, get rid of your earbud. We can't risk him finding it."

"Will do."

"Keep your watch on at all times. Okay?"

"Yes."

"Honor, I—"

Voices and the light sound of footsteps headed her way. "Gotta go."

"Just remember, I'm close. Say the word and I'll come in and get you."

Honor closed her eyes. Yes, he would do that, but she

had to play this all the way through. Locate the girls, communicate what information she could, and then an LCR team would swoop in and rescue everyone. Now she had to survive to put that plan into place.

"You're awake."

The cold, hard tone of the childlike voice was creepy. Honor twisted her head so she could see. Continuing her role, she said, "What happened? Who are you? Why am I tied like this?"

Still so oddly innocent-looking and almost too beautiful, the girl smiled with a mocking sweetness. "You'll get your answers soon enough."

"I'm so groggy."

"Just a mild sedative, nothing that will affect you permanently. We don't approve of recreational drugs or alcohol."

"'We'?"

"Silence!" Thin, delicate-looking fingers grabbed Honor's right nipple through her clothes and twisted hard. Unable to control the gasp, she closed her eyes and fought the need to cry out. Seth didn't need to hear her pain.

Finally the pressure eased on her nipple and Honor opened her eyes to see the excitement on Tabitha's face. "You're going to be one of them, aren't you?"

"One of what?"

"The stubborn kind. Pretending you're not scared. Acting like what we do to you doesn't hurt. Those are my favorites."

"There are others?"

Going to her knees beside Honor, Tabitha whispered softly, as if sharing a secret: "I'm not allowed to cause permanent damage or severe bruises, but if you ask another question, I'll show you some methods I've learned that provide excruciating pain without leaving a mark anywhere. Want to test me?"

Honor shook her head. If asking questions would give her pain but no answers, she'd wait.

"Good girl." Tabitha rose to her feet and sat on the bed above Honor. "Now, there's something else you need to know before we get home."

Unwilling to risk another cruel pinch or worse, Honor merely looked at her.

A smug smile curved Tabitha's lips. "You're a fast learner. That will be most pleasing to your new mate. However, there is something you need to understand." She leaned down and whispered again: "Father has taken a liking to you. I don't know why. You're skinny, ugly, and have freckles all over you. Whatever the reason, know this: do not try to come between us. He may allow you in his bed and even give you his seed to bear a child, but he is mine. You'll die before I'll allow him to take you as his mate. I've done away with three of them, including my mother. One more will not make any difference to me."

Grabbing a fistful of Honor's hair, Tabitha jerked hard until her neck was painfully strained. "Do you understand?"

More chilled than she wanted to admit to herself, Honor whispered, "Yes."

Apparently satisfied that her warning had been heard and understood, Tabitha let go of Honor's hair and stood. Lifting her foot, she nudged Honor's shoulder, causing her to roll over onto her back. "Get used to being on your back, whore."

Honor watched as Tabitha straightened her dress, finger-combed her hair, and smiled into the mirror as though practicing. Then she turned and strolled out of the room.

That bitch had hurt Honor. He'd heard everything. The gasp had been telling . . . the silence even more so.

And he knew the reason she'd held back. Honor didn't want him to know she was suffering. They'd agreed that unless she was in imminent danger, he wouldn't come in after her. And though he'd known he would have to listen to shit that was going to drive him crazy, damned if he wanted her to hold back her need to scream if necessary.

Well aware that speaking too loudly with Tabitha so close would be dangerous, Seth kept his voice low and even. "You okay?"

"I'm fine."

"Honor, do not hold back for me."

Her soft voice held a trace of amusement. "Trust you to read my mind, Cavanaugh."

Not feeling the slightest bit humorous, he said, "Just don't. Okay? You hurt, you scream. Burst the bitch's eardrums. Understand?"

"Okay."

Breathing only slightly more easily, he asked, "I'm assuming she's gone?"

"Yes."

"Let's go over what she said."

"She mentioned there were others." The excitement in her voice warmed him. That was so like Honor. "That means the girls are most likely alive."

"That's what I'm thinking. And she said something about mates."

"You think that's why he's taking the girls?"

"Could be. Which means there's going to be more than just Tabitha and her father to deal with. I'll alert McCall . . . make sure he brings enough people." And because it was an additional complication, he added, "Sounds like the creep's got the hots for you."

"And his daughter doesn't like it. Apparently they have some sort of sexual relationship going."

Deviant minds and sick, sadistic behavior had long

since stopped surprising him, but he had to admit that this seemed sicker than most. "Watch your back. She's not going to tolerate him giving you attention."

"I can handle her . . . don't worry. So, where are we now?"

"Still on Cody Highway."

"Okay, I'll—" She stopped abruptly.

Seth tensed. Had something happened? Had he lost contact with her?

"Gotta go. Something's up."

With his eyes trained on the RV far ahead of him, he saw the brake lights come on. "Looks like he's about to stop." And because he couldn't not say something, he added, "Don't do anything foolish, Honor. Promise me."

"We make a good team, Cavanaugh. I'm not going to screw that up now."

The lump in his throat developed quickly. His bright, courageous Honor. He might never have the future he'd once fantasized about with this beautiful woman, but one thing he could guarantee: she would live through this mission. No matter what he had to do, Honor would survive.

twenty-six

It was with immense satisfaction and a sense of peace that Alden drove into the storage container that housed the RV through the winter. Shifting into park, he sprawled in his seat and breathed out a long sigh of relief. Tranquillity was only about thirty miles away. Soon they'd be going through her gates, secure and safe from the outside world. He and his people would stay nestled together for months, content with the paradise he had created for them.

Hunting season was now over. The woman he'd found was as unique as a mountain orchid. A couple of men would no doubt be disappointed that they wouldn't have the chance to bid for her, and Brother Baker would have to make do with the stable girls for one more year. Their disappointment was nothing. He was their leader; his happiness meant much more than any of theirs. They knew this.

His daughter, on the other hand, was a different matter. Even though she understood that his happiness should always be her ultimate goal, apparently she needed a stern reminder. Her defiance when he'd told her to bring the woman to him wasn't something he would tolerate. How dare she not want him to have what he desired.

Though he knew he should be weary from such a long trip with no respite, the excitement spiraling through him prevented true exhaustion. The woman who called herself Maggie had kept his adrenaline going, and now his blood felt like it was on fire. With every hour that had passed, his anticipation had built. Now he was ready to see, up close and personal, the uniqueness that had drawn him to his future bride.

He stood and stretched his big body, wincing as his muscles protested and his bones popped. A long soak in his hot tub would ease the aches. And Tabitha would take care of another ache. Normally he would reward her with a job well done by allowing her pleasure. This time, he would be the only one to achieve satisfaction. Her punishment needed to be swift. The next few days would be critical as he oriented his new addition. And then for months, all of his time would be spent initiating the four new women to their future life.

"She's ready, Father."

Alden eyed his daughter suspiciously, noting that the mutinous tone was back in her voice. "You gave her just enough to knock her out for about an hour. Correct?"

Blue eyes skittered away as she said, "I didn't know you wanted her awake so soon."

"Daughter, I have reached the end of my patience. How long will she be unconscious?"

"Only a few hours. Enough time to get home and allow you rest before you begin the grueling days ahead of you." She blinked innocently up at him. "I was only thinking of you."

He continued his perusal of his daughter for several long seconds. Tabitha's defiance was getting out of hand, making him wonder if her punishment should be more severe than he'd first considered. She knew he was displeased. However, instead of feeling distressed, she was aroused by his anger. He could see the tight, hard peaks of her nipples through the material of her dress, and her eyes glittered with a hot, greedy light he often saw seconds before they coupled.

Alden made a decision that would be painful for them both. However, he had no choice. "You will not share my bed for at least a month."

Her eyes wide with shock, she fell to her knees. "Father, I'm sorry. I won't defy you again. Please don't deny your pleasure on my account."

"I will be finding pleasure. You can be assured of that." He felt not the slightest remorse as he headed to the bedroom, where the woman lay. "Start the Hummer. I'll bring the woman."

Leaving a desolate Tabitha to prepare for the last leg of the journey, Alden entered the bedroom and stood, transfixed, over his new mate. To make carrying her easier, his daughter had untied her. Now she lay unconscious and vulnerable on the bed. Desire pulsed through him, and it was all he could do not to strip her here and wake her with a long, hard ride. He wouldn't. There were rules and rituals. He had created them as safeguards against the lust women deliberately incited in men. Ignoring his own rules just because this woman teased him like no others would make him appear weak.

"The vehicle is ready." The husky tone in Tabitha's voice told him she'd been weeping piteously. That pleased him.

He scooped the lovely woman into his arms and carried her from the bedroom. She mumbled something he couldn't make out. Not that it mattered. Every thought, word, and action would soon be given to her. Her only desire and wish would be for his comfort, pleasure, and happiness.

He couldn't wait to get started on training her for her new life.

As her eyes blinked open this time, Honor woke up angry. Tabitha had jammed a needle into her neck with the glee of the truly sadistic. Odd: she remembered waking earlier with a nice, lethargic buzz. Not so now. She hurt everywhere, her lips were dry, her tongue felt swollen and parched from lack of moisture . . . and she badly needed to go to the bathroom. Her arms were above her head and tied to something she couldn't see. Her legs were bound together at the ankles.

She moved her head left and right, realizing that she was in a different location. Apparently that was the reason she'd been knocked out again. The room was small and, with only one overhead bulb turned on, dimly lit. No window; the walls were pale-cream-colored—squinting, she peered closer—cement blocks.

Seth was probably going crazy not knowing what had happened to her. She glanced up at her arm, relieved to see that her watch was still intact. What about her earbud? She hadn't been able to get rid of it. Had they found it?

Figuring there was a camera somewhere, Honor turned her face against her arm to hide her mouth "Seth?" she said urgently.

No answer. Her heart pounding with dread, she spoke again, this time louder: "Seth, can you hear me?"

Still no answer. Crap. Did that mean they'd found the earpiece? Or had it fallen out? If they'd found it, she'd just tell them she was hearing-impaired and the earbud was a device to assist her.

Even though she could no longer hear Seth's voice, she knew he was listening. She had to give him as much information as she could—though, admittedly, she didn't know much more than she had before. Dammit, she had to make sure she stayed conscious.

"I've lost my earbud, so I can't hear you. I'm all right. They drugged me again. I'm in a room, almost like a cell. I'm tied to a bed. There are no windows." She closed her eyes and concentrated on what she could hear. *Nothing*. Where were the missing girls? Were they close?

"I can't hear anything. It's dead silent. I'm going to call out and see if anyone answers."

She shouted, "Can anyone hear me? Is anyone there?"

No answer . . . just the same eerie quiet.

Honor blew out a resigned sigh. If the girls were close, she would love to give them some hope and reassurance. However, since she could hear nothing, chances were, they couldn't hear her, either.

Turning her face against her arm again, she said, "I can't hear anything, so there's no way for me to know if the other girls are close. I know you want to come in, but you have to wait. Until I know where they are, there's no point in blowing our cover. If they're here, we could be putting their lives in danger even more. If I think you need to come in, I'll tell you."

A key jiggling in the lock told her someone was coming. "Someone's at the door."

Honor held her breath as the door opened and a large man entered. Middle-aged, maybe early fifties, salt-and-pepper hair, sherry-brown eyes, and an oddly ingratiating expression on his hard, weathered face.

"Welcome to my home, Maggie."

"Who are you?"

"My name is Alden Pike." He sat beside her on the bed and patted her cheek. "Alden means 'old friend.' Did you know that? Very soon, we'll be the very best of friends." Apparently not expecting a response, he continued: "You may call me Brother Alden. Later, when we know each other much better, we'll discuss a different title."

"Why am I here? What's going on?"

"I know you're afraid, but you have no cause to be. I mean you no harm. You're in a new home now, filled with people who will love and care for you." He smiled again and added, "You're in Tranquillity."

"But . . . why?"

"My daughter described you to me. I sensed your deep loneliness. Your need of a place to belong. A people you can belong to. In Tranquillity, you'll find everything you've ever dreamed of and you'll never want for anything ever again. I'll make sure of it."

"But what if I don't like it here?"

"You will, my dear. I promise you that. In Tranquillity, you'll have everything you could desire."

"But I'm a student. I have to go back for my classes."

"We have schools here. Excellent teachers. You'll learn everything you need to know. You'll have a family, friends. Everything you could want."

Honor was fast getting the picture of why'd she'd been taken. And she could only assume the other girls had been taken for a similar reason. Part of her felt enormous relief. If they'd been brought here, then they should still be alive. Another part was furious that this creep believed he had the right to kidnap people and impose his will. She looked forward to wiping that smug smile off of his face.

"But I don't know what it looks like here. How will I know if I like it?"

Pike's face brightened. Apparently she'd said the right thing.

"Let me take you around, show you your new home."

Twisting her head, she looked up toward the ties on her wrists and tugged. "Why do I have to be tied?"

"Because I was afraid you'd try to run away and become lost. You're far up in the wilds now, and it's bitter cold. If you wandered off, we'd never find you. You would freeze to death or be eaten by bears. It's for your protection."

"If I promise not to run, will you take the ties off?"

"Of course I will. I want you to feel at home here."

"May I go to the bathroom?"

"Absolutely." He stood and drew out a knife, cutting the ties at her hands and then her feet. Honor sat up slowly, not wanting to startle him and make him think she would try to make a run for it.

"Let me help you up." A giant hand, almost twice the size of hers, was presented to her.

Maintaining an "I'm too stupid to know you're a perverted freak" expression on her face, she placed her hand in his and allowed him to pull her up.

Honor rarely felt at a disadvantage. She was above average height, strong, and well trained in self-defense. She had taken down large men before. However, not only was Alden Pike tall and thick, but she could feel the strength in him. It was going to take stealth to bring down this gorilla. That or a gun.

As he led her out of the room, Honor tried as inconspicuously as possible to look around. Ten doors in the hallway, five on each side. They looked identical to what she had just left. Was each one filled with a young, terrified woman?

He opened a door that led to another, similar room. Instead of a bed, it held a toilet and a sink. Thankful that relief was in sight, she walked inside and the door was shut behind her.

"I'm right here, waiting on you."

Not caring where he went as long as she was left alone, Honor hurriedly took care of personal matters, feeling enormous relief. Standing at the sink, she washed her hands thoroughly and then cupped her hands to hold water and drank her fill. She rinsed her face to erase the remaining grogginess and dried her hands on the paper towels beside the sink. Finally she felt almost human.

Holding the watch to her mouth so she wouldn't have to talk as loud, she said, "I've seen ten doors, similar to what I just left. The girls could be there, but I still didn't hear anyone. Will let you know as soon as I learn something."

She took a step to the door and was startled when Pike pushed it open.

"You were taking too long, my sweet. We have rules everyone must abide by, so this will be a good opportunity to let you know. Only five minutes are allowed for a bathroom break."

As if a time limit on a bathroom visit was a totally acceptable concept, Honor nodded her understanding and followed him out the door.

He held out his hand again and gave her another oddly kind but creepy smile. "Come, let me show you your new home."

Seth's breath created puffy clouds as he leaned against a tree for a quick rest. He'd parked the Wrangler and half-run, half-climbed the last mile. The terrain had gotten steeper with each step. Wouldn't have taken near as long to get here, but he'd had to hoist on his gear and then spend time hiding the SUV in the woods, covering it with shrubbery. Having someone notice it would cause suspicion they couldn't afford.

An hour ago, he'd watched a large, middle-aged man load an unconscious Honor into a Hummer. The girl, Tabitha, had calmly gotten into the passenger seat, acting as if it was an everyday occurrence to have kidnapped a woman. Hell of it was, for them, it *was* a common occurrence.

The only bright spot, and he was digging deep to find it, was that after the Hummer had taken off, Seth had driven slowly by and had seen something glistening on the ground. Honor's earpiece. He'd stopped and grabbed the thing. Though it'd been a small worry—they'd discussed explaining it away by saying she had a hearing impediment—at least now she didn't have to think about it.

The road the Hummer had taken had been a carved-out path in the midst of wilderness, but easy to follow. Now Seth was about three hundred yards from a giant iron-and-brick gate. Though he hadn't seen the vehicle go inside, the path it had taken dead-ended at the gate.

Before the RV had turned off Cody Highway, he'd made another call to McCall to give an update on the location. An LCR team would arrive in a few hours. While he waited, he planned to scout out the area. If nothing else, that would keep him from going crazy, thinking about what Honor was going through.

After they'd started off in the Hummer, there had been very little back-and-forth conversation between the father and daughter. Whenever the bastard did say something, it had been terse and his daughter's response had always been a "Yes, Father."

She might be acting like the submissive now, but Tabitha was no victim. Maybe she had been originally, but no more. The conversation she'd had with Honor and her cruelty had revealed that she was totally on board with what her father was doing. Hell, what *she* was doing.

Several hours passed before he heard from Honor again. Waiting in silence was almost as bad as hearing Honor's pain. Then, finally, he'd heard the sweetest sound of all—Honor's voice reassuring him that she was okay.

Then the man had arrived. He'd introduced himself as Alden Pike, and from the sounds of it, he was more than enamored of Honor. Being on the sick bastard's good side might not necessarily be a good thing.

Either way, Seth could do nothing until Honor confirmed their suspicions. Going in without knowing exactly where the girls were would be pointless. It could also get Honor or one of the girls hurt. He'd wait and watch. He trusted Honor.

Staying busy while Honor was in the midst of danger was the only way to keep his sanity. He dropped his backpack onto the ground and went to work rechecking weapons and organizing explosives. The methodical routine soothed him. Once he finished, he'd do a search of the area. By the time Noah and his team arrived, he would have all the knowledge he'd need to infiltrate the compound.

With the sounds of Honor's innocent questions and Alden Pike's creepy answers in his ear, Seth continued his task. And then, as the tour of what Pike called her "new home" began, Seth listened with growing alarm.

As Alden led the woman out of the training building and into the bright new world to which she would soon belong, he took a long breath of cold air and felt revitalized and as youthful as a teenager. Long past the days of romanticisms, he couldn't help but feel that a certain kind of magic had brought them together. He couldn't think of a woman better suited for him than this girl.

She was taller than average, so he didn't tower over her as much as he did with some of the other women. Her strawberry-blond hair was thick and shiny, and hung past her shoulders like smooth silk. She wore no makeup and wasn't flashy the way so many girls her age tried to be. When he'd carried her inside last night, he'd gotten a glimpse of her creamy skin under her shirt. Not only was her face covered in delightful freckles, but apparently her entire body had them as well. He couldn't wait to discover each and every one.

Her demeanor was perfect, too—timid and shy, with just the right amount of respectful curiosity.

"There's snow everywhere. Did it snow while I was sleeping?"

Disappointed that her first reaction to the beauty before her was related to the weather, he said, "Yes, we had several inches of snow come through overnight."

Maybe the girl was a little slower than he'd first thought. Why wasn't she exclaiming over her new home? "What do you think about Tranquillity?"

She gave a small jerk, and then the brilliance of her smile made him forget his earlier irritation. "It's beautiful . . . almost like a fairy tale. And it's so large, too." Green eyes blinked up at him with a sweet innocence. "How many people live here?"

With pride, Alden looked around. They stood on the main road, in view of most of the public buildings. The houses he'd allowed the older married members to have were on another, smaller street.

"We have over one hundred residents now."

"Where did they come from?"

He frowned down at her. "What do you mean?"

Her slender shoulders lifted in a shrug. "I just wondered if they were all related to you in some way."

"Not by blood. Only by loyalty and a shared belief system."

"What belief is that?"

Taking her hand, he led her down the main street. "You'll soon learn about our beliefs. You'll be able to quote each one from memory. But for now, let me show you around."

Dammit, she had almost blown everything with her initial reaction, but the snow had stunned her. Had Seth had difficulty following them? Was he okay? And what about the rest of the LCR team? Had the weather slowed them down? Were they outside, just waiting for her word to come in, or were they hundreds of miles away?

She shook herself from her momentary panic. All of that had to be put aside. Playing the wide-eyed, clueless innocent would take all of her concentration. She had to trust Seth and her team. They would get here . . . she had to believe that.

Fortunately, Honor didn't have to feign interest in her surroundings. She was fascinated to learn that this community had been here for so long, hidden away from the authorities and able to get away with everything.

"How long has Tranquillity existed?"

She knew she was going to have to intersperse her probing questions with wide-eyed, awed remarks that would feed Pike's massive ego.

"Almost fifteen years."

She gasped, again not having to fake her response. Had he been kidnapping women since then? And was it only women he had abducted? "All of you have been here for fifteen years?"

His hearty laugh, filled with condescension, grated on her nerves. "No, no. We've grown over the years. I started our community in another state, with just a few people." He stood in front of a large, one-story brick-and-aluminum building that resembled a warehouse. "This is our community sleeping area. Our unattached men and newly married couples live here."

"If I stay here, is this where I'll live?"

With a grin that told her there was no "if" to her staying here, he shook his head. "You'll be given a very special place to live."

She didn't have to ask any more about that. The lascivious looks he'd been shooting her told their own story. Did he use the other girls the same way? Keep each as his until he replaced her with another?

No, that didn't track with what Tabitha had revealed last night. She'd said her father had taken a particular interest in her. Gee, didn't she feel lucky?

"Where do the unattached females live?"

Another smug smile lifted his thin lips. "That's the beauty of Tranquillity. There are no unattached females. That's why our women are so happy and satisfied."

A chill zipped up her spine. It was as she and Seth had discussed yesterday. He abducted women and brought them here as brides for the male members of the community.

"So Tabitha is married, too?"

The smile disappeared. "Tabitha is attached." He pointed to another building, this one almost quaint-looking, like a small church. "This is our schoolhouse. Training begins very early for our little ones."

Holy hell. Honor swallowed the bile that shot up her throat. Of course they'd want to impregnate the women. Not only would this bastard want to increase his numbers, but getting their captives pregnant would provide extra incentive for the women to stay here. Few women would try to escape if it meant leaving their children behind.

Working harder this time, Honor exclaimed her delight. "Oh, I love children. How many are here?"

He beamed down at her, and bile surged up her throat again. That look was one of pure delight, and the gleam in his eyes told her that he clearly intended that she have his children. *Over your dead body, asshole.* And she meant that quite literally.

"Right now, we have nine children under the age of ten and five teenagers. However, that will soon change."

"Really?"

"Seven of our women are pregnant."

Great. Children and pregnant women. Storming the

compound had been her initial thought. Now that wasn't going to be possible. A dozen or more LCR operatives coming in with guns a-blazing would endanger the innocents. Their first priority was rescue, which meant stealth would have to be used.

Even though she knew Seth was hearing all of this, she nevertheless had to reinforce that message. "Protecting the children and the pregnant women is of utmost importance," she noted.

Pike gave her an odd look. "What makes you say that?"

"Because they are the future of Tranquillity. Are they not?"

Surprising the hell out of her, he picked her up and whirled her around. "I knew the moment I saw you that you were the one."

Wishing with all her might to be able to kick him deep in the balls for even daring to touch her, she gave him another shy smile. "Really?"

With her feet back on firm ground, Pike continued that sickly adoring look. "You'll be held in esteem over all the other women."

Honor favored him with what she hoped was an appropriately grateful look and glanced around again. Spotting what seemed to be a large structure up above the community, she pointed to it. "What's that?"

"That's where I live. Where you'll live, too."

"Really?" she breathed. "It looks so grand."

"We'll have dinner there tonight and I'll show you around. After your training is complete, you'll come live there with me."

"Training?"

"Yes, all new members must be trained in the proper laws and procedures."

"How long will that take?"

"It depends." Eyes that had been gleaming with approval and desire suddenly turned cold. "Those who resist learning don't fare well here in Tranquillity. You must remember this."

She nodded hesitantly and said, "Thank you, Brother Alden."

As if he'd never issued that chilling warning, he took her hand and said, "Come. There's more to see on the next street."

Knowing she looked like the most curious of sight-seers, Honor twisted her head left and right, taking in all the different buildings that made up the community of Tranquillity. All the questions she asked were eagerly answered by Pike, who seemed so incredibly thrilled with her questions, she began to see the sick mind that existed underneath that evil. She didn't bother to ask herself which had come first. Either way, the man's atrocious community had to be destroyed.

She stopped in the middle of the intersection. On one side stood a row of small, charming houses. On the other side, isolated from the rest of the community, was another large building that also resembled a warehouse. "Oh, what's that building over there?"

"A place where our unattached males can enjoy companionship until their mates arrive."

So apparently Tranquillity had its very own red-light district. Had these women been abducted, too? Of course they had. How many women would willingly lock themselves away inside a community that apparently believed women were here to serve men in whatever capacity the men wanted?

Covering her disgust with a veil of stupidity, she pointed to the houses on the other side of the intersection. "Who lives in those houses?"

"Our older, married members move into the homes just before their women are ready to bear children." He smiled down at her. "Our women are supremely happy.

Talk to any of them and they'll all tell you the same thing. That's why we call it Tranquillity. It's the way the world was meant to be."

Though she knew that Pike was telling her these things to convince her of the community's goodness, she saw behind his words. The man might be able to sell others this bill of goods, but he had his own private agenda. His bullshit about "the way the world was meant to be" was nothing more than a ruse. The bastard had set himself up a little kingdom with his own community of slaves, along with a harem and a nice little breeding farm, too.

She gestured at a man standing on a high platform on one wall, holding a high-powered rifle. "What's he doing?"

"He's there for our protection. Tranquillity is a special place and must be guarded and protected at all costs."

As if in awe of the beauty that surrounded her, Honor turned in a circle and glanced around the perimeter. Though they were a distance away, she could just make out the other armed guards, one at each corner. When rescue did arrive, these men would have to be neutralized, and it would have to be done quietly. Just because the few people she'd seen on the streets had looked harmless, that didn't mean there weren't more men on the lookout. That also increased her concern for the women and children. Would Pike's men turn their guns on them? Yet another reason stealth would have to be used. This crazy freak believed he owned this community and its inhabitants. What would keep him from killing them if he felt threatened?

Pike grabbed her arm and pulled her close. "Come. We'll have a bite to eat at our dining hall. You'll get to see several of our members there. And tonight, you'll be treated to an extraordinary gift."

Her heart thudded with dread. "A gift?"

"Yes, dining alone with me is an honor few are granted."

The dread increased. Dinner alone with him she could handle. Anything else and the man was in for a seriously painful surprise.

twenty-seven

Honor opened her eyes and allowed her fogged brain to catch up. She hadn't thought she'd be able to sleep, but she had managed a few dreamless hours. Yesterday's ordeals had apparently exhausted her reserves.

Sitting up on the small cot, she put a pillow behind her head and gazed around at the blank walls of her cell. Since she was quite sure there was a camera hidden somewhere, she'd taken care not to seem too curious about how to escape. Pretending to be content to be locked up was ludicrous, but it was what Pike seemed to expect, so she would continue until she was ready to make her move.

The room was a small square space, made completely of cinder blocks. An explosive could crumble it in seconds. The stainless-steel door, however, would be difficult to penetrate. The thing looked more like a refrigerator door than anything else. There was no escaping this place until she was let out of it. Though she hated waiting for that, after last night's conversation with the man, she figured something would be happening soon.

After she had been closed in for the night and all the overhead lights turned off, she had spent over an hour with her head under her pillow, whispering to Seth. Though she'd known he'd heard every word Pike had spouted, she'd described in detail everything she had seen. When Seth and LCR came in, they would know as much as she did.

Yesterday had been enlightening, giving her and Seth an opportunity to see what they faced. During lunch at the dining hall, she'd noticed that there were only men at the tables. The occasional woman did pass by, but apparently only to see to a man's needs. At first, a few curious looks had been thrown her way, but once the men saw Pike's hand on her elbow, his possession clear, they quickly glanced away and never looked again. Not one person spoke to them.

After lunch, they'd walked down the main road again. Pike had pointed out a small general store, a library he'd described as having only "the right kinds of books," whatever the hell that meant, and a building he said housed their "healer." When she'd inquired if the man was a licensed doctor, he'd frowned, saying, "That's nothing to concern yourself with."

She'd seen several women on their walk, all of them dressed modestly in long corduroy dresses and with pleasant expressions on their faces. None of them seemed desperate or anxious to escape. In fact, they looked too damn happy. Their appearance had given her pause. Were some of them here because they wanted to be?

When Pike had received a call on his cellphone he'd said he had to take, Honor had gotten an answer to her question. An answer that had left her chilled to the bone.

Looking a bit put out at the unexpected interruption in their tour, Pike had glanced around and spotted two women sitting on a park bench at a small play area. Three young children were in front of them, having fun in the snow. He'd guided Honor to the women and said, "Sisters Sharon and Linda, would you two be so kind as to visit with our newest member while I take this call?"

The women, both in their early twenties, had shot to their feet, their expressions of reverence sickening. Having Pike talk to them was apparently seen as a rare privilege. After he'd walked away, she'd soon learned why they'd acted enamored. For at least half an hour, Honor had listened while the women extolled Alden Pike's virtues and how much they loved living in Tranquillity. When she'd asked where they were from, both had answered with wide-eyed sincerity and identical words: "We lived nowhere before Tranquillity."

By the time Pike had returned for her, she'd concluded that brainwashing was the only explanation. She'd seen no evil, no subterfuge in their answers. The women truly believed all the crap they'd told her because that's what they'd been conditioned to believe.

On the surface, if she'd known nothing else about this community, she could almost have convinced herself she was visiting some kind of extreme religious cult. Only problem was, she *had* seen beneath that surface. "Extreme" was a good word for this place, but whatever their belief system, God had no part in it.

Last night at dinner, Pike had treated her with an odd, pseudorespect. He'd never touched her inappropriately or said anything overtly sexual . . . for which she was extremely grateful. The man's attitude had been more that of a superior being condescending to spend time with an underling. Though repugnant, his narcissism had been reassuring. An ego that huge would never suspect an infiltration of his kingdom. She looked forward to showing the arrogant asshole how very fallible he was.

By worldly standards, his home was upper-middle-class modest. Compared to the small houses of his followers, it was palatial. He made no attempt to hide the immense pride he felt in what he had accomplished. And though it was nauseating, she had to admit to being impressed with what he'd managed to get away with for so long. He had his very own kingdom, with people falling all over themselves to please him. Convincing one person to do something against their will could be difficult; doing that with dozens of people and being able to maintain that power and control was phenomenal. Scary as hell, too.

A middle-aged blank-faced woman who never made a sound had served a surprisingly nutritious dinner of grilled trout, brown rice, and steamed vegetables. During their meal, Pike had asked her no questions, making it obvious that her past didn't matter. No doubt because he intended for her to forget that past. Instead, he had continued his diatribe about the benefits of living in Tranquillity . . . a sales job she had pretended to buy.

After showing her around his backyard, which included a swimming pool and a Jacuzzi, along with a breathtaking view, Pike had escorted her back down the hill to her small cell. Before locking her inside, he'd given her another one of those smiles that creeped her out, along with a warning: "Training begins tomorrow. Remember all you've seen, especially tonight. The more cooperative you are with your training, the faster you'll be able to enjoy all the luxuries I'm willing to give you."

What the hell that training would include, she didn't know. She'd yet to see any of the girls they were looking for. A couple of times, she thought she'd glimpsed a familiar-looking face, but Honor wondered if that was wishful thinking on her part.

She hadn't been tied down last night, so apparently she had convinced him that she wasn't a flight risk. That one blessing of not being restrained was severely diminished by what she'd found in the corner after she'd been locked in for the night: a plastic bucket. This was apparently for toilet purposes, since toilet paper had been placed beside the bucket. As much as she'd hated to use it, she'd had no choice. The act was demeaning, which was exactly what, she knew, it was meant to be. What else did he have in store?

A sound outside alerted her that someone was coming. Was her "training" about to commence? Tense with equal parts anticipation and dread, Honor waited. A slot at the bottom of the door opened and a tray appeared. Instead of her training, breakfast had arrived.

Honor stood and picked up the tray of cold cereal, milk, and hot tea. She didn't hesitate to eat the meal. She'd already been drugged a couple of times. If Pike wanted her unconscious again, the sadistic Tabitha would likely be happy to jab another needle into her neck.

Just as she took her first bite of cereal, a creaking sound caught her attention, alerting her that she was being given another surprise. Honor looked down at the slot and watched as a toothbrush, toothpaste, and a glass of water appeared. So Pike encouraged good dental hygiene in his slaves. *How thoughtful.*

Honor finished her cereal and tea and then retrieved the toothpaste and toothbrush. Resenting the inhumane treatment would do no good. She was sure he intended much worse. So she took a few moments to appreciate the small convenience and relished the feeling of a clean, fresh mouth.

Breakfast and teeth cleaning out of the way, Honor sat down to wait. While eating her cereal, she'd noticed a minuscule black dot in a corner of the ceiling. Though she couldn't get too close since she didn't want Pike to think she was becoming suspicious, she was almost sure it was a camera.

So instead of pacing around the room or looking for an escape, she sat on the bed and acted as if being held captive by some sort of maniac was just where she wanted to be. Sure, a normal person would have put up resistance, but so far, Pike seemed to be buying her act. If he thought she would be an easy one to "bring over" or whatever the hell he called it—maybe he'd let his guard down sooner.

On edge to get this thing started, Honor stared hard at the solid steel door, willing it to open. Finally a sound outside had her attention. Was this it? The door opened and two women and a man entered. The tall, almost emaciated-looking man was in his mid-sixties, wore glasses, and had deep furrows on his forehead. He gave her a cold, clearly sadistic up-and-down glance. "Strip."

Honor stood. Playing this thing out was going to take every bit of the courage she had and then some. Noticing her hesitation, the women who'd come in with the man began to tug on her clothes. Jerking away from them, she snapped, "I can do it."

She took everything off, but she'd fight them to the death before she removed her watch. Right now, that was her only connection with Seth and freedom. Damned if she'd give that up.

Thankfully, no one seemed to care that she'd retained it. The man nodded at the bed. "Sit."

Honor sat down and watched in surprise as he withdrew a stethoscope from his pocket and approached her.

"What are you doing?"

"Nothing more than a physical exam. We like to make sure everyone in our community is well."

Several sarcastic responses came to mind, but Honor held them back. Staring straight ahead, she submitted to a humiliatingly thorough exam—one that included checking her teeth and gums.

Half an hour later, the man stood back and gave a satisfactory nod. "You're in excellent health. Brother Alden will be most pleased."

He turned and went out the door. The two women, who'd never said a word during the entire ordeal, followed him. One of them carried her clothes.

"Wait. Let me have my clothes back."

As if they didn't hear her, they closed the door behind themselves, and she heard the lock click again. Hell, what next?

She didn't have to wait long to find out. The lights went off, creating an inky blackness her eyes couldn't penetrate. Then Alden Pike's voice boomed into the room:

"The time has come for you to learn our ways. You will memorize our mantra and recite it repeatedly until it is ingrained so deeply inside you that it is a part of who you are. The laws and mandates of Tranquillity will be your companion, your ally, and your security.

"Welcome to your destiny."

Honor took a breath. Okay, so this was the true beginning of her indoctrination. Knowing she was strong enough to resist the insanity the bastard was about to enforce didn't negate her dread. Though the room was dark, Honor closed her eyes and thought about Seth. About the last time they'd made love. Keeping him at the forefront, she knew without a doubt, she could survive whatever these monsters threw at her.

Seth would be her light in the darkness.

twenty-eight

Pacing back and forth, every muscle screaming with tension, Seth listened to Alden Pike's insane manifesto. As the man bellowed his beliefs, Seth pictured a naked, vulnerable Honor sitting in a small, cold room having to endure his teachings.

He told himself she was a strong woman. Never had he known anyone more grounded or stable. He told himself she could withstand anything Pike could dish out. Seth believed that. What he was having trouble dealing with was listening as Honor endured.

The information she had unearthed yesterday had been remarkably revealing, giving them insight into not only Pike's twisted mind but also what his victims had been through. Had Kelli gone through the same thing? If so, how had she fared? She was twenty years old and still trying to find herself. What kind of effect would this maniac's brainwashing have on a young, impressionable woman? He knew the answer to that question. The young women Honor had talked to yesterday had given a good indication of what Pike's victims became. Was Kelli there yet? Would she be able to recover and return to the innocent young woman he remembered?

Yesterday, Seth had done a thorough search of the area. Situated between two large hills, Tranquillity was a formidable fortress. The armed guards had changed shifts at midnight. And this morning, at eight sharp, they'd changed again. With LCR's help, they should be easy to take out.

McCall, Livingston, and Thorne would be here soon. The decision had been made for the rest of the team to wait a couple of miles away. When Honor signaled for them to come in, he and the three men would go in as quietly as possible. Any other way could get someone killed.

After listening to the tour Honor had been subjected to, he'd called McCall again. Learning that many, if not all of the women had been abducted wasn't that big of a surprise. And it didn't surprise him that several of those women were pregnant or that there were children in the community. It did ramp up his concern, though. As much as he'd like to go in like gangbusters with the strength of dozens of LCR operatives behind him, the risk was too great. Silent stealth was the only way to ensure the safety of the innocents.

The light crunch of leaves had Seth whirling around. McCall, Thorne, and Livingston stood about five yards behind him. Hell, either he was getting rusty or these men could move in like fog. All three were dressed in full camouflage, and their serious, determined faces reflected Seth's own feelings.

"What's happened?" McCall asked.

"You bring a radio receiver?"

Dropping a bag to the ground, McCall nodded. "Yeah, it's designed to pick up Honor's mic."

"Get it out. Honor's training has begun."

The grim expression on McCall's face echoed Seth's terse words. Retrieving the radio, he adjusted the setting, and soon all four men were listening to Pike's tirade.

Noah propped the radio against a rock, and the men began to unpack their gear. McCall cast an approving eye at the weapons lying on a sheet of canvas—weapons Seth had checked and rechecked, all in an effort to keep himself busy. "Looks like you came prepared. We'll have plenty of firepower. Doubt we'll be able to use much."

Seth gave a grim nod.

Pulling his backpack from his shoulders, McCall said, "Any new information?"

"Not really. Breakfast was delivered to her this morning, and then some man I think Pike calls 'the healer' gave her a physical examination. The man said Pike would be happy about her physical health. It's clear the bastard intends to keep her for himself."

"And still no sounds indicating that the other girls are there?" Livingston asked.

"Not yet. She's in a place with several small rooms, so they could be there and unconscious." Seth shrugged. "Or they might be in another building."

"So what's the plan?" Thorne asked. "We going in?"

McCall shook his head. "We wait. There's no point in going in until we know exactly where the girls are. If anyone gets the idea that Honor isn't one of their victims, we'll be placing her and the others in even more danger."

As much as he hated this plan, Seth had to agree. "Honor will alert us as soon as she sees one of the girls."

"What if she doesn't see anyone?" Thorne said.

That was the easiest answer of all. "We go in and save Honor."

"How long do we wait?"

"We play it by ear," McCall said. "Let Honor make the call. If she's in danger or can't handle this part of the training anymore, she'll let us know."

"Any idea what other kind of training this guy was talking about?" Livingston asked.

Seth shook his head. He didn't want to speculate out loud, but he'd spent a sleepless night thinking about just that. Anticipating what a sadistic psycho would do was difficult.

The men fell silent, listening as Pike continued his insane ravings. Had the volume been turned up? It seemed the man's voice had gotten louder and harsher. Though he had seen Pike only from a distance when the man had carried an unconscious Honor to the Hummer, Seth could imagine the bastard standing before a microphone, his eyes gleaming with an unholy excitement, spittle on his lips . . . maybe even standing and pacing as his disturbed brain issued its rules and regulations to his "people."

His gut twisting into knots, Seth turned away from the too shrewd eyes of the LCR men. Though Honor couldn't hear him, he closed his eyes and spoke softly to her anyway: "Be strong, sweetheart."

"Father, may I approach you?"

Alden looked up from his account books. He had much to do this morning. Training had already begun for his woman. He had stayed for a few minutes to watch the beginning . . . he loved to see the initial reaction. It was almost always one of sheer panic, at least at first—an "Oh shit, what have I gotten myself into" moment.

As time went on, myriad expressions would cross their faces. Pain, confusion, anger, despair, and then that edge-of-insanity moment when each one finally accepted the inevitable. That look always gave him the biggest rush of all.

Once that initial phase had passed, it would be time to step up the game. A joint orientation to give the girls a chance to not only see one another but to observe how the others reacted. Sometimes their fear for the other girls was as fulfilling as their own.

The group training also showed him each girl's threshold, both physically and mentally. After he learned that, he would have little free time until he was able to gauge each individual's breaking point. Once that was determined, he'd structure a training session based on their needs. After that was decided, Tabitha would assist him. But until then, the time-consuming, backbreaking, yet admittedly enjoyable work was all his.

"What is it, daughter?"

He saw Tabitha move toward him until he said the last word. When he referred to her as "daughter," it was an indication of displeasure. Had she really thought he would forgive her so soon?

"I wanted to apologize once more. Beg your forgiveness."

"Has it been a month since you defied me?"

She lowered her head. "No, Father."

"Then what makes you think I'd consider granting forgiveness so soon?"

"Because I know what a forgiving, loving man you are."

That was true. Many people had betrayed him. Years ago, he had punished them without remorse, his only desire to appease his rage. Once he'd realized his potential in controlling others, however, he had gained control over his temper, too. Now when he punished, the results were rarely fatal. If behavior could be controlled and then changed to his liking, what was the point in killing, other than self-gratification?

Ruling over his followers allowed him to be the gracious, forgiving leader his people worshipped.

"What do you believe would be a just punishment for what you did, daughter?"

Tears appeared in her eyes. "I can think of no greater punishment than to have you withhold your pleasure from me."

Tabitha rarely cried. Even during his most enthusiastic

punishment, when his enjoyment overcame his caution, she remained dry-eyed. But now he could see that his desertion was indeed hurting her. How very interesting.

"The punishment stands. Is there anything else?"

Surprise flickered in her eyes, and he almost chuckled. She had thought he would give in. Did she think him so weak as to be moved by tears?

Visibly collecting herself, she finally said, "The promise you made about John. Did you mean it?"

"You know I always keep my promises."

Her face brightened. Yes, he was being overindulgent, but how could he not give in to her? And though doing away with his son wasn't his preferred solution, having John gone would make life simpler. Plus, it would give Tabitha happiness. Despite his anger at her disobedience, he couldn't help but spoil his angel.

"Do with him what you will, however you like. Just make sure it brings no questions from our people. Our family affairs are none of their concern, and speculation can cause worry, disrupting the community."

"I have already determined the method. No one will ever suspect."

"Excellent. Now leave me to my accounts. Orientation has already started for our newest member. You know I hate missing one moment of progress."

Her entire body jerked at the news. "You've begun already?"

"Are you questioning my judgment?"

"No, of course not. I'm just surprised you've started so soon with her."

Only to himself had Alden admitted that he had made an exception for this new female. But never had he seen one so ripe or ready. Under ordinary circumstances, orientation with his manifesto was the second phase of training. Weeks of incarceration, along with deprivation of food and sleep, and the occasional drugs, softened their senses, readying each girl to hear his message.

Though he resented his daughter's question, perhaps this was a good opportunity for her to learn what he had in mind for their newest member. "She is special. It's as if she was made for Tranquillity." He deliberately paused and then added, "Made for me."

A small lip tremble was Tabitha's only indication of upset. Then she backed away silently, as she had been taught.

Satisfied that he'd made his point, Alden returned to his accounts. Now if only the new girls would be so co-operative. And his newest one? It was all he could do not to single her out and begin the intensive training with her immediately.

No, that would be breaking more of his own rules. He'd already deviated with her orientation. Any other change was out of the question. Discipline flowed from the top down. If he made another exception for her, others might learn of this. They would question his strength.

The fact that she'd already made him desert his long-standing rules concerned him. Was he seeing the qualities of subservience and obedience because they were truly there? Or did he want her so much that he had exaggerated them? A chill swept through him. A woman who made a man so weak as to question himself had an evil inside her that needed to be exorcised.

No, he wouldn't break any more of his own laws. However, her influence over him could not go unpunished. She would pay a stiff penalty for being such a temptation.

twenty-nine

Seth sat on a rock yards away from the others and listened to the nonstop bullshit blaring at Honor. Alden Pike's manifesto, in his earsplitting voice, was a blast of insane meanderings. He went on and on about perfection and tranquillity and how he offered both. His ego had no boundaries as he extolled his own achievements and how he offered solace to those who'd lost their way. He'd yet to say that he was a god, but the inference was there. Or if not a god, at the least, some kind of supreme being.

The message was thirty-seven minutes long. Rules, regulations, what could and couldn't be planted in the garden. What food should be prepared for a man. What sexual services a woman should give to her mate. How they were to dress and conduct themselves. Those and a seeming thousand other ridiculous mandates blared as if they were being yelled through a bullhorn.

Once the message ended, it started again. This was the beginning of the fourth hour. Just how much more could Honor take? He wanted . . . God, how he wanted to go in and get her now.

An hour ago, he'd been ready to do just that when, in the midst of Pike's recorded rant, he'd heard Honor's voice. Out of necessity, her words had been soft. He pictured her putting her mouth directly over her watch to speak.

"Hopefully you can hear me over this crap. I'm okay.

Don't come in. Got a headache from this asshole's ramblings, but nothing worse. I promise."

Though the message had been too short, and he'd heard the tension in her voice, her iron will had been there, too. He had to trust her judgment. She had asked for his trust . . . for him to have faith in her abilities to handle this job.

She believed he hadn't trusted her before with the truth. Maybe he hadn't. His main concern had been protecting her. To Honor, not telling her the truth had been like a slap in the face to her integrity.

So now, here he sat, trusting her judgment and cursing himself for doing it.

"You okay?"

Seth looked around at Noah McCall. "This may not drive her crazy; I can't say the same for me."

"She'll tell you if she thinks you need to come in."

"Yeah, I know. She told me you worked on some cases together before she came to LCR."

McCall nodded. "First case was a few years back. Takes a lot to impress me, but she did it in spades. Compassion combined with a steely strength is a rare quality. Honor never lets her kindness control the job she needs to do. Nor does she allow her experience to jade her. I don't have to tell you that she's seen a lot of bad things and though she's tough, she's not hard."

Seth couldn't have said it better himself. That was Honor in a nutshell. Every person had a breaking point, though. No way in hell did he intend to find out what hers might be. Seth knew he wouldn't be able to wait much longer. Hell yes, he trusted her judgment, but he also knew that Honor was all about service and sacrifice. That had been ingrained into her DNA. Damned if he'd allow that sacrifice to include her torture.

She wouldn't forgive him if things went sour and he charged in too early. Living without Honor's forgiveness was painful but doable. Living without Honor in the world wasn't.

Soon, he'd have no choice but to act on his instincts.

Seth's mouth moved softly, sweetly over hers, their lips sipping at each other's, his spicy taste sweetly addictive. Large, callused hands, so very gentle, caressed as they glided, covering every inch of her body. Honor groaned her arousal. The image was so clear in her mind, she could almost feel the stinging stubble of his beard against her skin.

Fantasies and memories were keeping her sane. For five hours, nonstop, she'd listened to the same message. When would it end? What indication did she need to give that she was fully on board with Pike's bullshit message?

An incessant ache throbbed in her head, created not only by the loud, booming voice but also by the lights. She'd remained in the dark for the first hour and then all the lights had been turned on, brighter than they'd ever been. So bright, she'd gasped at the pain in her eye sockets. Two minutes later, she'd been plunged into darkness again. And then the lights had gone on again. Then darkness once more. This had been repeated every few minutes.

She'd received no food or water since this morning. An hour ago, she'd drunk the water she'd used to swish out her toothpaste earlier. Damned if she'd die of dehydration. This bastard would not defeat her.

She figured Seth must be going crazy—listening to this and feeling helpless to do anything but wait for her signal. And he would be questioning the promises he'd made to her. Not because he didn't trust her but because of who he was—a protector through and through. He would wait, though . . . she trusted him.

She couldn't give the go-ahead yet. Yes, this was painful and, yes, she wanted it to end. However, if she called the team in now, without any idea of where the girls were, this mission could well end without them being found. Worse yet, making the call too soon could put their lives in danger—Pike would have no qualms about killing to protect himself. Honor refused to accept either outcome.

At some point, Pike would believe he had achieved his goal. Was that five minutes from now or five months? At that thought, Honor sat up in bed. No, she had to find a way to convince him that she had succumbed to his will. What would it take to convince the bastard?

Think, Honor, think!

Alden stood and stretched his achy muscles. This was always the most tiresome part of the process. After enjoying their initial reaction of terror, watching and waiting for each girl to break could become tedious. The average girl could take anywhere between two days and a week before he broke her into a gibbering, slobbering idiot.

For entertainment, because of the boredom, he often placed bets with himself on how long it would take each girl. So far this year, he had a perfect score.

The runaway had taken the longest—six days. The skinny blonde had taken four. The fat blonde with the pretty blue eyes had surprised him the most. With her subservient attitude, he'd figured he was being way too generous when he'd wagered three days, but that's exactly how long it'd taken before she was mumbling his words like a jabbering moron.

He always rewarded the ones who took the shortest amount of time with something special. After all, when they gave in, his real enjoyment of the process could truly begin. So though she'd taken three days, he'd rewarded the girl with an extra glass of water.

Alden checked his watch again. Five hours so far . . . she was holding out moderately well. The tiny camera attached to the ceiling had shown the normal amount of restlessness. She'd tried covering her ears, putting a pillow over her head, and even singing. Watching her methods of avoidance had been quite amusing.

It was time for a bit of relief. One solid hour of stark silence, during which she would be fed and watered. She would receive another glass of water to brush her teeth. Then music would be piped in. He'd never cared much for music . . . had never seen the point to it. However, he'd found it had a soothing, if inane quality that calmed. He'd noticed that in the course of a day, many of his people would go around humming the tunes they'd heard during their training. Now, to him, that was beautiful music.

Her musical therapy—or lullaby, as he liked to think of it—would last for fifteen minutes. She would believe the training was over for the night. She would grow sleepy. Weary from the stressful day, she would lie down and begin to doze. And then, like lightning, it would all begin again.

He blew out a tired sigh. Exhausting work, but eventually fulfilling. His future bride deserved only the best of him.

Five hours later

"I'm going in."

McCall looked up from his crouched position. The man didn't seem surprised by Seth's declaration. He shrugged and said, "It's too soon."

Too soon? The urge to slam a fist into the man's implacable face was strong. "How the fucking hell can you think it's too soon? She's listened to that shit for ten hours."

"Yes, and she's given us a message every hour that she's fine. You go in now, everything Honor's gone through will have been for nothing. Do you want that?"

Hell no, he didn't want that. But neither could he just stand by and listen to her continued torture, either.

When Seth didn't answer, McCall stood and placed a hand on his shoulder. "Believe it or not, I know what you're going through. Before Samara and I married, she went through something similar. I wanted to kill the men responsible as soon as I could. If I had, the entire mission would have been screwed and several young girls would have been sold into sexual slavery. Waiting saved them."

"And Samara?"

Seth had never seen McCall smile. The one that spread across his face now was filled with pride and love. "She's one of the gutsiest women I know. She survived that and so much more." He eyed Seth again. "She wouldn't have wanted the outcome to be any different. The hell she went through is something I'd give my life to prevent, but we saved lives by waiting until the time was right."

Nodding, Seth looked away from McCall's penetrating black eyes. Yeah, he was sure every emotion of his was there for the world to see. Didn't take a psychic for McCall or anyone else to know his feelings for Honor.

"Thorne and Livingston come up with anything?" Seth asked.

"Last time I heard from them, they'd spotted two more soft areas."

"Good."

While Seth had been listening to Honor's torture, the other men had kept themselves occupied by looking for areas to breach. Seth had identified two the first day. Finding the best one was imperative. When they got the go-ahead from Honor, their plan would need to be in place so they could execute it immediately.

"If they find—"

Seth held up his hand for Noah to stop talking. Was that Honor's voice? Even though he still had the earbud in his ear, he'd listened to Pike's noise for so long, he wasn't sure if he had imagined Honor's whisper.

He shot a glance at McCall. "Did you hear—" He broke off when Honor's voice came through louder. "I'm going to try something," she said.

Frozen in place, he waited. What the hell did that mean? What was she going to try?

Curled up in a corner of the room, Honor was creating what she hoped was a picture of a broken mind. Pulling at her hair, twirling it with her fingers, alternately rocking back and forth and jumping up to pace, she mumbled Pike's insane mantra, rules, and manifesto. After hours of hearing it, she had no problem reciting it verbatim.

Would this work? Was this what he wanted to see?

When she'd been given an hour of silence and a meal, she had come up with this plan, but waited a couple of hours before putting it into action. The creep had to be convinced that she was well and truly indoctrinated. Was this too soon? Who knew? She only knew she wasn't going to listen to this crap any longer. With Pike's ego, he would probably congratulate himself on bringing her over so soon.

She'd started her act by pacing back and forth. Knowing where the camera was, she made use of it by giving Pike a show she figured he wanted to see.

After ten minutes or so of pacing, she'd dropped into a corner. With her legs curled up for warmth, she'd stared blankly into space and begun to fiddle with her hair. Then, as if it were just a natural occurrence, she'd begun to mouth the words blasting through the loud-speaker. Able to match the words exactly, she'd gone on and on, hoping that at some point, Pike would get the idea that his manifesto was the only thing occupying her head.

She had allowed herself to talk to Seth for only a couple of minutes every hour. Covering her head with her pillow, she'd given him updates on her condition and nothing more. If she let loose all the things she wanted to say to him, she greatly feared, she would lose the ever-present control she'd worked so hard to achieve. When this was over and she was back in his arms, she would tell him what was in her heart. Things she should have told him before. Her pride had stood in the way of giving him the forgiveness he'd asked for. How silly all of that seemed now.

Picturing Seth had helped keep her sane as had re-membering his passionate lovemaking, his tenderness, and those little quirks that made him unique. Did he know that when he was angry, it showed in his mouth first? Those sensual lips would curl ever so slightly; then his eyes would turn flinty blue. Had he ever noticed that he always put his left shoe on first? Or that after they made love, she often put her head on his chest just to listen to his heartbeat?

She remembered all of these things from the past, and had picked up new memories lately. Had she ever told him how she admired him, adored him, loved him? Of course she hadn't. She'd fallen back into his arms and into his bed so very easily, but never had she given him the words she should have. Words he deserved to hear.

What they had was too wonderful to let go of again. Yes, she knew he still had some issues to sort out. But those things, whatever they were, had to be minor com-pared to living without each other.

Now she had to convince Pike that she was ready for

his next round of training, then find and rescue Kelli and the other girls and get the hell out of Tranquillity . . . and then she would tell Seth what was in her heart.

Alden was in the control booth, eating his dinner, when he noticed the delightful change in his woman. Enthralled, he watched her mumble the words that would stay in her head forever. She had gone over the edge even more quickly than he had ever hoped. From the moment he'd seen her, he'd felt their deep connection, and their discussions yesterday had only confirmed his belief—she had indeed been made for him.

Her coming over so quickly would make his life so much easier—another indication that she was meant to be his mate. Even subconsciously, she was trying to please him.

Finishing his meal, Alden barely saw the old hag who took his tray. His mind was on the upcoming event. It was time to begin the next phase. Group orientation. The women would be allowed to see one another for the first time—a bonding moment.

He always found it interesting how they reacted to one another. Some seemed so pleased to see another human being, they actually cried. Others acted as if they didn't even see anyone at all. Of course, all of that changed when the training began. Hard to ignore shrill screams when they were right beside you. And then each one would wonder when it would be her turn.

Alden stood and headed to the cell. First he would give his woman the brief reprieve of a bathroom privilege, including a shower. A small amount of water to sustain her—no food, though, since vomiting was often a distasteful result of this phase of training.

A soft female sigh stopped his forward progress. He turned and gasped at the sight before him. Tabitha stood several feet away. Earlier, she'd been dressed in a flowing white dress, one of his favorites. From what he could tell, it was the same dress, only it was no longer white. Bright, vivid splotches of red covered her from head to toe. *Blood.*

"What happened, daughter?"

"John has left. He won't be back."

"What did you do?" Alden didn't think he'd ever been so shocked in his life. "Is this your idea of taking care of the matter quietly?"

"No one saw me. I drove from the garage at the house to the underground garage here." She shrugged. "My brother was more resistant to leaving than I'd anticipated. He was also more healed than I'd thought he was. He fought hard; however, he was no match for my determination."

"Where is he now?"

"In garbage bags in the trunk. Since he was so large, I had to drain the carcass in the bathtub and then take him apart there."

"But why?"

Her eyes still as innocent and sweet as always, she said, "He was too heavy for me to carry out in one piece."

Alden felt a strange sadness. It had been inevitable, but still, he hadn't expected to face it this soon. His little girl had grown up. Though only twenty, Tabitha had achieved a maturity it had taken him many more years to attain.

Not wanting to give away his emotions—after all, she was still being punished for her insubordination—he asked, "What do you intend to tell my people?"

"That he left us."

He stiffened in anger. Had he been mistaken about her maturity? "Absolutely not. That could give others the impression that leaving Tranquillity is an option. You know there's only one way anyone can ever leave here."

"My apologies, Father, for not being clear. We will tell them you forced him to leave."

Once again, Alden was stunned—this time, by his daughter's brilliance. If his followers thought he might expel them from Tranquillity, their efforts to obey would only be heightened. Fear of rejection was a powerful motivator. That's why many of them had come to him so easily—castoffs from a cruel society. If they worried that he might kick them out, his control over them would be even greater. His mind exploded as he considered all the additional benefits he could enjoy.

A rush of love flooded through him as he gazed at his daughter. What a treasure she was. Alden knew he was being much too lenient, but how could he continue to punish her when she had done something so extraordinarily useful?

"Let's go back up to the house."

Tilting her head hopefully, she said, "But what about the training?"

"That can wait a little while longer." He held out his hand. "Your reward can't."

Her face took on a glowing happiness as she rushed into his arms.

Alden held her tight, the dampness of her gown in no way deterring his passion. "Come, let's celebrate your brother's life in the best way possible. Tomorrow, I'll call a town meeting and announce John's departure."

Turning away from the monitor, he ignored the woman in the corner, rocking back and forth and mumbling his words. Another few hours of his manifesto would only reinforce his will. When he returned, she would be even more pliable.

But for now, it was time to reestablish his bond with his angel.

* * *

The first nursery rhyme came around midnight. Seth and the others had been staring at the radio and listening intently, assuming Honor's mumblings of the manifesto had been her attempt to get Pike to think she was completely under his spell. Since she'd done that for over two hours without any sign that the bastard was even watching, it apparently hadn't worked.

When she began to recite "Humpty Dumpty," he and McCall met each other's eyes. The second time, Seth got to his feet and went for his supplies. He didn't give a damn whether she had given the signal or not. He was going in.

He heard a sound behind him. Figuring it was the LCR leader ready to stop him, Seth whirled around. What he found was McCall, Livingston, and Thorne gearing up, too.

"I can go in alone," Seth said. "If it doesn't work out, then you—"

McCall's head shot up. "We're a team, Cavanaugh. Get used to it."

With a brief nod of thanks, Seth shrugged into a Kevlar vest he'd previously packed with weapons and medical supplies. Zipping it closed, he glanced down at a sheet of canvas on the ground. Working from Honor's descriptions and instructions, along with their own observations, they'd drawn a map of Tranquillity.

Using a stick, McCall pointed to each platform where a guard stood. "Livingston, you take these two up front. Thorne, you take the east corner; I'll take the west." He looked up at Seth. "Cavanaugh, go down the back alley Stone mentioned. The instant you identify the building she's in, radio its location to us, but hold your position until your backup arrives."

Seth nodded and took off, barely hearing the three men behind him. Running alongside the brick wall, he located the weakest area they'd been able to find—a patch of darkness where the distance between two lights was too great. Thorne and Livingston had tested the area and assured him that the wall was bare—no barbed wire at the top or electrical current running through it.

He withdrew a rope attached to his utility belt, then threw it up and over, pulling sharply till the grappling hook caught the edge. Climbing with sure, even strokes, Seth was up, over, and on the ground in less than two minutes.

After he unhooked himself, he left the rope in place for the other three, then turned to assess his location. A dark structure loomed high in the distance. Was that Pike's house? If so, he was going to have to hike upward and then go down into the valley to where the community lay. He spared a glance back to see that two of the three men were now on the ground and Thorne was coming down the wall. He gave a quick nod to McCall. Then, knowing that the other men were set to their tasks, Seth turned and pulled his Glock from the holster in his jacket. Focused on the tall structure ahead of him, he began his climb.

To take his mind off yet another nursery rhyme Honor was reciting in his ear, Seth concentrated on picturing the town the way Honor had described it.

Once he reached the main road, the school, dining hall, and hospital would be on one side, the communal living quarters, a small store, and the library on the other. The smaller road held eighteen homes, nine on each side. On the other side of that road was what Pike had referred to as the stable. Up on a hill, separate from his followers, was the bastard's home.

Right now, Seth was interested in only one location. About a hundred yards past the "stable" was where he believed Honor was being held.

Eight minutes later, he caught his first clear glimpse of

the community in the valley below him. He took off downhill at a run, dodging bushes and rocks and trying like hell to avoid falling. Dressed in camouflage, he wasn't worried about stealth until he got closer to town. The nearer he got, the more likely it was that there would be people on watch. Evading the moonlight, staying in the shadows as much as possible, Seth ran down the hill toward a grouping of buildings.

Finally on more level ground, he stayed low and chased shadows as he headed toward the main road. At the side of one building, he stooped and peered around the corner. Everything looked exactly as Honor had described it. Lights lined the street, but they were dimmed. The buildings were dark. Since the time was well past midnight, Seth saw no one. He had a feeling that wasn't an unusual occurrence at any time. These people might have believed they'd achieved tranquillity, but it was pretty damn clear that their lifestyle didn't include downtime for enjoyment. Alden Pike seemed to be the only one who had that luxury.

Even though there were no people milling about, he had no way of knowing whether the armed guards at the walls were the only lookouts. Trying to determine his best course of action to get to the next street, he went to the back of a building and ran through the darkness. Once he got to the end of the street he'd veer right to go toward the building where Honor was most likely being held.

A sound in his ear caught him in mid-stride. Seth stopped abruptly and listened.

Pike's slimy voice said, "Time for the next phase, my dear."

Seth heard heavy panting, as if Honor was scrambling, trying to get away. Then a small, gasping cry.

"Now, now . . . don't fight it. Everything will be much easier once this is all over."

Seth took off running again. No way in hell was he waiting until the bastard did something else to her.

In the midst of his flat-out dash, he heard the most chilling sound of all: Honor's scream of agony.

To hell with stealth. Seth shifted direction and darted between two buildings. Running as fast as he could, determination and fear giving him speed, he zoomed out onto the main street and raced through the middle of town. Honor's scream echoed in his head, a chilling reminder of another woman he'd failed to save.

Not this time. And not Honor. Dammit, this time he would not be too late.

thirty

Helpless in the grip of horrendous pain, Honor felt her muscles spasm out of control and then lock. The bastard had held out his hand to her and she, acting like the brainless twit he wanted her to be, had thought he was helping her up from the floor. Instead, he'd stunned her with that fucking Taser again.

Breathlessly, she glared up at him through eyes glazed with tears. Hiding the pain would get her nowhere. Working to recover, she didn't have to fake the quiver in her voice. "Why are you doing this to me?"

"For purification purposes, of course." That slimy smile came back as he held out his hand again. "Come. No zapping, I promise."

She had some choices . . . all of them sucked. If she ignored his hand, he'd see it as defiance and might keep her locked up even longer. If she tried to fight him now, as tired as she was, she stood a good chance of losing. Her last option sucked the most, but it was the one she had to take. Releasing a long, silent breath, Honor took the giant hand and allowed him to pull her to her feet.

Embarrassment because of her nudity never occurred to her. The slime of his smile extended to his eyes as, like a lascivious lecher, he allowed his gaze to roam over her. Let the bastard look his fill, maybe he'd drop the damn Taser. She'd be more than happy to show him how it felt.

"I hoped you would have freckles all over your body."

He reached toward her breast and Honor jumped back, out of his way.

His laughter sounded the way it should—evil and filthy. "You're shy. I like that. I had planned on allowing you a shower and some water, but that spark of defiance needs some quick taming."

When she stared mutely up at him, he gave her another sick, twisted smile. "And though you don't deserve it, I have a special gift for you. Several other girls will be joining you for training. You'll finally have some friends."

Other girls? Now, that was music to her ears. Offering him a trembling smile, Honor took a half step. Once more, agony zoomed. Screaming, her body jerking uncontrollably, she fell forward. Strong arms caught her. A burlap sack was shoved over her head and then tightened around her neck. With effortless ease, Pike picked her up and threw her over his shoulder like a bag of flour.

Dammit, she should have tried fighting him before. Struggling, she pounded on his back, screaming. He stopped in mid-stride and dropped her to her feet. Though blinded with the bag over her head, Honor tried for a quick punch and kick. The punch hit what felt like a shoulder and the kick made a nice thudding noise as it slammed into a fleshly part of his leg.

Pike grunted and then pain slammed into her jaw. Stunned, her ears ringing, she was once more picked up and slung over his shoulder, where she hung limply. Seconds, minutes later, he released her . . . and her back was slammed down onto something hard and long. She felt her hands and feet being tied to it. The sack kept her from seeing anything, and the blow to her face had frozen her into an almost numbing submission. Just what the bastard wanted.

"I'll be right back."

Honor pushed past her anger at allowing herself to get caught like this. Analyzing her stupidity in believing she had control of the situation would have to be dealt with at another time. For now, she had to figure out how to get out of this mess.

After hearing her screams, Seth wouldn't wait any longer. He and the others would be here soon. Had they heard Pike's comment about the other girls? She needed to make sure. Turning her face toward her arm, she whispered harshly, "He's bringing the other girls out. I have a sack over my head and can't see." And then, because she knew Seth would be worried sick, she added, "And I'm okay. Honest."

How long would it take them to get to this building? Would they encounter more resistance than the men at the towers? She couldn't say. Right now, her priorities were to stay healthy and delay whatever kind of group torture Pike had planned.

Squinting with all her might, Honor tried to make out, through the thin fabric, what kind of room she was in and what was going on. She saw movement to her left and two blurred images.

His voice filled with approval, Pike said, "Very good, my dear. Lie down, just like that."

The blurred movements stopped momentarily, and then he said, "I'll be right back."

As soon as she heard him retreat, Honor whispered, "Who's there?"

A trembling female voice said, "My name is Anna."

Gratitude flooded her. *Thank you, God.* "Anna, do you know if there are others?"

"Two more, I think."

"Do you have a bag over your head, too?"

"No, I can see."

"Can you describe what you see?"

Honor heard the young woman swallow and then she
started giving a litany of terrifying descriptions. "We're
tied to long boards that kind of look like seesaws. There
are four of them. Each board has a bucket of water, one
in front and one behind." Anna paused for a breath and
then continued: "There are hooks and tethers hanging
all over the room. I see several kinds of machines behind
you . . . I don't know what they're for . . ." She swallowed hard and added, "They look hideous."

"Okay, what about doors or windows? Any kind of
exit?"

Seconds later, Anna said, "From where I am, I see only
one door. It's the one he brought me through. I don't see
any windows."

"You're doing great, Anna. What about—" Honor
broke off and then said, "Shh, he's coming back."

Silently, Honor listened as Pike returned and apparently tied another girl to a board. Saying the same
words—"I'll be right back"—he left the room again.

"Who's there?" Honor asked.

"Who . . . who are you?" The voice sounded young
and female, and it quivered with terror.

Concerned that Pike could hear, she maintained
her role and answered, "My name is Maggie. What's
yours?"

"Kelli . . . Kelli Cavanaugh."

Emotions soared so high inside her, she almost started
crying. Knowing that Seth could hear his niece's voice
made up for every pain and indignity she'd suffered.
Soon . . . very soon, he and LCR would arrive, giving
Alden Pike exactly what he deserved.

Footsteps grew closer, letting her know Pike was returning, hopefully this time with Missy. She lay still and
listened as he tied the third girl down.

Seconds passed without movement in the room. Other
than the sniffling and soft crying of the girls, Honor

heard nothing. And then a new sound hit her ears: Pike's breathing. Not normal breaths either—heavy, excited, rough rasps of air. The sounds grew harsher, escalating in speed. Grating grunts echoed around the room, followed by rapid pants like those of a gasping, wild animal. The perverted freak was getting turned on.

Fury beat down the bile surging up her throat. Determined to ruin the sadistic bastard's good time, Honor said, "Hey, mister, are you some kind of a pervert or something?"

The silence was deafening, and then the bag was ripped from her head. Ignoring Pike's furious face in front of her, Honor took a quick glance around. Just as Anna had said, she was in a semicircle with three other boards, a girl tied to each board—Kelli, Missy, and Anna.

A thrill of happiness surged through her, followed by a scream of agony as Pike zapped her with the Taser again. Her body twitching in pain, he put his nose against hers and snarled, "You'll pay dearly for that insult."

Seth stood at a closed door at the back of the building. The description Honor had given was right on target. Honor, Kelli, and the other girls were inside. He'd heard her reassurance that she was fine, and he'd heard Kelli's sweet voice. His adrenaline surged, urging him to go inside.

He spoke into the mic on his shoulder: "I'm at the building. Things are heating up . . . I can't wait much longer. Anyone close?"

"Livingston and I are headed your way. Thorne ran into a problem . . . he's a couple of minutes behind us."

"Hey, mister, are you some kind of a pervert or something?"

Seth almost smiled at Honor's cutting question. Seconds later, she screamed in pain. Fuck waiting. Whispering harshly, "I'm going in," Seth pushed open the door.

One of the men issued a soft curse, but no one protested. Seth paused inside a small, dark hallway, his ears alert for sounds . . . muffled voices came from the other end of the hallway. Gun at the ready, he ran toward a closed door. Turning the knob, he eased it open a slight crack. He peered in, his breath suspended as he took in what could only be called a modern-day torture chamber.

The room was a giant cavernous space. Hooks, ropes, chains, and leather halters hung from the ceiling. Narrow tables that resembled doctor's examining tables were interspersed with some of the oddest and most horrific-looking equipment and machinery Seth had ever seen. He recognized one contraption that resembled a pillory; in a corner, he spotted what looked like a modified electric chair.

A soft sob drew his attention to the left, near the far corner of the room. Bent low, Seth crept inside and then crouched behind a table.

Four slanted boards were arranged in a semicircle. Each board resembled a child's seesaw. Four nude women, including Honor, were tied to the boards. A bucket of water had been placed under each of their bare feet. Pike lowered a board holding a woman . . . Seth peered closer. Anna, he thought. When her feet dipped into the water, he tilted the board again until she was out of the water. Taking several steps back, he pointed something toward her feet. What the hell . . . ?

"Pike, you bastard. Don't you fucking dare!" Honor shouted.

Pike turned to stare at Honor. "You can't talk to me like that."

"You're a monster and a sadistic pervert. I'll talk to you any damn way I please."

"You've been faking." He sounded like a bewildered child.

"Your kidnapping and torturing days are over."

"This is my kingdom, my rules. I can do what I please. No one can stop me."

"Think again, asshole," Seth snarled.

Pike whirled around. "Who the hell are you?"

"I'm the man who's going to shoot your head off if you don't drop that Taser and back away from the women."

Alden shook his head slowly, disbelief and fury culminating in a mass of volcanic emotions. No, this couldn't happen. This was his home—his paradise. He had safeguards set up for protection. His people were supposed to die before they let anyone get to him.

Who was responsible for allowing an infiltrator inside his kingdom? The realization came quickly. He whirled around and stared at the traitorous female. The woman who should have been honored to be his chosen mate had betrayed him in the worst way possible. "You," he whispered hoarsely. "You brought him here."

With the look of innocence and fear now gone, her face showed a maturity that stunned him. Where was his lovely, submissive female? For the first time ever, Alden felt a blow to his heart, almost as if she'd ripped it from his chest and squeezed it with her fist. She was to have been his queen.

"I'm not telling you again, Pike," the man behind him growled.

Barely hearing the threat, Alden shook his head, almost dazed with hurt. "I was going to make you my queen. You would have had everything any woman could want."

"You're a pervert and a freak, Pike," the woman said. "And you're going to prison for a very long time."

The bitch hadn't deserved him. His broken heart now fully healed, his mind grappled with a plan. Indecision battled with supreme confidence. This was his world . . . his rules. No one told him what to do. He turned to look at the man holding the gun. "This is my home. What I say goes here."

As if he hadn't heard him, the man motioned with his gun. "Walk toward me, slow and easy."

No, he'd worked too long and too hard to create this world. He would damn well not allow anyone to destroy it. Staring intently at the man for several more seconds, Alden huffed out a long breath and slumped his shoulders as if accepting defeat. He dropped the Taser onto the floor and began walking in front of the women.

"I said 'toward me,' asshole," the man growled.

The man wouldn't shoot . . . not if it meant endangering the four females. Alden continued walking slowly. Then he darted sideways, running between two women.

"Dammit!" the man shouted.

Withdrawing a knife from his pocket, he held it to the betraying bitch's throat. "Drop your gun or I'll slice her head clean off."

"And the instant you do, you're dead."

The man's hard voice and icy expression gave Alden pause for only a second. If the girl was his partner, he wouldn't risk her life. Smug with his superior knowledge of human behavior, Alden pulled hard on the bitch's hair, stretching her neck. With the knife firmly against her throat, Alden smiled and said, "Drop your gun and slide it over to me. If you don't, she's dead. Your choice."

His face twisted with indecision and then frustrated defeat, the man lowered his gun to the floor and slid it several feet forward.

Triumphant, Alden eased the knife back slightly. Even though he had every intention of killing the man, Alden couldn't resist offering him instructions on what he had done wrong. "You made several errors in judgment. Your first was daring to infiltrate my kingdom. And your second was caring what happened to the bitch." Tightening his grip on the knife, he whispered in her ear. "Say goodbye to—"

A noise sounded behind Alden. *Tabitha?* Good. She could help him do away with the intruder. Alden lowered the knife and turned. Searing pain shot through his hip; an instant later he heard a sharp blast. Stunned, he turned back to see that the man was down on the floor, holding another gun. The gun he'd slid across the floor was still there. How had that happened?

Knife still in his hand, Alden jabbed down toward the woman. Another shot blasted through the air—this time, from the other side of the room. Alden glanced down to see blood staining his shirt, and then pain exploded in his chest. His legs went out from under him and he fell forward. Men were shouting. Where had all of these people come from? How had this happened?

Fury dimmed the pain. Alden lifted his hand and, with the last of his reserves, threw the knife at the bitch who'd caused his kingdom to fall. In his last moment on earth, he heard a man's tortured voice shout, "Honor!" And then he knew nothing more.

A furious howl of grief exploded from Seth as he ran forward. Pike had found his target . . . a knife was sticking out of Honor's chest. His entire body close to meltdown, he raised a shaking hand to the knife.

"It's not deep," she whispered.

His gaze flew to her face. "What?"

"It's barely inside me, Seth. Look. It hit a bone."

Relief and happiness flooded him. She was right. The blade had pierced her sternum enough to make the knife stand up, but it hadn't gone deep at all.

"She all right?"

He looked over his shoulder at McCall, who stood several feet behind him. "She's fine. Knife hit the bone."

Behind McCall, Seth saw Livingston untie Kelli and then cover her with a blanket. Assured that she was fine for the time being, he turned back to Honor. Unzipping one of the pockets of his vest, he pulled out gauze and bandages.

"We need to get everyone out of here as soon as possible," Honor said. "Someone might have heard the gunshots."

"Let's take care of this first." Gently, he tugged on the knife, more relieved than he'd ever be able to express that it almost fell into his hands. Though blood oozed from the cut, the tip of the knife hadn't even penetrated a quarter of an inch.

Placing gauze on the wound to stop the bleeding, he held it with one hand and cut the ties at her hands and then her feet with the other. "I'm sorry, sweetheart. I should have come sooner."

"You came at exactly the right time."

He shoved the bucket of water away and helped her stand. Tugging at his Kevlar vest, he dropped it on the ground, then unbuttoned his flannel shirt and pulled it off. "Let's get this on you."

"Thanks—it was getting drafty in here."

Grinning at her unbelievable spirit, Seth stooped down and pulled a space blanket from his vest. "Wrap up with this. I'm going to check on Kelli. Okay?"

Honor nodded. "I'm fine. Go."

Seth turned to see Kelli sitting on the floor, her face almost hidden by her long hair. Though she was wrapped in a blanket, he could see her body trembling. Feeling unusually tentative, he went to his knees before her and said softly, "Kelli? Honey?"

Her blond head came up. Her face was paper white, and tears filled her eyes. "Uncle Seth?" Her disbelieving whisper clutched at his heart. "Is it really you?"

"Yeah, it's really me."

An expression of such joy came over her face, it was all Seth could do not to grab her and hold her close. Not knowing what she'd gone through, he hesitated to make the first move. Kelli, apparently, had no reservations as she threw herself at him. Seth's arms closed around her and held her as she sobbed against his chest.

Tears stung his eyes, and he looked upward as he whispered a prayer of thanks. He had never given up hope that she was alive, and despite the thinness of her body and her obvious distress, she looked unharmed and whole. God only knew what Pike had done to her, but Kelli was a Cavanaugh through and through—a survivor.

She pulled away slightly and peeked up at him. "I'm never leaving home again."

Laughter erupted from him. "I think that's something your parents will wholeheartedly endorse."

Shivering from equal parts shock and cold, Honor grabbed one of Pike's buckets. Dumping the water out, she tipped it over and sat down abruptly. Her legs felt like overcooked noodles and her entire body was one mass of quivering nerves. She couldn't believe it was over.

"Listen up, everyone," Noah said. "Thorne's on watch outside. He'll alert us if anyone's coming this way. A chopper's on the way . . . ETA three minutes. It'll land as close to this building as possible. We took care of the guards at the walls, but we don't know what kind of resistance we'll face once the chopper lands."

Honor tightened the blanket around herself and took deep breaths, hoping to calm the jittery nerves that continued to send jolts through her. The shocks she'd received hadn't been high voltage enough to do any real damage; they'd just caused sudden, tremendous pain. The knife wound, other than the scare it'd given Seth, was a small, insignificant throb just over her left breast. All in all, other than being weak as a kitten, she felt damn good.

And what made it all the better was seeing Seth hold Kelli in his arms. Honor's relief that the young woman was safe was almost overwhelming. She could only imagine what he must be feeling.

How much had these poor girls been through before tonight? Their recovery was going to take a while, but thank God they were alive so that could happen.

The other women in the community would have to be dealt with delicately. Noah had probably already talked with the authorities. And though she knew that most, if not all of the women had been abducted and abused, she couldn't help but hurt for them. Their lives were going to be torn apart once again.

She took in the room that Pike had apparently used for his training purposes—every available space filled with some sort of contraption or device meant to inflict pain. Never had she seen a more classic example of a sexual sadist. Problem was, not only had he used the torture devices for his own sick enjoyment, he'd somehow managed to control his victims' minds. There was no telling what kind of therapy it was going to take or how long it would be before his victims were able to regain their lives.

A movement in her peripheral vision caught Honor's attention. She stiffened. Was that someone or had she imagined it? She went to her feet and took a step forward, trying to peer into the darkness. "Is someone there?"

A shrill scream of rage echoed through the room. Tabitha appeared like a ghostly specter from a darkened corner and walked slowly toward her father's body.

Tears streamed down the young woman's face, her expression ravaged with horror and grief. Honor couldn't help but feel sorry for her. She had, no doubt, been a victim of Pike's incredible cruelty since her birth.

"Tabitha, I—" Honor jerked to a halt when the girl's hand flew up . . . she had something in her hand. Dammit, a weapon . . . she had a weapon. "Gun!" Honor shouted.

Too far away to tackle her, Honor focused instead on where Tabitha was pointing the weapon. Seth! The distance seeming insurmountable, Honor began running toward him. Her legs felt weighted and heavy, her body sluggish, as if she were moving in slow motion. Seth . . . she had to reach Seth!

He had been stooped down, holding Kelli, but when Honor shouted, he went to his feet. Standing in front of his niece to shield her, he never had the chance to defend himself.

Before Honor's horrified eyes, she saw his body jerk. Terror almost locked her limbs as, helplessly, she watched Seth fall face-first to the ground.

More gunfire erupted. The sounds were dim, almost as if they were miles away. A part of her mind acknowledged that one or more of the men were shooting back at Tabitha.

Denial screaming through her, Honor gently rolled Seth over. He'd taken his Kevlar vest off when he'd given her his shirt, and he hadn't put it back on. Why, oh God, why hadn't he put it back on? A thin T-shirt was the only thing that covered him. He'd had no protection at all.

A litany of prayers repeated in her head: *Please, God, please, let her have missed.* Even as Honor uttered the prayers, she already knew the truth. A cry of denial echoed in the room. Tabitha had found her mark . . . Seth had been shot multiple times. A bullet hole high up on his shoulder, one right above his heart, another below his heart.

"Honor, hurry or he'll bleed out."

She turned to see Noah on his knees beside her. Holding a cloth against one of the wounds on Seth's chest, Noah handed her another cloth. "Keep the pressure hard and steady."

Nodding numbly, she did as she was told. She vaguely heard Noah yell for a medic. Apparently the chopper had arrived, bringing much-needed medical help. Her eyes were glued to Seth. He was unconscious, his face slack and pale.

Her hand shaking, she pressed her fingers against his neck. His pulse was weak, almost nonexistent. She leaned over him. "Seth . . . can you hear me?"

No response.

She put her mouth to his ear. "You're going to be fine. Hang on. Please. Just hang on."

His eyelids flickered as if he knew she was there, but they never opened. "I love you," she whispered hoarsely. "Please don't leave me again. Please."

"Step aside, ma'am."

Gentle but firm hands pulled her away. The medics had arrived. Backing away, knowing there was nothing more she could do, she watched as one man started an IV and another fastened a protective collar around Seth's neck. Frozen from the inside out, she kept her eyes on his face as the medics lifted him onto a stretcher.

She shot a glance at Noah. "I'm going with him."

His face grim, he nodded. "Call me when you know his condition."

Barely hearing him, she ran to keep up with the men racing Seth to the helicopter. Honor tried to deny the facts, but she knew it was useless. She'd seen mortal wounds too many times not to know the truth. People didn't live through those kinds of injuries. Seth was going to die.

thirty-one

Two days later
Janisville Medical Center
Janisville, Wyoming

Beeping machines were the only sounds in the stillness of dark midnight. Honor sat in a chair, as close to the hospital bed as she could get. Though there was a couch across the room, she had yet been able to move that far from Seth. The only time she'd left him was to go to the bathroom. Any other time, even when the doctors had given her an order to leave, she'd stubbornly shaken her head.

She would stay out of their way, she wouldn't make a whisper of a sound, but she would not leave him.

His family was on their way in an LCR jet. They would have been here sooner, but the blizzard that had held off for three days had finally blown in, holding up their flight. Honor was expecting them at any moment. She hoped they'd make it in time.

Seth had held on longer than anyone had thought he would. An artery in his heart had been severely damaged, and his liver had been punctured. The wound in his shoulder was the least significant of his injuries, requiring nothing more than extraction of the bullet. After ten hours of surgery to repair the artery and the tear in his liver, along with two blood transfusions, the doctors had emerged with weary, defeated expressions and offered little hope. The artery in his heart was badly torn, the damage more extensive than they'd thought. They'd repaired the tear . . . done what they could. Now it was up to Seth.

After the surgery, she'd been told the next forty-eight hours were critical. With that news, she'd let herself believe there was hope. If he could hang on for forty-eight hours, he could recover. Seth was strong and tenacious . . . incredibly stubborn. She knew he could make it!

The hospital was small but well equipped. Noah had offered to fly Seth to a larger facility, but the doctors didn't believe he would survive the trip. And when Honor had asked if there was anything she could do, one of the surgeons had taken her hand and gruffly whispered one word: "Pray."

Twelve hours after his surgery, Seth had gone into cardiac arrest. A medical team had worked on him for a full three minutes, until finally, blessedly, she'd heard the *beep . . . beep . . . beep*. His heart had started beating again.

Honor had been standing in the corner, out of the way. Pressed against the wall for support, she had been praying fervently for a miracle. After Seth's heart had started beating again, that same doctor had turned toward her and she had seen the knowledge in his eyes. They had bought him some time, nothing more.

Seth's family was bringing one additional person with them. The family priest.

Honor still hadn't accepted that she was going to lose him. Maybe at some point, it would take hold, but as long as that machine kept beeping, she could not, would not, lose hope.

He hadn't regained consciousness during the entire ordeal. Skin that had been bronzed from the sun now looked almost bleached white. The lines around his mouth and his eyes indicated that, though he wasn't conscious, somewhere deep inside, the pain was there and he was suffering.

She had gone over in her mind, again and again, the last few seconds before Tabitha had shot him. She should have been able to stop her. She should have screamed faster, louder. Found a way to jump in front of Seth. She should have had a gun. She shouldn't have screamed . . . he'd stood up because she'd screamed. She should have done something, anything, to save Seth's life. If he died, it would be her fault.

Dear God, how was she going to live without him? Sobs built in her chest; her breath hitched. How could she live without this heroic, wonderful, loving man who'd done nothing to deserve what had happened to him?

Unable to be even this far away from him, Honor got to her feet and stood at the side of the bed. Though wires were attached to him, they were on the other side. She grasped his hand and held it to her mouth. Once his family arrived, she might not have this chance to be alone with him again.

Lowering the railing at the side, she eased down onto the bed and curled up next to him. Careful not to touch any wires or tubes, she placed her cheek against his and held him lightly, tenderly. If these were the last moments she would have to be close to him, he needed to hear all the things she'd held back. All the things she could have told him five years ago. And all the things she should have said in the last few weeks.

"Seth, I need you to know how much I love you. You're the finest man I know. I blamed you for breaking us up years ago, but I never told you how heroic and wonderful I think you are. You did what most people wouldn't have been able to do. You've got more honor and integrity in your pinkie than most people have in their entire body.

"I'm so sorry I didn't tell you this before. My stubborn pride . . ." Pressing her forehead against his shoulder, she whispered, "Please forgive me."

Swallowing hard, the painful lump in her throat ever present, she whispered one more plea, praying that if he heard anything she said, this one would get through. "Please, please, don't leave me alone. I'm begging you, darling. Please don't leave me again."

"Honor?" a soft female voice whispered.

She lifted her head, her eyes so blurred with exhaustion and tears, she could barely make out the woman standing at the door. Older, with grayish-blond hair and a grief-ravaged expression on her face. Seth's mother.

Releasing a shaky, resigned breath, Honor pressed a kiss to Seth's cheek and whispered in his ear, "You will always be the only man I'll ever love, Seth Cavanaugh."

She sat up and put her feet back on the floor. "I needed to say goodbye."

Mrs. Cavanaugh's mouth trembled uncontrollably for a moment, then she said, "He never stopped loving you."

"How do you know that?"

"When he came to tell us the truth about his undercover work, we were all shocked. Even though I'd never believed most of the things people were saying about him, I can't deny that I'd almost given up on him. Months would go by without me even hearing from him. When he did call, he just wasn't my Seth anymore. And when I found out what he had been doing and why he'd pushed us out of his life, I was stunned. We all were." Her wrinkled throat worked as she swallowed. "Some of the family didn't want to give up their anger. I should have put my foot down harder, called them out for being so stubborn and childish." She shook her head. "We just didn't really consider what Seth endured all those years."

She gave a small, apologetic smile, as if she realized she'd gotten off track. "Anyway, I asked him if he was going back to you, now that it was over. He said that you had gotten on with your life. But I saw the deep pain in his eyes. He still loved you."

Standing on shaky legs, Honor turned to put the bed's rail back up. Unable to look at Seth's mother without losing complete control, she gazed down at Seth. "I never stopped loving him, either. I never will."

She gave one last fleeting caress to his hand and then focused on the door behind Ruth Cavanaugh. His family deserved to have time alone with him to say goodbye. "I'll be just outside." She cleared her throat and added huskily, "If it looks like he's letting go, would you call me back in? Please."

Mrs. Cavanaugh opened her arms, and Honor flew into them. Though unable to shed the tears that filled her eyes, she held Seth's mother, who sobbed out her grief. At some point, Honor knew, she would need to let go of the emotions that swamped her, but not yet. Letting go meant giving up, and she resolutely refused to do that.

Steeling her spine once more, she gently disengaged herself from Ruth Cavanaugh's arms and stepped back. "Is the rest of your family outside?"

"Yes, all of his brothers and sisters are here. And our priest, Father Dawkins. I asked them to give me a few minutes before they came in."

Before leaving, Honor turned to see the older woman bend over Seth and gently kiss his forehead. Unable to watch the tender goodbye between mother and son, she went out the door.

* * *

"Honor?"

Her head jerked up. Noah stood at the entrance to the waiting room. They'd talked very little since Seth's surgery. She knew he'd been in discussions with the doctors several times a day. She knew he had offered anything and everything to help.

"How are you doing?"

Unable to form words past the giant lump residing in her throat, she lifted her tired shoulders in a helpless shrug. What could she say, anyway? She wasn't doing well at all and doubted she ever would again—that fact would not change.

His expression grave, he nodded his understanding. "The nurse told me his family was in with him. Thought, if you're interested, I'd catch you up on what's been going on with the case."

Focusing on something other than losing Seth sounded like a small reprieve from hell. She managed a husky "Yes."

Noah dropped into a chair across from her. "The FBI took over the case. They raided the community and gathered everyone they could find. The women and children have been separated from the men. Don't really know what's going to happen to the men. Just from general discussion, sounds like Pike might have brainwashed some of them, too."

"He abducted men, too?"

"Don't know yet, but from the sound of it, looks like he convinced them to join and then coerced them to stay."

"Does anyone know who Pike was? Where he came from?"

"Real name was Leonard Sykes. Years ago, he served three years in a California prison for rape. Found religion while he was there . . . or at least his self-made, twisted version. Got out for good behavior and started collecting people. Not sure how he hooked up with his first followers. He fell off the grid after his parole was up. The land in Wyoming once belonged to one of his members. Apparently, that member mysteriously disappeared.

"So far, they've identified eight other women as missing persons. There's one woman who's been missing for over twelve years. Thank God for police and FBI records, because getting any of the victims to open up has been almost impossible. It's going to be slow going figuring out what happened to each of them."

"What about Drenda or Karen . . . has anyone seen either of them?"

"Yeah, they're both there. Both married." Noah sighed and added, "And both pregnant."

Honor closed her eyes. The horror these girls had gone through was something she could barely comprehend. "And Kelli, Anna, and Missy—how are they doing?"

"They're all back with their families, but they're going to need extensive counseling."

Honor nodded. She knew that Joel had flown in with his family, but Beth, Kelli's mother, had stayed in Texas with their daughter.

"I'm assuming the girls were subjected to what I went through, only more?"

"More and much worse." Noah's mouth tightened. "Sadistic son of a bitch alternately drugged and starved them. I'm surprised they're in as good health as they are."

"Sounds like they're strong women."

Noah nodded. "Oh . . . and we found a body, cut up into pieces, in the trunk of one of Pike's vehicles."

"Do you know who?"

"Pretty sure it was his son."

"He killed his own son?"

Noah shook his head. "Coroner doesn't think so. Thinks the daughter did it. She had blood under her nails and in her hair that matched her brother's."

Honor swallowed. She knew she shouldn't be shocked. These people were the sickest of the sick. Still . . .

"We found an underground tunnel . . . that's apparently where the daughter came from. And how Aidan missed her."

Honor nodded. Blaming Aidan, or anyone else, for Tabitha's crime would be ridiculous. If anyone was at fault, she blamed herself. After witnessing the girl's cruelty firsthand and seeing her insane devotion to her father, she should have known to be on the lookout.

"So what now? What happens to all those people?"

"That's up to the authorities. We rescued the girls. They'll take care of the arrests and prosecutions. And they'll find and notify the relatives of the other women who were abducted. Our job is done."

Yes, that was good. A case solved, victims rescued. A successful mission was complete. With only one hitch: a very good man had given his life.

"I don't suppose it'd do any good to tell you that you need to get some rest."

"I can't leave him . . . I just can't."

"Is there anything I can do? Anything I can get you?"

"No, I'm just going to stay in here until his family is through visiting. Then I'll go back in and sit with him."

A warm hand touched her cold ones, gripped together in her lap. "I'll check in with you a little later. Call me if you need me."

Honor nodded tiredly, and vaguely sensed Noah leave the room. Her head pressed back against the wall, she closed her eyes and drifted in limbo, waiting for either Seth's family to leave or for that dreaded moment when the doctors and nurses would rush to his room once more and Seth would be gone for good.

Allowing her memories to comfort her, she returned to one of the sweetest in recent memory. She and Seth in the bedroom at her mom's house, naked-dancing to sappy old love songs. Gliding around the room, getting lost in the music and each other's arms. Had it only been days ago? It seemed like forever since she'd felt his lips moving over hers, felt his warm, hard body against her, or heard that beautiful husky voice of his whispering softly.

She had lived for five years without him and cursed herself for not seeking him out and discovering the truth. They had lost all that time together because she'd been too angry and hurt to find him.

"Honor!"

Her eyes popped open. One of Seth's brothers stood at the entrance to the waiting room. She couldn't place his name. Tears pouring down his face, he waved at her to follow, then turned and disappeared before she could speak.

Every instinct inside her told her to run the other way. She didn't want to say goodbye. If she followed him, she would face a finality she wasn't sure she could handle.

As if she were walking through molasses, her feet shuffled slowly down the hallway, toward Seth's room. She stopped at the door . . . heard sobbing. Pressing her forehead against the doorjamb, she whispered a short, silent prayer for courage.

She pushed open the door, then stopped abruptly. The room was filled with people. All of Seth's family was there. Her eyes darted to the still figure on the bed. Two doctors stood beside him. She moved closer. She could do this . . . she had to do this.

As she drew nearer, a movement caught her attention. Her heart raced. Had Seth moved? What was going on?

Dr. Benson, Seth's surgeon—the one who'd told her to

pray—looked up at her, his face wreathed in smiles. "Look who's awake."

She dropped her gaze to the man on the bed. Though his eyes were dull and glazed, she saw life there. Something she never thought she'd see again. Almost too afraid to hear the answer, Honor looked at the doctor and asked, "What does this mean?"

"It means he's out of the woods, my dear. That miracle I told you to pray for actually happened."

thirty-two

Eighteen days later

The hospital door swung open. Seth looked up in relief, only to curse under his breath at the sight of yet another nurse. Honor hadn't come by today, and it was getting close to lunchtime. Where the hell was she?

"Don't you look cheerful?" the nurse chirped.

He glared. "You get poked and prodded at all hours of the day and night and see how cheerful you feel."

A sly look crossed her face. "I saw that pretty little freckle-faced woman who makes goo-goo eyes at you coming down the hall. Guess I'll just have to tell her you're too grumpy for visitors today."

"Like hell."

When she didn't change her expression, Seth gave in and sighed. "I'll be good."

Chuckling, she said, "That's better. You're getting out of here tomorrow. One would think you'd be in a better mood."

Yeah, one would if one knew where the hell one stood with a certain beautiful freckle-faced woman.

Honor spent hours with him each day. They read newspapers, talked about current events, watched television, read books, and chatted about the weather. It was like they'd been married for about eighty years. Either that, or they now had a platonic relationship.

Every time she left for the night, he kept expecting her

to kiss his forehead, the way his mother used to, or kiss his cheek like a sister. Hell, she never even got that close. She probably knew better, since he'd pull her into his arms if she did.

Death had come so close that his mother had tearfully described the last rites Father Dawkins had been in the process of giving him when Seth had suddenly opened his eyes. He remembered very little of the shooting. One minute he'd been reassuring Kelli that she was safe. He remembered someone screaming, a sudden searing, paralyzing pain, and then nothing more.

Waking up to see his entire family standing at his bedside, along with the priest who had heard every confession from him until he'd stopped going to confession, had been a shock.

Then Honor had been there. Her eyes bloodshot, her face ash white. He'd been drugged and in pain, but one thing he knew for sure: he never wanted to see that look on her face again. Seeing her like that had hurt him a hell of a lot more than three bullets. Though those had hurt like a bitch, for sure.

His family had stayed for a couple of days, but he hadn't talked with them much. It'd taken six days before he could speak with any coherency. By that time, they were gone. Though each of his brothers and sisters had come by, one by one, and said goodbye, Seth still felt like a stranger with them.

His mother had wanted to stay, but he had insisted that she leave with the rest of the family. She had looked so worn out and worried, he'd been more concerned about her health than his own. Seth had promised to come home for a long visit as soon as he was able.

Tomorrow he was being released. He was still as weak as water, had several weeks of physical therapy to get through, and couldn't work for at least two months. Not that he had a job to go to. In fact, he wasn't sure where he was headed. His doctors had told him he could do his PT anywhere.

The door opened and Honor came into the room. Would he ever get to the point where his heart didn't skip beats when he saw her? He knew the answer to that. Problem was, he still wasn't sure what her thoughts were. Right now, it seemed as if they had a nice friendship going and nothing more. Damned if friendly was what he felt.

"Good morning. How are you feeling?"

"Why does everyone keep asking me that?"

She grinned, not one bit put off by his bad mood. "Well, let's see. For starters, you have three extra holes in you that you weren't born with and you look like something the cat gnawed on and then dragged home. Other than that, I'm not sure."

Seth held out his hand to her. "Come over here and put me in a better mood."

Instead of coming to him, she settled on the couch by the window. Seth almost growled at her again, but the sunlight on her face gave him pause. Though she looked a hell of a lot better than she had three weeks ago, he noticed that she was paler than she should be and her mouth looked tense and taut.

"Are you ready to talk about it?" he asked.

"Talk about what?"

"What that bastard put you through. Every time I've brought it up, you've tried to tell me you're fine. You don't look fine."

She shook her head. "I won't deny an occasional nightmare or the incredible anger I still have against the creep, but I've had no real residual aftereffects."

"Come on, sweetheart. This is me you're talking to. I heard the shit you had to go through."

Her lips trembled as if she was trying to keep from

crying. Unable to watch that without holding her, Seth put his feet on the floor.

Her eyes wide, she held out her hand to stop him. "You shouldn't be out of bed."

He snorted. "I'm getting out of the hospital tomorrow. I damn well better be able to walk a few steps." Despite his cocky self-assurance, when he reached the couch, he felt like he'd run a marathon. *Damned weakness.*

Sitting beside her, he said softly, "Talk to me."

She swung her face toward him and Seth lost his breath. Tears glistened in her eyes, her pretty mouth twisted with emotion, and her breath hitched in an effort to hold back her sobs.

"Honor . . . sweetheart. Tell me, please."

"Do you honestly think that what I went through with Alden Pike is what's bothering me?"

"Then what?"

"Seth, you almost died."

He shook his head, still confused. "But I didn't."

Honor swallowed, trying to articulate something Seth couldn't seem to comprehend. How could she tell him that he might be well on the road to recovery, but she wasn't? The nightmares she had weren't of her experience with Pike. They were of Seth getting shot. Seth dying. Every time she closed her eyes, she saw his face, ghost white and still as death. She couldn't get the image out of her head.

"Come here."

With infinite gentleness, Seth pulled her into his arms. She knew he was still sore, so she tried not to lean into him too much, but when he bent his head toward her and whispered gruffly, "Let go, sweetheart," she could no longer hold back.

With her face buried against his chest, sobs ripped through her body with the force of a tornado. Anguish, fear, grief, and every other emotion she hadn't allowed herself to express for almost three weeks erupted from her like a geyser.

How long she stayed like that, she didn't know. Seth's arms were the best things she'd ever felt in her life and she didn't want to leave them. From time to time, she heard him whisper soft endearments, and he kissed her hair several times. For the most part, he just let her cry.

Finally, feeling like a freight train had been dropped from the sky on top of her, she pulled away. Seth produced several tissues, and Honor tried to set her face to rights.

Knowing she looked like the wrath of hell, she lifted her head and said, "I'm sorry."

His smile achingly tender, he touched her cheek with his fingertip, catching a teardrop. "Is that the first time you've cried?"

She nodded. "I couldn't let go before. I knew if I did, I'd never make it back."

"My brave, beautiful Honor."

She felt neither brave nor beautiful. Though the doctors had assured her that Seth would live, and each day, she saw that he was getting better and stronger, she hadn't really trusted them. Not until she came in this morning and saw him so gloriously grumpy, obviously more than ready to leave this place, had she finally allowed herself to believe he would be all right.

"I never want to have to go through something like that again."

He shrugged. "Not a lot of crazed maniacs on my little island in the Keys."

Pain speared through her heart. He wanted to go back to his home in Florida. They hadn't discussed the future. Hell, she'd just finally accepted that there could be one. But now that the future loomed before her, "lonely" and "empty" were the only two descriptions she could think of if Seth wasn't there with her.

"So you're going back to Florida?"

"It's where I live."

She knew he was eyeing her carefully. Suddenly, Honor didn't care who said it first and maybe he would never say it, but they'd gone through too much for her to let pride or fear get in the way. If she had told him years ago, things might have been different then.

She straightened her shoulders and faced him with the truth: "I love you and I want a future with you."

There, it was out there. Was he going to stomp on her heart all over again or tell her what she so desperately wanted to hear?

Seth, being Seth, surprised her again. Taking her hand, he held it to his mouth, pressed kisses all over it, then put it against his heart. "I loved you from the moment I saw you across the room at that party. That's never changed . . . never will change, no matter what happens in the future."

Honor didn't know whether to be elated or broken-hearted. "What are you saying?"

"Just that the Seth Cavanaugh you fell in love with five years ago doesn't exist anymore. I need you to know that."

Confused, she shook her head. "What?"

"Those years, that experience, changed me. You said that you never stopped loving me. Well, that man you once loved doesn't really exist any longer. I don't think he ever will again. We've spent almost no time getting to know each other since we've been together again. I just think—"

Honor pulled her hand away and sat back against the couch. "You need to tell me what happened."

Seth sighed. Hell, might as well. She needed to know

not only how he'd changed, but why. Maybe talking would give him some kind of closure.

Refusing to look away from the possible judgment and disappointment he might see in her face, he held her gaze and said, "The things I had to do to keep my cover . . . the filth I was surrounded by daily—they changed me. Turned me into a man I no longer recognized.

"I tried to keep a distance from Clemmons's raunchier side of life. Most times that worked, because Hector wanted me to maintain a semirespectable façade. Avoiding everything wasn't possible, though." Disgust filled him as he remembered some of the things he'd seen and done to keep his cover. "His weekend parties were notorious. Drugs, sex, women. I couldn't not go. Not only because Clemmons insisted, but a lot of his business transactions took place then. I had to be around in case something came up I could use against him later.

"Close to the end, Hector became a desperate man. So many people had betrayed him, or he'd gotten pissed at people and found a way to ruin them. He had few friends left. I was still part of his inner circle but not exactly a part of it—still maintaining my halfway-legitimate businessman persona. He trusted me, but he didn't trust me enough. Getting dirt on him was taking much longer than we'd expected. I had some things that would put him away for a few years, but nothing that was going to do away with him permanently, like we had planned.

"Even though we couldn't pin anything serious on him that would stick, with my connections, I was able to provide intel the department needed to make it worth their while for me to stay undercover." He shook his head. "I wanted out . . . God, how I wanted out. And then one day it all came to a head."

The compassion and understanding he saw in her eyes almost shattered his control. How the hell had he gotten so lucky to have a woman like Honor love him?

She asked softly, "What happened?"

Breaking eye contact with her, he looked toward the window, but in his mind, he was hundreds of miles away, seeing the horror, the absolute carnage of Clemmons's final fury.

"Have you heard of Kings Run?" Seth asked.

"I remember that it's one of the most exclusive resorts in Texas. I went there once because of a case . . . had to interview one of the employees. Never went there for fun, though . . . it was a little above my lifestyle."

"But the murders, you heard of them?"

"Yes . . . it was called the massacre at Kings Run. Some wealthy businessman rented the entire place to celebrate his birthday. Gunmen broke in and killed a bunch of people."

Too often, when Seth closed his eyes, he still saw those lifeless bodies scattered around the resort. To his eyes, it had looked like hundreds. "Fourteen, to be exact. Women, men . . . five children. The gunmen planned to take out everyone."

Honor gasped, and he could see that she'd finally caught the connection. "My God, how could I have forgotten? That's what brought Clemmons down. Three men were found tied and gagged in the middle of the hotel lobby. The survivors claimed that a masked man attacked the gunmen and single-handedly took down all three of them. They were contract killers and testified that it was Clemmons who hired them." She paused to stare at him and then whispered, "You were that masked man, weren't you? You saved all those people."

Seth swallowed the bitterness at her words. Saved *all* those people? No, he had saved some . . . but not all of them.

Rubbing his wounded shoulder, which was beginning to ache, he said, "Clemmons wasn't one to do his own dirty work, even in hiring people for a kill. This job was different for him—personal. I knew something big was going down, but I didn't know what or where. I overheard some whispers and managed to catch the word 'King.'" His mouth twisted. "You know how many places in Houston start with 'King'?

"I told my handler what I could. The only thing the department could do was cover as many King places as we could."

"And then it turned out not to be in Houston," Honor murmured.

"Yeah. We had ten different locations in Houston staked out. The ones we thought would be the most likely. Instead, he went about thirty miles outside the city."

"How did you find out?"

"Dumb luck. I remembered that Herman Oakes, the man who was celebrating his birthday, had been in one of my restaurants the week before and had mentioned that he was having a big birthday bash out at Kings Run. Oakes and Clemmons had done some business deals but had parted ways, seemingly amicably, the year before.

"I had nothing to go on but a hunch. I went out there expecting nothing, really. The instant I drove into the parking lot, I heard the shots. Before I got out of the car, just as an afterthought, I grabbed a ski mask I had stuck in my console from a skiing trip a few weeks before."

"What happened?"

"Hell happened. I walked into a massacre in progress. The men didn't care who they shot. Their orders were to murder everyone . . . leave no witnesses." He closed his eyes as the most heartbreaking image came to his mind. "A young mother ran toward me, holding her four-year-old daughter." He still remembered the hope and desperate horror in the woman's eyes. "Before I could get to them, they were both killed."

"And you think all of this was your fault?"

He turned to glare at her. "Do you know how many times I could have killed the bastard? I spent years watching shit happen and allowing it to happen because we wanted him permanently . . . not just for a short run. But if I'd had the balls to take him out years before, do you know how many lives I could have saved?"

"Seth . . . listen." She took his hand and held it tight. "Do you know how many people I've seen walk out of a courtroom, free and ready to go out and kill or rape again whenever they pleased? And days later, that's exactly what they did.

"Every time that happened, I was furious, and part of me wanted to hunt the bastard down and take justice into my own hands."

She shook her head. "Injustice like that sickens me, too, but we don't get to choose who lives or dies. All we can do is do our jobs to the best of our abilities. Killing one man to save many may seem like an easy answer for some, but that's not the right thing and you know it."

Yeah, he did know it wasn't the right thing, but that didn't change his regrets. How many times could he have put a bullet through Clemmons's head in those six years? His only consolation was that the bastard had finally received his just deserts. And though it'd taken more of him than he'd been prepared to give, Seth finally allowed himself to feel peace in knowing that he had been instrumental in the man's downfall.

"I think about those years . . . what I wasted." He kissed the hand that held his. "We could have been married during that time. Had a couple of kids by now."

Her mouth trembled with the beginnings of a smile. "That's in the past. It does no good to dwell on what might have been. One of my dad's favorite sayings was 'Dwelling on the past is a sure way to ruin the future.'" She turned over the hand she held and pressed a kiss to his palm. "Don't give Clemmons that kind of power."

Honor was right. He'd been a fool once. And letting the past taint him forever was not only self-indulgent, it was pointless.

Taking the hand that held his, he put it to his chest once more. He might not be the man he'd been when they'd first met, but damned if he'd let her go again. "Marry me, Honor."

The smile he hadn't seen in five years brightened her face into an ethereal beauty. With his heart in his throat, he waited what seemed like a lifetime for her answer.

"Yes," she whispered. "A thousand, million times yes."

Pulling her back into his arms, Seth claimed Honor's lips, much the way she had claimed his heart years ago.

epilogue

One month later
Houston, Texas

Honor released a silent, satisfied sigh as Seth rolled the SUV to a stop in front of his mother's house. The crowded driveway and the cars lining both sides of the street were an indication that the gang was all here—just as Ruth Cavanaugh had promised.

His body tense, his jaw granite hard, Seth stared at the large, white two-story house where he'd grown up and then shot her a small, wry smile. "You're sure you want to go in with me?"

Honor rolled her eyes. The man was more nervous about this than he'd been about getting shot. "They're not going to eat you, Seth."

He gave a short bark of laughter. "You've never seen my brothers eat."

"You did tell them you were coming, didn't you?"

He shrugged. "Not really."

"So you're planning to just spring this on them?"

"Calling and telling my family I'm coming for Sunday dinner was never a requirement before."

She heard the hurt behind the words, and her heart ached for him. Though Seth's entire family had come to Wyoming when he'd been shot, things were still not easy between them. There was still an awkwardness between family members—a division Seth blamed himself for. But now it was time to put all of that behind them.

His mother was his biggest supporter, but she had admitted to Honor that she hadn't made her position known as loudly and clearly as she should have. That was about to change.

And Honor was ready for the battle, too. If even one of them made the slightest rude or disparaging remark, she had her plan of attack all set. Seth had suffered more than any man should. He'd brought down Clemmons, an evil man who'd ruined many lives, protected his family even when they'd practically disowned him; then he'd saved his niece from a sick, twisted pervert, and had almost died because of it. Damned if she would allow anyone to say anything against him.

"Uh-oh. You've got that look on your face."

She tilted her head, confused. "What look?"

The grin she so loved brightened his expression. "The 'mama bear defending her cub' look. Between you and my mom, I'm well protected."

"I just don't want them to hurt you anymore."

"And that's one of the reasons I love you so much."

"Because I'm protective?"

"Because you forgave me and you think everyone else should, too."

She shook her head. "I'm not sure there was anything to forgive you for."

"Why would you say that?"

She blew out a sigh and looked at the house. Was that drapery being moved aside? Turning back to him, she admitted, "After I almost lost you, I finally got it."

"Got what?"

"Since I was a little girl, I've understood all about the need to protect and defend. What I didn't understand, until you were shot, was what it felt like to have the need to protect someone you love." She whispered fiercely, "I would have done anything, and I mean anything, to keep you from being hurt. And it made me realize that that's what you felt back then. You gave me up to protect me."

Tears glazed her eyes, blurring the beautiful man in front of her. The man she would literally die for, if she had to. "I'm sorry it took you almost dying for me to understand that."

"Come here."

Tugging her over to him, Seth lowered his head and kissed her as if it had been days since she'd been in his arms. They were lost to everything but each other, until a tap on the driver's side window broke them apart.

They turned to see a little boy of about six grinning at them.

"Who's that?" Honor asked.

"My nephew Andrew."

Seth pushed a button for the window to come down. "What's up, Drew?"

"Grammy told me to tell you that you need to stop kissing and come inside before all the turkey's gone."

"Well then, we'd better get going." Seth turned to Honor. "You ready?"

She nodded and watched as Seth got out and grabbed his nephew into his arms, whirling him around.

She checked her makeup in the mirror once more, then reached for the door, but Seth was there already, opening it and helping her out. She wondered if, at some point, she'd ever take Seth's manners for granted. The answer came immediately: there was nothing about Seth she would ever take for granted.

Still holding his nephew with one arm, he took Honor's hand and said, "No matter what, we'll always have each other. Right?"

"Always." Squeezing his hand lightly, she matched her steps to his as they headed to the house. No matter what they faced in the future, whether it was Seth's stubborn family or another dark moment, Honor knew they would face it together.

Seth stood at the threshold of his mother's front door. He'd walked through this door a thousand times before, but this time, he had to stop and stare in wonder at what was waiting for him. Damned if he would cry. He shot a questioning glance at Honor.

She shrugged and said, "I might've mentioned to your mom that we were stopping by."

Since they'd flown from Florida to Texas this morning with the singular intent of seeing his family, he sincerely doubted the "might be stopping by" part of her statement.

Leaning down, he pressed a quick kiss to her smiling mouth, then looked around, more overwhelmed than he'd ever been in his life. Every member of his family, all forty-seven of them, was in the living room; they were crowded together under a giant sign that proclaimed, WELCOME HOME, SETH! WE LOVE YOU!

Realizing that Drew was squirming to get out of his arms, Seth stooped low to let him down. Everyone stood still, silent and waiting. Seth barely knew what to say. He sure as hell wasn't much for speeches, and the clogging of his throat told him he'd make a garbled mess if he tried.

Drew took off like a rocket toward his daddy, his shrill voice echoing through the room: "Uncle Seth was kissing that pretty lady and I made him stop!"

The entire room exploded in laughter. The tension and silence disappeared, and Seth and Honor were suddenly swamped with hugs, kisses, and "When's the wedding?" questions.

In the midst of the madness, Seth looked up to see his mother standing several feet away, tears pouring from her eyes. Mouthing the words "I love you," Seth watched as her face took on a beautiful glow. And at that moment he knew that whatever had happened in the past between him and everyone he loved was all truly in the past.

Lying beside Seth in his old bedroom, Honor snuggled closer to him, relishing this long-awaited quiet time with the man she loved. The last few weeks had been so crazy busy, she and Seth had barely had the chance to hold each other, much less discuss the future.

Much to her delight, as well as her mother's, Seth had agreed to stay with Beverly Stone while he went through his physical therapy. Not only was her mom a former nurse, but Honor had known nothing would delight her more than to take care of the man who'd saved her daughter. And though Seth had grumbled good-naturedly, she could tell he thoroughly enjoyed the attention.

Honor had been going back and forth between Florida and Paris, and then she'd headed back to Wyoming to give testimony about her experience at Tranquillity. After hearing what some of the others had gone through, she knew she'd been fortunate to have been with Pike for only a few days. The man had been a true sexual sadist. And he'd trained his children to be just like him.

With Pike and his two children dead, hell was now even eviler.

"I spoke with Joel . . . he apologized." Seth's voice vibrated beneath her cheek. "It was awkward for both of us, but I think we're going to be okay."

"And Sandra?"

"She finally stopped hugging my neck long enough to say she was sorry."

Honor sighed her contentment. Ruth Cavanaugh had told her twice on the phone this week that everything would be all right. Not knowing the Cavanaughs that well, she had reserved judgment. Being back in his family's good graces meant the world to Seth, and since Seth meant the world to her, she couldn't be happier about the way things had worked out.

"I saw you talking with Kelli," Seth said. "I only got to spend a few minutes with her . . . how do you think she's doing?"

"Remarkably well . . . considering. She's in counseling and is probably going to go back to Rice for the spring semester." Honor propped herself up on one elbow to look down at Seth. "Did you know that she, Anna, and Missy have become good friends?"

"Yeah, Kelli told me. I'm glad, but it was a hell of a way to find friends."

Laying her head back on his chest, Honor said, "Yes, but at least something good came out of it."

"McCall told me what Livingston did. Surprised the hell out of me."

Honor smiled as she thought about the seemingly hard and emotionless Jared Livingston, who had not only accompanied Missy back home to Indiana, but had also arranged for her counseling and found her a nicer apartment and a job at a bank. "I don't know him well enough to understand why, but I think Jared somehow identifies with Missy. He was furious about how her employers treated her at that pizza place."

"Guess you're right that some good things did come out of it. I heard that Anna has moved to Wyoming temporarily and is helping with the Tranquillity residents."

Honor nodded. She had been there the day Anna had described her escape and survival in the wilderness for four days, only to be brought back to where she'd started.

"She said that there were several people who'd been kind to her, two in particular, and that she wanted to make sure they were treated fairly. No matter what she ultimately decides to do with her life, she's going to make an impact on this world. She's a remarkable young woman."

A thought suddenly hit Honor. Raising up on her elbow again, she asked curiously, "How do you know all this stuff?"

Seth shrugged. "I talked to McCall a few times. He mentioned some things."

Nope, she wasn't buying that for a minute. Noah McCall, no matter how grateful he might be to a non-LCR person, would not reveal to them the things he'd obviously discussed with Seth.

Her eyes narrowed in speculation. "You got something you want to tell me, Cavanaugh?"

Seth's mouth twitched, then curved into a full-fledged grin. "I'm never going to be able to surprise you, am I?"

Little did he know that he surprised her with the depth of his love every single day. Refusing to be sidetracked, she said, "What?"

His expression went from teasing to serious in an instant. "How would you feel about me working for LCR?"

Her breath hitched and tears glazed her eyes. Dammit, how was it he was the only one to ever make her cry? Seth working for LCR had been a thought that'd been going through her head for weeks. She hadn't mentioned it to him because she didn't want to influence his decision. His past experience had colored his outlook on so many things. She would never doubt Seth's courage or skill. What she wasn't sure about was his willingness to immerse himself again in a world of secrecy, flying bullets, and danger.

There was one thing she had to make sure of before she answered his question. "You're not doing this for me, are you? Because you're afraid for me?"

Seth shook his head. "I never questioned your abilities . . . not five years ago and not on this mission to rescue Kelli. So, the answer is no, I'm not considering joining LCR to watch over you." He shrugged. "Rescuing victims feels damn good and is a hell of a lot more rewarding that watching people get away with shit that you can do nothing to stop."

Grabbing her shoulders, he pulled her inches from his face and growled softly, "You haven't answered my question."

As usual, arousal sprang quick and urgent through Honor's body. Loving the strength in the hands that held her and the desire on his face, she gave her heartfelt answer: a deliberately brief "Yes."

"Yes, what?"

Lying completely over him, Honor put her lips to his and whispered, "There's nothing I'd rather do than work with you."

She felt his smile beneath her lips as his hands cupped her bottom, pressing her against his arousal. "Nothing?"

"Okay," she said softly, "almost nothing."

With a groan, Seth rolled her onto her back and devoured her mouth. Breathless moments later, he said, "So when you do want to get married?"

"Next weekend too soon?"

Keeping the steady, deliciously throbbing pressure of his erection against her mound, Seth pushed up on one arm so he could see her face. "You don't want a big wedding?"

She laughed softly. "It's going to be big no matter what with your family there, but no, I don't want a huge, elaborate wedding. Just your family and mine." And once again, that wave of emotion flooded her eyes as she whispered, "I've waited so long for this . . . I can't wait any longer."

Seth lowered his mouth to hers and gave his answer in the best way possible. Once again, the world and its problems fell away.

Honor didn't know what she'd done to deserve a second chance with this heroic, gorgeous man she adored. Seeing him again at LCR had been a twist of fate, but Seth surviving his wounds had been nothing short of a miracle. Now their future was spread out before them like a bright, shining beacon, and she planned to do everything she could to make the most of the glorious gift she'd been given.

acknowledgments

Thanks to my loving and supportive family, especially my wonderful husband, who keeps me sane and does so much to make my life bright and beautiful. And to the precious, furry creatures at my feet who keep me company as I pound the keyboard.

To my wonderful editor, Kate Collins, for her insight and kindness. And to the entire Ballantine team, especially Junessa Viloria, Beth Pearson, and Bonnie Thompson.

Thank you, Kim Whalen, my incredibly supportive agent, for your energy and enthusiasm.

Special thanks to Crystal Scott for patiently answering my endless questions on Wyoming. Any mistakes are entirely my own.

Thanks to the Recommend Monday gang on my blog, who love to talk books as much as I do.

And to the readers of the Last Chance Rescue series, thank you for asking for more LCR stories. I hope you enjoy this new addition.

Read on for a preview of

Sweet Revenge

the eighth novel of sexy suspense and
thrilling adventure in Christy Reece's
Last Chance Rescue series!

Bustarviejo, Spain

The night was silent and still. The air, thick and humid, held a feeling of expectancy—as if it were aware that rescue had finally arrived. Stooped behind a low brick wall, his eyes narrowed into a squint behind powerful binoculars, LCR operative Dylan Savage surveyed the perimeter of the massive property owned by Stanford Reddington.

The house in front of him held Jamie Kendrick—a young woman who'd been abducted by a maniac and then sold to Stanford Reddington. Purchased for what purpose, Dylan didn't even want to consider. Their mission was clear: rescue. Their plan: a soft entry. Grab Jamie and get the hell out, hopefully without firing a shot.

"Everyone in place and ready?" Noah McCall asked quietly. The Last Chance Rescue leader kept his voice calm and low, his tone betraying none of the tension Dylan knew he must feel.

On missions, McCall acted as though ice ran through his veins. That was an attitude Dylan had adopted long before he'd joined LCR. Never let them see you flinch. He'd learned that lesson as a child. Staying expressionless had saved his ass more than once.

Dylan answered with a soft "Ready."

Adrenaline surged as the three other people on the op answered in the affirmative. Any second now . . .

"Go," McCall whispered.

Staying low, Dylan and McCall ran toward the back door that their informant, Raphael, had promised would be unlocked. Noah eased the door open . . . Dylan peered inside. Scanning the large kitchen, he briefly noted that not only did the room look like a pigsty, it stank of old food and stale alcohol. The messy space had one thing in its favor: no people.

Dylan entered first, McCall behind him. Dim light filtered from a greasy bulb over the stove revealed the remains of last night's dinner and four dirty plates on the counter. Four here, including Jamie?

In the middle of the kitchen, the men stopped . . . waited . . . listened. On cue, a loud, thudding knock sounded at the front door. A moment of dead silence, then lights came on as someone stomped toward the door. The instant the front door opened, Dylan and McCall moved.

Guns at the ready, their steps silent, they made their way to the next room. At the entrance to the living room, McCall went in one direction, Dylan the other. Sticking his head into a small den and a bathroom, Dylan found nothing other than furniture and more evidence that slobs lived here.

One minute later, they met in the middle of the living room. The loud protestations coming from the front of the house reassured them that the home owner would be occupied for several more moments.

His black eyes glittering with cold determination, McCall mouthed silently, "Anything?"

Dylan shook his head.

Both men turned and headed up the stairway. Halting at the top of the stairs, they assessed the area. Bright lights from the first floor allowed them to see three rooms to check on this floor. McCall jerked his head at the stairs to the third floor.

With a quick nod, Dylan headed upstairs. At the top of the small landing, he stopped and listened. The only sounds were the distant mumblings of Reddington as he argued with the Spanish police. Two rooms to check here. The door to one of the rooms stood open. Easing his head in, he looked around. A storage room, filled with furniture and boxes.

Swiftly, silently, Dylan moved across the hallway, toward the closed door of the other room. His ear to the wood, he listened and heard a soft, trembling sigh.

He put his hand on the doorknob. Locked. Pulling a small tool from the belt at his waist, he inserted it into the keyhole. At the sweet sound of a click, he twisted the knob, eased the door open, and stepped inside. The room, midnight dark and deathly quiet, held the musky scent of sour sweat and felt heavy with fear, confirming what he already knew: she was here.

The softest whisper of sound put him on alert; half a second later, a small body leaped onto his back. Not wanting to hurt or frighten her further, Dylan dropped to the floor with Jamie Kendrick hanging on to his shoulders.

She ground her knee into the small of his back and spoke in a harsh, raspy voice: "Touch me and I'll kill you."

Admiration and compassion slammed into him. She was tough. Good. She would need to stay that way. "I'm here to rescue you, Jamie."

With a soft, laughing sob, she said mockingly, "Yeah, my knight in shining armor."

"I'm with Last Chance Rescue."

After a long pause, she whispered hoarsely, "What's that?"

"A rescue organization."

Another long pause. Finally, a shaky, tear-filled voice asked, "Are you for real?"

"Yes." He waited two heartbeats, giving her time to absorb the information. Then, since time was of the essence, he said, "We need to get out of here."

Her slight weight eased off his back, and he felt her shift away from him.

Getting to his feet, Dylan took a flashlight from his utility belt and clicked it on. His heart thudded and crashed as he got his first glimpse of slender, petite Jamie Kendrick. Untamed, golden-brown hair draped over her bare shoulders. Gray-blue eyes shimmered with tears; white teeth bit at her lips as if to control their trembling. The thin sheet covering her nude body couldn't hide her uncontrollable trembling. Despite his reassurance, she was terrified that this was a trick.

"Found her," he whispered softly into his mic.

"Get her out," Noah answered softly. "Reddington's still at the door, arguing. I've got one bastard down, two more on the run."

"Affirmative," Dylan answered.

There was no time for more reassurance. They needed to get their asses out of here . . . now. He took a step toward her. "Let's go."

When she lifted her hands to tighten the sheet around herself, he saw the cuffs on her wrists. Pulling a standard key from his belt, he reached for her hands. Admiration grew in him as he watched her stiffen but refuse to back away from him. He unlocked the cuffs from her bruised, raw wrists and then let her go. The last thing she probably wanted was for a man to touch her. Unfortunately, he was going to have to do more than just touch her if they were to get out of here in one piece.

With a sweep of his flashlight over the room, Dylan

took another quick scan. No clothing. He pulled his black cotton T-shirt over his head and handed it to her. "Put this on." Giving her a brief moment of privacy, he went to the door to peer out. Still quiet.

At the sound of a small, relieved sigh, he glanced over his shoulder. She was ready. Her feet were bare, and her body swayed as she tried to stand. The T-shirt swallowed her, landing in the middle of her wobbling knees.

"It'll be easier for both of us if you let me carry you out." He wasn't asking for permission, but he didn't want to scare her by just lifting her without warning.

"I can walk."

"You're barefoot and weak. We need to get out of here as fast as we can." Giving her no time to argue, Dylan reached for her and scooped her into his arms. Her body was shaking with terror, but she didn't fight him, and that was all he needed.

Making a rapid exit from the room, he strode quickly toward the stairway. As they got halfway down the stairs, the distant blast of gunfire ramped up the tension. *Shit!* No way was he not getting her out of here alive. Holding her tighter against his chest, he whispered, "Hang on, sweetheart."

Lowering his head, Dylan ran like hell.

One month later
Charles de Gaulle Airport
Paris, France

"Ladies and gentlemen, flight 231 to Atlanta, Georgia, U.S.A., will begin loading in ten minutes."

A bright, sunny smile plastered on her face, Jamie turned to her sister, McKenna. This stiff-upper-lip thing was a lot harder than she'd thought it would be. This wasn't goodbye forever, but still . . . "I'll see you soon again . . . I promise."

McKenna's face, so similar to Jamie's, revealed the same turmoil. "You're sure you don't want me to go with you? It's not too late for me to buy a ticket."

The lump grew in Jamie's throat at the offer. McKenna's anxiousness was sweet but unnecessary. She wasn't nervous or worried. After everything that had happened the last few months, she felt insulated from the trivial stuff. And she'd been given a miracle: her sister. Her biggest concern was being separated from McKenna again.

"I'll be fine. I just want to get this behind me so I can move forward."

"Will you have to see him?"

Funny, even the thought of seeing her ex-husband again didn't cause the thud of dread it once had. "I don't think so. My attorney assured me I'd just need to appear before a judge."

"You know I'll be there for you if you need me. Right?"

Jamie hugged McKenna again. After her rescue, they'd spent almost a month together and had gotten even closer than they'd been as kids. Having both survived their own hell, being together again made them appreciate each other so much more.

Pulling away, Jamie smiled through her tears. "You need to go see Lucas."

At the mention of Lucas Kane, a breathtaking expression came over McKenna's face. Never had Jamie seen anyone more in love. And just from the short amount of time Jamie had spent with Lucas, she knew he felt the same way. Other than her parents, she had never known a couple who loved each other like that.

"You promise to come back to Europe soon?"

"Cross my heart. And if not, you can always come see

me." She gripped McKenna's hand and held tight. "We'll never let each other go again."

Tears sparkling in her eyes, McKenna nodded fiercely. "Never. I promise."

"Jamie? McKenna?"

They both whirled around at the sound of the familiar masculine voice approaching them. A gasp escaped Jamie before she could stop it. She hadn't thought she'd ever see him again, and yet here he was. *Dylan*.

"Hey, what are you doing here?" McKenna asked.

"I heard Jamie was headed back to the States. I've got some business to take care of there, so I thought I'd tag along." His emerald gaze turned to Jamie. "That okay with you?"

It had been almost a month since she'd seen him. Dylan had been the one to carry her out of that house, the one to rescue her from hell.

Her rescue had been as dramatic as any television drama, with Dylan and the other LCR operatives swooping down in the dead of night and rescuing her from Stanton Reddington and his vile son. Jamie barely remembered the event other than Dylan's gruff, reassuring voice, his strong arms carrying her out of the house, and him saying "You're safe now, Jamie" as he handed her over to the EMTs.

Then she'd been lifted into a helicopter and taken to the hospital. She'd gone from abject misery and terror to comfort and safety in a matter of seconds. And she had thought Dylan was the most wonderful of heroes.

For the first couple of days after her rescue, he'd been kind and wonderfully attentive. Then something had happened, and for the life of her, she didn't know what. The day of her release from the hospital, Dylan had turned noticeably cooler. She'd tried to tell herself she was just imagining it, but when he'd given her a barely perceptible nod after she'd thanked him once more for her rescue, she had known it wasn't her imagination.

Those words of thanks were the last ones she'd thought she'd ever get to say to him, and now here he was, going to the States with her.

Realizing that both McKenna and Dylan were looking at her strangely, Jamie knew a deep blush covered her fair skin as she stammered, "Yes . . . of course, that's okay with me."

"Ladies and gentleman, flight 231 to Atlanta is now boarding."

As the airline personnel gave boarding instructions, Jamie forgot everything other than the knowledge that she was saying goodbye to her sister. Throwing her arms around McKenna's neck, she whispered in her ear. "I love you, Kenna."

Her voice thick with emotion, McKenna answered softly, "I love you, too. See you soon. Okay?"

Unable to speak for the ginormous lump in her throat, Jamie nodded and tightened her arms around her sister one last time . . . then made herself let go. McKenna didn't need to see the uncertainty and dread that had suddenly swamped her. After everything she'd been through, what was there to fear?

McKenna's eyes glittered with emotion. "Call me as soon as you land. Okay?"

She nodded again. "I will."

She wasn't surprised to see McKenna hug Dylan—he seemed to have an affectionate rapport with her sister. Something that was sadly missing with her.

With her carry-on gripped tightly in her hand, Jamie headed to the ticket agent. At the door, she turned back for one last glance. McKenna waved and blew a kiss. Jamie gave her the best smile she could muster and turned to walk down the narrow tunnel to the plane.

"Want me to take your bag?"

Despite the massive willpower she thought she had, tears were flooding her eyes. Not looking at Dylan, she shook her head.

"You okay?"

"Yeah, just hate saying goodbye." She straightened her shoulders, determined to get past her weepiness. "Where are you sitting?"

"First class, row two, seat A."

Startled, she jerked her head up. "I'm in row two, seat B. How'd you manage that?"

He shrugged as if it was nothing and stopped at the entrance to the plane, allowing her to go first. As she passed by him, his closed expression told her he wasn't going to explain anything. Not why he'd arranged to sit with her, and probably not why he'd just shown up, out of the blue, to travel with her. Telling herself she didn't need an explanation, Jamie settled into her seat and watched as the most handsome and infuriatingly mysterious man she'd ever known dropped into the seat next to hers.

Would nine hours of sitting beside him give her any insight? Like why he'd made the effort to travel with her but still treated her as though she'd done something to offend him?

Dylan stretched his long legs out and cursed himself once more for coming. She would've been fine traveling on her own. He hadn't seen her in almost a month, and during that time, she'd obviously recovered. So why the hell was he here, like some sort of guard dog? Hell if he knew.

She looked healthy. No, not just healthy . . . she looked beautiful. When he'd rescued her from that hellhole, Jamie's golden-brown hair had been almost to her hips. Now it was shorter, just past her shoulders, with subtle blond streaks. The bruises and swelling on her face and neck were completely gone, and her silky, fair skin glowed. Even the dark, haunted look in her eyes had vanished.

This morning, he'd been at LCR headquarters giving a review of his last op. After his meeting with McCall, he'd anticipated going back to his apartment and healing for the next few days. The job had had gotten a little dicey, resulting in a couple of bruised ribs and a deep thigh bruise. A long soak in a hot tub and about ten hours of uninterrupted sleep had been his only plan. The instant McKenna had called McCall and mentioned that Jamie was headed back to the States, alone, his plans had changed. Dylan had shot out of his chair and, on the way to the door, asked McCall to arrange a seat on the same flight. If he hadn't been in such a hurry, he would've stopped to snarl at his boss's amusement.

Had anyone asked him why he felt the need to be with her, he wouldn't have had an answer. He'd rescued dozens of people for LCR. And while he wished them well, not once had he felt any real desire to see them again, much less accompany them home.

What was it about this woman that made him react in a way opposite to what was normal for him? Nothing could happen between them. She was going back home to live in the States. He lived in Paris.

Yeah, like that's the only thing keeping you from pursuing something.

"What kind of business are you going back for?"

Jerked out of his dark thoughts, he shrugged. "Family stuff."

"Where does your family live?"

He didn't hesitate with his answer: "Florida."

So what if "live" wasn't exactly the right word? While he was in the United States, he figured he might as well visit his mother's and grandmother's graves in Florida. He could rent a car and be in Jacksonville in a matter of hours. And he'd be visiting the only family he'd ever wanted to claim.

"Are you flying out of Atlanta to Florida?"

Dylan shook his head and asked, "What about you? You headed to Louisiana?"

"Yes, I have a connecting flight to Baton Rouge about an hour after I land."

"You going to have to see your ex?"

She grimaced. "You know about him?"

"I know that he hurt you."

Her chin came up in a defensive gesture. "Just once. He never got the chance again."

"Will you have to see him?"

"I don't think so. My attorney seems to think that I can just file another complaint against him and then appear before a judge. He was only in jail for a few days. . . . He deserves a longer sentence."

"You want me to go with you?" The words were out before he could pull them back. Hell, what was it about her?

If Dylan was surprised, Jamie was apparently stunned. Her eyes widening, she blushed a crimson red and stuttered, "Oh . . . I . . . well . . . that's so swee—" Thankfully she stopped before she got the word out. Even when he'd been a baby, "sweet" was one description that had never been attributed to Dylan. She swallowed and said, "I appreciate the offer, but I need to handle this myself."

He shrugged. "Yeah, that's what I figured." He was relieved she'd said no, so why did he have this odd letdown feeling? Damn weird.

"Besides, I'd hate to take you away from your family."

He looked away from her, to the flight attendant headed their way with the drink cart. "Yeah, they'd be disappointed."

"How long are you going to be in the States?"

He shrugged, not really wanting to go back to that discussion. "Just a day or so."

"Wow, you came all the way from Paris just for a day? Won't your family—"

"You want something to drink?"

Looking startled at his abrupt question, she said, "Oh . . . yes. Hot tea. Thanks."

Dylan gave the order, hoping that once Jamie had her drink, she'd forget what they'd been talking about. Discussing his family—or, for that matter, his life—wasn't something he liked to spend a lot of time on.

There was an awkward silence while Jamie accepted her hot tea and Dylan chugged down his black coffee. By the time she'd sweetened her drink to her taste, his cup was empty. Though a slug of bourbon or a Scotch neat would have been his preference, coffee was the only drink he could allow himself. Maintaining his wits would keep him from uttering another stupid comment. Offering to go to Louisiana with her had been lame-brained enough.

She took a sip of her tea, and Dylan felt his mouth twitch with a smile. Everything Jamie did was feminine and . . . what was the word . . . dainty. She even made drinking a beverage a feminine action. Where he swallowed in gulps, she sipped like a delicate sparrow.

Mentally rolling his eyes at the stupidity of his thoughts, he said, "You and McKenna enjoy your time in Paris?"

Her eyes glowing, she nodded. "It was wonderful. I've always wanted to visit, and Kenna knows the city so well. We did all the touristy stuff, along with lots of things people who have never been to Paris might not know about."

"You probably had a lot of things to get caught up on."

Her eyes dimmed for an instant, and Dylan felt like an

ass. Bringing up the past meant reminding her about all the crap she'd been through. Not only had she been brutalized by that scumbag Damon Hughes, she'd been held captive by the human slime Stanford Reddington and his son. Of course, it wasn't something she'd ever be able to forget, but his comment sure as hell hadn't helped. This was just another reminder that he needed to stay away from her. His late wife had told him more than once that he had the tact of a water buffalo.

Thankfully, Jamie's smile returned. "We had years to get caught up on. Our lives have been completely opposite."

"What was it like, living with your aunt?"

Her pretty mouth twisted in a wry smile. "The best description I can come up with for Aunt Mavis is a cross between an elderly drill sergeant and Miss Manners. My aunt had an opinion on everything and felt it her duty to share that opinion with everyone."

"Doesn't sound like a lot of fun."

"It wasn't." Jamie's slender shoulders lifted in a delicate shrug. "But I was safe and warm, had good food to eat and a place to sleep. Kenna didn't have those things."

"Are you going to see your sister again soon?"

She nodded. "I haven't told her because I wanted to surprise her, but as soon as I settle things in Louisiana, I'm going back there to live."

Dylan felt a kick to his gut. "In Paris?"

"Yes. I fell in love with the city, and being so far away from Kenna isn't something I want to do again. Family is so important, don't you think?"

Since everyone in his family was dead and most of them hadn't been worth much alive, he didn't have an answer that wouldn't cause more questions. He settled for a vague nod and another question: "Are you going to continue teaching?"

For the first time since he'd known her, he saw a flicker

of secrecy in her expression. She shrugged and took another sip of her tea. "I'm not sure yet. There're a lot of possibilities out there."

That was about as vague as one could get. "McCall has a lot of contacts," Dylan said. "He could probably help."

Yet another slight flicker, but all she said was "That's a great idea. I'll give him a call as soon as I get settled."

The seat-belt sign went off, and Dylan used that as an excuse to get up and walk around. He needed a few minutes away from Jamie, not only to come to terms with these damn odd feelings of protectiveness but also to deal with the news that she was moving to Europe. It'd been easy enough to stay away from her the last month. He'd been away, working, and Jamie had been recovering. What was he going to do now that they would be living in the same city? How was he going to stay away from her when he hadn't gone a day without thinking about her since they'd met?

Hell!

Jamie took one last sip of her now tepid tea and grimaced. Aunt Mavis had been a hot-tea drinker, and it irritated her that she'd instinctively requested what her aunt would have expected her to order. Though she'd had only five years of living with the woman, her aunt had worked hard to fit a lifetime of strict lessons into that time. Aunt Mavis had been gone for several years— she had died peacefully in her sleep. Jamie couldn't help but wonder if she'd just decided to die that day and had then done it. The woman had had that much iron-willed discipline.

"You want to get up and stretch your legs?"

Swallowing a gasp, she jerked her head to gaze at the man standing beside her. He moved so quietly, she hadn't heard him. "Quiet" was a good description for Dylan

Savage. He didn't talk a lot, and when he moved, he barely made a sound.

She smiled her thanks. "No, I'm fine."

As he eased into the chair beside her, she noticed a slight wince, as if he were in pain. "Are you okay?"

"Yeah, just a couple of bruises."

"From a job?"

He nodded.

"Did I ever thank you?"

For the first time ever, Jamie saw a small smile at his lips. "Yeah, about twenty times that first day."

"I wanted to send you something, but McKenna said that wasn't necessary."

He looked over at her, a slight softening in his eyes. "I don't think anyone's ever done that before. What were you going to send?"

"For saving my life?" She laughed, pleased that she actually found some kind of humor in referring to those dark days before her rescue. "I was torn between a fruit basket and a bottle of Scotch. McKenna said Scotch was your favorite drink."

"You didn't need to send anything. It's my job."

She ignored the sting of his comment. Of course that's what she was to him: a job. How silly to think he'd be attracted to someone he'd rescued. "Are you married?" Oh God, had she just asked that question?

"No."

Feeling like she'd opened a giant hole and was teetering on the edge, she added, "Me neither."

"Yeah, I know."

Jamie fought hard to control the blush that spread over her entire body, knowing it was useless. When she said stupid or inappropriate things, her fair skin glowed like a beacon. And this had to be one of her stupidest comments to date. Of course he knew she wasn't married; they'd just talked about her ex-husband. Besides, there was little the man didn't know about her life—at least, he'd heard about the awful parts. Whereas she knew next to nothing about his.

She looked up as Dylan stood again and pulled something from the overhead compartment. He handed her a small pillow and then, sitting back down with a pillow of his own, reclined his seat, put the pillow behind his head, and closed his eyes.

And just like that, all conversation stopped. Not that it was his responsibility to entertain her. Still, she couldn't deny the sting. His response to her single status wasn't exactly encouraging, even if it had been an inane statement.

Jamie looked out at the bright blue sky. Okay, so what if he had no interest in her. She had more on her mind than starting a relationship that could go nowhere. The news she'd received this morning before leaving—news she hadn't shared with McKenna—was going to occupy all of her thoughts. Because if things progressed as they looked like they might, she was going to have to figure out how to not only hunt down and capture a fiend but also find a way to stay alive.

headline
ETERNAL

FIND YOUR HEART'S DESIRE...